True

a novel

Melinda Field

Published by Wise Women Ink 2011
Printed in The United States of America

ISBN: 978-0-9762008-3-3

First Edition

Wise Women Ink
P.O. Box 1450
Mt. Shasta, California 96067

info@wisewomenink.com
www.wisewomenink.com

love

melinda

Hold me, hold me, never let me go,
Hold me like the leaves on the ends of the branches…

Autumn

Chapter One

The girl flipped her long black hair out of her eyes. She stood looking at the empty motel room's dirty carpet and cracked walls. She'd cleaned it as best she could, hoping that Mr. Monsoon, the manager, would give her what little was left of the deposit. The girl and her mother had lived there for six years, until last week when the cops busted her mother for heroin and prostitution. She opened the window—dusk in downtown Phoenix, the crowded boulevard, a cluster of gangs, pimps and drug dealers, shouting people, heavy traffic, honking horns and the constant screams of sirens. She looked around the place one last time. The big closet with shuttered doors had served as her room. Most of the time she'd slept there on the mattress or listened to the radio.

"Goddamn her!" she yelled into the disinfected air of the bathroom. In the daytime she was gone, at school or work, while her mother shot heroin and nodded out in front of the TV. Most nights her mother went out, but once in a while she'd bring a man back; then the girl slept in the tub so she could lock the door.

Her mother had been arrested before but her pimp, Eddie, usually bailed her out right away. This time he'd been arrest-

3

ed too. The Monsoons let her stay in their guest room in the apartment above the decaying motel. When her mother was allowed her one phone call, she'd told the girl, her voice soft and weak, "I'm gonna be in for a long time; call your grandmother, Jenny Brown, Green Valley, California."

"No, mom, no way! I've never even met her!" she fired back. Then she heard a gagging sound like vomiting and the phone line went dead.

At first she'd thought, *No fucking way I'm calling the grandmother.*" Once when she was ten she'd found a picture in a box her mother kept under the bed. In it, a small dark woman held a little girl who was laughing. On the back it said, "Morning Dove and Mamma, 1959." She'd asked her mother, who went by "Dovie," if that was her real name.

"It's my Indian name, Green River Tribe. That's your grandmother holding me. You too, you're Indian, maybe more than Mexican, not East Indian like the Monsoons, but more like…" she'd paused, "like cowboys and Indians. But don't tell anyone, say you're Mexican, they won't treat you so bad." Ever since that day the girl had checked the box next to Hispanic.

The last few days she had been desperate to find a way to stay in school and keep her job. She needed to find a safe place to sleep. She'd wondered if the Monsoons would let her rent their guest room, but she knew better; the cops were always on their back for one reason or another. Then, yesterday, after Child Protective Services called, Mrs. Monsoon had drifted across the room, her sari edged in gold, and handed her a cup of tea. She'd moved to the altar that they kept in their living room and lit a stick of incense. "Kali," she'd said tapping a framed picture, and "Ganesh," pointing to an elephant god. Then, with her eyes on the floor, in her broken English, she'd told the girl, "Good luck with grandmother," and handed her the push button phone. Reluctantly, she'd called information; the number was listed.

At first, the old woman on the phone didn't understand. "Dovie's girl? Where? Arizona? Who? Caterina?" The girl explained about her mother and jail. She bit her lip and fought back angry tears as she spoke the words, "I have nowhere else to go."

It took forever while her grandmother copied down the Monsoon's phone number and address. For the next few days she'd helped Mr. Monsoon move furniture out of a room, shampoo the carpets, and hang drapes. He'd had another sudden vacancy and she'd worked with him to get it ready to rent. There had been no word from her grandmother. Then, on the third day, Mrs. Monsoon had set a letter with the words Express Mail stamped on it by her plate. She'd held it in her hands a long time, knowing her life was somehow bound to it. She'd left the table and walked out to the balcony to read it.

Dear Caterina,
Here is a bus ticket to Green Valley.
Someone will pick you up at the Post Office.
Your grandmother, Jenny Brown

It was all happening too fast. She looked up Green Valley, California, on the library computer. Three hundred miles north of San Francisco, a rural, secluded ranch valley…

Shit! Did her grandmother live in a tipi? she wondered. Surrounded by three wilderness areas…Boasts a rich history from the gold rush days…*Boasts!? Who uses words like that? Who!*

She straightened her small body, pulled the fitted shirt down over her tight black jeans. She picked up the new black backpack she'd saved all summer to buy, the one that was supposed to be for her junior year, not to carry her pathetic belongings to some godforsaken place. She put on dark glasses and the head phones that plugged into a small AM/FM radio and CD player she carried in her pocket. She almost always wore the headphones whether she could afford batteries or not. Wearing them stopped people from talking to her. She heard Mr. Monsoon's horn, looked one last time at the room, blinked hard, shouldered the pack and hurried outside.

In the parking lot of the Greyhound station, Mr. Monsoon, after double checking that the Honda's doors were locked, took the backpack from her. He'd worn his brown Nehru jacket and shiny black shoes. She'd noticed in the car that his clothes smelled like curry and incense. She wondered if she'd miss that smell. Probably not, she decided, trying to keep up with his clipped pace. The terminal was packed with people. Buses lined the street, their engines running, the visible exhaust rising up into the orange, dirty ceiling that passed for air.

After reading the destinations lit up on the back of each bus, she finally found hers, Phoenix to Sacramento. She pointed and Mr. Monsoon veered with her to the left. Once she'd gotten into line she noticed that Mr. Monsoon kept looking around nervously, adjusting his turban. She saw relief in his eyes when she told him that it was okay to leave her. His face was blank; he stepped towards her, bowed, pressed a ten dollar bill into her hand, turned and was gone.

Right then, as Mr. Monsoon disappeared into the crowd, a man in the line winked at her and grabbed his crotch. She looked away, hiding behind the curtain of her hair. After handing her ticket to the bus driver she stepped up into the bus, the heavy air freshener not able to completely cover the faint smell of sweat and dirty diapers. It wasn't until after she'd found a window seat and stashed the backpack underneath it that reality slammed, her heart raced, she felt nauseous, hot, sweat on her palms and across her lips. She turned to the window and pressed her cheek to the cool glass.

Stop! she wanted to yell, *Let Me Off!* As if he knew, the bus driver buckled the seat belt over his pot belly, glanced in the overhead mirror, nodded, reached out and pushed the double levered doors shut. They closed with a loud intake of air as if the people on board were vacuum packed, sealed in.

She woke in the dark, the black windows and dim blue lights more like a space ship than a bus. Most people slept, even the crying baby in the back. After using the cubicle bathroom she ate the food that Mrs. Monsoon had packed—an apple, an orange, and a naan filled with meat and vegetables. She flipped through a *People* magazine she'd found in the bathroom. **"Back to school fashion, looking great in 98."** She fingered a hole in the knee of her jeans and yawned. She watched the wide, dark desert pass by; jagged shadows of cactus were backlit by a half moon. Stretching out her legs, grateful for the space of three seats, her stomach full, the repetitive swish of the tires lulled her and she slept again.

On and on and endlessly on, the bus crossed the swaths of farmland and freeways through central California. Identical freeway towns with carbon copy restaurants, stores, and malls spilled into new suburbs with look-alike houses and beige cars in every garage.

The bus stopped morning, noon, and night. She couldn't tell one Stop n' Shop from the next, from the people, to the familiar merchandise; they were even arranged identically so you could always find the chips no matter what town you were in. And she wondered, were Greyhound stations located in the worst neighborhoods, or had bad neighborhoods sprung up around Greyhound stations?

In the early morning of the second day, they dropped off and picked up passengers in the Sacramento station, where huge, carved balustrades told the story of the discovery of California. A lot of people got on the bus, and this time she was in the middle between an old man who started snoring the minute he sat down and a boy about her age who kept staring at her. She glared at him.

Four more freeway hours later, her body cramped and in need of a shower, she tried to read her worn copy of *Jane Eyre*. Just outside of Churncreek, the bus driver announced over the loud speaker the sighting of Mt. Cloud, fifty miles away. He referred to the double humped mountain reclining on the horizon as *She*.

That was really weird, she thought, *giving a sex to a pile of dirt...*

At the Mt. Cloud Stop n' Shop she reached into her pocket and counted eighty-three cents. She bought a candy bar, then filled her empty Pepsi bottle with water at the drinking fountain. Outside she stared at the huge mountain, so close she felt like she could have reached out and touched it. 14,351 elevation, said the engraved plaque. She was only about an hour away now. Her stomach growled, so she unwrapped the chocolate, letting the sweet bitterness melt on her tongue. In the bathroom she'd washed up, reapplying the heavy black eye liner and maroon lipstick she always wore. When she came out, the driver had called for people to board.

Miles more of brown stubble fields passed, some dotted with a few horses — or were they cows? The old houses seemed to all have a falling down barn nearby. Where the hell were the neighborhoods and shopping malls? After forty miles they exited the freeway into Butte City and drove a short distance past the main street which held a grocery store and gas station.

Here I go, she thought seeing a sign that said, To Green Valley. Twenty-three miles of steep winding road, unmaintained in the winter.

Does it snow here? she wondered. They trundled uphill, nothing but heavily forested mountains on either side. She felt sick, the alien landscape and high elevation twisting in her gut. The summit looked down on a valley imprisoned by mountains. The highway narrowed to one lane, then abruptly dropped. In a few moments, she'd told herself, she would get off this bus, step into a place she'd never been, a place where she knew no one.

My life is over! her mind screamed, while the bus's brakes bleated a series of short shrill shrieks as it hurtled downhill.

Chapter Two

Emma Cassady's farm sat in the middle of the Green Valley, on the far west side, on the bank of Serpentine Creek. The creek flowed out of a narrow jagged canyon that cut through the blue-green-grey Serpentine Mountains. The creek was awash with huge boulders and fast water in winter, but now, a week into September, the slow summer wash licked its way over the ever-widening alluvial fan of the rocky bed. The lazy trickle spread itself through the stands of cottonwood and willow that grew along the shore. The big trees, autumn tinged, their leaves beginning to fly, flanked one side of the twenty-acre farm while a narrow, rock-lined irrigation ditch skirted the other. The constant calming sound of running water surrounded the property.

Established in the 1800's, the small finger of land cradled a varied terrain. At the eastern end of the farm a rivulet wound through red clover pastures and stands of tall oaks. The middle ground was wooded, arched over with both young and mature fir, cedar, and pine. The small forest sheltered deer, grey squirrel, fox, coyote, raccoon, skunk, opossum, and even bear and mountain lions in search of water. Many birds, both native and migratory, traveled the tree tops—woodpeckers, jays, robins, hawks, turkey vultures, ravens and crows. Canada geese nested near the creek during spring flows.

Just beyond the woods, up over a green hummocked pasture, the farmhouse knelt in an old apple orchard. The well kept, two-story, white clapboard house had old bubbled glass and double hung windows framed by faded blue shutters. A gnarled elm leaned into the front porch. The house, more like a cottage, was squat, built on a low foundation of creek rock. A weathered shingle roof peaked up and over the dwelling. Ivy twined itself around the stone chimney. Chinese lanterns, hollyhocks and bleeding hearts grew in the dooryard where a double-dutch back door opened into a large kitchen. Big beams hung with drying flowers and herbs spanned a low pine ceiling. Baskets of ripe fruit and vegetables lined the pocked wooden floor. White cotton curtains hung in the windows. In one corner stood an original cream and green wood cook stove that warmed the drafty room on cold mornings. The chunky stove had four burners and an oven, which came in handy for cooking during the frequent power outages in winter. A round table and four chairs looked out to the orchard and the rivulet.

The kitchen opened into a long, narrow dining room which held only a table and chairs and an oak hutch. The room's large window faced the garden. A bedroom and bath sat back under the eaves. French doors framed the entrance to the living room, bright with sunlight reflecting off the low cream ceiling. The room looked out to the front porch and the orchard beyond. Comfortable overstuffed furniture circled the simple stone fireplace. Deep chocolate chenille sofas and love seats rested on a flowered wool rug. Tucked back under the stairs was a small office area. Upstairs there were two bedrooms and a bath. A long low library which also served as a guest room fronted the house.

A few flagstone steps away from the back porch was a

large garden that looked west to the Serpentine Mountains. Rather than being laid out row by row, the garden was a lush impressionistic tangle of flowers, herbs, and vegetables.

Emma stood under an umbrella of sunflowers squinting into the sun. She reached up, taking the prickly stalk into her hand, which caused the heavy flower head to shower black seeds on her silver streaked hair. Her strong legs flexed as she snipped the flower and put it in her basket. As she turned towards the gate a large green and gold dragonfly hovered before her, then lighted on the sunflower she had just cut. Slowly, she extended her hand, the Emerald looked up at her and cocked its head. She hummed as she stroked its back, where delicate, copper wings met the long body. A moment of stillness, then the dragonfly levitated and was gone.

Three cats, a long-haired black one, a calico, and a tortoise shell, meowed at her feet. "It's coming," she told them as she closed the gate. Before going in, she paused to look at the orchard, the weighted branches bent with red and gold apples, the same trees that she had climbed each summer of her childhood. Every year when school was out her parents would travel from San Francisco to visit her aunt's family in Green Valley, and Emma would be allowed to stay all summer. Every day, up with her cousins at dawn, they combed the vast mysteries of the farm, exploring its blackberry brambled tunnels, treetops and creek beds, its animals and insects.

In her early forties Emma had the opportunity to buy the farm after her aunt died. She'd been ready to leave her busy nurse/midwife practice in San Francisco. Green Valley and its familiar roots had called to her at the right moment. She'd loved her life at the farm the last fifteen years. Working out of the house and keeping her practice down to three days a week allowed her to have the time—although there was never enough—to care for the farm and garden and animals. A tremendous amount of work for a single woman but, she thought to herself, *I wouldn't change a thing...well, maybe one thing.*

Her old dog, Bear, smiled and wagged his tail as she passed. The kitchen was cool and dim as she set down the basket of flowers. She chose a vase from the top shelf of the hoosier, a burnished copper one that complimented the rose, pink and orange zinnias she arranged with the sunflowers. Her friends Lilly, Clare, and Midnight were coming over to celebrate the birthday of their youngest member, Briar, with an afternoon horseback ride and birthday cake. Emma had seen four patients that morning—a cold, stitches, and two pre-natals. She'd baked a chocolate cake with coffee icing, and looked through a junk-filled drawer in the oak hutch in search of candles, finding two half empty packets.

While placing the candles on the cake, she thought, *Thirty five! How was it possible that Briar was 35 years old?!* She put the flowers on the table and picked up the picture of the five of them she kept on the hutch. Taken last summer in the Big Meadow Wilderness Area, it captured all of them on their horses grinning into the camera. Emma had embroidered "Yee Haw Sisterhood" on the cloth frame. She remembered how they'd come up with the name years ago, up in horse camp. One morning Lilly was sitting by the fire reading a book titled *Divine Secrets of the Ya-Ya Sisterhood.*

"Hey!" she'd announced, "we're the Yee Haw Sisterhood! Don't you think?" They'd all agreed, laughing.

She looked at her watch. "Yikes!" she said out loud, hurrying into the kitchen, where she pulled on her boots and grabbed Mav's rope halter which hung by the back door. She found the bay Arabian gelding underneath the oaks, his eyes half closed. "Hey, Mav," she called to him, "want to ride?" He stretched his elegant body and lowered his head into the halter and sighed while Emma tied a knot. They walked to the corral as locust leaves blew through the air. She tied him and brushed his burgundy coat and combed out his long black mane and tail. While putting on the bridle he nuzzled her palm with his soft lips. Mellow on the ground yet spirited and energetic on the trail, she'd bought him as a green five-year-old soon after she'd come back to the valley. Briar, then only 19, had helped train him. A smart, honest horse, her friends had dubbed him "Mav, the wonderful." She buckled the chest strap and tightened the cinch, then checked his hooves for stones.

"You ready?" She put her left foot into the stirrup and swung her right leg up and over the saddle. As she slipped her other foot into the stirrup and settled her rump, Lilly's truck pulled into the turnaround. Emma watched as Lilly and Clare jumped out, waved, and went to the back of the horse trailer to let out their horses. The sisters, although they shared a resemblance, differed in height and coloring. Lilly, just fifty, was tall and blonde, while Clare, five years younger, was short with brown hair. Predictably, they grumbled at each other as they mounted their horses.

Midnight arrived next, driving her brother Liam's truck and trailer. She slid out of the truck cab, her tall body formidable, her toes pointed in descent. She called out, "Yee Haw" with a smirking smile on her brown face. Flipping her long braid, she opened the trailer latch and backed away in anticipation of her snorting mare shooting out backwards, which is exactly what she did. Because of her wild mustang, dominant mare history, the horse was named "Ever Be Wary Molly." Midnight's timing was close but flawless. "Get a grip, woman," she told the horse as she led her out. "Happy Birthday, Briar!" she called as she climbed into the saddle.

"Hey, it *is* Briar!" called Lilly, as Clare gave a little wave.

Briar had ridden over to Emma's on Elvira, a big taffy-colored quarter horse mare with blue eyes. "Salutations, tis' me, the birthday girl," her hazel eyes teased, "Jeez Louise, do you think you'll have enough candles?" And then, as she knew they would, they'd joked back.

14

"Oh, shut up," said Midnight,

"You are such a baby," called Lilly.

"Just wait," offered Emma, "forty is looming."

They rode out under a buttermilk sky, the clotted clouds rippling with sunlight at their edges. The horses were excited as they crossed the wide, almost dry, creek bed. Once on the other side, they rode through brown fields. Emma's neighbor, Bob, saw them from his front porch and waved as they passed by at a trot. The horses, familiar now with the terrain, chomped at the bit, anxious to be given their heads. The women too, momentarily free of their complicated lives, let go. Giddy, whooping, and laughing, they galloped the horses over the hills. Briar, the most competent and fearless, led the race, shrieking as she passed them one by one. At the top, there was a comfortable silence as the horses stood, sweat soaked and breathing hard. The women looked down on the valley, the drought-drained Green River, a slim ribbon moving across the fields.

On the ride back, they wound down through the hills and back onto the littered alfalfa fields. With only two fields left to cross, they let the horses canter one last time, the cardinal rule being, "Never let them run home." The women rode in a V-formation, two in front, two behind, and one in back. Underneath the warm, mild Indian summer air was a subtle chill heralding the turning of the season.

They were moving at a good clip across the brittle open field when suddenly the horses slowed as Lilly called out, "What the...?" A shining, flashing apparatus was approaching from about three hundred yards away. Like nothing they'd ever seen, it seemed to have wings—shiny, square metal wings with a span of at least sixteen feet. These appendages reflected the lowered sun, flashing blinding light into the perplexed faces of the riders. It moved steadily, if not slowly, towards them. Not identifiable as a tractor or four wheeler, the horses panicked in unison. Midnight's mare Molly snorted and rose straight up, turning a full three-sixty circle in midair, and galloped off with a swearing Midnight barely on board. Mav jerked under Emma. No question of flight or fright, he ran as fast as he could away from the menace. In the second row, Lilly and Clare's horses skidded and froze staring at the advancing enemy, then turned and ran, leaving Briar the lone one still riding toward the bulky, winged creature. Coming closer she moved her horse out of its path and told her to"stand," so she could get a good look at it. *Jeez Louise, what **is** that?* she wondered as it came nearer. And then it registered. A huge red bull was balancing a metal livestock gate on its wide shoulders. She heard shouting and saw Bob, the neighbor, yelling and waving his arms as he ran towards her.

"George! George! Oh, so sorry, Briar, I saw the whole thing from my porch." He turned to the massive animal who stood about ten feet away. "George!" he yelled, "take that gate back now!" he shook his fist at the bull, "Now!... Bad Boy!... Look how you scared these women!" The bull looked at him and slowly turned a two thousand pound cloven-hoofed pirouette, the livestock gate still across his shoulders, and walked back towards the corral. "Sorry, Briar, he's found out he can stand under it and lift the gate off its hinges, but that's the farthest I've ever seen him carry it! Where are the others?"

"Here they come," said Briar pointing. The women steered their reluctant horses closer and watched in fascination as the bull walked away.

"Sorry, ladies, he's just too smart."

Shaking their heads, laughing, they turned and rode back to Emma's through Serpentine Creek. After unsaddling the tired horses they turned them out together to graze.

In the long dining room Emma poured a cup of tea and handed it to Lilly.

"It's not caffeine, is it? I already can't sleep because of these damned hot flashes." She blew down her blouse a few times. "God, how can I sweat buckets and still be bloated?"

"It's my herbal blend, but there is a little coffee in the icing," said Emma lighting the candles.

"Jeez Louise, it's a torch!" cried Briar. Just as they began to sing Happy Birthday, Emma noticed a faint bruise around Clare's left eye. They sat contentedly at the long table, enjoying seconds of the rich cake while Briar opened her cards.

"Thanks, you guys, for the nice afternoon. I think from now on I'll remember this birthday as the Day of the Flying Bull."

Midnight shook her head, "God, wasn't that something! Molly spooked when she saw it coming; she went straight up into the air and when she turned the saddle slipped sideways and I almost fell on my ass."

Clare laughed softly, "Our horses just froze."

Emma put her cup down. "Mav saw it before I did. I noticed his ears twitching frantically back and forth, and by the time I saw what he saw, he was out of there."

Briar folded her napkin into neat little overlapping squares, "I figured bombproof Elvira could face it off and she did. Before you all came back, Bob told me the bull even attempts to drop the gate back onto the hinges. So much for dumb animals."

Clare cleared her throat, "We should go, I've still got to make dinner for Don and the boys."

"Okay," said Lilly getting up, "but couldn't they do it themselves once in a while?" Clare shot her a look.

Midnight stood, "Oh yeah, me too, I forgot I've got a bottomless pit of a teenage boy to feed."

Emma rose, the teapot in her hands, "Hey, before you all go, are we on for horse camp? When is it? Weekend after next?"

"Clare and I are, right Clare?" Her sister nodded,

"Me too," said Midnight. "The tribe's salmon festival is the week after. I just need to clear using the trailer with my brother. I'm sure it will be fine. By the way, Em, Liam asked about you." They followed her to the kitchen.

Emma's cheeks burned but she asked casually, "Oh yeah, what did he say?"

"Oh, just 'how is she' and 'what's she up to?'"

Briar piped in, "Your face is red, Emma!"

"Ooh, look how aloof she seems, but we know better, don't we, girls," sang Lilly.

"Oh stop it, all of you, Mary mother of god, I'm fifty-eight years old!"

"You don't look it!" shouted Midnight.

Briar smiled, "You don't act it either."

"And the past is the past," said Emma, setting the cups and saucers down in the sink with a clatter. After they'd all put on their jackets and gone off to load the horses, Emma was at the sink when Midnight came in the back door.

"I almost forgot to ask you, did you know that Jenny Brown's granddaughter has come from Arizona to stay with her?"

Emma dried her hands on a towel. "I didn't know Jenny Brown had a daughter, let alone a granddaughter."

"Oh yeah, 'Dovie'. She went to school here. She left and never came back. I guess she got into hard drugs and worse. She's in jail. That's why the girl is here. She's sixteen."

"Hmm," Emma said, "what do you think? It might be good for Jenny…"

"Members of the tribe have been concerned, seems the girl is trouble."

"I'll check in on her this week, take her some vegetables, see how she's doing."

"That would be great. She's fragile, Emma, and proud. The tribe's been helping her financially; she's down to choosing between food or medicine."

Emma ran her fingers through her hair and sighed, "That is so wrong. Okay, I'll call you after I see her."

"Thanks, I'd better go, Molly is probably having a cow."

Chapter Three

Cat hit the snooze button for the second time, then pulled the stiff, wool blankets over her head, burrowing deeper. She dozed, sinking into the quiet nothing. When the alarm went off for the third time she bolted upright, disoriented, not recognizing the room at first. Small and dark with peeling wallpaper and broken linoleum, it was furnished with just the sagging bed and a beat-up dresser. Dread filled her as she heard the voice of the ancient grandmother calling up the stairs.

"Caterina! you're gonna be late! Hurry, or you'll miss the bus."

Good, she thought. She didn't know what was worse, riding the bus to the small stupid high school, or staying here in this haunted house right out of a Stephen King book. Loose floorboards creaked under her bare feet as she stepped out of the shower, twisting her long thick mass of black hair. She squeezed out as much water as she could and put it up in a ponytail. She pulled on black jeans, a black sweater and black boots. She drew dark lines around her eyes and put on lipstick.

"Who cares…," she said to her reflection in the old mirror, "I'm not going to make any friends in this hick valley."

The first day of school they had stared at her and pointed

and called her names. She grabbed her long black coat off the bed and took the stairs two at a time. She sighed as she came into the dark kitchen. Her grandmother stood at the stove frying eggs. The short, stooped woman wore a stained housedress and bedroom slippers. The girl watched her as she pulled a bobby pin out of her bun, scratched her head with it, then stuck it back in.

"Come, Caterina, come on and eat before the bus comes."

"No," she said going for the coffee that perked in a dented aluminum pot on the stove.

"Girl, you need food. These are fresh from the hens this morning."

"I don't eat eggs *because* of where they come from," she said, sitting down at the table. The local announcer on the ancient TV droned on about the boring events of a small town. She turned it off and looked defiantly at the old woman. The grandmother held a paper bag out to her.

"Here, I made you a sandwich."

"Wow," said the girl, turning her back to her and putting five spoonfuls of sugar in her coffee. "Double wow!"

Jenny's reaction was slow; she sighed. "Girl, watch yer mouth, and look how tight yer pants are. Go change 'em!"

"Go change your diaper, granny, and leave me alone!" She picked up her backpack.

The old woman shook her head slowly back and forth. She clucked with her tongue. "Don't you care, girl? Don't you care about anything? Just like your mother, aren't you?"

"No! I don't fucking care!" she yelled, slinging the backpack over her shoulder as she slammed the back door. The bus was leaving, farting exhaust into the chilly air. She had to run and wave her arms. All eyes were on her as she sat down attempting to be invisible, her face in her notebook. Something slimy glopped onto the window next to her. She looked at the English assignment: **"Write two or more paragraphs about** *yourself.*" She clicked her pen as if cocking a weapon. "Okay, you asked for it."

> *My mother had me on a dirty blanket in the motel where she hooked. My life has been about learning to stay out of her way. Everything went to hell when she was busted again for heroin. She's shot up every day that I can remember. Now she's in Arizona State Prison for five years. That's why I came to Green Valley (believe me, it wasn't by choice) to stay with my grandmother. Everyone in Arizona said I'd love it in California, but this place is so northern, I could spit into Oregon.*

She looked up from the notebook as the bus pulled into the small high school parking lot and felt a rush of panic at the thought of spending the next seven hours there.

Yesterday, during PE, the kids had made fun of her clothes, her hair, her name. RJ, a boy in her history class, had followed her from class to the cafeteria, all the time poking an umbrella at her. When she'd finally spun around to face him, he'd laughed and spit a wad of chew on her boots before getting into the lunch line.

Asshole, she said to herself.

"Hi, I'm Amy Lee." The blonde girl palmed a paper napkin from a table and handed it to Cat.

"Sorry about your boots. Don't worry about RJ, he's not even from here. Got kicked out of Butte City and sent here. He's a jerk. Some of us are nice; let's sit over here." The girl sounded sincere.

"Thanks," said Cat turning away, "I've got to use the rest room, maybe another time."

She ducked out of the crowded room, her small body disappearing into the dim hallway. The boy, RJ, was standing in front of her locker. There was no one around. She froze, and he didn't see her. She watched him. He was turning her combination lock one way and then the other. She quietly walked to the girl's bathroom where she hid until she heard the end-of-lunch bell.

Up all night attending a birth in Butte City, Emma drove down into the valley as the sun cleared the Eastside Mountains. Even though she was exhausted, hungry, and in need of a shower, she turned off the highway onto Jenny's road. She had been a home nurse for the woman a few times. Once after Jenny fell and broke her hip, and last year when Emma had followed her through a bad case of pneumonia. She slowed, so her beloved blue Toyota pickup could take the pothole bumps as easily as possible.

The property was littered with rusted cars and old farm and logging equipment. The rickety house sat in the back. The siding peeled off in places; a cracked window had been taped. She hefted a cardboard box of vegetables and remembered to sidestep the stair that was rotted through. She knocked loudly, knowing Jenny didn't hear well. She opened the door to the familiar loud TV, and the odors of Pine-Sol and Crisco.

"Jenny?...Hi, it's Emma!" She found her in the spotless kitchen sitting at the table, a cup in front of her, a framed picture beside it.

"Oh, Emma! I didn't hear you knock, come in, come in! Oh, you already have, I see." She eyed the box.

"My garden just won't quit: broccoli, kale, carrots, potatoes, some nice heirloom tomatoes. Can you use them?"

"Oh, thank you, I sure can," she took a handkerchief out of her cardigan sleeve and dabbed her nose and eyes, "especially with the girl here...you heard about her? My granddaughter?" She turned the TV off.

"Yes, Midnight said something...she's from where?"

"Arizona. The streets. One good thing, she's always gone to school though, even skipped a grade."

Emma looked at the picture of a girl with long dark hair.

23

"Is this her? What's her name?"

"Her name is Caterina, but that's not her, that's my daughter, Dovie."

"I didn't know you had a daughter, let alone a granddaughter, Jenny." There was a very long silence. Emma recognized the moment as Jenny gathered herself. She put the tomatoes in the fridge, which was almost empty. She knew not to ask any more questions.

After another minute, Jenny sighed. "This is my daughter, Dovie. Did I tell you that?" Emma nodded. "She was one angry girl. She left after high school, got into booze and drugs, and never came back. I didn't hear from her for, oh, maybe ten years. Then she called one night out of the blue. 'Ma! I had a baby,' she says, 'a girl, Caterina.'" The old woman paused, "Oh? I say... Dovie? Where are you? Give me your number. She tells me she's gotta go...Sixteen years I don't hear another word, Emma, sixteen years, until the girl called. Dovie's in jail for a long time I guess."

Emma's exhaustion and the woman's vulnerability made her feel suddenly weak. She took a breath. "What's she like? Is she helpful, Jenny? Could it be a good thing to have someone here with you?"

"Oh, no!" Jenny shook her head back and forth. "Oh, no! She's bad, Emma. So wild and mad. She has a filthy mouth, just like her mother. She doesn't help."

"Well, she's only been here what, a month or so? In time she'll adjust. Sixteen is a hard time to change schools. It will get better." *Or not*, she thought to herself. "How have you been feeling, Jenny?"

"Fine, fine, I'm much better since I went back on the diabetes medicine. The tribe's helping me pay for it."

"Well, let me know," Emma said, "I can probably help you get it. And if things get out of hand, you can call me or Midnight. I'll check in with you soon."

The old woman had a faraway look in her eyes. "Okay," said Jenny, staring at the photograph, "thanks again."

Emma left, feeling like she was leaving a sinking ship. In the truck, she wrote in the date and details of her visit, although it was unofficial, and a reminder to call Jenny in a few days.

On the way home she turned into the valley's one shopping center which sat at the end of the little town's mile-long stretch of shops and small businesses. She remembered that she was out of half-and-half but knew that she was too tired to grocery shop. She pulled into a parking place in front of the Goldrush Café, which was flanked by Willard's Market and Drugs on one side and by the Stay County Bank on the other. A big ornate sign read:

Goldrush Café
Est. 1898, or thereabouts

The historic building resembled a saloon. Bells on a leather strap announced her arrival as a rush of dry, hot air followed her in. It was cool inside, and the smell of bacon and coffee made her mouth water. Rudy, the owner and cook, stood by the register. A country music song—the long sad twangs of a guitar—drifted out from the kitchen.

"Emma! Well hello, what are you doin' out so early?"

"Good morning, Rudy," she smiled absently, reading the specials printed neatly on a blackboard, "Oh, you know, helping people populate the planet...hmm," she couldn't decide. "I'll start with coffee, okay?"

"Cream, right?"

"Yes, please."

He set the mug and creamer on the counter. A group of men sat at the big round table near the window. Many of them greeted her or nodded.

"Good to see you,"

25

"Hey, Emma,"

"Join us?" She waved.

"Nice, I'll just order. Okay, Rudy, I shouldn't but I'll have the maple glazed pecan waffles."

She swirled cream in her coffee and turned towards the table, spilling a little across her scrub shirt. The men met every morning at 7:00. Mostly retired, they were grateful for a reason to get up and get dressed and for a place to go. The regulars were joined by others over the course of the morning, coming in from the fields or doctoring cattle; some were on breaks from their jobs. They sat under the watchful eyes of the deer, bear, cougar, and bobcat mounted on the wall behind them and engaged in heated debate and fierce gossip. Both local and national newspapers were strewn across the table. Lilly's husband, Bud McLaine, stood up and pushed a chair back, signaling Emma to sit. His father-in-law, Ralph Rawlins, smiled. Emma noticed how much he had aged. They no doubt had been up since 4:00 or 5:00 dealing with chores on their big ranch.

"Hello, Bud, Ralph," she settled herself in.

"Well? Did somebody get born or croak?" Ralph inquired.

"Nine pound baby boy, 3:00 in the morning."

"Emma, good to see you," Bud said, his big open face clean shaven in spite of the early hour.

Bill Plainsford in white shirt and tie gestured to her. He was a tribal member, and the only lawyer in the valley.

"Hey, Bill, you're all dressed up?" Emma said.

"Yeah, got court today."

"Hi, Harry," Emma turned to the short, older man who helped Briar run her place.

"What's up guys? Have you figured it out? Reinvented the world yet?"

"Well, gas is up to $1.67 a gallon...," Bill said between sips of coffee, "that should be number one on the reinvent list."

Ralph suddenly burst out, his face turning red, "Yeah,

well, get used to it. As long as the goddamn ragheads are in charge, it'll keep going up." Ralph sounded so upset, Emma understood why Lilly was concerned about her dad.

Rudy set the plate in front of her, plunked down silverware and a napkin. Pools of maple syrup and butter filled the waffles' little reservoirs.

"How's your truck running, Emma? Any more problems with that oil leak?"

"No, Bud, it's fine, running just fine after you fixed it." He nodded and drank his coffee.

Harry spoke around his chew. "Did you...," his cheek puffed out, "ever see the river lower?" He set his trademark Pepsi down.

"Midnight said not in her lifetime," offered Emma.

"Me neither," agreed Bill. "Droughts yes, but not like this. Salmon will be in trouble. *Farmers' Almanac* says it's supposed to be a heavy winter—let's hope so."

Emma listened to the men, saw their frustration. It seemed that everywhere she went recently control of water was the main subject.

"You watch, if we have a steady drought the next few years, the government will want to regulate our water," Harry announced quietly.

Carey Jackson, the barber, approached their table, his bill and wallet in hand.

"It's already happening," he held up a newspaper. "The *Butte City Star* says the state's proposal will eventually charge land owners to use their own water."

"Yeah, I saw something about meters and such," sighed Harry.

"Goddamned government! Close the valley off at the pass, that's what I say," shouted Ralph.

"Come on, Dad," said Bud, "it's just a proposal, that's why we're organizing; it's okay."

"No, it's not!" said Ralph, breaking a piece of bacon in half.

Emma relished the last bite of her waffle and took a sip of coffee. "What's Lilly up to today?" she asked Bud, hoping to change the subject.

He picked up his bill. "She and Clare are going to see their mom this morning."

"Oh, how *is* Dora? She doing okay at Wrenwood?"

Ralph looked at her and frowned, "You want to know the goddamned truth, Emma?" He leaned forward. "She just sits there and stares, doesn't know me after fifty goddamned years. People in the dining room all out of their minds, pissing their pants. The whole place smells like crap and cooked carrots."

Emma reached over and patted his shoulder. "I know, Ralph, it must be so hard and I'm sure you miss her, but at least she's safe. Could you look at it like that?"

"Safe! Safe!" he bellowed, "it's way more dangerous there. She should come back home goddamn it, that's all."

Bud stood up. "Come on, Dad, let's go, we've got a lot to finish on that corral."

They got up and paid and said their goodbyes. Emma yawned.

"You up all night partying?" Harry's blue eyes teased.

"You know better," she smiled and picked up her wallet.

"Got a lot of patients today?"

"No, luckily I'm going to go home and sleep."

"See ya, Emma," called Bill over by the front door, putting on his suit jacket.

She waved. "Okay, Harry, me too, time to go, say hi to Briar."

"Will do; she's working that new stallion this morning."

"I swear that girl is fearless!"

"Yeah," said Harry, "she's got a gift, that's for sure…take care."

Dora Rawlins smiled at the morning attendant whose name tag said, "Ruth, Wrenwood Alzheimers Care." She came up to Dora's room every morning to help her eat and get dressed. Dora liked it at Wrenwood. She was grateful that her daughters...*what were their names? One was a flower name, Daisy? Rose?... Lilly! That was it!...The other was Clear? Carol? Clare?...Yes! Clare,* had brought her here. She chewed her scrambled eggs neatly before Ruth fed her another bite. Her small body rocked in the chair while Ruth put jam on a piece of toast and gave her sips of coffee. It was so nice not to have to do anything. No cooking, cleaning, nothing to think or worry about. All of these years of doing, doing, doing had filled her so past overflowing that when the spilling started she'd hemorrhaged seventy years of names and faces, days, weeks, months, and years—a lifetime of appointments and meetings, commitments and deadlines.

Ruth brushed her hair and buttoned her jacket. "The blue looks good with white, don't you think?"

Dora, unresponsive, looked at her hands. Days, weeks, months, years, jumbled out of time. Sometimes they came back to her and she ricocheted...reminded...remembered. The best was when the words had gone. No inquiry, deliberation, analysis. "Yes's" just floated upwards and soared. "No's" froze and faltered, broke apart and fell to the ground. "Maybe's" hid behind invisible excuses, and adjectives described themselves out of existence. No more talk or questions, trying to communicate, mediate, understand, teach, argue, blah, blah, blah. Just this mostly empty, blessed silence.

"C'mon, Dora," said Ruth, "let's go downstairs, the nail technician is here today. Won't it be nice to have a manicure?" Ruth led her to the elevator, the long hallway dark like a tunnel. The doors opened, bells rang, and lights flashed. Once inside, Ruth steered her towards the back. A soft ding and then, just before the doors closed, they saw a man in pajamas who waved and smiled as he was chased by two attendants.

"What a clown, that Mr. Justice is," said Ruth.

Dora smelled cotton candy and heard children laughing and shouting. She heard carnival music and saw her many faces in the funny mirrors. She put her hands flat against the back wall of the elevator, sucked in her breath, and waited for the floor to drop out beneath her. But the elevator just stopped with a soft bump, and the doors opened.

In the dining room several women sat at the long table, their hands spread out before them. Ruth helped Dora to a chair.

Vera, the nail technician, had set little colored bottles on the table. She turned to the first woman. "Hi, Mrs. Ravelli, what color for you today? Your usual purple or something different?" Mrs. Ravelli nodded and pointed. "Lavender Lane? Okay." She handed Ruth the bottle, which she shook by hitting it gently on her palm. Mrs. Ravelli, usually loud and combative, watched quietly as Ruth began painting her nails. It was Dora's turn next.

"What color for you, Mrs. Rawlins?" When Dora didn't answer, Vera reached for a bottle, "Okay, what about this bright pink? It's so cheery."

Dora watched as Vera fanned the air over her wet nail polish. She had the feeling that sometimes came over her, usually when she was alone in her room, of being in her chair, just quiet and content, her body relaxed, almost sleepy, while her mind took her away on the most amazing adventures, so real and colorful, sometimes even dangerous. When it happened she was transported to places that no one would believe or understand. It felt like a shifting of energy that swirled up from her toes and through her body, moving one reality out of the way to make room for another. Sometimes it was so glorious she didn't want to come back.

"Alright, Mrs. Rawlins, I think your nails are dry, how about a little art?" Vera opened the bottle that said Pearls in the Mist, and carefully painted little white polka dots over the bright pink.

Dora kicks out into the warm pink lake. She holds onto the white polka dots to stay afloat. She sees the shore lined with tall cedar trees and steers herself towards it. She steps on the bank. It's evening in the high mountains. Dora walks into the forest. She is welcomed by the big old female whose wise eyes light up at the sight of her standing in the clearing where they groom each other before dark. Dora sits next to her on a rock while a few young ones wrestle in the shadows. She is content as the faint last light falls through the overstory of trees, and night birds call to one another. The old one takes Dora's small hand and presses it to her graying muzzle. Dora looks down at their hands, fingers intertwined, hands so alike except that the big one's are covered with long black wiry hair.

Chapter Four

Lilly was loading her camp gear into the truck when she saw the broken fence. The young steers must have Houdinied right through.

Shit! She looked at her watch; good thing she'd spent the night before packing for Hidden Horse. The girls were going up to horse camp for the weekend and she was supposed to pick up her sister Clare in a few hours. She whistled for Joe. The dark brown gelding came into the barnyard with a look of "Did someone call my name?" on his big long face. He stood untied waiting for her to saddle him. She began to brush him, first his back in long strokes from his neck to his tail. Dust rose up off him.

"God, Joe, you must have just rolled, huh?" Faking a few coughs she ran a comb through his tangled mane and tail. She went to the tack room and brought out his blanket and saddle. She spread the faded red wool blanket over his broad back, then lifted the worn saddle over the pad. Squaring the saddle up, she moved it side to side and back to back until it sat right. Reaching underneath the horse's belly she found the cinch and looped it through the metal ring several times. The horse began to dance a little.

"Whoa, Joe, easy, easy." She ran her fingers underneath

the leather strap to make sure it wasn't too tight. "You're okay." Had her mother been there she would have scolded her for not tying the horse up while she saddled him. A stickler for following rules and procedures properly, Dora and Lilly had butted heads all through Lilly's teen years. Of course her sister Clare had been a perfect angel as a teen, too timid and shy to rebel against anything. She checked the stirrups and put the bridle over the horse's head and gently set the bit in his mouth. Again she thought of her mother, now sitting mute in a room at the Alzheimer facility in Butte City. Tears welled up as she remembered the day, only a few months ago, when after much family deliberation they had taken her there. Dora had waved gaily, a big smile on her face, as she and Bud turned to walk down the long hallway. *Damnit!* She hated being this emotional. She mounted the horse and led him across the alfalfa fields to the hills behind the ranch.

Unexpected heat flushed her face. She blew down her sleeveless blouse, waiting for her body temperature to peak. She'd flared up more and more often these last few months. She felt angry, raw, ragged and prickly. Everything irritated her. *Damned cows.* She'd barely have time. She urged the horse up the spine of the mountain. The scraggly junipers emitted a sickly whiff of gin and tonic in the already hot air. A tunnel of dust followed them. At the top, she let the horse rest. He blew and sneezed, then snuffled the ground. She got off and sat on a big rock. Her family's ranch lay below. She could see the hundred-year-old farmhouse and the modern ranch style she and Bud had built in the eighties. Clare and Don's place was to the east. The Green River threaded through grazing cows and fields of ripe alfalfa. Mountains surrounded the bowl of the valley, a circle within a circle.

She watched the sun crest the mountain; a slow orange light spread across the sky like a broken egg yolk. Normally she would have sent one of the boys to find the cows. But this year, less than a month ago, her youngest had left for college. She missed his activities and games, and even his rowdy friends. The house was too quiet. She sighed and brushed off her jeans and climbed back on the horse. "Come on, Joe, let's find those cows." They cut down the far left side, privileged to a stunning view of the next valley over, the black oaks already turning.

What if her dad was right? Could the boys lose this way of life? Again she felt flash lightning beneath her skin. She missed her mother, wanted to talk with her about this menopause, this change of life. They sure got that right. Well, her mom didn't talk with anyone anymore. And Clare, God! Lilly couldn't get through to her at all.

She spotted the runaways under a tree. Flies buzzed around their heavy eyes. She herded the slow-moving steers back to the top. They speeded up going downhill, tumbling rocks with their hard black hooves. They reminded her of the boys, kicking up their heels, bumping playfully into each other.

She was covered with a fine powder of dust by the time she came into the north pasture, opening the gate while still on Joe. The cows ran straight for the water ditch. Lilly tied the horse and walked to the house. She wondered if Clare had given up on her.

Clare stood on the braided rug and set the basket of eggs down carefully. She removed her muddy boots, putting them on the old newspapers covering the linoleum. She poured a cup of coffee, glancing at the clock—still time to sit a minute. She placed the basket of eggs on the table, admiring the Araucana colors: pinkish brown, teal blue, mint green. Easter eggs every day. Her fingers brushed the smooth shell of one, palming the perfect oval shape.

She took her coffee into the spare room that was really her art studio. But she hesitated to call it that, not knowing how her husband, Don, would react to her having a room dedicated to what he perceived as a useless hobby.

Her ongoing collection of paintings hung on the walls. The newest one, on the easel, was a study of leaf patterns overlaid with the orange, black, and white design of a flicker feather. She studied the watercolor, seeing the need for a lime wash over the leaves. She took another sip of coffee. In this moment she belonged only to herself. Most of the time she was divided into so many pieces—clerk at the feed store, cook, laundress, volunteer, cheerleader, maid. She moved to the kitchen, picking up discarded socks, candy wrappers and even *What! a packaged condom.*

She slathered mayonnaise onto a piece of white bread. Each set of sandwiches would be different. Boy #1, mayo, no mustard, cut the crust. Boy #2, extra mustard and no mayo, leave the crust. And the husband, the husband made yesterday's lunch *the* topic of last evening.

"Not enough mayo or mustard, don't be stingy with the meat, and what in the hell is with the wheat bread?" She'd explained that it was better for him. But he said, "Shut up and make it right next time."

He came into the kitchen, "Why is Red tied outside?"

"Remember? I'm going to Hidden Horse with Lilly this weekend."

"No, you're not!" he said angrily.

"Oh, come on, Don, this has been planned for weeks. The boys are going to my dad's; you'll have the whole place to yourself."

"Well, you're not taking Red; ride Bandit, he needs the experience," he said with his mouth in a tight line.

"Don, please, I don't want my weekend to be about a green horse."

"Too bad!" he yelled.

In the silence that followed, Clare watched the flies at the window. Born of attic bat shit, they buzzed dumbly and bumped their tender yellow-blistered heads against the dirty glass.

Don moved to the window to investigate. "What's up with all the flies?"

Clare took a breath, her voice quiet. "Another hatch out," she told him turning. "It always happens at this time of year."

Don moved to the back door and took the fly swatter off the hook. She stared at the sandwiches waiting, ready. She barely flinched as the perforated square of plastic stung her cheek.

"Get rid of 'em! This house is a sty!"

She nodded, her hands shaking as she added meat and cheese, salt and pepper.

Don stood over her as he put on his coat. "And as far as your weekend, it's Bandit or you're not going, understand?" He stomped hard on her bare foot and slammed out the back door.

Hurry! Hurry! she thought as she wrapped the sandwiches. *Go!* Her mind pounded.

Her sons came into the kitchen. "Here's your notebooks, quit hitting each other. Here's your lunches and jackets, take Dad his." The back door slammed. She turned, her foot throbbing. She got an ice pack out of the freezer. She sat breathing, trying to release the pressure in her chest. *Please don't come back in, please,* she prayed, waiting to hear Don's truck starting up outside. *Where in the world is Lilly?...*

Midnight drove home from the tribal meeting. The sun had not yet cleared the steep river canyon. She turned onto the narrow, winding road towards home. The Green River was lower than she could ever remember. The slow water pooled around boulders, whose striated tips could barely be glimpsed in a normal water year. The meeting this morning had been about water. The government, both feds and state, the environmentalists, the ranchers and farmers, all had their agenda for the river. The tribe hadn't even been asked, but she and Bill Plainsford, whose generosity provided her with a part-time job at his law office, had decided to send a letter. She knew that as such a small tribe they didn't have much clout. She felt the old anger boil up. Her people had lived on the river for a thousand years, for god's sake. Frustrated, she pulled her long salt-and-pepper braid over her shoulder and twisted it. Hidden Horse sounded good.

She was so deep in thought that she almost missed the turnoff; she had to step on the brakes to make it. The old wood-slatted bridge made the truck bump and jerk. The next part was all uphill, a mile or so. Huge madrones lined the road. She slowed as she passed through a dark cluster of cedar and fir, their scent imprinted in the air.

She pulled into the clearing, parking next to the cabin. She jumped out and stood a moment, listening. Except for the river far below it was intensely quiet. She found the fire still burning. Her son, Julian, had left the milk out, cereal spilled on the table. *God!* she thought, *is that kid six or sixteen?*

After a scrappy lunch of salad and cold fry bread, she settled into the old recliner. *I'll just nap a minute*, she thought, *then go to Liam's to pick up Molly and the trailer.*

She tried to sleep but flashbacks from the meeting kept spinning in her brain. The look of surprise and then arrogance on the forest ranger's face as she and Bill Plainsford sat down in the small meeting room. The ranchers' outrage about their threatened adjudicated water rights to use the river for irrigation. The dreadlocked environmentalist with her piles of data.

She heard a loud screeching ruckus outside. She opened the cabin door, yawning. Wing, the raven, was on the picnic table, his blue-black feathers flashing as he hopped and squawked. It had been ten or more years since Julian had brought the injured bird to her. She had removed the buckshot from his wing and splinted it, and amazingly he'd made a full recovery. He and his tribe lived up the mountain but he had never forgotten her. He flew back to the table, flapping and dancing. There was something small and pink on the table. He often brought her small gifts. Once when she had been feuding with a neighbor over a destroyed beaver dam, Wing had brought her a pair of the man's underwear, stains and all, and she swore he had laughed with her, as his feathers shook.

The most precious gift had been a small fossil with a shell embedded in it. More often than not, he brought a brightly colored piece of plastic ribbon used to mark timber sales or a piece of blue bandana. He was definitely doing his "look what I found" dance on the table, strutting, turning, picking something up in his strong beak and dropping it.

"Okay, okay," she said, "let's see it." She moved in closer and studied the small, pink object. It was a tiny baby doll, maybe two inches long, naked and wrinkled like a newborn.

A wild ringing neigh exploded from the throat of the roan stallion. The horse reared, his front legs pawing the air, his head thrown back, ears plastered. Briar loosened her grip on the rope, moving her tall, thin body a small step closer to let him know she wouldn't retreat. The two-thousand-pound horse came down with a heavy thud onto the dry sand. She threw one long ripple into the lunge line and clicked her tongue twice, asking him to move in a circle. The horse had been labeled a dangerous troublemaker, but she could tell by his reactions that somebody had abused him. Obediently, he trotted clockwise. She asked him to change direction, and he did.

"Ho," she said approaching him, her eyes meeting his, "good job!" He snorted and threw his head in a circle. She unhooked the rope, leaving the halter on. He was being picked up that afternoon. "I hope your owner's on time," she said, climbing out of the round pen and throwing him a flake of hay. Walking back to the barn her mind went over all she still had to do to get ready for Hidden Horse camp.

As she pushed open the heavy doors, the horses she boarded and trained called to her with soft nickers. She breathed in deeply; so many times she had tried to define the unique smell of horses—a combination of sweat, leather, and molasses.

Greeting each horse, she delivered a flake to all seven stalls. She paused, scratching the forelock of the blue-eyed mare that belonged to Harry, the ranch hand. "How's Elvira today?"

She hurried quickly past the last empty stall, where a hand-painted sign read "**Swift T Bar One**." She sat down on an old barrel, listening to the horses' rhythmic chewing. Through the rough windows the morning light was purple and teal, the stars just blinking out. She listened to the old building's strange music. The banging and flapping of loose metal roofing, loft shutters creaking. She heard the coded clickings of mouse feet in gutters, the quiet unbraiding of rope hung on walls. She couldn't stop herself from looking over to Swift's empty stall... remembering their seventeen years together... the first time she'd seen the palomino colt, a gift from her parents for high school graduation... their instant connection. His love of running and her fearlessness and training ability had won them countless ribbons for barrel racing over the years. In her late twenties they'd retired from the circuit. Their accomplishments had put Green Valley on the rodeo map. Up until the accident last year, they were still inseparable.

Unstoppable random images of their last day reeled across her mind. The hometown rodeo arena had been full to capacity. She'd felt the wild anticipation of the crowd, their impatient enthusiasm and vicarious need, the announcer's excited voice.

"Ladies and gentlemen, let's all stand for the final ride of our own Green Valley Queen of the Barrels, Briar Terry and California's Grand Barrels Champion, Swift T Bar One!" Boisterous applause, blaring cheers from the stands.

Swift gathered, blonde, beautiful, snorting, tense and hard muscled, waiting for the gesture. The bell rang as Briar's heels signaled the moment of thrust, then off, brief fusion, true unity as they joined for the run. Crouched low, her heart pounded adrenaline as she gave him his head. He'd galloped out, shot forward, full force then slowed, turned a perfect degree as dun dust rose to meet the first barrel. Their choreography innate, throbbing hooves rotated, wheeled as he cleared the second. He moved out, held fast, her hands loose on the reins as he rounded the third. Then, their circuit completed, in dangerous ecstasy they'd raced for the buzzer, drunk on speed.

In the final echoed applause she'd seen his ears twitch, felt a subtle withholding as he stumbled in staggered increments. She'd pulled back, but momentum propelled his jerky stride, and he'd groaned a whinny of caught breath just before the loud snapping crack. She'd flown off before he'd buckled and watched from the ground as he fell, the crumpled legs in slow descent, churning beneath him. She'd run to him, helpless, as he rolled onto his back, one front leg a scissored angle, the exposed bone skyward. His eyes were wild with agony when he looked at her as she called out, "Swift! Swift!"

Then his panted breath became a dark coughing of blood on the sand. People ran in, shouted. She heard her name, "Briar! Briar! Briar!" as she knelt down and stroked his quivering neck. Something cold was slapped into her palm. She looked from the gun to Harry's questioning eyes and back to the gun. "No! No! I can't!" she screamed.

Harry took the gun; she turned away in sickened dread as the shot exploded.

Trembling with the memory, slowly she raised herself up from the barrel where she sat.

Enough! she told herself. She slapped at tears as she hurried towards the house. She heard the rooster crow and saw light break over the rim of the Eastsides. She scraped her boots and stood in the little kitchen, breathing hard. She looked around the room desperately. Noticing the spice cupboard door was open a crack, she crossed the room and turned the little wooden knobs. Inside, she found the labeled bottles out of order and arranged them alphabetically—cardamom, chili, cinnamon, cumin, curry—making sure that their sides didn't touch each other.

Chapter Five

Emma's cell phone rang in her pocket.

"Emma? Emma, it's Briar. I'm running late, still waiting for the owner of the stallion to arrive. I wanted to let you know to go ahead, and I'll come up this evening. I hate it when people are late!"

Emma laughed. "I know...okay...have a safe trip. I'll see you tonight." She dialed her office. "Hey, Carrie, it's Emma. I'm leaving for the weekend soon. I told Dr. Drew about it, but you might want to remind him. How is it going? Is he swamped as usual?...Sounds like a Friday...I'll be back Monday morning. Sheila is going to cover my patients, and I don't have any babies due this week...yeah, Hidden Horse...have a good weekend."

It would take about an hour to drive up to the wilderness area. She went over her list one last time: food—scones, salad, dressing, stir fry; foam pad; flash light; cooler; ice. They always brought too much, but part of the pleasure was camping in utter comfort and even elegance. She knew that by the first meal the old picnic tables would be covered with tablecloths, garden bouquets and even candles.

She remembered July's hailstorm and grabbed her rain poncho from the coat rack. After everything was boxed, bagged, packed, and loaded into the truck, Bear came out from under the porch and looked at her sleepily. She helped him up into the pickup and watched him settle in. She opened the door to the horse trailer, then went around to the side to check gear in the small tack area. Saddle, blanket, bridle, halter, rope, salt lick, hose, water bucket, hoof pick, herbal fly spray, fly mask, first aid kit, hay, grain, dog dish, kibble, leash. "Nothing like traveling light," she said to herself.

Mav was running around the pasture with excitement. "Yes," she called to him, "we're going to Hidden Horse, you smart guy." She opened the gate; the horse was eager. Right before she loaded him into the trailer, she patted his big soft cheek. After she swung herself up into the cab she paused, looking at the house and orchard. A second bloom of old English pink roses climbed over the split rail fence, and the slow summer creek flowed by, barely covering the pale stones. She felt at once so grateful for her home and yet somehow not worthy of it. She couldn't keep up with it—the roof needed repairs and the paint on the shutters was a faded blue. But there was never enough time or money.

On either side of the highway there were fields of freshly cut alfalfa; the sweet hot scent drifted through the truck's open windows. Aspens along Rawlins Creek were tinged with brown. Farmhouses and outbuildings dotted the vast expanses of fields. Late afternoon sun shimmered on asphalt. She took a drink from the water bottle and settled into the seat. It would be so nice to relax for a few days. Her practice had been crazy busy. She'd had little time for friends this summer. A weekend with the Yee Haw Sisterhood was just what she needed.

As she slowed for the turnoff, the air was noticeably cooler. Huge firs and cedars towered above the truck. She glanced at the rear view mirror; Mav and the trailer seemed steady. The steep road rose up, mile after mile. As she neared the top, the wilderness area loomed before her. The Trilogy Mountains took up half the sky. At their base was a small valley.

Dust clouded the pickup as they passed the larger camp. The truck and trailer edged slowly down and around; on the left was a small sign that said Hidden Horse Campground. Bear was sitting upright, his ears twitching with excitement. The campground was laid out in a circle. There were six camps, each with a small corral. Each site had a water hookup, fire pit and picnic table. Over the years, they had all established their favorite camps, and Emma knew who would greet her first.

"Yee Haw!" shouted Lilly, coming out from around her camp stove and wiping her hands on her jeans. "About time, Emma!"

Emma helped Bear down; he took off immediately to join Clare and Lilly's dogs barking at the base of a tree. She let Mav out of the trailer.

"Hey, Emma," said Midnight, "hey, Mav." The horse snorted and looked around. Lilly's horse, Joe, whinnied a greeting, and Emma led Mav towards the corral.

"Where's Briar?" asked Midnight. "It's her first time without Swift, huh?"

"Yes, so sad. The owner of the stallion was late; she should be here soon."

Clare came from the bathroom, greeting Emma with her shy smile.

"We're going to Midnight's for horse d'oeuvres," said Lilly, grinning.

"I'll be over in a second." Emma set Mav up with water and hay. She took her duffle bag and box of food and stashed it in the cab. She spread the foam pad with old sheets, quilts and a sleeping bag. Bear's bed fit into a corner. The sky was silver and pink. Mav chewed slowly, his eyes closed. She put all the salad stuff into a bag, found her flannel shirt and camp chair and headed towards the laughter coming through the trees.

The kitchen was always at Midnight's camp, and though they had all contributed items over the years, Midnight kept the big wooden box. She had come up early, and everything was set up and ready. The fire pit coals were glowing, the steaks lined up on a plate. The meat was fresh from the slaughter last week at the Rawlins' cattle ranch.

Lilly sat at the picnic table, "This is the life, huh, Emma?"

Emma set her chair down and put the salad on the table. "I am so glad to be here."

Lilly handed her a glass of wine, knowing she would take only a few sips and set it down, the same way she would probably only take a bite or two of meat, sneaking the rest to Bear. Lilly didn't understand her dear friend's strange ways but she accepted them, dubbing her "Mrs. Natural" years ago.

Midnight spread an herb and garlic rub on the meat. "God! That smells divine," said Emma. "Let me know when we're five minutes away and I'll do the salad."

Lilly got up and stirred a small pot of beans at the edge of the fire.

"How's Clare doing?" Emma asked her.

"That's a whole other story I need to talk with you about."

Clare, who was just out of earshot, came into camp, her brown hair in a ponytail. She pulled a sweatshirt over her head. "Just so you all know, I fed everybody and they all have water." She took a dark beer from the cooler and sat down.

"Are you limping?" asked Emma.

"Yeah, I dropped a pan on my foot at breakfast, I'll be all right. Where *is* Briar?" she asked, changing the subject.

Lilly looked at Midnight who was sipping a soda and shook her head. Midnight flipped her braid over her shoulder, her face expressionless. They heard a truck coming up the hill. It was Briar; she pulled around to the camp and jumped out.

"Jeez Louise! I thought I'd never get here. I'll just settle Elvira and be right back. Smells great! Save me some!"

45

The fillets were crusted brown as Midnight turned them. "Okay, Em, it's salad time!"

Briar came into camp carrying a container, her tall thin body elegant even in jeans and a tee shirt. Clare handed her a beer.

"You cannot believe how wrong the end of my day was," she said, her light green eyes wide. "The stallion I've had all month, well he's a real sweetheart and he did great, I mean really made progress, until today. The minute his owner showed up the horse went berserk. Broke away from him, ran all over. Jeez Louise! Of course that tells me all of my work with him was for nothing. I told the man if he ever wanted to sell him to let me know. I also suggested that he would make a great gelding. It was definitely something between them... Oh well... how is everybody?"

"Starving!" laughed Midnight.

They feasted. The steaks were butter tender, the salad and fry bread crisp.

"Everything is so good," said Clare taking another spoonful of Lilly's beans. "Mom's recipe, huh?"

Briar took more salad. "Who else is in camp? Anyone I know?"

"Oh, there's a family from Butte City over in #6. And I thought I saw Bethany Wineman," said Midnight. "Not sure though."

Lilly dropped her fork in the dirt, groaning as she retrieved it. "Damn! I hope not. I came up here to get away from the world, not to be reminded of people like her and her weird enviro cohorts."

Emma cleared her throat, "Have you ever met her?"

"No, and I don't want to either. These people move up from the city, tell us what to do, how to run our ranches, try to take our water away, think they know it all from their junk science...You know her?"

"She's actually an interesting person."

46

"Hmm," said Lilly sighing.

Clare started clearing dishes, pouring hot water into the rubber tub.

"Okay, Briar, what did you bring?" said Midnight, eyeing the plastic container.

"Oh, just my special fudge in case anyone has a chocolate attack."

They ate almost all of it.

"Get this away from me!" said Emma, pushing the candy towards the middle of the table.

It was almost dark. The horses stood quietly in their corrals; the dogs dozed at the edge of the fire. Lilly brought out her guitar and played the *Tennessee Waltz*. Clare sang harmony. Their sweet voices drifted over the campground.

Emma pulled her flannel shirt closer. After a few more songs, the warm fire and her full stomach set off a series of yawns. She finally stood up to say her goodnights.

"Me too," said Midnight, heading towards her tent.

Bear waited for Emma at the bathroom. She walked to the corral and checked on Mav, who sighed sleepily through his soft, loose lips. She helped the old dog get into the truck bed and climbed in after him; he curled at her feet. Her tired body sank into the comfortable bed. Above, the Milky Way was thick and bright and close.

Emma woke to Bear's face right above her own. "Gotta go, boy? Me too; hold on a minute." She opened the tailgate, hopped out and then helped the dog down. The camp was quiet. Thin clouds scudded across a pearl sky. On the way back from the bathroom she picked a few late-blooming St. John's Wort plants. She lit her one burner stove and boiled water for tea.

Bear was cruising for ground squirrels with Lilly's lab, Jonboy.

Smoke rose from Midnight's camp and Emma walked over, the cup of tea warming her hands. She found her friend feeding wood to an already hot fire.

"Morning, Emma, guess we're always the first ones up, huh? Think we'll ride out by noon?"

Emma laughed, "It's one of the Yee Haw rules to sleep in as long as we like."

Mav whinnied, starting a chain reaction of horse calls. "I'll go feed everybody, or no one will be able to sleep in." When she came back Midnight was sewing beads onto a leather shirt.

"God, that's pretty!"

"It's for the Salmon Ceremony. We're trying to outfit each kid with one."

"How are your classes doing?"

"Real good; we got a room to use at the community center. I teach dance Tuesdays and Thursdays. The Green River language classes are full. I'm glad the kids want to learn about their heritage. Julien is not too excited about it though. He's in a new rebel stage, partying all the time. After all that crap with his dad, I don't get it."

"Peer pressure, genetics—high school is a tough time," Emma tried to console her.

"Yeah, well I just want to shake him."

"You wouldn't be the first to feel that way," Emma chuckled. "What about his relationship with Liam?" As the name came from her mouth, her heart jumped, but she recovered herself.

"Yeah, my brother's a good role model and he tries to spend time with Julien, but you know, you can lead a horse to water but you can't make him think!" Emma laughed. "Julien chooses to be with his so-called friends 24/7."

Briar appeared and waved to them, then headed towards the corrals. Lilly wandered in, dressed in the sweats she'd slept in. Her blonde hair was ruffled and her half-lidded eyes searched for the coffee pot.

"Mornin', early birds," she mumbled, reaching for a cup.

Clare came out of the big tent she and Lilly shared with the dogs. "Are you alive, Lilly? I woke up sometime in the night and the whole tent was full of the foulest dog stench. No more beans for them!" said Clare, heading for the bathroom. Emma noticed that she was limping less.

Midnight turned the bacon, the salty smoke rising. Emma took a cantaloupe from the cooler and sliced it into eighths. Lilly brought out her special scrambled egg mixture, shaking the plastic pitcher before pouring it into the butter that sizzled in the pan.

Emma made a fresh pot of coffee. She heard the voices of children filter through the trees. She moved away from the fire. An unexpected sadness swept over her, and she breathed it away. The dogs, exhausted from their pre-dawn mischief, slept in the dirt.

"Okay, it's ready," called Lilly.

Briar came in and offered to slice the loaf of raisin bread that Clare had just put on the table. "I got hung up talking with Bethany Wineman. She was having trouble loading her mare."

"What kind of horse does she have?" asked Lilly, pouring half-and-half into her cup.

"Well, she's new at it, that's for sure…you guess."

"Well, let's see…I know, a Tobiano paint."

Briar started giggling. "God! How did you know that, Lilly?"

"Because that's the most popular horse today."

"Anyway," said Briar, helping herself to large portions of everything, "I helped her load her horse. Hey, Clare, who did you bring? I don't recognize him."

"That's Bandit," Clare said, "Don got him a few months ago. He's totally green."

Briar ran her hand through her dark hair. "When will people learn that you never name a horse Badger, or Bandit, or Buster? You were smart, Emma, calling your Maverick, Mav, as soon as you got him."

"Better than his registered Arab name, which is Zee Mousad," replied Emma.

"Oh, fancy!" said Lilly. "He's a good boy though, not a hyper airhead like some of them."

Midnight got up and moved a frying pan to the edge of the fire. "Well, what do you think? Be ready at 11:30?"

"Twelve would be more like it; I'm on dishes this morning."

Emma caught Midnight's look and held her thumb up in response. "You were right," she mouthed to her.

"Oh! I know what I forgot to ask you guys." Briar stood up, coffee cup in hand and moved with her backside to the fire. "You know my friend Marlene, over on the coast? Well, she and some of her friends have rescued these promarin mares."

"What's a promarin mare?" asked Clare, clearing the dishes.

Midnight poured bacon grease into the dog dishes. "Is it a breed? I've never heard of it."

Lilly looked up, suddenly interested, "Did you say _pro mare in_?"

"Uh huh," Briar answered, her mouth full of toast.

Emma wiped down the vinyl tablecloth. "You mean as in hormone replacement therapy?"

Lilly blurted, "That's what I'm taking for my hot flashes! I don't understand—what does it have to do with rescue horses?"

"Everything!" said Briar. "You see, somehow the hormones in pregnant mares' urine are used in many medicines for woman who have had hysterectomies or are suffering from symptoms of menopause. Note the word 'mare' in the name. Millions of women unknowingly put pregnant mare urine into their bodies every day."

Midnight smirked, "I probably shouldn't bring this up, but how in the hell do they collect it?"

"That's the awful part," said Briar sighing. "These poor horses are hooked up to catheters 24/7. They're kept in concrete cubicles in these giant factories. They kill their foals and breed them back over and over..."

"Okay, that's enough," said Emma. "Mary Mother of God! What will humans think of next? And Lilly, there are other meds that are made from plants that work."

"Good! I'm not taking horse pee for no reason, no way!"

Briar continued, "They, my friends, need a place for an extra mare they were able to rescue. Anyone have room or time?"

"Not me," said Clare.

"Or me either," chimed Lilly.

Midnight looked thoughtful. "It would be up to Liam to decide, but I don't think so."

"I could," said Emma. "Mav seems lonely since Cherry left. Is she pregnant?"

"Well yeah, that's the catch, but Marlene says the foals should be healthy. This one's due in the spring. I'll help you place them after that, okay?"

"Okay," said Emma, "it might be nice to have a baby around."

"Oh! be careful what you wish for," laughed Lilly.

"I'm gonna get Molly ready now," said Midnight. Walking to her pickup, she grabbed a muck shovel and swung it over her shoulder.

"First me, then the horse," said Emma, getting up.

The camp was quiet as the women prepared for the ride. Emma dressed and took Mav out and tied him to the fence. She scooped last night's dung into the wheelbarrow that the Forest Service provided. As she pushed it towards the pile at the center of camp, she caught a glimpse of Clare tying the buckskin to the side of the trailer. She had just stepped behind him to get to the saddle when the horse spooked. Rising straight into the air then pulling back with all his might, his haunches fell under him onto the ground, while his neck and front legs were arched and stretched by the taut rope. Emma saw Briar and Lilly running towards Clare and the horse.

"Whoa! Whoa!" said Briar, pushing the frozen Clare out of the way. In a flash her knife was in her hand. "Watch out! He could go down!" yelled Briar just before she cut the rope. As if in slow motion, the freed horse flew backwards, sliding on the ground, his front legs splayed out before him. When he finally got up, he was breathing hard and trembling.

"Easy, easy, boy, you're okay," Briar spoke to him. Frantic calls came from the other horses; although out of sight they had sensed trouble.

"Everyone all right, Clare?"

"Yeah, I'm fine," she said under her breath.

"Has Bandit ever been to the mountains?"

"I have no idea, Briar. I doubt it."

"Why don't you ride Elvira today? I'd like to get to know this guy. How old is he supposed to be?"

"I think five or six"

"Here, I'll switch saddles with you," she said.

By the time every buckle, snap, tie, bit, strap, hook, cinch, and loop was fastened and secured, the sun was high overhead.

They went out of the campground the back way, heading west. The horses were excited. Midnight led the way, her mustang, Molly, being the fastest. Next came Emma, Lilly, Clare, and finally Briar. The horses picked their way through the small logs and slash on the ground. The smell of dried pine needles followed them down the hill.

Some of the barefoot horses walked lightly on the graveled road. Their destination was Hidden Lake, about eight miles in. They rode up through a series of woods, meadows, and rocky plateaus. The climb was gradual at first, and soon they were in deep old growth. Emma wondered about the first people here, how beautiful and peaceful the natives' lives must have been. She thought about Lilly's ancestors who came in the 1800's to mine gold in the valley's boom time, then turned to logging the huge trees. Once, in one of the meadows, Lilly had shown her a stump as big as a car.

It was cool and dark, the forest floor cushioned with twigs and bits of decaying bark. After a few miles, a tunnel of light appeared and they came out into a meadow. On both sides the mountains rose to an elevation of 6,000 feet. The meadow, although not as soggy as it had been in July, was still green and dotted with skunkweed.

They stopped to let the horses drink from the cracked creekbed. Briar got off and adjusted Bandit's cinch. So far, he had followed the other horses, but Briar could feel his fear of the unknown just under his skin. Mav stood in the water making gulping sounds; afterwards, he raised his head, his muzzle dripping.

Again they climbed upwards, terrace after rocky terrace, the boulder-laden switchbacks so steep that one horse would make the traverse while the others waited, dancing in place to keep their footing. Bandit started rearing, refusing to move forward, and trying to turn around on the narrow path. Briar spoke softly, looking to see what might have frightened him. She saw something move just ahead of them. The snake was curled on a rock, its head lifted, tongue darting. It was so close she could see the diamond patterns on its body.

"Hey, Lilly?" she shouted. No one had spoken for so long that it woke the women up, and when they heard the word *snake* everyone pulled their horses up short and stopped. They all edged their horses as close to the uphill slope as possible so Lilly could get to Briar. Like stones in a dry gourd, the snake's rattles hissed in the air. Lilly took the gun out of her saddlebag and was releasing the safety when the snake disappeared, as if it had been sucked back into the pile of blonde boulders.

"Ha!" Midnight yelled, "one for the snake." They all laughed and started up the hill again.

The afternoon heat was intense. The horses were lathered up and breathing hard. They crossed the last creek and Briar urged Bandit through the water. Clare turned towards her and said, "I can't believe how great he's doing, Briar, thank you!" She then patted Elvira's rump, "Vi is so easy."

"She's one of a kind," said Briar, "I wish we could clone her."

They were getting close to the lake, but it wasn't visible until they were almost to the shore. Slowly the horses made the last effort. They pushed forward, breaking through an area of small pines and scrub. The lake, cupped on three sides by huge mountains, lay like a calm green stone before them. They were the only people there, and after a moment of quiet, Lilly started yelling. "Yee Haw! Yee Haw! Last one in is a rotten hag."

The women dismounted, and their saddles thunked to the ground. All except Clare kicked off their boots and peeled off their clothes. Briar handed over Bandit's reins and got on Elvira, feeling the ring of sweat from the saddle on her thighs.

They rode into the lake. The horses let the sandy bank give way beneath them, as their strong legs paddled in place. Molly tossed her head, whipping water all over Midnight. Lilly's horse, Joe, swam out to the middle. Lilly stood up and dove off. "Oh my God! Heaven!" she called, as she surfaced and scrambled once again onto the horse's broad back.

Elvira swam, prancing through the water, thunderous splashes stirring up flecks of gold. Briar leaned forward and embraced the copper mare's throat.

After the swim, the women dressed and tied the horses to small trees to dry out in the sun. Each rider had brought an apple, and the tired beasts munched peacefully. The women lounged on the rocks. Their clothes felt warm against their lake-cooled skin.

The ride back was uneventful except for some lightning and thunderheads that boomed in the distance. The horses were grateful to be penned and fed. The women ate a late dinner: Briar's garlic bread, Emma's stir fry with noodles, and Midnight's salmon to top it all off. After only a few songs around the fire, they agreed that their bodies felt good but tired. Camp was dark and quiet by ten o'clock. A light rain fell as the last lantern went out.

On Sunday morning Lilly and Clare packed up early. Midnight was gone by noon. In the late afternoon Emma and Briar took one last ride through Big Meadow. They paused after crossing the creek, where sun speckled a small pool.

"Emma? When I was taking a shower last week, I think I found a lump in my breast. I'm not very good at these self-exam deals. What should I do?"

"Come see me. Let's see, Monday afternoon, are you free?"

"Yeah, I'll be there." She looked away.

"I wouldn't worry about it. Thirty-five is very young. It's just good to check it out."

"Okay, thanks. Race you to the top!" she said, turning the blue-eyed mare around.

"God have mercy, Briar, I'm an old woman."

"Bull Crap! Your horse is twice as fast as mine." Briar shot back, then took off at a dead run. Emma felt Mav meet the challenge and relaxed in the saddle. The only thing left to do was give him his head and hang on.

By the time they returned to camp and packed up, dusk had fallen. On the way down the mountain, Emma realized that although her body was exhausted, she somehow felt renewed. She looked forward to a hot bath. Light rimmed the valley. The first stars pocked a Prussian blue sky. It would be good to be home.

As night fell, the house waited. Cool air caused beams to creak and contract. The wind from an open upstairs window, slithered downstairs and softly banged the wooden screen door. In a downstairs closet six newborn mice slept against their mother's brown fur. At exactly sundown, crows cawed on their way up the mountain to roost, while little birds flew at them, pecking at their ragged feathers. Bats flew out of their attic cave one at a time, each one jumping into mid-air as if to say *Ta Da!*, then free-falling away towards an insect buffet. Cats dozed near the back door, waiting to be let in. The elder of the raccoons, a tall thin one with a grey speckled mask, led the raid on cat food. As Emma's truck pulled into the driveway the house sighed and settled into its worn wooden floor. Sleep at last.

Chapter Six

RJ pulled the black Lexus into the driveway. Hard to tell if the old man was home, because he often walked to his office near the Butte City courthouse. *Well, no car,* thought RJ, ducking through the big double garage instead of going to the front of the lavish house. He heard the maid, Frita, singing in the kitchen.

"Shut up, Fritolay!" he told her, slamming his books on the table. She started and turned. "What's up, Mamacita?" As he knew she would, she smiled her grandmotherly smile at him. She'd worked there ever since his mother left when he was four. Frita pretended she didn't understand a word he spoke, but he knew better. "Where's the old man?" he asked her.

"Trabajo," she said, taking a sandwich out of the fridge and handing it to him. He wolfed the sandwich down and gulped the milk she'd set down before him.

"Those cats still in the wood pile?" Frita became agitated and started waving her arms and shaking her head "no" over and over. RJ got up and strutted out the back door. The wood pile was behind the garage. The mother cat eyed him warily. "Here kitty, kitty," he called in his high-pitched voice. A little yellow one poked its head out of the wood pile and meowed hungrily. RJ leaned down and slammed a log down on its back. It struggled, shaking its head and tail, then convulsed and went still. He picked up the limp kitten and threw it behind the wood pile.

Back inside, he climbed the stairs. He washed his hands in the bathroom. In his room he sat at the computer and Googled the Aryan teen website. Lots of kids from all over wrote on it. It made sense, he thought. If the world was rid of all the non-whites, it would be a better place. He took out the swastika he kept hidden in his sock drawer and put the pendant around his neck. Hitler had it right. Even his asshole dad told him that he was lucky to be a white boy, because they were better than other people and smarter. Oh yeah, his dad, the important Butte City County Commissioner—*what a joke*—pretended to like people of color in his job, but RJ knew better. And besides, the whole county, *what, maybe 40,000 people?* was almost all white. There were more Indians in the school in Green Valley than there had been in Butte City. He didn't like Green Valley school, but it was better than the lockdown private school he'd almost had to go to before his dad had "pulled strings" after RJ was kicked out of Butte City High.

He opened the desk drawer, took out a razor blade, looked at it, and put it back. He put a heavy metal CD in the player. He clicked on a photo he'd taken of the new girl at school.

Cat! What kind of name was that? And what the fuck was she? Sure not white. He didn't like the way she looked at him. *Weird little bitch…*

Cat and Amy Lee walked up to the football field to eat their lunches. Cat still wasn't used to the wooded mountainside behind the high school. There was even a waterfall where some of the kids went to smoke during lunch. The football and track team ran the trails during PE. Football seemed to be a big deal in the valley. Amy Lee had invited her to the first few games, but Cat hadn't gone. She'd found the girl to be sincere and friendly so far, way more than some of the other kids.

The bell rang and they walked back to the quad. An hour later Cat came out of English, stirred. Literature was her favorite subject, and the young teacher was pretty good. They'd discussed *The Scarlet Letter*, which Cat had read when she was twelve, and considered required reading for the daughter of a whore. The teacher had asked her to read her paper out loud. She was really scared, but she did okay. It had been a week without an incident at school; as she looked back on it, she must have relaxed her guard.

RJ was waiting for her with some other boys. He grabbed her arm and she froze, letting her arm go limp. He leaned down and put his pale, pocked face near hers. He smelled like alcohol.

"Hey you!" he said, pinching her arm hard, "I been wantin' to ask, you dress all in black to match your face?" Her heart banged.

"Aw, come on, RJ," said one of the boys, walking off a little, "leave her alone." Some more kids gathered around.

"Shut the fuck up!" he shouted back. He got in her face again, his eyes wild. She wouldn't look at him, so he took his other hand and turned her head towards him.

"C'mon little girl, you a midget too? Cat got yer tongue?" He laughed in a strange demented way. More kids stopped and listened. Cat felt the backpack strap cutting into her shoulder. A boy with a long red ponytail passed by and turned, staring.

"Are you a spic? A dreadlock jew? Your hair is kinky enough," RJ said, reaching out and touching the wiry black halo.

"You Indian? Hey, Julien, is she Geek River? Is she your

cousin?" Julien's face was serious as he walked away. A fat kid laughed.

"Tell me!" RJ said under his breath, "what are you?"

She yanked her arm out of his grip and put it through the backpack strap. The crowd was quiet, waiting. She took her time. "Well I been wantin' to ask you, cowboy, that big belt buckle, is it making up for something?" Someone chuckled. "Maybe something that's too small?"

RJ glared at her.

"And as far as *WHAT I AM?*" she nodded her head slowly, "I'm a lot of things, but at least I'm not a redneck white ass John Wayne wet dream!" There was a stunned silence, followed by wild laughter.

"She got you, RJ!"

"Dang! She's little but tough!"

RJ looked shocked. For a moment Cat stood there and faced him off, then spun around and walked away.

Chapter Seven

Emma pulled the last vegetables out of the garden. Several small pumpkins were piled in a basket, and a good crop of red potatoes would keep well underground. She'd cut a large bunch of kale, its crinkled leaves still green. Now she needed to pull out all of the brown, leafless stalks. She yanked hard on the rooted sticks.

It had been a stressful three weeks since horse camp. Briar had waited for over two weeks before coming for a breast exam. Emma had never seen her so nervous, and in the end she had a right to be. Emma had found large masses in both breasts. Briar was undergoing a series of mammograms and sonograms to determine malignancy this week. Emma had a very strong feeling it was cancer.

"No!" she said firmly out loud, as she shook the spidery root balls free of dirt. "She's too young! Why Briar?" *Briar, who had been through so much as a child.*

Standing near the sunflowers she heard her grandmother's voice, *"Never ask why; why is only for God to know."* Emma missed her then, like an ache. Always the matriarch of their family, Gran Genevieve, an RN herself, had kept the big Victorian in San Francisco running like a well-oiled machine. This was no small feat, considering that Emma's father had his medical practice downstairs. Gran could make ten pounds of stew in the morning, work in the garden, take off her gloves and wash up to help her son, Marcus, deliver twins, and be there after school for Emma and her brother, Thomas, with steaming mugs of black tea and hot scones. To this day, Emma continued the traditional English ritual of tea. Gran had taught her that no matter what was going on — good news, bad news, indecisiveness — it was easier to celebrate, grieve, or take the time to *"think about it"* with a warm cup of tea.

Emma's mother, Katherine, had loved Gran too. Her presence in the house had given Katherine the freedom she needed to raise funds and attend her beloved social engagements. It was Gran who taught Emma about herbs. They would spend hours in the terraced garden, the moist air blowing in from the bay. Then Gran would invite her into the basement, which she called her "laboratory." The small earthen room was lined with shelves full of jars, bottles, and tins. It smelled of wintergreen, lemon balm, and the clean scent of drying lavender. Emma never tired of the stories Gran told her about her mother and grandmother. They'd lived in a small village in Cornwall, England. She described the cobbled streets and whitewashed houses, the hilly farms that overlooked the sea. They were known as wise women, or good women, healing with herbs, midwifing babies, and helping people die. Emma's identification with Gran and her love of gardening had inspired her to be a nurse/midwife. Now, she and her brother Thomas were the only ones left.

A flock of little black and grey birds flew into the brittle cornstalks, rattling them like castanets. *Don't ask why*, she told herself, pushing the wheelbarrow over to the compost pile. How many times had Gran told her this same thing? When Liam married Gretta and Emma thought her life was over at eighteen. Again, when her husband Ronnie and their child died in a car accident. She stood looking at the raggedy, dry garden that had, just a few months ago, been green and plump and ordered. She could remain detached from her practice most of the time, but this was Briar.

Emma didn't know what to do with herself. She'd been faxed the results of Briar's tests and scans the night before and had gotten little sleep. She'd cleaned, organized and straightened the exam room and still there was an hour before Briar's appointment. She opened the back door; wind-blown leaves spiraled in the corner by the potted lavender. She sat down under the arbor. The old grapevine was sticky and heavy with ripe concords. She picked one and sucked it. She'd given out a lot of bad news but never to someone this close. *I better not cry*, she thought.

The old, portly, tortoise shell cat toddled over to her. The calico came out of the shed and stretched and yawned. The young black hellion leapt down from the trellis and head butted her ankle, purring. A timed trio of meows started and built to a frenzy. They might as well have been yelling at her.

"What?" she asked them, then remembered that she was out of cat food. "Good, something to do."

She grabbed her purse from the house and drove the few miles to Willard's Market. She was thinking about what else she needed when she saw Liam's pickup parked in front. She felt a rush of panic; her gut instinct was to leave, turn around and just drive away. *This is ridiculous*, she told herself. She turned into the parking lot and sat looking at her face in the mirror. *Nice dark circles*, she scoffed, finger-combing her hair.

Inside the store she walked down the aisles, all her senses heightened with the anticipation of seeing him. She heard his deep voice before she saw him. It triggered a purely visceral physical response that she couldn't control. She willed her body to be steady.

"Emma," he said in his low slow voice. She turned; his six-foot-five height always caught her off guard. "Emma, how are you? It's been so long."

It had been so long. It had been almost five months since she'd seen him. She looked up into his craggy face. He had his sister Midnight's hazel eyes and dark skin. She noticed the silver threaded through the braid that fell in a straight line down his back. He waited for her to answer. She couldn't find words for a moment, the pleasure of standing near him all mixed up with memories of the exquisite pain he'd caused over her lifetime. *No! no! no!* she stopped herself. *What had he asked her?*

"Um…oh, just busy with the patients and babies, not much else. Went to Hidden Horse with the ladies a few weeks ago. Teaching a class for foster parents…What about you?"

"The same, not much going on. Sometimes life's a torrent…I guess I'm in an eddy right now." She studied his face and hands while he spoke. "Kinda looking forward to winter though. I'm working on several pieces."

She looked at his long fingers, so feminine compared to the rest of him. "Pieces" was all she heard. "Uh huh, are you still showing in Wolf Creek?"

"The gallery owner said they'd take as many as I can give them." He looked at the floor, then shyly into her eyes. "It's been good; the more I carve the more I learn." Emma shifted the bag of cat food to her other arm.

"Want me to take that to the check stand?" He was looking at her in a way that made her feel both intensely present and not in her body at all.

"No thanks, I've got it." She looked at her watch. "I really have to go, I've got an appointment…Well," she started to move away from him, "good to see you, Liam."

He followed her a few steps then stopped. "Okay, you too, Emma, you too."

She knew he'd watch her walk all the way down the aisle. She didn't dare look back. *Go quickly*, she thought, heading for the checkout with no line. Back in the truck she stepped on it and drove out of the parking lot just as he came out. She chanced a look back; he was standing there, his face serious, both arms holding bags, watching her drive away.

After she fed the yowling cats, whose demanding meows sounded like "Now! Now! Now!," she put the kettle on and laid out a tray, cups and saucers, sugar, milk, and spoons. She hugged Gran's brownstone teapot to her chest and prayed, *Be with me, dear one.* She poured the boiling water over the teabags. How would she find the words to tell Briar? The phone rang, and she stood looking out the window as she answered a new mother's questions. She saw Briar's pickup pull into the driveway and watched her get out. Old Bear wagged up to her and smiled as she petted his head.

Emma went to the door, phone in hand, and waved Briar in, pointing to the steaming teapot on the table, then disappeared into the exam room. Briar hung her coat. Emma came in then and hugged her lightly.

"Let's go into the living room." She picked up the tray. The living room windows poured light into the room. Emma moved a vase of flowers and set the tray down. She watched Briar place her long feet on the flowered wool rug. She poured the tea and handed Briar a cup. "How are you, honey?" A blue jay screeched outside; the fire popped.

Briar didn't meet her eyes. "I'm nervous, just tell me?" she swallowed.

"Well, it's not good." Briar looked at the vase of flowers

and counted…*one, two, three, four, five daisies.* "Both masses are malignant."

"God," she fingered her jacket buttons up, down, up, down. Emma sipped her tea and let her take it all in. After a long silence, which felt like lifetimes to Emma, Briar asked, "They're sure?"

"The oncologist will have films to show you."

Briar closed her eyes, then looked at Emma. "Okay, now what?"

"Probably surgery, check the lymph system to see if it's spread. I suggest Dr. Carter in Bradford. I can set it up, even go with you. Dr. Drew says he's the best."

Something declared itself in Briar. She slumped forward, literally weighed down with the realization.

Emma moved to her, sat down, and put her arm around her thin shoulders. "You must be overwhelmed. Just remember there are many options to cure it."

She felt Briar stiffen, take in a breath, then get up abruptly. "Okay, Emma, thanks for your honesty. I've got to go feed… I'll call you in the morning."

"Walk you out?"

"No thanks." She buttoned her jacket. Emma opened the door and Briar slid past her, walking quickly to the truck.

Emma cleared the tea things. After drying her hands she took a sweater off the coat rack. She found Mav in the northeast pasture, dozing under a big pear tree.

"Hey, boy," she moved into him, leaning her head against his massive chest. The horse nickered softly and stood solidly, calm and steady, while her sobs broke against him.

Chapter Eight

Cat, alone in the locker room, heard loud cheers from the football field. She looked in the mirror. It was Halloween; most of the kids were dressed up and wearing weird make-up.

Hell, she thought, *it's the only day I'll ever fit in around here.* She had always worn costumes. When your clothes came from Goodwill or the free box, you had to be creative. She'd always had a thing for putting together something crazy but cool, and she'd always worn weird make-up. Her small self looked back at her, long black hair down and wild today, black sweater, black skin-tight lace-up pants, good ol' black high-heeled boots. She puckered, applying maroon lipstick.

It seemed random how Amy Lee had come up to her at lunch. Cat was reading and picking at her sandwich.

"You want to party tonight after the game?"

Cat didn't know what to say.

"Me and some of the other kids, we're going up to the cabin on Halfway. C'mon, it'll be fun. We're leaving right after the game."

"I'll think about it," Cat had muttered, hurrying off to class. She was so bloody bored; in the end, she'd decided to go.

Wind whipped the black and orange streamers wrapped around the flagpole in the high school parking lot. Cat and Amy Lee climbed into the car that belonged to Josh York's girlfriend, Liz. The couple sat in front, while Amy Lee, Cat, and Julien were wedged into the back seat.

"That team sucked! What a bunch of jerks." Liz opened a Silver Bullet and drank daintily; she wiped her mouth on her sleeve.

"Yeah, Fort Wisdom. They're always jerks and they always win."

Josh turned onto Highway 1 and drove across the valley. Clouds circled a big rising moon. Wind gusts jerked the tinny little car. They passed the beer around. Julien opened another and handed it to Cat.

"Where are we going?" she asked no one in particular, as they started to climb towards the summit.

"It's an old cabin up in the mountains; we party there a lot," Amy said. Cat still hadn't gotten used to the jet-black nights here—no lights stretched across a city, only black forest and steep narrow roads.

"It's called Halfway because it's halfway between the valley and Butte City," said Liz.

Josh looked in the rearview mirror. "I think that's Bobby behind us." Lights lit up the inside of the car for a moment.

"Hey, could we pull over before you head up?" asked Julien, who already sounded drunk. They stopped and the boy disappeared into the trees. Josh and Liz were making out, Cat and Amy Lee quiet in the back. Julien came into the headlight beams still zipping his pants. The wind blew his long red hair out of its rubber band, and it flew around his face as he got back in. Another car full of kids passed them.

"Yup, it's Bobby… anybody have a hair tie?" he asked the girls.

"I might," said Cat, reaching into her pocket. The small car snaked up the mountainside. Wind ravaged the needled branches of giant pines and cedars, their long arms swaying frantically. Cat screamed as an owl, its wingspan wide as the car, almost flew into the windshield, then floated off above them.

"Shit!" she said.

"It was a big one," Julien speculated calmly.

"We're almost there," said Amy Lee, as they rounded a steep curve.

Tucked up in a stubbly draw, the property held a log cabin, some out-buildings and an old orchard, where there were still a few apples left on the trees. The night air carried the vinegary scent of rotted fruit. Used as a hunter's dump, scattered deer entrails, legs, and heads without horns gave off the rusty smell of dried blood. Inside the cabin someone had left tattered, overstuffed furniture raided by mice. Horsehair stuck up out of it like cowlicks.

Calvin Drucker popped open another beer and guzzled it down until a thunderous belch came up his craw, spraying beer over the other boys.

"Shit, man!" said Hubert Ross, wiping his hands on his No Fear T-shirt. Already drunk from shots in the school parking lot, he punched Calvin in the arm.

RJ Dobson lit a cigarette and blew out perfect smoke rings. "The game should be over; are you guys still up for it?"

"Up for what?" asked Chuck Gallegar.

"You know the plan," said RJ, not wanting to describe it.

"I'm in, but I want to live to see seventeen. You sure you got the right stuff?" asked Calvin.

"Don't worry," said RJ, touching his pocket, "I'm a pro."

Headlights appeared at the bottom of the hill.

"Then let the party begin!" screamed Chuck, waving his bottle of bourbon in the air. "No cops though, ya promise? That scared the fuck out of me last weekend."

"You drunk shit," said Hubert, "then don't pick a fight."

They tumbled out of cars and pickups, about a dozen kids pent up from losing the homecoming game. RJ, Hubert, and Chuck had built a bonfire in the field in back of the cabin, and everyone headed there. Several joints were passed, people were laughing, someone barfed in the shadows, and Josh asked if anybody had a condom. One of the cheerleaders gave him one, and he and Liz walked to her car. Julien took another swig from his bottle and passed it to Cat. She already felt dizzy, but took another gulp anyway. *What the hell.*

"Hey, cowboy," she shouted. Standing on the other side of the fire, RJ looked over at her. "Don't bogart that joint." Amy Lee giggled, RJ just smiled.

Someone started throwing pine cones into the hot fire. They exploded in fits of pitch, little bombs going off one after another. A drunken Hubert threw one at Chuck. It sparked loudly at his feet. Chuck grabbed him and started punching. It didn't last long; neither boy really wanted to fight.

Cat could feel RJ staring at her. She shuddered, suddenly chilled, and walked over to Amy Lee.

"Hey, Cat, how ya doing?" The girl was buzzed. With her genuine bubbliness she offered Cat a smile. They heard Liz's car start up.

"Shouldn't we be going?"

"Let's stay and have one more shot."

"I don't know…," Cat hesitated.

"It's okay, my cousin Chuck will drive us home, c'mon."

The boys were already in the cabin, where someone had lit a candle. They had dragged a very drunk Julien into the room; he sat slumped on one of the old chairs. RJ poured the shots and handed each girl a glass. Amy Lee gagged, but Cat just downed hers. Hubert and Calvin slouched on the mattress in the middle of the room. Amy Lee's head kept nodding towards her chest. Cat yawned. She tried to get up from the chair but stumbled. RJ caught her from falling and lifted her into his arms.

"Move!" he yelled at the boys on the bed. He tossed her onto the mattress.

"Hey, RJ! you didn't say anything about Amy Lee. She's my cousin and…"

"Shut up! I just had to knock her out too."

Julien looked up. "Whaass going on?" he slurred.

"Yeah well, first the pact. Raise your right hand and promise that you will never speak of this night. SWEAR!" RJ ordered.

They all raised their hands and mumbled their creed, then quickly stuck their hands in their pockets. Hubert licked his lips.

"Okay, you dumb shits, let's start. I'll go first." RJ turned towards the bed and took a knife out of his pocket.

"Whoa! Whoa! Wait a minute!" a panicked Chuck yelled.

"Shut up! I'm getting her pants off." RJ laughed and took his knife and carefully slit the soft vinyl material from Cat's inner thigh to her ankle. He did the same on the other side, then lifted the pants up behind her. She wore a black thong, and he pulled it over her boots and tossed it on the floor. He lifted her shirt, revealing a pierced navel and small breasts. He unzipped his jeans. He mounted her, but couldn't get it in at first. There was heavy breathing in the room. Then he pulled back and rammed her hard again and again.

"There! There!" he yelled, his contorted face a sweaty sheen. Afterwards, out of breath, he stood up, turned to the boys, and zipped his pants.

One by one they did her. RJ went over to Julien.

His hair hung in his face. "Hey, don't!" he batted at RJ.

"Okay, Redboy!" said RJ, "how's that Vee-agra working for ya?" He laughed. "It's your turn." He and Chuck lifted him off the chair.

"Stop it," mumbled Julien. They took off his pants and lifted him on top of Cat. RJ grabbed him, yanked on it, then pushed it into her.

"No! No!" Julien moaned, rolling off the girl and falling on the floor.

RJ's high-pitched laughter rang out. "Oh, Julien! You are in big trouble. Shit, man, we saw the whole thing…"

"Hello, hello?" Emma groped for the phone. The clock on the night stand said 3:55 a.m. She heard a woman screaming incoherently. The only words she could make out were "Caterina, Caterina."

"Jenny, Jenny? Is that you? What's wrong?" Then the phone went dead.

She pulled on her sweats as she hurried downstairs. Not knowing what to expect, she grabbed the medical bag that had once been her father's and rushed towards the truck. During the five mile drive she thought about Jenny, who could barely care for herself, let alone anyone else.

The night sky was a clear deep blue; stars glittered coldly overhead. Along the rind of the Eastside Mountains a band of gray indicated dawn. Smashed and broken Halloween pumpkins littered the vacant highway. She turned down Jenny's road, the wood and wire fences collapsed in on themselves. As the truck bounced down the dirt road she spotted a small figure on the old porch huddled over something. She reached for her bag and fumbled as she jumped out of the pickup, hurrying towards Jenny's keening.

A teenage girl lay on her back, spread-eagled, her pants slit up to her thighs; congealed blood covered her pubic area. "She's dead, Emma! Oh my God, Caterina's dead!"

Emma wasted no time with comforting words. She opened the bag, simultaneously bending down to listen for the girl's breath.

"No, she's not, Jenny; what happened?"

"I don't know," the old woman wheezed. "I heard a loud thump on the porch and a truck pulled away, fast, down the driveway."

Emma took a gauze pad from the bag and dabbed gently around the vaginal area. No new bleeding. She guessed the girl was either drunk or drugged. The word "rape" crossed her mind. She took her phone out of her pocket and punched in 911.

"Sit down now, Jenny, the ambulance is coming." She knew that it would take awhile. Because of budget cuts, the paramedics had to travel over the mountain from Butte City.

The old woman was breathing hard and shaking. The front door was open, and Emma entered the shabby living room. She grabbed two quilts off the torn couch and, moving quickly to where Jenny sat, she tucked a blanket around her and bent down to look into her eyes. "It's alright, Jenny."

Then she covered the girl with the other quilt and took her pulse. She saw lights turning onto the road and thought it would be the sheriff or a fire truck. The vehicle sped towards them, raising dust, then stopped. Jim Collins, one of the valley's two policemen, asked, "What's up, Emma?" while taking the steps two at a time.

"Not sure yet," she replied, "possibly drunk or drugged, maybe rape."

"I just heard on the radio. The ambulance is halfway over the mountain," Jim said hurriedly. "If it's ok, I'm gonna go. Almost all of the crews are down river—we've got a hell of a fire over at Carlotti's. Are you alright by yourself?"

"I think so; her vitals are good."

"Ok, Emma." His car raced back down the road.

She heard a strangled gurgle and got up, turning towards Jenny. The old woman's eyes were rolled back, and Emma caught her just before she fell. She laid her down on the porch and started CPR, slowly pushing, then breathing, pushing, breathing. She put her ear over the woman's mouth, nothing. She took her pulse, nothing. Jenny stared up as if interested in the papier-mâché hornets' nest on the porch ceiling. Emma tried a few more times then stopped. Jenny was gone.

"Mother Mary." She pulled the blanket from the metal chair, and covered Jenny's body. Emma sat down on the worn boards and waited. Half light, laden with bird song, rose around her. Trees, sheds, and a large pig rooting in the garden revealed themselves.

Emma rode in the ambulance with Jenny and Cat. She wanted to be there in case the girl woke up en route. At the hospital they checked for semen, stitched her torn labia and hooked her up to an I.V.

A nurse tiptoed into the room and asked Emma to sign papers so Jenny's body could be transported to the mortuary. After the door closed, Emma stood over the girl, who looked so peaceful and innocent against the white sheets. Her long, black hair splayed across the pillow; her small dark face, although smeared with mascara, was delicate and beautiful.

The girl's long lashes quivered as she tried to open her eyes. She looked up into Emma's face, disoriented, and asked quietly, slurring slightly, "Where am I?"

Emma explained that she was in the hospital and why. At the word "rape" the girl's face melted, and she turned into the pillow. Emma told her about the stitches and the I.V., and asked her about birth control. Cat looked up at her, confused, and nodded yes.

Sensing the girl needed to be alone she said, "Caterina, my name is Emma. I'll be right outside the door if you need me." Once in the hallway Emma leaned against the antiseptic wall and closed her eyes.

By midmorning the girl was lucid, and Emma stood near her bed while the police questioned her. She told them of the party at the cabin—how she'd come with Amy Lee, and about the boys who were there at the end. With an expressionless face, a policeman asked if she'd had consensual sex with all five boys. After a moment Cat glared up into his face and hissed, "I wouldn't touch any of them with a ten-foot pole."

Chapter Nine

The girl was released to Emma temporarily until Child Protective Services decided what to do with her. She was mute on the ride home, sitting as close to the window as possible. They stopped at Jenny's briefly, so she could get some clothes. As she waited in the truck, Emma saw the rundown house through the girl's eyes. Green Valley must have been a drastic change from the streets of Phoenix. From what Emma understood, she had no other relatives except her mother, who was in jail.

Cat came down the ragged steps carrying a duffel bag. She was still in scrubs from the hospital, as her own clothes had been taken for DNA testing. *God!* Emma thought, looking at her face, *she's just a baby.*

Emma knew by the loud old pipes in the house that the girl had taken an hour-long shower, which had given her time to make up the bed in the library upstairs. The room looked out over the orchard. Bookshelves lined the four walls, and a double bed and dresser stood at one side. She had decided that the upstairs room would offer more privacy than the downstairs guest room. Emma looked out at the dark sky, the thick, snotty rain. She made up the bed with flannel sheets and turned up the space heater. By the time she returned with a tray of tea and sandwiches, the girl had closed and locked the door.

"Okay, Caterina, there's some food out here. Get some rest; I'll check on you later."

On the way downstairs she made a mental note to set her up with counseling right away. The kitchen was chilly, and she turned on the kettle. Her phone rang.

"Hello."

"Emma, it's Lilly."

"Hi."

"Did you hear about Jenny Brown? Evidently she had a heart attack and died."

"Yeah, I know."

"There are rumors all over the valley that her granddaughter was involved with some of the kids from the high school. Clare called and said Josh was at the party."

Here we go, thought Emma, *not twenty-four hours later and the story is already out.*

Lilly rushed on, "Clare said the girl in question is accusing some of the boys at the party of rape! She's beside herself, although Josh said he left early with his girlfriend...Emma?... Emma?"

"I'm here, Lilly." She took a deep breath, "Yes, I know about it, but I can't say much yet, confidential you know. As a matter of fact the girl is here with me."

"She is?...Why?"

"Because she didn't have anywhere else to go, and..."

"Oh! be careful, Emma. Connie Parker told Clare that the girl is a real case. Dresses all in black, wears weird make-up. Connie said that her mother is in jail...maybe you shouldn't get involved."

"I already am, Lilly. Let's wait and see what happens when we learn the facts."

"Do you know any of the boys that were there? I heard Julien was involved."

"I can't say. Lilly, do me a favor and don't talk about it, okay?"

"...Okay, Em, I'll change the subject then. How is Briar?"

"She's doing as well as can be expected I think; it's such a shock, you know."

"Well, she won't answer her phone, I've left several messages."

"I think she needs some time to herself; don't take it personally, sweetie. She only found out a little while ago, and the surgery is soon. Keep trying though, I know she appreciates the support."

"God, Emma, she's gonna be okay isn't she?"

"Honestly, Lilly, I don't know, let's hope so." Emma heard a door upstairs open. "I've gotta go, Lilly, I'll be in touch." By the time she got upstairs the door was locked again. The tray hadn't been touched.

Midnight paced the length of her small cabin trying to make sense of the phone call she had received from the high school principal that afternoon. Mr. Janus told her that Julien had been involved, along with other boys, in an "incident" after the homecoming game on Friday night. When she had asked him what kind of incident, Mr. Janus said that he wasn't sure of the details yet, but that it might possibly involve the alleged rape of another student. He needed permission from her, as the police would be questioning the boys after school. As she hung up the phone, her mind had raced in a thousand directions. Julien had spent the weekend at the Gallegars. She had only seen him briefly Sunday night. He was his usual sullen self, and she had gone to bed early.

She had been waiting for him ever since the call. She moved back and forth on the worn rug, pulling at her braid. She couldn't imagine that Julien, quiet, gentle Julien, could be a part of something like this. *Where was he? It was after five now!*

She went outside to get some wood. The tall cliffs above the cabin were draped in fog, and thick shrouds hung in the trees. Below, the river's distant roar echoed up to her. She split a chunk for kindling, the hatchet slicing sticks of pungent cedar. Fear overtook her momentarily. She knew that he had been drinking, and recently, when she had smelled alcohol on his breath, they had gotten into it. But rape? She couldn't go there. *Wait and see,* she told herself.

Where The Hell Was He? she thought, dumping the wood into a bucket. She moved towards the cabin, but the sound of his truck bumping up the hill stopped her. She set the wood down, vowing to herself to stay calm. The small blue truck edged slowly towards her; Julien's face looked blank. Then, full of fear, he eased his tall body out the door and stood before her, his eyes on the ground.

"Well?" she said.

"What?" he answered defensively.

"Mr. Janus called; where have you been?"

"The police kept us after school."

"What's going on, son? Mr. Janus said that you may have been involved in a...," the word lodged in her throat, "that something happened after the game Friday."

"Mom, I don't know! I don't remember anything."

"You don't remember? Come on!"

A minute passed before he spoke. "Mom, I was drunk, ok? We were up at the cabin on Halfway; a bunch of kids were partying after the game..." He ran his long fingers, so much like his father's, through his red hair.

He's stalling, she thought. "I'm waiting, Julien…"

"I don't know anything. Most of the kids left. The last thing I remember, I was in the cabin sitting in a chair. I think I was passed out."

"You *think* you were passed out?"

"Mom! I don't know what happened."

"Who else was there?"

"This kid, RJ, Chuckie, Hubert, maybe Amy Lee, this new girl, I don't know."

Her voice rose, "What happened, Julien!"

"I swear to God, Mom!…I swear on Dad and Grandma's graves, I don't remember!"

She bit off each word, "What are you being accused of?"

He shuffled his feet, swallowed and mumbled, "Rape."

"Shit, Julien!…What did the police say? Who were they?"

"Two sheriffs from Butte City. I didn't know them. They said this new girl had been drugged and raped in the cabin."

"What did the other boys say?"

"They all said the girl had sex with them willingly."

"And you, what did they say was your part in it?"

He started to cry then, big loud, gulping sobs. She stopped herself from going to him. He looked twelve years old, not sixteen. Her nails dug into her palms; she was trying to stay in control. Her mother's heart wanted to hold him. She waited. The lower limbs of a big pine lifted and swayed before her.

"They said, they said," he hiccupped, unable to catch his breath, "they said… I did it, that I had sex with her too. Mom! Mom! You've got to believe me, I wouldn't…couldn't DO… THAT!…I don't remember…any of it."

Her voice was hard and cold. "And why, Julien? Why don't you remember anything? Tell me, son, tell me now!"

He broke again and fell to his knees. "Because, because I was drunk," he wailed, "really drunk."

"Precisely," she spat out, "because as you well know from your father's sorry life, when you are drunk you do things like die in a motorcycle accident. Or maybe even rape someone..."

Furious, she picked up the wood bucket and stomped into the cabin. She crushed sheets of newspaper into tight balls and threw them into the stove. Grabbing a handful of kindling, she layered it on top, arranging the sticks in a criss-cross pattern, piling them just so. The wooden match scraped across the rock hearth. The paper caught fast, and the dry wood crackled, pitch popping, as flames shot up. She stood and looked out the window. Julien was laying face down in the dirt, his hands over his head, his plaid flannel shirt rising and falling with the rhythm of his shame.

Emma's life had turned crazy so suddenly that she found herself forgetting little details. The girl, Cat, who had asked Emma not to call her Caterina, needed so much. Emma arranged for counseling. It was decided that Cat would apply for emancipated minor status and stay with Emma for the time being. She was still withdrawn, but cooperative.

She had been interviewed again by the police and had stuck to her story. In a way, Emma was glad Cat didn't remember anything. DNA tests had shown five individual sperm samples. At least four of the boys said she had taken the drug willingly and consented to sex. Julien still claimed he was too drunk to remember the act. Luckily, while still in the hospital, the girl had told Emma that she was on birth control. Emma meant to ask her if she needed her prescription refilled.

Cat now came down for meals, but was still holed up in the library most of the day. Emma noticed her choice of books on the night stand: *To Kill a Mockingbird*, *Of Mice and Men*, poems of Anaïs Nin. Not your usual sixteen-year-old street person's interests.

Jenny Brown's funeral had been a simple affair with mostly members from the Green River tribe in attendance. Cat sat stoically next to Emma throughout the short service. Bill Plainsford was working on the estate, and Midnight had offered to help. In the middle of all of this, Emma had seen a dozen or so patients. Mary Milich had her baby at home, an easy, joyful birth for a mother of now eight children.

Thanksgiving was right around the corner. Briar's surgery was the Monday after. Emma's brother Thomas had other plans, so Emma was going to cook for Cat and Briar. The Yee Haws would go for their annual Turkey Trot ride the day after, preferring riding and picnicking to the traditional busiest shopping day of the year at the mall in Bradford. She looked forward to the ride, having had no time for Mav in the last month.

Chapter Ten

Bud came up behind Lilly and kissed her neck. "Nice way to wake up," he whispered.

"Yeah, better than coffee," she smiled, adding cranberry sauce to the turkey sandwiches she was making.

"Not bad for an old man and woman," he joked, while lacing up his boots.

"Speak for yourself," Lilly laughed. "The boys are still asleep, huh? What are you and Dad up to this morning?"

"Oh, moving the heifers over to the back side, fixing that strip of fence, not too much. He seemed tired at breakfast; think yesterday was hard on him?"

"It was such an up-and-down day—so much joy with the boys at the table, so much sorrow as Mom just sat there. Then of course the tension between Clare and Don could have been cut with a knife. God, Bud, I don't get it. Did you see the way he grabbed Josh during dessert?"

"I know, honey, nothing you can do though. Okay, Ralph's waiting for me. Have a good ride."

She heard a truck and looked out the window. Clare had pulled into the turnaround. Lilly finished wrapping the sandwiches.

"Anybody home?"

"In here," said Lilly, "in the kitchen, where a good wife belongs. Hey, baby sister!"

"Hi," said Clare, heading for the sink. "Bandit took a giant dump as I unloaded him; need to wash my hands," she said, rolling up her sleeves. "The boys are all going quail hunting today. Nice to see the cousins together, huh?"

"It really is. Are yours sleeping in too? They were all up pretty late. Sweet that they volunteered to take Mom back to Wrenwood. Clare! What the hell?" Lilly moved closer to the sink. "What happened?" There were four blue bruises on the inside of Clare's wrist.

"Oh, it's nothing, really," she said, rolling down her sleeves.

"Goddamn it!" yelled Lilly, slamming her fist on the counter. "Tell me the truth — what happened? Why don't you get it? He's not going to change! Leave him! What are you waiting for?"

Clare buttoned the cuffs. "Calm down, Lilly. Don had too much to drink last night. I got between him and Josh, that's all. He's been really hard on him lately."

"Lately!" Lilly snorted, "you mean his whole life." Her ice-blue eyes burned into her sister's face, "What's it going to take, Clare?"

The front door opened. "Yee Haw!" called Midnight, "I come bearing gifts." She entered the kitchen carrying a box and then set it on the antique oak table. "Wild strawberry jam for your fam. Hey! didn't know I could rhyme this early in the morning. How's everybody?" she asked, feeling the tension.

Lilly turned, "Good, and you? Oh! thank you! I've just run out of this wonderful stuff."

"This new batch has a little elderberry too, gives it a nice bite. My contribution to the picnic is in the truck. Where's Emma and Briar?"

"They're coming together, should be here soon," said Lilly, putting the saddlebag over her shoulder. "I still need to get Joe ready."

"Molly's not saddled either; I'll come too."

Clare followed them out the door. Joe was tied to a post. Bandit, ready to go, stood next to him, pawing the frozen ground.

"Damn, it's cold." Lilly shivered as she spread the saddle blanket over the horse's back. "Are we nuts or what?"

"It's supposed to clear up later this morning," called Clare, then ordered her horse, "Quit it, Bandit! Just stand!"

Midnight's tall, strong body moved slowly as she led her mustang over to another section of fence where the horse could be tied. "When is Briar's surgery?" she asked.

"Monday," said Lilly. "Oh, here they are."

Briar's truck pulled into the area and she waved, moving swiftly to let the horses out.

Emma took Mav's rope and walked toward them. She carried a small saddlebag, the kind that fits over the horn, and a thermos in a canvas holder. "God, I can barely walk, I ate so much yesterday. I can't believe I'm about to do it again," she said, patting her stomach. She certainly wasn't fat, but they had all teased her over the years about her full, voluptuous body.

"Hi, everybody," said Briar cheerfully. "Hey, Clare! You brought Bandit! How's he doing?" She hoisted a backpack over her shoulder and pulled a bright blue wool hat over her ears.

"I've been riding him a lot; he's doing good for a horse that doesn't know much."

Mav and Elvira were ready except for their bridles. "They look like wooly mammoths with their winter coats, don't they?" asked Lilly.

Midnight threw back, "Wish I'd grown one. It's freezing ass."

One by one the women mounted. The horses sidestepped and circled in anticipation, their breath steaming in the frigid air. They rode out of the ranch's east gate and began to climb. Low fog hung in the junipers. It would be a steep traverse to the top. The hillside was splotched with black oaks that had turned red as far as they could see.

Three quarters of the way up the sun broke through, igniting prisms on the hoarfrost that clung to the buckbrush. They stopped to rest then, the horses in a half circle, panting.

"Would you look at that!" declared Emma as the valley lay before them. The women were quiet for awhile, letting the sun warm their faces and hands.

"Are we thankful?" questioned Emma.

"You bet!" said Clare.

"Is this a thanksgiving thing?" asked Midnight, "because I'd be a lot more grateful if we had poisoned the white people starting with the first one." Her eyes danced as she looked from face to face.

"Oh, you bitter old woman," said Briar. "I'll race you!"

Midnight let out a yelp and turned Molly uphill. They all screamed and whooped as the horses galloped the rest of the way.

Emma poured turkey soup into tin cups and passed them around. The smell of sage and rosemary wafted up through the steam. Lilly handed everyone a turkey sandwich, her specialty, made with a honey mustard mayonnaise and cranberry sauce. Midnight poured pink manzanita berry juice out of her canteen into paper cups.

"It's been so long since we've had this," Clare said, swirling the fruity liquid on her tongue.

"It was a good year," said Midnight. "We must have canned 110 quarts between me and Aunt Ada. It's gotta sit from spring to fall for the right ferment."

"I'm finally warm," breathed Emma. "So how was everyone's turkey day? Briar and I...," she paused for a moment, "and the girl, Cat, stuffed ourselves silly; of course there was enough for an army." There was an awkward moment. The call of a red-tailed hawk punctured the silence.

Lilly felt no reaction from Midnight at the mention of the girl's name. She decided to stay quiet about the situation, remembering Emma's gentle reproach a few weeks ago.

"We went to Lilly's," Clare piped in. "It was great to have all of the boys home."

Midnight looked right at Emma, "What's she like, Jenny's granddaughter? Does she look Indian?"

Emma cleared her throat, "She's small and dark. She's been really quiet and withdrawn though, hasn't told me much about herself. I guess her father was Mexican; she never knew him though." She paused, "How is Julien doing, Midnight?"

Midnight's jaw tightened, "He's okay. I've turned him over to Liam and some of the other male members of the tribe."

"I'm so sorry, Midnight, it could have been any of our boys, what with alcohol and testosterone," Clare added.

"Yeah...thanks," said Midnight, flipping her braid and looking away.

After the picnic things were packed up, they readied the horses for the ride back. As Lilly tightened Joe's cinch she turned to Briar, "Hey Bri, got everything covered at the ranch next week? Need a ride to the hospital or anything?"

"Harry Cash is watching my flock, and Emma's offered to take me and pick me up. But thanks, Lilly, I appreciate it."

"Just let me know, okay? Should I call the church for prayers?"

"Hey, can't hurt can it?"

"The women in the tribe will be dancing for you Saturday night," said Midnight.

The ride back was quiet and seemed to take less time. Sun lit the valley, and a low steam rose from the ground. The horses moved faster, maybe because it was downhill or because they knew they were going home.

Briar was in the lead, and Lilly couldn't stop thinking about her. So young and vibrant, she steered her copper-colored horse down the rocky path. They startled a covey of quail that exploded from the brush with a loud whoosh. The high-pitched call of their lookout sounded like, *I need you, I need you, I need you.*

Briar was cleaning the barn. She wanted everything in order before the surgery. Her pop's old friend, Harry Cash, had offered to feed while she recovered at Emma's. He had helped her many times after her parents had died. Harry and Pop had been in the Navy together and were always close after that. Harry was a drifter. He had probably worked on every ranch in a hundred mile radius, and he knew every facet of the job. He was a small man, now in his seventies, with a white beard and kind eyes.

The ranch, although only thirty acres, was still a handful for one person. Luckily at this time of year no irrigating needed to be done, and the few cows she raised had gone to market last week. Harry would just need to feed and care for the horses. She had eight that she boarded, all with their own special needs. She stopped sweeping and sat down to make a list.

The three young ones, Sonny, Lad, and Spirit, would not only need to be fed, but put through their paces daily. All of them were with her for three months to be trained. Harry knew exactly what to do. She just needed to write out a schedule for him. The other five, all retired and living out their lives at Briar's, would need grain and vitamins. She knew Harry would camp out in his little trailer and stay there the whole time. This made her feel better, since besides feeding, training and bedding them down at night, you never knew what kind of trouble the horses might get into if no one was around. This was, after all, her job, and it was how she made her humble living. The ranch was paid for, and she did almost all of the work herself. But thank god she had been able to board and train so she could pay for the truck and medical insurance. That was really important now. She felt so healthy; with no outward signs of the disease, it was hard to fathom the battle her body was having with itself.

She finished sweeping and looked around frantically for the next chore. She decided to clean out the tack room and found herself suddenly throwing the bridles and halters and ropes onto the ground. Rage and frustration overtook her, and she yelled into the rafters, "Why me, God? What did I do to deserve this?"

As she untangled the tack, she found Swift's yearling bridle. She looked over to his empty stall. She sat on a sawhorse, remembering. It calmed her to buckle the buckles, straighten ropes, and make sure each horse's tack was in the exact right place. What had Emma told her? One in every nine women gets breast cancer. *Well, Jeez Louise! Crap!* she thought, *why NOT me?*

Obediently she swallowed the sleep medication the young nurse gave her. She changed into her old Eeyore pajamas; their warm familiar softness felt good on her skin. She was grateful to have the room to herself. After brushing her teeth she tried to watch TV but then turned it off. She sat in the visitor's chair fingering the cracked, green Naugahyde, thinking about the short journey that brought her here.

The clock in the room said ten minutes to midnight. She lay on the bed counting minute perforations on the ceiling above her. *She knows that the surgeon will make a long incision across her breastbone, peeling back the flesh, cutting the pectoral muscles. Then the lymph nodes and fatty breast tissue will be sucked out. Once both breasts are removed, she will be stitched up and transferred to the recovery room. Only later will reconstruction be an option. Once healed, chemotherapy and perhaps radiation will begin.*

She heard the sound of a bed being wheeled by, the silken swish of legs hurrying somewhere. She heard muffled telephones ringing, and that indecipherable vibration at the heart of it all, perhaps a giant generator in the basement, or a wave of pain so palpable it becomes a subtle noise.

Feeling weak in the knees, she got up and quietly closed the door. Searching through her suitcase, she placed two votive candles on the tray table. The match scratched the still air. Watching the flames grow and rise, she sat on the edge of the bed for a long time. Tenderly, she cupped one breast and then the other in her hands and wondered what her body would be like without them. It'd been almost two years since she had a lover, but she remembered what wonderful pleasure toys they were, how Aaron, her last boyfriend, called them "perfect." She'd always hoped for marriage and motherhood, dreaming of the day she would hold and nurse her baby.

She was startled when the door suddenly opened. She let her hands fall into her lap and looked up into the face of a nurse, a big smiling woman with poufy red hair.

"I saw the light under your door. Are you Briar Terry?" she asked, looking at the chart she carried.

"That's me," said Briar, trying to smile.

"Hi, I'm Estelle, I'll be your night nurse." She frowned looking at the candles, "You're not supposed to have those, you know."

"Oh, alright… I'll blow them out."

"No wait, it's okay, leave 'em a minute, they smell really good. You're scheduled for surgery in the morning, right?"

Briar let the words "double mastectomy" come out of her mouth. Her voice was soft and slurry from the sleep medication. "I was just having a little going away party for my breasts."

"Hmm," said the nurse, fastening a blood pressure cuff around her arm and efficiently squeezing the black bulb. After a few seconds she pulled the Velcro apart and wrote on the chart, "good, healthy blood pressure."

"Now let's check your temp." She placed the thermometer in Briar's ear until it beeped. "Okay, just where we want it. Now you know you can't eat or drink anything, right?"

"Yes, they told me…shall I put these out now?"

"Yeah, probably should. What's the scent, it's really nice?"

"Rose, I think."

Briar lowered her head and blew both candles out at once. She watched the smoke spiral until it disappeared, then pushed the tray table back and stood. The nurse bustled over to the bed.

"Aren't these just the most godawful pillows?…Hey, cute pajamas. Gosh you're tall. Let's get you settled; why don't you get in and I'll fix the blankets. I don't know why housekeeping always short sheets the beds."

Briar waited for her to finish then slithered her long body under the covers and sat back against the hard pillows.

"There you go; can I get you anything else? Another blanket?"

"No thanks, but could I ask you something?"

"Sure, anything!"

Briar picked at the blanket, uncertain, and then said, "Do you remember the first time you were aware of your…um…breasts?"

The nurse paused, her face thoughtful. "You know, I can't say that I do. I was an early developer though, seems like I'd always had 'em."

Briar's eyes felt heavy; she closed them for a moment. "Well, I had to convince my mother that they were really there. But I remember in seventh grade I entered the doors of penney's department store a child, and came out wearing my badge of womanhood—a soft white, cotton training bra with a pink rose sewn in the middle."

The nurse nodded and smiled. "I had the same one, and I always wondered what we were in training for."

Briar laughed. "Me too, and by high school I realized that none of the girls really liked theirs; they were either too big or too small."

"Well, I'll tell you," the nurse giggled, "it took me a hell of a long time to like mine. Goat tits! You could have literally tied 'em in a knot." They both laughed. "I gotta go and check on some other patients." She looked at her watch. "Now," she said in a solid, motherly way, "do you think you can sleep?" Briar nodded.

As the big woman moved towards the door she turned and faced Briar. "Hey, can I share something with you?" She put the chart on the chair. Briar's eyes widened as the nurse began to unsnap her scrub shirt. She pulled it back, exposing a broad scarred chest with no breasts. Bright colored flowers, birds, and butterflies were tattooed all across it.

All Briar could say was, "Oh."

"You get some rest now," Estelle said, snapping the shirt back up. "I'll be here in the morning when they come for you, okay?"

Briar looked into the woman's face before the door closed quietly.

Winter

Chapter Eleven

Emma sat up in her quilt-layered bed after a long, slow awakening and looked out the window. The sky was a low gray ceiling, threatening snow. The lilac and plum trees were bare and ragged, the branches almost skeletal. After last year's drought, the *Farmers' Almanac* predicted a heavy winter.

The seasons always crept up on her, but she felt especially unprepared this year. Yesterday, walking across the pasture on the worn footpath to the barn, she had been shocked to see the last of the crisp oak leaves lying in windblown piles.

With Cat's and Briar's needs at hand, there was even less time. It was like racing daylight, now that the sun set before five o'clock. She started a mental list. Buy more hay—and it needed to be purchased from someone who would deliver and stack it. One of the most frustrating aspects of getting older was not being able to lift anything heavy. She used to be able to stack a ton of hay in an afternoon. Mav's feet should be trimmed. More grain and vitamins purchased and stored. Then there was that leak in the barn's tin roof that should be patched. The ancient rain gutters on the house needed cleaning.

Her supply of wood had dwindled, and she reminded herself to call the Stover brothers for at least two cords of cedar and two of oak. It would be worth it to pay extra to have it delivered and stacked. She looked out to the garden, the summer furniture still there. *Shoot, can't lift that either... God I need a...*, she refused to even think the word "man"... *I need to hire a sherpa.*

"Up, up," she told herself. She pulled on a pair of jeans, glanced in the mirror. "Mary Mother of God!" She sucked her stomach in and zipped the jeans, ran her fingers through her tangled hair. Braless, she pulled on a turtleneck and wool socks. The silent house told her that Cat and Briar were still sleeping. She crept downstairs as quietly as the creaky stairs allowed. A few embers glowed in the woodstove; she poked at them and added a small log. Because Briar was in the yellow room, she turned up the thermostat on the heater. The house had no real insulation, but if she warmed it up early, it might stay tolerable throughout the day. Yawning, she boiled water for coffee. Bear, curled on his rug, opened his eyes, then rolled over and started snoring again.

Briar had been there for a week, and although her recovery was going well, she still required a lot of care. The mastectomy drains needed to be dealt with three times a day; the medicines given every few hours; and of course she needed to eat and start putting the weight she'd lost back on. The Yee Haws had been generous, dropping off salads, casseroles, and baked goods.

Cat had been very helpful, doing laundry, feeding the chickens, and really anything that Emma asked of her. Still mostly silent, at least she had finally come out of the library to be part of the household. The preliminary hearing on her case was next week. Emma sat in the dining room sipping the bliss of French roast, grateful that it was Saturday, a day with no patients to see. She gazed at the garden beyond the big window. A strong wind blew the branches of the plum tree, and the old window chattered in its frame.

After coffee, she put on her hooded flannel jacket and went out to the pasture. Mav was inside his little barn, head down, obviously asleep. "Hey, buddy, come and get your flake." He looked up with a low nicker. "Here, have some horse granola too. It's going to storm, don't you think?" she asked, pouring oats over his hay. She leaned into him and he returned the weight of her affection, then began to chew.

She walked to the garden and steadied the gate banging in the wind. Putting the garden to bed was always such a sad day. The winter garden seemed almost a graveyard, holding memories of the season's yields and its idiosyncrasies—the volunteer cilantro that had pushed up in all the corners, and the weird-looking hard green squash with little frowning frog faces. She'd thought that the seed packet said "Patty Pan."

Zipping up her jacket and putting the hood over her bed-messed hair, she walked the rows, saying goodbye. The rosemary looked as if it wanted to spend the winter on a sunny Greek island. The sunflowers bowed low on their spindly stalks, their hearts an empty geometry of brown disks. The green beans, now a deadened rust, slumped over the trellis as if admitting defeat. The sky darkened even more. An unclaimed melancholy swept over her as she stared at the tomatoes, withered and pleated, deflated like the shriveled balls of old men.

Above the farm the storm gathered, as wind spiraled inward, circled by warm humid air. Moist clouds rose and cooled; frozen particles found one another and merged. She looked upward as snow fell softly on her face.

Emma came downstairs the morning of the hearing, willing herself to put on a positive face for Cat. But when she saw what the girl was wearing—big hoop earrings, a skin-tight short black skirt, a rather revealing scoop-necked black sweater, and calf-length black high-heeled boots—she suggested that perhaps, considering the circumstances, she might want to rethink her appearance, assuring her that she did look beautiful, but that a little less make-up and a more appropriate outfit might help to make a better impression.

"No!" the girl said. These were her clothes, this was how she liked to look, and if they wanted to judge her for it, then let them. She *was innocent,* and that was all that mattered.

It was raining heavily as they drove over the mountain to Butte City. A huge storm had moved in the night before, and the small town's streets were flooded. The old courthouse stood looming and angular, set back from the street. It was fronted by a set of steep stairs whose rise somehow indicated that one was now leaving earthly ground to ascend to a place of higher significance. The Stay County courthouse wasn't unfamiliar to Emma, who had attended many hearings there in her role of foster care advocate. She also knew too well the sadness and sense of loss instilled in both children and adults as they descended the steep stairs.

On that morning, two of the boys in question, RJ Dobson and Chuck Gallegar, waited with their parents by the huge doors at the top of the stairs. As she and Cat approached the door, there were openly hostile looks from both the boys and their parents.

Mary Mother of God, she thought, *wait until she takes her coat off.* Amy Lee and her parents came in behind them. No eye contact was made between the girls, and Emma wondered about that. Amy Lee's mother, Eva, had come to Emma's once to get stitches on a Sunday afternoon, so she wasn't a stranger. But she had chosen not to look at her either. Calvin Drucker and his bleary-eyed father shuffled in.

They waited in line to enter the courthouse. Ever since a distraught elderly man had drawn a gun in the lobby a few years back, a set of armed policemen checked purses and sent them through to be X-rayed. Everyone entering stood in a booth to be scanned for weapons, car keys, certain kinds of jewelry or pocket knives, which often set off a loud alarm. After passing through, Emma and Cat climbed more marble steps and entered the courtroom. Only parents and guardians were allowed to accompany the minors involved, so it was a fairly small group in attendance: the boys and their parents, Amy Lee and her mother, the girl and herself. She did notice a reporter from the *Butte City Star* seated outside in the hallway, writing in a small notebook.

Cat was stoic and quiet but held her head high as they entered. The boys, already seated, stared openly, and RJ even smirked as the girl removed her long black coat. Chuck Gallegar's father gave Emma a nasty look, then turned away. The courtroom was stark except for a mural of the history of the town on the back wall and an American flag with a gold braid near the witness stand. Emma understood it was to be a preliminary hearing, mostly to garner information.

Midnight and Julien were the last to arrive; they seated themselves in the back row. The tension in the room was palpable, and the smell of coffee, too much perfume, aftershave, and a tinge of nervous stomach permeated the air. As the clock ticked nine a.m., a court recorder entered and announced the presence of the Honorable Judge Raymond Throckmorton. The elderly judge, his thick glasses resting on his nose, read the charges from an affidavit.

Amy Lee, who was not being charged or accusing the boys of anything, was called first. She told the judge that she had invited Cat to the party at the cabin, how they had ridden up together and stayed late, having one more drink before leaving. She listed who was there, and said that after the shot RJ gave her she remembered no more until she woke up in her bed at home the next morning.

99

The boys were called next. The judge said five DNA samples had been found. He spoke of the seriousness of the charges against them and the consequences if the boys were found guilty. He reminded them that they were under oath to tell the truth. One by one they were called forward to tell what had transpired that Halloween night. The stories of four of the boys were almost identical, detail for detail. Emma felt that in itself should have raised a red flag.

Their story was that after school on October 31, 1998, they were in the high school parking lot when the girl in question approached them, saying that she had some really good drugs she'd gotten from her mother in Phoenix. Out of curiosity, they'd asked her what kind of drugs, and she'd told them it was a kind of Ecstasy that made you really want to have sex. They had all told her "no," but she insisted that she was really horny and they could all have a great time together at the party after the game. One after another they testified that she'd danced naked in the cabin and begged them for sex. The four admitted to intercourse with her. Cat squirmed in her seat, turned to Emma, and shook her head *No!*

Julien was called last, and he mumbled quietly into the microphone that he'd ridden with Amy Lee and Cat up the mountain, had drunk too much, and passed out before they'd left. He said he'd woken up in his uncle's barn the next morning and didn't remember anything else. The judge asked him if he heard anything about a plan to rape the girl. Julien said, no, he hadn't. The boy's face was solemn. Emma caught Midnight's look as he made his way back to sit beside her.

Cat was called to the small table. She rose and turned to the boys, giving them a look of utter defiance. Then, as Emma cringed, Cat all but sauntered up to the table. Even the court reporter raised her eyebrows as the girl sat down.

"Please state your full name," the judge began.

She spat out, "Caterina Maria Ramos," then tossed her wild head of black hair.

"Where did you live before you came to Green Valley, Miss Ramos?" He peered at her owl-like.

"Phoenix, Arizona."

"Where were you living at the time of...," he stuttered a little, "at the time of the alleged incident?"

"With my grandmother."

"Your grandmother? Would that be Jenny Brown?"

"Uh huh?"

"Please answer 'yes' or 'no,' Miss Ramos."

"Yes."

"Why did you come to live with your grandmother?"

"I had to, it sure wasn't by choice. My mother went to jail for five years."

"And what were the charges against your mother?"

Her shoulders moved up, then down as she sighed audibly. Quietly she said, "Prostitution and possession of heroin."

"Speak up, Miss Ramos; please repeat your answer."

She leaned forward, reached out with one hand to grab the neck of the microphone, and bellowed, "Prostitution and possession of heroin."

One of the boys in the back laughed. The judge fanned the edges of the thick pile of papers in front of him. He took his time, cleared his throat.

"Alright, Miss Ramos, please tell us what happened on the night of October 31st."

"Amy Lee came up to me in the lunch room and asked if I wanted to go to a party at the cabin after the homecoming game." She took a deep breath, "At first I didn't think I would go, but in fifth period I told her I would...We left the game early and me, Amy Lee, Julien, Josh York, and his girlfriend Liz, left the school and drove up to the cabin on Halfway Mountain."

"And who was there that night?"

"Um…me, Amy Lee, Julien, Josh, Liz, Chuck, RJ, Hubert, Calvin, and then a bunch of kids… I don't know their names; they came after the game was over."

"Were you all in the cabin? Was there drinking? Drugs?"

"No…sir. There was a big bonfire in the field; we couldn't all fit in the cabin…Yes, people were smoking pot."

"Did you imbibe, Miss Ramos?"

"I'm sorry…what?"

"Did you drink and smoke marijuana?"

"Yes."

"Please go on…what else happened?"

"Not much, we all just hung out around the fire. Josh and Liz were leaving and I asked Amy Lee, shouldn't we get a ride with them? And she said no, let's have one more drink, and we could go home with her cousin Chuck. Then we went into the cabin."

"Who was there?"

"Me, Amy Lee, Chuck, Hubert, Calvin, RJ…and oh yeah, Julien was passed out on the chair. RJ handed me and Amy a shot glass and we drank it." She paused, lowered her head. "That's all I remember until I woke up…in the hospital."

"I see, and that's the whole story, Miss Ramos? Remember you're under oath." He peered at her with an intense stare, adjusted the glasses on his nose. "Miss Ramos, did you ingest the drug you told the boys about after school? And did you have consensual sex with all of them?"

A long moment of silence floated above the room, and then the girl jumped to her feet. "NO!" she screamed, turning and facing the boys, "I never had any drugs! They're lying!" Her voice rose in anger, "And no, I didn't," she turned back to face the judge, "have sex with any of them…I swear!" She sat back down and crumpled into the chair.

"You understand, Miss Ramos, that you are under oath,

and lying now will have serious consequences. You're sure? You're telling the truth?" he asked piously.

Cat pulled at her shirt and put her hands over her face. She sucked in air, trying not to cry. "Yes, sir!" she hiccupped, "I'm, I'm sure…"

After it was over, Emma rose, taking Cat's coat off the back of the chair. She walked to Cat, put the coat around her shoulders, and hustled her out of the courtroom. They left through the back door of the family law office. She would never forget the ride home. The storm peaking, with violent rain pelting the windshield—each swipe of the wipers like the metered rise of her anger—and the girl's hysterical wails all the way down the mountain.

Cat held the towel over her mouth. She was crouched in the upstairs bathroom, head over the toilet. Again she retched, desperately trying to be quiet. Quickly she wiped the vomit off her mouth and flushed the toilet. The vomiting had started a week ago. Even smells made her sick, especially the odor in the room where Emma's friend Briar was recovering from surgery. Cat had been helping Emma as she changed the drains in Briar's mastectomy wounds this morning. After handing Emma an alcohol swab, she had bolted from the room. When she returned, she had brushed it off as an upset stomach, but Emma had given her a questioning look.

Returning to the kitchen, Cat let the warm water run over her hands as she rinsed the dishes. She was always cold here, dressing in layers of tights, sweatpants, and two or three shirts. She had never experienced a true winter, and she found herself seeking out places near the woodstove or a sunny spot in the living room. At night she piled on as many quilts as she could find in the upstairs linen closet. Emma had layered the old quilts she collected with lavender sachets. At night, as Cat lay in her bed crying, overwhelmed with the uncertainty of her life, the smell of lavender somehow soothed her.

God! What if I am pregnant? She knew from her mother's past that she had all the symptoms, but how could it be possible, when she distinctly remembered Emma asking her at the hospital if she wanted birth control? She had said "yes", thinking that one of the medications they would give her would be a morning-after pill. She closed the dishwasher and turned to find Emma standing in front of her.

"Thanks for helping me, Cat," she said, putting the kettle on the stove. "Let's have a cup of tea; it's been a busy morning." She reached for the small brown teapot and filled it with dried peppermint. After the water boiled, she poured it into the teapot, then strained the liquid and carried two mugs to the kitchen table. Cat was sitting, head down, waiting.

"How are you feeling?"

"Okay, I guess."

"Have you been sick long?"

"Just this last week."

"Have you had your period?"

"No, it's late, three weeks or so."

Emma looked at the girl's face and felt her fear. Her own stomach lurched. "What kind of birth control are you on? I've been meaning to ask if you needed it refilled."

"Excuse me, um, I've never been on birth control," Cat answered.

Emma set her cup down. "But I asked you in the hospital, and you said 'yes'."

"I thought you were asking me if I wanted it, a morning-after pill or something."

"Mary Mother of God," Emma frowned. "You're not on birth control then?"

"No, I've never been sexually…I am…I mean…I was a…virgin." She dropped her head and put her small hands over her face.

Emma got up and stood behind the girl, putting her hands on her shoulders. "Alright…I see…well…go ahead, let it out, honey; it's okay to cry." The girl sat up straight and stiffened. Emma could feel her holding back. She removed her hands from the small thin shoulders.

The pregnancy test was positive, and for the rest of the day, as snow fell outside, Cat opened up her life to Emma. She told her about being raised by a prostitute, that her mother had had several abortions. Once, she'd become infected afterwards and lay in the dirty motel room feverish and delirious. Cat was only ten then and had to go get Mr. Monsoon to help. She had also seen her mother have a miscarriage, the tiny fetus floating in pink water in the toilet. She told Emma that most nights her mother was gone, but that sometimes she would bring men back to their room. The men were usually drunk or on drugs, and at these times, Cat would lock the bathroom door, make herself a bed in the bathtub, and drown out the sounds by turning up the radio.

During the weekdays after school she stayed at the public library. The women who worked there always made her feel comfortable in her little corner. She ate breakfast and lunch at school, qualifying for the low-income meals, but dinner was more of a challenge. Her mother shot up heroin every day and rarely gave her money. Cat started bussing tables at a diner when she was thirteen; part of the pay was a free meal. On holidays, both American and East Indian, the Monsoons, who were childless, invited her to their apartment above the motel.

She kept to herself at school. Everyone knew about her life, but it was hard to put down a straight-A student who never caused trouble. She had a few friends through junior high and high school, other girls from rough families, but when they started drinking and drugging and having sex, she quietly dropped out of their circles.

Emma asked her about her father. Cat told her that she'd never met him or his Hispanic family. She also said that she'd never met her grandmother, Jenny, before she came to the valley.

By late afternoon the snow began to stick, and a mauve light gathered around the house. While Emma was peeling potatoes, Cat broke down again, telling her that she was terrified of an abortion but that she definitely couldn't have the baby. Her words came quickly. She wanted to go back to Phoenix and finish high school. Her plan was to enroll in the junior college and get her general education out of the way. Eventually she wanted to become a psychologist.

"That would be a good calling for you," Emma offered, "a way to use your life experiences to help people."

"Yes…," said Cat, tearing lettuce.

Emma was about to apologize for her part in the misunderstanding when there was a knock on the back door. She saw Harry Cash through the glass window, hat in hand. His smile lit the gloom around him.

"Come in, Harry, good to see you!"

"Hi, Emma," he said, wiping his feet on the rug. "It's a blizzard out there; how are ya?"

"Good, good. Harry, this is Cat." Cat looked up from her place at the counter and nodded.

"Pleased to meet you. I'm here to see the Squirt. How's she doin'?"

"Really well," said Emma, "nothing is going to keep that girl down. Come with me. She's in the yellow room; she'll be so glad to see you." He followed Emma down the hall. "Harry, stay for dinner; Briar would love that."

"Well, okay, if it's not too much trouble. It smells good."

Emma poked her head through the door. "Bri, Harry's here, are you decent?"

Briar sat on the edge of the bed dressed in flannel pajamas. "Harry? Oh good! Just the man I want to see."

Harry shuffled in.

"Let me take this," said Emma, reaching for his ancient cowboy hat. "Briar, how's your appetite? I've got a roast and such."

"I'm famished."

"Good! Harry's going to join us. Shall I fix him a tray for in here?"

"No, I'll come to the table, Em."

"Okay, I'll set it up while you two visit." She took the empty water pitcher and left.

"How are you, Squirt? You look chipper, feelin' okay?"

"I'm doing well, Harry, plan to come home week after next. How are you and the horses? Everything okay?"

"Fine, fine, everybody's been good. The trainees are making progress. I got Sonny under saddle yesterday. Just took my time, started with the blanket like I told you on the phone last week. The first time I carried the saddle into the round pen he balked and snorted. Then for the next few days I just left it on the fence, put his hay by it, held it up to him, leaned it on him. I felt after awhile he was thinkin', *Okay, okay, Harry, just put it on my back and get it over with,*" he chuckled. "Elvira's cut is healing, just superficial. Bradshaw delivered hay; it's stacked in the barn. Looks like some good orchard grass too."

"Thank you, Harry," said Briar, taking his tan, veiny hand. "No one knows how to take care of them like you. I haven't worried a second about the ranch."

She had loved this gruff, gentle man since childhood. She had been "Squirt" to him ever since she came to the Terry's at age eleven. Even though she towered over him now, she still loved hearing that nickname.

Emma called them into the big kitchen. The pot roast was surrounded by brown glazed carrots and potatoes. There was a big salad, and Lilly's home-baked bread. Steam covered the windows as a satisfied quiet came over the table. Emma noticed Cat picking at her food. Soon after, she got up and excused herself.

"Is she alright?" asked Briar.

"Yes," said Emma, "she doesn't feel good today." Turning to Harry she asked about his summer, where he had traveled. He spoke in his quiet way, telling story after story about the big ranches he had worked on in Wyoming. After coffee and apple pie, Briar began yawning, and Harry got up and put on his coat. He hugged Briar, told her to behave herself, and thanked Emma for the fine meal.

After Briar went to bed, Emma cleared the table and loaded the dishwasher. Her mind shot questions in all directions. How could this have happened? Why hadn't she checked with the girl sooner? The consequences of the miscommunication overpowered her. Enough had happened to the poor child without having to deal with this too. Quickly she calculated. Cat must be about six weeks along. She sliced two pieces of Lilly's bread and put them in the toaster. She found the vanilla yogurt in the fridge and spooned some into a bowl. Upstairs it was quiet; she knocked hesitantly on Cat's door, waited, then turned the knob and heard a soft, "Come in."

Emma went and sat down in the purple chair by the window. "I brought you some toast and yogurt; it will settle your stomach. Cat... I am so sorry about the...," she searched for the words, "about the misunderstanding. I feel just awful. I want you to know I'll help in any way I can. You're welcome to stay here, honey, as long as you want, okay?"

"Okay," said the girl.

"Tomorrow we'll talk about options and figure this out."

"Okay," said Cat passively, scooting further down under the quilt.

"Goodnight now." Emma rose and started for the door.

"Please try and eat."

"Emma?" the girl spoke in a whisper.

"Yes."

"It's not your fault...or mine. It just is."

Chapter Twelve

On Christmas Eve day, Briar sat in her living room watching thick snowflakes fall, spiral, and dissolve. *How appropriate*, she thought, yawning. Although she was beyond tired, she looked forward to the Yee Haw's tradition of caroling in town that evening. It had been a little over three weeks since the surgery. She was regaining her strength on her body's time clock, slowly. She sipped the foul-tasting Chinese tea that Emma had prescribed and gagged a little. Still weak, she was limited to light chores. Harry did all the heavy work, even saddling the horses for her, which drove her crazy. It still didn't feel real.

That morning, in a hurry for a shower, she'd stripped off her pajama top in front of the bathroom mirror and was shocked by the puckered indentations that gaped back at her. She still automatically took a bra out of her underwear drawer every morning. Sighing, she'd fold the two cups into each other and put it back. She wasn't sleeping well. Emma said it was withdrawal from the pain medication. The cumulative exhaustion made her nervous and jumpy when she put the trainer horses through their paces.

Her friends had been wonderful and caring, but her own positive facade dissolved each night as a cruel lasso of doubt and fear tightened around her. Questions riddled her in the half-light. Would she live or die?...What if the treatment didn't work?...How long would the chemo last?...Could the healthy cells endure the calculated chemical demise of the cancer cells? She yawned again. The fire crackled, spitting more *"what ifs"* up the chimney. With the next yawn, her eyes watered and she thought *God, I'll never make it tonight if I don't rest.* She needed to go with the women and at least pretend nothing had happened. It wouldn't hurt to be around their warmth and laughter. The old, brown leather couch received her long limbs. She pulled the afghan her mother had made over her. Her unrelenting mind ticked on. *What if they treat me differently?...Have my looks changed?...Will people stare?* "Oh, stop it! Shut up! Please, stop it!" she pleaded.

"Are you sure you don't want to come with us, Cat? It's such a perfectly beautiful night. Did you celebrate Christmas in Arizona?" Emma pulled on the red wool gloves and hat that had, an hour ago, been under the lighted fir tree that stood in the living room. Clare had knit them, and that afternoon she had called and told Emma to open her present. Emma was excited to meet the Yee Haws in town for their traditional Christmas Eve caroling.

The little village put on quite a show for the holidays. Main Street was lit up, and cedar wreaths hung on the doors of every storefront and office. The stores would be open for last minute shoppers. Santa — always Gene Strawberry, who actually sported a potbelly and white beard all year long — would hand out candy canes. His eyes would twinkle too, and his smile would be warm, more from the flask of brandy in his deep velvet pocket than from the spirit of the season.

"Come on, Cat, honey, you haven't been out of the house in weeks."

"No thanks, I'm going to bed early."

"Okay, I have my cell if you need me."

"Have fun," said the girl grimly, "I've always hated Christmas."

Mary Mother of God, Emma said to herself, as she got into the truck and banged her boots together to remove the snow that had been falling all day. *Poor kid,* she thought, pulling out of the driveway. With no adult to sign for Cat, and her emancipated minor status still in process, they had petitioned the court in Wenachappee, a neighboring county, to allow Cat to have an abortion. Even though the rape happened in Stay County, Emma had known up front that a request would be vetoed. There had never been an abortion performed here, as far as she knew. Now, weeks later, they were still waiting for the judge in Wenachappee to grant permission for the abortion. The judge had told Emma, after her fifth call, that it wouldn't happen until all the ducks were in a row, and said not to call him again. Emma hoped for the girl's sake that it would be soon.

Briar's road was covered with snow, and the truck tires made two clean lines down the middle of it. She pulled in front of the log house and honked. Briar came out right away, pretty in a green tartan plaid jacket and a black angora beret.

"Hi! God, it's a great night, huh, Emma?" She swung her long legs up into the truck. They chatted on the way, admiring the houses along the highway that were decorated with lighted snowmen, reindeer, and even a giant red and green Grinch.

In town, Main Street was crowded with people moving from store to store. Children carried hot apple cider and doughnuts given out by the Kiwanis. A fifteen-foot tall Christmas tree stood in the middle of the square. The decorations, handmade by school children, only reached halfway up the tree. Popcorn balls, tin-foil wreaths, and glittered pinecones studded the branches; light and shadow made the ornaments appear more precious than their common materials. Briar and Emma saw Lilly and Clare in front of the hardware store.

"Hey, you two!" shouted Lilly.

"Merry Christmas," said Emma, hugging them and thanking Clare for the hat and gloves.

"Briar, you look great!" said Clare.

They all admired the new black leather coat that Bud had given Lilly.

"Well, look what the boys gave me," piped Clare, smoothing the ends of a soft burgundy scarf.

"Where's Midnight?" asked Briar.

"I heard they got a foot of snow in a few hours down river. Let's go find Patty. Midnight will find us," called Lilly, already crossing the street to the old fire house. "Patty, yoo hoo, where are you?"

"Oh, God!" said Emma, "Look! I never get used to them, you know."

Patty and Darrol Strong's pair of black Percherons stood in front of a wagon built to look like a sleigh. At eighteen hands high, they dwarfed the wagon, making it look like an ornate toy. They held their heads high, and their huge draft horse feet were as big as pie plates.

"Hi, Bonnie! Hi, Beau!" called Briar, standing on tiptoe to scratch their triangular ears.

"Hey, girls." Patty came out of the firehouse sipping cider. She was a smiling woman with a deep voice, her blue eyes shaded by a cobalt Victorian cloche. Her corseted dress was laced up the front, revealing ample cleavage. "Tally Ho," she said, pulling a black cape around her shoulders.

Everyone admired the Percherons' new Christmas outfits. Circlets of belled leather wrapped around the black fringe of their fetlocks. Bonnie had a red poinsettia garland around her neck, while Beau's was made of evergreens and red berries.

"Oh, they're so pretty, Patty! Did you make their new costumes?" asked Lilly.

"Yup, in my spare time," she laughed. "Darrol helped with the bells. I made my dress and cape. Gee, girls, I've worn the red one for what, ten years or so. Are you ready?"

Midnight appeared silently, sneaking up on them the way she always did. "Boo!" she exclaimed.

"How do you do that?" asked Clare.

"Oh, just practice I guess."

"She came upon a midnight clear," sang Lilly, giggling.

"We got a shit load of snow down river. I had to wait for the plow."

"Time to go," said Patty, climbing into the wagon.

Midnight's white alpaca poncho brushed the ground as she bent to step up. Her braids wound around her head like a crown. Patty took the reins and held them high in front of her. She clucked to the horses, whose moving feet sent out a crescendo of bells that rang out as the sleigh turned onto Main Street. People *oohed* and *aahed* as they passed and the women began to sing.

Soon they turned into the neighborhood. The older homes were lit and decorated with Christmas trees displayed in the windows. They knew each song by heart, but Clare still called out the titles. Patty would stop in the middle of a block as the ancient songs rang out. People came out on their porches to listen to "Silent Night," "Oh, Little Town of Bethlehem," and "Away in a Manger." As they sang "Mary's Angel," Emma thought of Cat.

And one of the angels saw Mary's face
Her youth and her beauty, her fear and her grace.

How sad the girl must feel. Emma realized that she'd played Gran's Christmas records all week, and almost every song was full of "mother and child. "

They turned down street after street. The moon clouded over, and it began to snow. During "Jingle Bells," Patty encouraged the horses to prance, and the ringing bells almost overpowered their voices.

On the way back to the firehouse, Main Street was quiet, a few inches of light snow covering stairs and railings. They all thanked Patty and Darrol, who had come to help load the horses into their giant trailer. The women stood in a circle saying good-bye. Clare reached out and touched Briar's shoulder, saying how glad she was that Briar was doing so well.

"Emma, do you still want to go to church?" Briar asked.

"I'd like to."

"Well, I'm really tired...happy, but tired," sighed Briar.

"I could drop you home if you want," said Midnight, "it's on my way."

Emma walked to the old Catholic church. Built of logs in the 1800's, it was one of the first buildings constructed in the valley. The town was now deserted, everyone home with their families. There were no cars in the parking lot; midnight mass wouldn't begin for a few hours. She could see the soft glow of the stained glass windows through the falling snow. She came every Christmas Eve, not because she was a devout Catholic—hardly. She had been the number one doubter in her family. She came to remember her mother and Gran. Her mother had never missed a service and had been part of the League of Catholic Women. She had raised her children with a good deal of love and guilt. Gran, on the other hand, was an old-country Catholic who, along with all the religious holidays, celebrated the solstices and equinoxes and believed in the pre-Christian goddess who had become Mary after centuries of matriarchy. Emma, who was quite the intellectual feminist in her day, liked the fact that a female deity was even included in Catholicism. She didn't believe literally in the virgin birth, but she loved the story of it. Once she had asked Gran, demanding an absolute in her teenage angst, what was the truth about religion?

"It's what is in your heart, Emma. If it's a debate between your mind and your heart, go with the heart."

In her heart she knew she believed in the "Great Mystery," whatever it was, and still she loved the quiet beauty of a church. She took off her coat in the vestibule. How lucky, she thought, to be the only one there. She entered the church and paused, taking in the smell of the damp hymn books and melted wax. Incense lingered in the corners; pine boughs were strung along the pews. She passed by the bowl of holy water and moved to the front near the altar. She slid across one of the polished wooden benches and sat for a moment. She was always grateful that the little church had no crucifix, only a small wooden cross. She vividly remembered the large crucifix in St. Joseph's cathedral in San Francisco, the statue of Jesus, his face writhing in pain, realistic blood painted on his palms and feet. Here, Emma looked at the Madonna of the Mountain, a simple but delicately carved wooden statue, the compassionate face of Mary gazing down at her baby boy.

She got up and moved to the side altar, lighting three candles, her own personal ritual. One for the past, and all of the loved ones who had crossed: Mother, Father, Gran, her husband, Ronnie, and their child, Theo. The old pain filled her momentarily. She lit the next candle for the present, asking for peace on earth. Lastly, she lit a candle for the future, hoping for a good outcome for Briar, and asking for guidance in the young heart of Cat.

She was so lost in thought that she didn't hear Liam's quiet footsteps coming down the aisle. But she realized that someone had sat down behind her. She remained facing forward, her eyes closed, then turned to go back to the pew. Liam looked into her face, the warmth of recognition spreading across his mouth.

"Emma," he whispered. She started down the aisle, but he signaled her to come to him. Her legs were quivering as she slid in, near him, but far enough away that they weren't touching. "We have to stop meeting like this," he laughed quietly, taking her hand. She gently pulled away to brush hair out of her eyes.

"Merry Christmas, Liam." Only silence moved between them.

Finally he said, "Did you know that my mother's uncle carved the Madonna of the Mountain about a hundred years ago? She's made of white oak, and the child is cedar. Behind her cloak on the back right side he carved an acorn, a symbol still important to the Green River tribe. Come with me; I'll show it to you." She felt light-headed as she followed him around to the back of the Madonna. "Right here, see it? And over here he carved a horse with wings." She bent to see the cross-hatched design.

They both stood up. He looked down at her, his eyes serious, questioning. His braid fell over the front of his broad shoulder. "Emma, oh, God forgive me, but..."

She was torn, ripped down the middle, panicked. Her heart wanted him so badly, but her mind screamed, *Don't!* Candlelight flickered a red warning.

"Emma...please," he whispered, close to her face, "can't we just...talk about..."

Her resistance faltered; her knees went weak; she couldn't look at him. "I don't know...it's been so long and I'm afraid..."

He smelled of soap and cedar. He took her hand and it burned into her palm. The quiet of the church seemed deafening. Then suddenly she was in his arms, his mouth warm on hers. She pulled back, but the old hunger consumed them as he kissed her neck and moaned, "Oh, God, Emma." The sweet strength of him wrapped around her as he kissed her forehead and cheeks and her mouth again.

They heard a car door slam and then another. Father Lawrence's voice called out, "Michael and Billy, you look festive. Do you think you can remember the words?" As the priest entered the church, Emma was walking up the aisle and Liam was seated in a pew. As she brushed past the priest her eyes were downcast and her face flushed.

"Merry Christmas, Father," she murmured.

"Ah, Emma," said Father Lawrence, "is your annual visit over already…?

Cat came out of the bathroom. It was the fifth time she had thrown up that day. She was so full of rage and anger that she didn't know what to do with herself. *I just want to go downstairs and smash every one of those glass balls on that Christmas tree!* She imagined throwing them against the wall one by one, the pastel shards shattering. *I hate all that crap about peace on earth, good will to men—what bullshit! And I hate those boys who raped me and left me with this…THING… inside me. Fuck them! And this place! How could they have told the judge that I screwed them all WILLINGLY! I've got to get out of here!* she thought, *as soon as that redneck judge says that I can have the operation.*

She sat down in the purple chair by the window and bawled. Since no one was there, she screamed and cried and pounded her fists on the arms of the chair. "I hate you too, you little bastard! Get out of my body you ugly little thing. I don't want you, do you hear me!" She pounded on her stomach. Emma's yellow cat Sam was suddenly in the room; he looked at her and meowed. "Shut up!" she yelled at the cat, "get out of here!" The cat turned and ran. She was hicupping, her chest heaving from all the crying. The cat came back into the room. "Get out, you freak!" But the cat jumped into her lap, circled and laid down. She started to push him away, but the contact of his warm body and his outstretched paw started her crying again.

Chapter Thirteen

Lilly put on her turn signal. "I need some caffeine, Clare; we'll still be there on time. Do you want something?"

"No, I had coffee this morning."

"Well, so did I," said Lilly, "but maybe a little more energy will make this easier. I don't know why it's always so hard to visit Mom, but it is. I know it's a good place and all, but it just makes me so sad."

"Yeah," said Clare, "I know what you mean."

The girl at the drive-thru opened the window. "What can I get for you?"

"A double latte please. Oh! and put some of those chocolate sprinkles on it, okay?"

"Be just a minute, ma'am." She closed the steamy window.

"God, it's cold!" said Lilly, turning up the heater in the truck. "Dad and Bud found two frozen calves yesterday..."

"Here you go, that will be $2.50," said the girl, handing Lilly the cup.

As they pulled away Clare asked, "How is Daddy, anyway?"

"Oh, I don't know. He seems okay, but I wish he'd move in

with us. We've got plenty of room, and he has all his meals with us anyway. But he says he needs his own house to sleep in. It must be really lonely over there without Mom. I asked him to come today, but he made an excuse. Damn, this coffee is hot! I never did learn how to drink out of these little holes either." She fanned herself with a napkin. "Great, now I'm hot again."

They pulled into the parking lot. "Wrenwood," the huge sign said, "Quality Assisted Living. Happy New Year!" The grounds, although frozen, were neat, with paths that wound through planted areas.

Lilly took a few sips of coffee, "I've got to psyche up, Clare, okay?"

"Okay," Clare said, "take your time."

"How can this happen, Sis? Mom was the most vibrant, intelligent woman I've ever known. How many years did she teach high school science?"

"Twenty, I think."

"She had so much energy, raised us, and helped Dad run the ranch."

Clare pulled at her bangs, "I know, it's weird, huh? Her body is still so healthy."

"Well, if it ever happens to me," said Lilly, crushing the cardboard cup, "just shoot me, okay?"

As they made their way towards the lobby, a man in pajamas and a robe suddenly darted out from behind one of the buildings.

"That's strange," said Clare, pausing.

Two attendants appeared and, seeing them, tried not to sound too frantic as they called to the man, "Mr. Justice, Mr. Justice." They each took one of his arms and led him back towards the building.

Lilly checked in at the desk and asked to see her mother's weekly report. *Dora Rawlins seems content to sit in her chair and is passive and cooperative with caregivers and routines.*

"Anything new?" asked Clare.

"No, I just wonder how they *know* she is content."

"Lilly, look at all of these beautiful bouquets of fresh flowers…in January. They must spend a fortune."

"Yeah, well, so do we."

Upstairs in her room, Lilly's and Clare's mother, Dora, sits in a chair. Her caretakers have dressed her, combed her hair, and reminded her that today is the day her daughters will visit. She is a small woman with cropped white hair and blue eyes. She stares intently at her hands, then pulls her cardigan around her shoulders and closes her eyes. She settles into her yellow velour rocker and wonders where she will go this time. It usually happens after breakfast.

She waits. Then her breathing slows and she is flying through space. *It feels so good to be free, flying further and further away from earth. She sees a big planet up ahead. It seems to have,* she squints, *rings circling it. Maybe Saturn?* she wonders. *It's as if the big planet draws her through clear uncomplicated space to its own surface. Above it, two pale pink moons are strung up by a bracelet of stars. The first moon, Rhea, whizzes past her, causing her heart to beat fast, as the moon, egg-like, fades into the black. Energy from the planet draws her now. She feels the pull and coolness on her face as she floats towards the first of the seven rings. She remembers that the diameter of Saturn at its equator is 74,600 miles or 120,000 kilometers. She knows its atmosphere is made up of helium, methane, ammonia, ethane and…one more. She turns over on her back as if floating on a mountain lake, only below the universe spins away in a freefall. She knows a version of her body is at Wrenwood, sitting in the yellow chair. She remembers the other element in the rings of Saturn, phospine… possibly phospine. She can see the words in her college text. As she flies through the first ring, prismatic ice particles burst like bubbles before her eyes.* "Oh, beautiful!..." she says aloud, "beautiful."

Muzak drifted through the lobby as Clare and Lilly approached the elevator. Just as the doors closed, they glimpsed the same pajamaed man, alone in the hallway. They stepped out of the elevator and entered Dora's room.

"Hi, Mom," said Clare, noting that her mother was wearing the bright pink pantsuit they'd given her for Mother's Day last year.

Lilly leaned down and kissed her mother on the forehead. "What were you saying when we came in, Mom? It sounded like…'beautiful'?"

Dora's face lit up for a moment, and then she said, "The rings, the rings."

Clare looked at her mother's small hands, her gold wedding band and the birthstone ring she never took off. How well she knew those hands. Small and thin, the fingers short and kept clean, even when she'd been helping with the cattle or gardening they were always neat.

Clare remembered the comforting touch of her mother's hands. If she had a fever as a child, those hands on her brow were soothing and cool. If Clare was cold, her mother would press her little-girl hands into her own to warm them. Her mother's hands were an extension of her quick, analytical, scientific mind. Whether explaining the reproductive cycle of the honeybee or showing her daughters the parts of a flower, she gestured with them, using them as a baton or teaching tool, pointing to minute details the eye might miss.

And those hands did so much. Clare could still hear the

click-clack of knitting needles after her mother had graded all her papers at night. Speed knitting, she and Lilly had called it. Out of those hands came white, ruffled dotted-swiss dresses, and homemade strawberry ice cream. They could also wield a mean willow switch.

Mom was there for the birth of both of Clare's sons, sitting back quietly as Emma delivered her grandchildren. Afterwards, stroking the umber down on the baby's head, she told Lilly and Clare about the fontanel, how the soft ring of bone was formed, and why. And when her own mother had died in her bed, Clare and Lilly watched her wash down their grandmother's body with warm clove water before the undertaker came to take her away. As the boys grew up, those veiny, brown-spotted hands flew kites and threw snowballs and buzzed their hair for summer. Her hands were shy and flirtatious when they covered her laughing mouth as her husband teased her unmercifully and called her the love of his life. Now, they rested in her lap, expressionless, useless and idle.

"Yes, Mama, your rings are beautiful. Let's go have lunch; are you ready?"

They found a table in the dining room, which was saturated with the smell of institutional food. The waiter came and they ordered soup and sandwiches. Other family members sat with their demented relatives. A man at the next table wiped the spittle from an elderly man's face. To the left, a loud scene played out as a woman, obviously upset and combative, screamed at the top of her lungs, "No, no, no!" Two attendants intervened and led her away. Her daughter kept saying, "It's alright, Mother, calm down." But the woman yelled even louder.

"How are you, Mom?" Lilly asked, taking her hand. Dora just stared, as if she wasn't there. "Did you have a good week? I see you had your nails done—what a pretty pink."

The waiter set down the food and asked if they needed anything else. As he walked away, Lilly looked at Clare and said, "Yeah, I'd like my mother back, please."

Clare tasted a spoonful of soup, made a face, and put the spoon in the bowl. Lilly sipped her water. At the same moment, they both looked up to see their mother take her sandwich apart. She picked up her empty coffee cup and used it to cut a perfect circle out of one of the slices of bread. She carved the center out of her tomato slice and placed the red ring over the bread.

"The rings! The rings!" she said excitedly.

They heard loud voices from the back of the room and turned to see what was causing the ruckus. The same pajamaed man was running from the attendants.

"Mr. Justice! Mr. Justice!" they called, "wait! wait!"

The man flung himself through the room and staggered to their table. Breathless, he stopped and put his hand on Dora's shoulder. He leaned down affectionately and blurted, "Dora! Dora! You were right! The roses do whistle when you touch them!"

Lilly and Clare watched their mother smile at him, lucid as ever, and heard her say, "Of course, Clarence, I told you so."

True winter came with the new year. Up in the mountains, rain followed by frigid sleet turned into a thick, creamy snow that fell for days. The draped trees allowed only glimpses of needled green, and the forest floor was covered with snowdrifts, banked and hummocked by freezing wind. Wind screamed in the hollows, and draws emptied of bird sounds. Hibernating animals rested in a thin margin between life and death. Beneath the snow, insects in the form of eggs and co-

coons lived a suspended existence under the insulated cover, while bacteria and fungi continued to decompose fallen leaves. Tree roots grew, and wild flowers made buds for spring, nurtured by last year's roots and bulbs. In the storm's interludes, chipmunks sleepily searched for seeds, bears turned and stretched and slept again in their rank torpor. Deer foraged for twigs not covered by snow. Fox and bobcat hunted tirelessly, and fish were held in icy limbo beneath the frozen lakes.

Down in the valley the storm wreaked havoc with the humans. Forty-mile-an-hour winds blew impenetrable veils of ice onto the windshields of cars and trucks. The pass between the valley and Butte City was closed for two days, due to a snow slide peppered with fallen boulders. The plows couldn't keep up, and people were snowbound, fed by what was in their freezers and pantries. On the third day, the arctic winds increased. Power lines fell and sparked; the main power station failed; and the ruddy glow of candles and lanterns in windows emitted a warm but eerie light across the valley at night.

Emma was dreaming, yet the pounding seemed so real and loud. When she heard a voice yelling, "Help us! Help us!" she sat straight up in bed. She switched on the bedside lamp but nothing happened. *Shit! the power is probably out again.* The noise was coming from downstairs. She fumbled in the nightstand drawer and found the flashlight. She took the stairs two at a time as the voice became louder. *Front or back,* she wondered, but then saw someone in the dim light of the front porch. She threw open the door. Jason Cooper grabbed her by the shoulders.

"Emma, Emma, I don't know what to do! Something is wrong with Kerry. She can't walk; she's been in pain all night."

"Where is she?"

"In the car. I think we're going to have the baby early."

"Okay, Jason, can you carry her?"

"Yeah," he said, holding back tears. "We tried to call, but

the power was out. Then we got the car stuck in the snow."

"Bring her to the back door; I'll meet you there." She ran back up the stairs and burst into Cat's room.

"What! What?" the girl murmured, half sitting up.

"Cat, wake up! Cat! Do you hear me? I need you downstairs, now!" Emma fled back downstairs.

"Yes," the girl called, "I'm coming. What's wrong?"

Emma's mind roared as she flew through the living room. *This was Kerry Cooper's first baby, and she wasn't due for another month.* In the kitchen she found a big pot, filled it with water, and set it on the woodstove in the living room. Cat came in and stood there sleepily.

"Get the fire going," Emma said.

Back in the kitchen she opened the door. Jason held his young wife in his arms. Huge white flakes clung to his hair and coat.

"Is she conscious?"

"Yeah."

"Okay, bring her in here, follow me." She held the flashlight in front of her and led the way to her exam room. "Put her on the table there," she said, shining the light as he laid her down.

"Oh no! Oh no!" Kerry moaned, "it's hurting again. I can't take it, Jason...Jason, where are you?"

"I'm right here, honey."

Emma found her medicine bag on the floor and put on latex gloves. She put Kerry's feet in the stirrups and was laying out the syringe and oxytocin when Cat appeared in the doorway.

"Cat, find the oil lamps in the pantry; light them and bring them here."

"Any bleeding, Kerry?...Kerry?"

The young woman was lost in pain, her eyes glazed over. "I don't know...Ow! Ow! Ow!" she screamed.

127

"Jason, how much?" Emma demanded.

"A little at first, then real watery. She got up at about two this morning. It came out for a long time."

"Hold the light, Jason, sounds like her water broke." As gently as possible, Emma pried the girl's legs apart. "Relax, Kerry, I need to see what's going on. There ya go, just let your legs open." The flashlight beam showed dark swirls of hair on the baby's crowning head.

"It's alright, your baby's coming," said Emma, grabbing the stethoscope. The heartbeat was strong and steady.

Cat came in with the lamps. "Put one here," said Emma, pointing to the counter top, "and one here," gesturing towards a chair near the exam table. "Cat, go get the pan of water. The hot pads are in the towel drawer in the kitchen. Grab some towels too. Hurry!"

"Is everything okay?" asked Jason

"I think so; your baby is on its way."

When Kerry started yelling again, Emma moved up and held her face close. "Kerry!" she said slowly, "look at me, honey. Your baby is coming...soon. I need you to focus and listen to me. Take in a deep breath; you're having a contraction. Now breathe like this: hee, hee, hee. Again, good, keep it up."

Cat came back in.

"But the baby," said Kerry, "it's too early...Ow! Ow! Ow!" she screamed.

"Focus on your breathing...good."

"Cat, open that drawer and get out scissors, olive oil, and something that looks like a small clamp. Jason, listen, reach up in that cupboard and get the oxygen tank down. Now, I'm going to tell you how to hook it up. Cat, hold the lamp for him. Jason, see the little hook? Put the tubing into the hole near it...good, turn it on...does it hiss, can you hear air?"

"Yes."

"Good." Emma poured olive oil on her fingers and began massaging the mother. "I can see the baby's head, Kerry; it's a boy, right?"

"Yes, oh, god!... I can't...Oh, Ow! Ow! Ow!" she shrieked.

"Now listen, Kerry, you're completely dilated and your baby will be born soon. I need you to do what I tell you." Emma kept massaging and softening the perineum with oil, stretching the circle of skin around the baby's head. *A month early*, ran through her thoughts again.

"Cat, get the roasting pan—it's in the drawer under the stove. Put it on the woodstove; get some bath towels and put them in it and cover it with a lid."

"Okay," said Cat, running from the room.

"Now, Kerry, when your next contraction starts, put your chin to your chest, take in a big breath, and push slowly.

Jason, hold her leg; I've got this one. That's great, Kerry, and again, chin to your chest."

Emma watched the head becoming more visible. "Take in a big breath and push, steady and slow. That's right...good, good."

"Jason, come here and look."

The young man came around while Emma held the flashlight. "Kerry, oh, honey, he's right there...Oh, Kerry, our baby's..."

"Help me...I can't...it hurts. Oh, god! Get him out!"

Emma stepped up to Kerry's shoulder, took her face in her hands, and looked into her eyes. "Kerry, *you* are going to get him out; you were made for this. Now again, chin on your chest." She moved back to see the head emerge.

"Cat...Cat!" she called. While she checked for the cord around the baby's neck, she looked up for a moment and saw a look of utter terror on Cat's face. "Go get the towels out of the roaster."

Emma rotated the head, and the shoulders came out. "One more push, Kerry, real gentle, one more and...here he is." The baby slipped into Emma's hands.

"He looks good. Jason, hand me that orange bulb syringe on the shelf." She suctioned the baby's nose and mouth, and he started to cry. "Come here, Jason, do you want to cut the cord?...That's it, right there, good." Blood poured out of Kerry.

Cat ran in. "Here take him," Emma plopped the squalling infant into Cat's arms and turned to Jason.

"Jason, I need your help here. Kerry, I'm going to give you a shot now; are you okay?"

"I'm so tired, I just want to sleep."

"Take some big breaths, honey, stay awake. Jason, put pressure right here," she said, guiding his hand to his wife's abdomen.

"How much pressure?" he asked, obviously frightened.

"About this much." She pressed on his arm.

"Okay, is she still bleeding?" He watched his wife receive the injection.

"The shot should stop it." Emma put her hand up into the young mother. She felt for the placenta—it was still attached.

"Keep the pressure, Jason."

Come on, come on, she said to herself. Blood was pooling on the table. Emma tugged ever so gently. *Please, please,* she thought. "A little more pressure, Jason, you're doing fine."

"Kerry, you okay? We're about to deliver the placenta. This may sting a little." Emma realized that it was quiet in the room. "How's the baby, Cat?"

"He's fine; his eyes are open and...he's holding onto my finger. What else should I do?"

"Just keep him warm, make sure his head is covered." Cat let the end of the towel fall over her palm and cupped her hand over his head.

"Alright, Kerry, one more time, I'm going to have Jason press...oh, here we go. The red mass came out onto the table. Emma examined it, holding the flashlight. It looked whole, thank god. The bleeding began to slow to a trickle. "Okay, Jason, I'll massage her a little longer."

"Cat, bring the baby here. Lay him down right there; just put the towel over the blood." The baby boy's eyes were wide open.

"Hi, little guy. Unwrap him, honey. Jason, hand me the stethoscope."

"Is he okay?" asked Kerry weakly.

"Just a minute." She listened to the child's heart and lungs. "He sounds fine." She noticed that although he was small, maybe five pounds, he was pink and alert. "He's great! Here, Jason, why don't you take your son to see his mommy."

The bleeding had stopped. Emma sighed, then noticed that Cat was standing next to her. She put her arm around the girl's shoulders, "Are you okay?"

"Yes... are they alright? That was...it was..."

Jason and Kerry nuzzled their new son. As the day's first light came through the windows, Emma put warm compresses on Kerry after she was cleaned up, and checked for tears. They put the baby to Kerry's breast, and he latched on right away.

"What's his name?"

"Jason Alan Cooper, Jr.," said the proud father, "but we're going to call him Jac."

"Oh, that's a nice name," said Emma. "I'm going to put some wood on the fire."

"I'll do it," called Cat, leaving the room.

"We'll give you two — I mean three — a chance to be together."

Emma left the door open slightly. On her way down the hall she noticed all the blood on her blue sheep-and-clouds flannel pajamas. *God*, she thought, *I need a cup of tea...*

The house, insulated by deep snowdrifts and warmed by the constant stoking of the fire throughout the night, leaned in protectively and welcomed the sound of the newborn's cries.

Jason and Kerry stayed for breakfast so Emma could keep an eye on them. She cooked eggs and pancakes on the little woodstove in the kitchen. Cat joined them, and they all admired and took turns holding little Jac. The power came on around ten, and the plows were running. The young couple prepared to leave to have Jac and Kerry checked out at the hospital in Butte City. Kerry's folks lived in Idaho, and Jason's were out of town, but his Aunt May would be meeting them at the house to lend a hand for a few days. After many "thank yous" and hugs, they pulled out of the driveway, the baby looking like a small doll in his car seat. Emma was suddenly exhausted and asked Cat, who was washing dishes, how she felt.

"I'm tired and wired," said the young girl. "I'll probably read and go back to bed. But I'll feed the animals first."

"Thank you," said Emma, heading towards the stairs. She ran herself a hot bath, then fell into bed.

Cat looked around the library. The room had floor-to-ceiling bookshelves on three walls. *Where to start*, she wondered. There were hundreds of books arranged in alphabetical order. A square of sunlight floated on the Oriental rug. After searching through the "M's" and not finding what she wanted, she pulled a wooden chair from the little antique desk and stood on it to reach the top shelf, which held Emma's obstetric books. Under the "F's" she found *Hansen's Fetal Development*. She stepped down and sat on the bed. She let the book sit on her lap a moment, hesitating. The cover showed a close-up of an unborn baby floating in *utero*. The big grandfather clock ticked into the silence. After taking a few deep breaths, she opened the book. The photographs ranged from conception to the ninth month. She counted on her fingers—end of October until third week in January—about eleven weeks. Slowly she turned the pages to what was called the first trimester, starting with pictures of an ovary, then an egg fertilized by sperm, then a blob with a tail, until, at about six weeks, the embryo began to look human. By ten weeks it had hands and little nubby feet and a face. She stared at it for a very long time.

Chapter Fourteen

Emma saw more patients than usual after the holidays. She and Dr. Drew called it '"Christmas-itis." They compared patients over lunch at the Goldrush Cafe. Both had treated overdoses, stomach issues, domestic violence victims, and plenty of flu. Andrew Baker had been Emma's overseeing physician since she started her practice ten years ago. She spoke with him often about patients, referred difficult cases to him, and they had attended many births together. A few times a year she handled his practice while he and his family went on vacation.

Emma fought back tears while sharing her feelings about Briar with him. He held her in his compassionate gaze and said, "It's a tough one, and such an aggressive kind of cancer. I'm so sorry." He asked about Cat, and Emma told him about the misunderstanding, the girl's pregnancy, and how bad she felt. They discussed the politics in Stay County, and he offered to call the judge, whom he knew personally.

Finally, they talked about Jason and Kerry's birth. He read through the chart. "God, Emma! Snowstorm, premature baby, retained placenta, hemorrhage, and all in the dark! Now you know you can do it with your eyes closed." He laughed.

"I really sweated the placenta. I was scared. The baby was

just so healthy and fine, though. They're nice kids; they'll be good parents."

"Well, back to the salt mines." Drew stood up and gave her a hug. "I'll call you next week after I talk to Briar's oncologist."

After running errands, Emma drove through the valley. A frozen fog had covered the fields for days. She was thinking about the new year and what it might hold, with all the changes in her life, when suddenly the sun broke through the slate sky and lit up every tree and bush. She marveled how one moment could be so cold, dank, and dark, and the next, sun-dazzled.

She had been so overwhelmed the last few weeks that she had barely thought about Liam and the incident in church on Christmas Eve. *My God! I'm in my late fifties, and still this man unravels me as if I were a young girl.* The thought of his whispers in the church and the warmth of his lips made her shift uncomfortably in the truck seat.

She was still deep in thought when the post office came into view. She parked and was walking towards the small building when she heard a voice call her name. She turned — it was Jason's mother, Molly Cooper.

"Oh, Emma, I just wanted to thank you again for, well, for just being there for those kids. You know, I never would have left town, but she was a month away from her time. Thank you so much. Kerry told me how wonderful you were. And that baby! Isn't he just the cutest little thing you've ever seen?"

"He really is," Emma said, smiling. "The kids did a great job, and you're welcome."

She turned and opened her post office box. A letter from the judge in Wenachapee County was on top. She opened it in the truck. Permission for the abortion had been granted.

Emma found Cat in the dining room. Little wisps of black hair that had escaped her braid were backlit by the sun slanting through the window. She was doing homework, having started home-schooling with Mrs. Fryer the week before.

"Hey, Cat, how's it going?"

"Okay," she said, not looking up.

"Anyone call?"

"There's a message from somebody wanting an appointment."

"Cat, the judge in Wenachapee has approved the abortion; his letter was in the mail today. Now we just need an appointment for the procedure. I can call the doctor right now."

Cat looked at her. She closed the book and put her pencil down. Her face was serious. "I was hoping to talk with you for awhile now, but you've been so busy, and I wasn't sure...Are you busy now?" She pulled at her braid.

"No, no, I've got the afternoon free, what is it?" Emma sat down across from the girl. Dust motes rose as she slipped her coat off and hung it over the chair. "What's up?"

"Well, I've been thinking...I know I can't...that I'm just not mature enough to...that I've got really nothing to give to this...I mean, under the circumstances, why would I?" She swallowed. "I was wondering if you might know of...I looked in your obstetrics book, and I saw that... You know, Kerry's baby was the first one I've ever held and...I saw that by twelve weeks the fetus looks like, not a baby really, but more human... And remember how we talked about our misunderstanding in the hospital, and you apologized and I told you that it wasn't my fault that this happened, or your fault? Well, I've decided that it isn't the baby's fault either..." A small bird landed on a branch outside the window. "I know that the easiest way for me to get over this and go back to Phoenix is to just have the abortion. But sometimes the easiest way isn't always the right way, and I wondered if you might know someone who...?" She rushed on, "And I know it won't be easy, and that I'd have to depend on you to help me, but I'll work for you and make myself useful if you think there might be a way to find someone to adopt it and give it a good home..." Her voice trailed off, and her big brown eyes looked at Emma, searching, waiting.

It took Emma a moment to respond; the girl's words took her by surprise. She moved her chair, leaning in. "Okay, well, yes to all you have said. It sounds like you have really thought about this. Yes, you can stay here, and I'm sure I can find a family out of the area to adopt the child. And, no, it won't be easy, especially when people know of your decision. But you are young and strong, and…"

"Thank you, Emma," the girl interrupted. "It's already three months. I could have it in July and be in Phoenix by fall…Do you really think I'm strong? Because right now I feel…," tears pooled in her eyes and were blinked away, "really afraid and weak."

"I know," said Emma. "We'll just take it one day at a time, alright?"

The girl exhaled, releasing a long sigh, then nodded, "Alright…thank you."

Unable to sleep, Emma walked to the pasture as a full moon rose over the eastside hills, pulling her out into the orchard. The apple trees stood in the soft light, their dark shadows more expressive and alive than the trees themselves. She listened to big rocks tumbling in the water-swollen creek.

Mav must have heard her footsteps on the frozen ground, because he appeared in the adjacent field and pranced towards her. She let herself through the gate and stood by him. She wondered if he was lonely since her mare Cherry had died last year. Briar always said horses should never be alone, because they are such herd animals. He moved away from her and began to dance a little, his tail up, ears erect.

"Playful, are we?" she said, moving towards him. They began their old game as she clapped her hands. The horse ran in circles, weaving, rearing, stopping, then turning and kicking up his heels. Moonlight glanced off his coat, the dark outline of his elegant body etched against a star-filled sky. He snorted, and she ran with him. She turned suddenly and so did he. "We're not so old are we, boy?" she called breathlessly. "No, we still get drunk on moonlight, don't we?"

Emma settled into the sofa the next morning, a cup of tea in hand, grateful for a free Saturday. She looked at the pile of mail on the end table. It had been a busy week, topped by yesterday's conversation with Cat. The implications of the girl's decision had kept Emma up most of the night. *Perhaps a nap,* she thought, unfolding Friday's *Green Valley Press.* "**Boys Cleared of Charges**," screamed the headline:

> *Stay County Judge Raymond Throckmorton ruled Thursday that all charges would be dropped against the five boys accused of raping a Green Valley high school student new to the area. The charges included kidnapping, rape, and administering an illegal drug. In his statement, the judge found insufficient evidence for prosecution.*

She put the newspaper down, her hands shaking. RJ Dobson's father, a Stay County Commissioner for Butte City, had done quite a job! No trial, no jury, just a hearing. *A complete rollover! Well, why am I surprised?* Emma fumed, getting up and pacing, *it still boils down to who you are and who you know.* The valley was just a microcosm of the larger corrupt world. She had never expected justice, but she admitted to herself that she had, deep down, hoped for it. *How to tell Cat?* she wondered. *What would be the best way to let the girl know?* In the end, she left the newspaper on the purple chair upstairs in the library, thinking that it might be better if Cat was alone when she read it.

That evening, as Emma sat by the fire looking at seed catalogs, she heard a loud crash from upstairs, then Cat yelling a series of expletives that could not have been imagined by even the surliest pirate. She knew that the girl must have read the paper, and she wondered what had been broken, but decided it didn't matter. She was, somehow, impressed. *God,* she thought, *the girl knows how to swear.*

The next morning Emma found the blue and white Delft vase that had belonged to her mother glued together and set in a sunny spot on the kitchen counter, next to a small note that said, "Sorry." When Cat came into the kitchen and offered to build a fire, Emma noticed that her eyes were red and puffy.

"Are you okay?"

"Yeah, I'm just mad," said the girl.

"So am I, honey. I'm so sorry, Cat. They'll get their just dues eventually. I'm a firm believer in the law of 'what goes around comes around.' We may not see their consequences, but they'll get them."

"Yeah? Well, they're going to have to *see me* and be reminded of what they've done!" said the girl, pointing to the small bulge on her stomach. "I'm not staying in this house anymore; I'm going to go out every day. I'll do errands with you and go to the store and the gas station."

"Alright," said Emma nervously.

"And maybe I'll go back to school and they'll have to deal with my belly and wonder whose kid it is. I'm not going to let this sick little redneck town forget." She narrowed her eyes, "They are so not ready for the revenge of Caterina Ramos!" The girl stormed out of the kitchen with paper and kindling in her arms.

"Mary Mother of God," whispered Emma under her breath.

Emma stood in the rain at the edge of the creek that was wild with fast water. Typical for February, it frothed with mud the color of coffee and cream. She looked west to the Serpentine Mountains. Snowmelt flowed down through the narrow canyon and braided its way into the wide, rocky creek bed. She was waiting for Briar, who was bringing the promarin mare any time now. Yesterday Emma and Cat had cleaned out the other stall in Mav's little barn. She'd gone to the feed store and bought vitamins and supplements for the pregnant horse. She knew Mav would be glad for the company.

The rain let up to a slight drizzle as she walked back towards the pasture and corral area. The bay gelding was standing quietly. She moved against him, scratching behind his ear; his eyes closed and his lower lip twitched loosely.

"You're going to have a friend," she told him, "won't that be nice?" He seemed to listen to her, his large brown eyes opening wide as she spoke. "This horse has had a rough time, not spoiled rotten like you, huh, big boy? We'll give her and her foal some shelter for a while, okay?" She realized then that she could have just as well been talking about Cat and her situation. The horse and foal would take care of themselves, but Cat—that was going to be more complicated, especially with the fiery attitude the girl had shown of late. And then there was Liam and Midnight; what would they think? And how would Cat feel, knowing that the son of one of Emma's best friends was involved in the rape? The enormity of her commitment to the girl overwhelmed her.

Dark purple clouds boiled overhead as she walked to the

corral. She saw Briar's truck and trailer coming down the road. Mav ran to the fence and whinnied as Briar pulled into the turnaround. Briar stepped down from her truck slowly.

"Finally a break in the weather, huh?" She seemed unsteady on her feet.

"Yes, finally, everything is drenched. I checked Mav for rain rot on his back, but he seems alright. How are you?"

"I'm okay, just really nauseous from the chemo. My friend Marlene didn't show up until after eleven; guess there was flooding along the interstates." She unlatched the doors of the trailer and Mav called again. This time the mare answered him as she backed out. She stood bewildered, looking at the unfamiliar surroundings. She was pathetic, a large dull brown horse with patches of hair missing, almost 100 pounds underweight. Her ribs jutted from under loose skin, and her hipbones stuck up at sharp angles. Her pregnant belly hung down, as if stretching all of her skin with its gravity.

"Oh, God!" said Emma, "poor thing."

"I know. We unloaded her in the dark, but when I got a good look at her this morning, I was shocked. It's amazing she still has the foal."

"When is she due?" asked Emma, reaching out to the horse, letting it smell her hand.

"As far as they can figure, sometime in May."

Mav was beside himself, running the length of the fence and calling to the mare. "Okay, okay, let's see how you two get along." Emma opened the gate as Briar led the mare into the corral. "I'm going to leave the halter on her, just in case," she said, unclipping the lead rope. The mare immediately kicked her hind legs at Mav, warning him not to come too close. He snorted and backed off, taking her in.

The contrast was pitiful. Even at twenty years old, Mav's shining red coat and the quick flick of his tail radiated health, while the mare had such a low life-force, not just in her body but in her eyes as well.

"What's her name?" Emma asked.

"Candy; here's her record," said Briar, getting a manila envelope out of the truck. "Candy Barr, approximately ten years. She's been at the factory in Canada for five years. Before that it looks like she had one, two, three different owners. This will be her sixth foal. No wonder she's in such bad shape."

"What are those scars on her withers?"

"From what I understand, the mares are cross-tied with some kind of strap over their withers to keep them in place. The scars must be where the harness rubbed her. Like I told you, these mares are hooked up to catheters twenty-four hours a day. The factory farms are huge, housing maybe five hundred mares at a time. It's a thriving business, as you can imagine, with women all around the world on estrogen therapy. The drug companies are cleaning up, and here is the end product," said Briar sighing, pointing to the mare who now just stood off to one side, head down. "They kill their foals as soon as they're born. After four or five babies, they kill the mares too. My friend Marlene knows a rescue group up there, and sometimes they can get a few of the mares out."

"I wonder if women would take the drug if they knew," wondered Emma out loud. "Well, I haven't fed Mav yet; let's give them a nice flake." It began to sprinkle, but Emma and Briar stood by the fence watching the two horses eat.

"So you're having a lot of nausea?"

"Yeah, I just feel like shit most of the time. I'll have the chemo and just start to recover, and then I've got to go again the next week. I'm not complaining; I know I've got to do this... I'm just so tired."

"I know, honey," said Emma, putting her arm around her. "It's awful, but it will end. Have you seen the oncologist, heard any reports on your progress?"

"Not until week after next," Briar sighed. "I'm gonna go

home and go back to bed. Thanks for fostering Candy, and I'll help out as much as I can. Dr. Alice will come check her out next week, and Harry will trim her feet soon. Mav looks happy."

The two horses were eating from the same pile of hay. Emma saw a ripple under the skin of the mare's belly. "Look at that!" she said, "what do you think? A little foot, maybe?"

"Maybe," said Briar, getting into the truck.

"Briar, you're coming for lunch Friday, right? Everybody is; we've all got cabin fever. It's potluck, but don't you worry about bringing anything. Take care and rest, alright?" Briar nodded and pulled herself up into the truck.

Emma turned and left the two horses in the corral. It had started to pour again; she pulled her hood closer around her face as she walked through the pasture. Back at the creek she squatted down, spread her hand over a round stone, and picked it up. She rose and aimed. The rock spun into the air and landed with a splash. She threw another and then another. Something about throwing the rocks into the dark water and knowing they were being carried away made her feel better.

Chapter Fifteen

Emma set a nice table in the long dining room. At the last minute she decided to use the good dishes that had belonged to Gran and her mother. She even set a delicate floral teacup at each plate. She had bought a bouquet in Butte City—the worst part of winter being the lack of flowers—and she arranged the hothouse white mums, daisies, and pink freesias in a milk glass vase. A big pot of vegetable soup simmered on the stove, and she had taught Cat how to make velvet crumb cake that morning. She knew the Yee Haws would fill out the meal with salads and Lilly's bread. The dining room window looked out on a lifeless garden, but there were little rabbit-ear buds on the lilac tree. Two straight weeks of rain had filled the creek; its muffled roar could be heard inside the house.

Cat was upstairs studying or watching television. Emma had invited her to have lunch with them. The girl had mumbled, "maybe," as she passed through the dining room. Briar was the only person who'd really had any contact with her, and Emma still didn't know how to tell Cat about Midnight and Julien. Word of the boys' supposed innocence had spread through the valley, but Emma hadn't discussed anything with her friends yet. She would be relieved when they all knew about the girl's pregnancy.

Soon the women arrived, carrying covered dishes, hanging up coats and hats, stomping their feet on the rug in the kitchen. Everyone talked at once, and a feeling of gaiety filled the room. Even Briar had come, looking much better than a few days ago. The pink stocking cap she wore over her thinning hair brought out the color in her cheeks. The aroma of Lilly's freshly-baked bread, a beautiful braid sprinkled with sesame seeds, was mouthwatering. Clare uncovered a huge tossed green salad, and gave Emma a watercolor of irises so real you could touch them. She smiled shyly when everyone complimented her on the colors.

Midnight had her hair in a bun at the nape of her neck and wore traditional Green River beaded earrings, black, white, and red, "like flicker wings," she explained, as Emma admired them. She slipped a pan of Indian tacos into the oven and winked at Emma, saying, "These at the end are no meat, for you, weirdo." She moved close to Emma and whispered, "Where's the girl?"

Emma, surprised, said, "Upstairs studying. I invited her, but I don't know." She shrugged.

"How is she doing?" Midnight's eyes were serious. "I mean about the verdict and all. When is she leaving?"

Clare asked for salad tongs just then, so Emma fumbled in a drawer without answering. Finally they all moved to the dining room, where there were two pots of tea: a chamomile-mint herbal blend, and a strong black with milk and sugar. Rain slid down the large old crosshatched window, and the women chatted, taking turns.

Lilly spoke about her oldest boy's phone call from college. He had said, "Mom, I met a girl; can I bring her home for Easter?" "Isn't that sweet, girls?" Then she asked Emma about depression, because her dad was more and more withdrawn or easily combative. He was having a real hard time with the environmental restrictions that were being imposed on the ranchers in spring, in an effort to increase the salmon run.

Midnight interrupted sarcastically, "Hell, there should be enough water for the ranches, Indians, and the fish. Hey, we used to have it all; tell him to get used to sharing." The women were accustomed to Midnight's blunt comments; they just smiled and moved on.

Clare talked about how Don was working with Bandit, and her concern that he was too hard on the horse. Lilly muttered, "No shit!" under her breath. Clare glared at her, then asked Briar for training advice.

Briar said, "Well, the key word is *training*. A lot of folks refer to it as *breaking*, and they sometimes use two-by-fours. That's about the worst thing you can do to a young horse." She offered her help, but Clare said Don probably wouldn't accept it.

They put the food on the table and began to eat. They laughed about how most of their get-togethers involved food, and they all talked about gaining weight since Christmas.

Midnight chortled, "We're supposed to hibernate and put on weight in the winter."

"Yeah," said Lilly, "but I can't get my fat, grizzly bear ass into my jeans."

Emma was slicing the bread when a sudden silence fell over the table. She looked up. Cat was standing there, and Emma saw the girl through the eyes of her friends: small, dark-skinned, her long black curly hair hanging down her back. She wore jeans and a pale blue sweater, without a stitch of makeup. Her dark eyelashes framed her huge brown eyes; her full mouth turned up slightly at the corners. She was in the room but looked like she might bolt at any moment.

Emma stood up. "Cat! Welcome! I'm glad you came downstairs. I want you to meet my friends. I'll introduce you around the table. This is Lilly and her sister Clare. You already know Briar."

Briar smiled, "Hi, Cat."

"And this is Midnight," Emma watched as Midnight eyed the girl unabashedly.

"Hello," Cat murmured, looking at the floor.

"Come, sit down, the soup is still hot. I'll get you a bowl."

"No thanks, I just came down to get my math book." She scooted out into the kitchen and came back with the book in her hand. "Nice to meet you all," she said, moving through the living room and up the stairs.

No one spoke until Clare said, "God, she's beautiful. How old is she?"

"Sixteen," said Emma.

"She doesn't look evil at all," said Lilly. Emma turned, frowning at her. "I mean, I've talked to the boys' mothers, and they've told me things about her. She did lie, right? That's why the boys got off?" Emma bit her tongue until she tasted blood. Lilly went on, "I'll bet you were happy about the decision, huh, Midnight?"

"I don't know about that," she responded, with a question in her voice.

"But, Midnight, Julien is free now. If the judge had determined that they were guilty, those boys' lives would be over."

"But Julian still has to answer to the tribal elders, a different kind of judge and jury. We'll see," said Midnight.

"Where's the girl from?" asked Clare, "Arizona?"

Emma nodded. Suddenly she didn't want them to know what was really going on with Cat. "I've got to get the recipe for that salad dressing, Clare."

"That was so good. I'm stuffed." groaned Lilly.

"Room for dessert?" asked Emma, cutting the cake.

"Always," said Briar, who was famous for her sweet tooth.

More tea was poured.

"So what's in the salad dressing, Clare?" asked Emma.

"Oh, it's so easy—olive oil, good garlic, salt, and rice vinegar, that's all."

"She's pregnant, isn't she?" Everyone turned towards Midnight.

"What!" exclaimed Lilly.

Emma looked at Midnight's folded hands, the hard question in her eyes. She hesitated, "Yes, how did you know?"

"A little birdie told me, actually a big black one."

"What do you mean?" questioned Lilly.

"Jeez Louise! What's she going to do?" asked Briar, swirling her spoon in her tea cup. "Will she have an abortion?"

Emma squirmed. "Actually, after much thought and deliberation, she's decided to have the child." The women's faces were incredulous.

"Why would she want a baby that's the product of a…was it rape, Emma?" asked Clare, her eyes wide.

"Yes, I believe it was. She told me that she was a virgin. She's planning on giving the baby up for adoption and has asked me to make the arrangements."

"Where will she go during her pregnancy?" asked Briar. "Does she have family in Arizona?"

"Not a soul," said Emma. "She's asked to stay here until the birth, and I told her she could."

Lilly's voice was loud, "Oh my god, Emma! Do you know what you're doing? What are people going to think? Harboring a girl that accused our boys of rape, dragging them through the courts for months. Why would you do this for someone you don't really know?" She rushed on, "Emma, I've heard all kinds of stories about her life in Arizona—gangs, prostitutes, drugs. The girl's dangerous!"

Emma stood up, "Stories and facts are two different things." She started clearing the dishes.

"But Emma, I'm just being protective of you. Why would you put yourself in this position?" pleaded Lilly.

"Let's not talk about this anymore," said Midnight, "since the girl is just upstairs." She got up, pushing her chair back, and stood facing Emma, giving her a curious look.

No one spoke as Briar, Clare, and Lilly got up, collected their plates and cups, and carried them into the kitchen. Lilly rinsed while Clare loaded the dishwasher. In the tension of the moment Briar said, "Hey, the rain has let up. Anyone up for a walk out to the pasture to see the mare?"

Midnight reached for her poncho, "Yeah, I'm curious; a walk sounds good."

Lilly yanked her coat off the rack. "I've gotta go," she said abruptly, "you coming, Clare?"

Clare gave Emma a look that said, "uh oh," then answered her sister, "Sure, okay."

Lilly stomped out the back door without saying a word.

Chapter Sixteen

True to her word, Cat went back to the high school, choosing to take classes in the mornings so she could help Emma in the afternoons. Emma, who drove her to the office to enroll, wasn't surprised by the cold demeanor of Vida Clause, the school secretary, who, once she understood what the girl wanted, promptly left and came back with the principal.

Mr. Janus' face was serious and pinched as he explained that he didn't know if the board would allow the girl back. Word of the girl's pregnancy had traveled like wildfire across the valley, and Mr. Janus couldn't stop glancing at the small but obvious bulge underneath the tight sweater that Cat wore. It might be better for all involved, he explained, pleading with Emma, if the girl continued to home-school. Emma turned to Cat, who strongly protested, "No!" It was her understanding that Green Valley was a public high school, and she was determined to attend her classes there. The principal said that he would have to call a special board meeting, and that he would let them know the decision soon. Mr. Janus called that evening, saying that as long as there was no trouble, Cat could come back.

The first morning of her return to school, Emma cleared

the breakfast dishes and found herself full of anxiety for what the day might bring.

Cat seemed relaxed, gathering her backpack and coat. "Okay, I'm ready," she said, pausing by the back door.

"Are you sure you don't want me to drive you? It's snowing really hard out there."

"No, I'll just walk down to the bus stop. I've got my hat and gloves."

"I'm worried for you, Cat. I'm only seeing a few patients today—you call me if there's any problems, okay?"

"Okay." She turned to face Emma, "Don't worry about me, and remember I'll be home on the noon bus. See you then."

Emma stood at the kitchen window and watched the small figure disappear down the road as a heavy and determined snow fell straight and fast.

Cat saw the big bus coming up the highway, black smoke spewing out the back. As if surprised, the driver braked quickly, used to passing by this stop. The tires made a loud squealing sound. The door opened; she took a deep breath and stepped up. There were lots of empty seats. She took one near the front, pulled the backpack onto her lap, and stared straight ahead. The bus driver, a woman, stared at her in the mirror. Cat met her eyes, and then the bus driver looked away and shifted the bus into gear.

Cows speckled the long white fields. Snow shook itself off trees and power lines. They stopped to pick up some kids on Rawlins Creek Road. One of them, a boy she'd seen at school, gave her a puzzled look as he sat down across from her. Two dogs, a shepherd and a collie, trotted on the side of the road. She kept her eyes on the window. Someone touched her shoulder.

"Hey," the boy across the aisle said, "aren't you that girl that...that..."

"Got raped," said Cat, looking right at him.

"That's not what the judge ruled," he fired back. "I heard you left town."

"Don't you wish?" she said, flashing him a big smile.

Cell phones were taken out of pockets, purses, and backpacks. A low buzz of whispers moved up and down the aisle. By the time the bus had traveled the remaining five miles, word of Cat's return was all over the school. The driver pulled into the bus lane. Cat saw a group of kids standing in the parking lot as she came down the steps. A boy's voice yelled, "Go home, slut!" She continued walking towards the office.

As she took the stairs, Amy Lee came up beside her. "Cat! Hi, I thought you went back to Arizona. I wanted to call you... um...afterwards, but my mom wouldn't let me. How are you?"

Cat slung the backpack over her shoulder. "Okay," she said, "considering."

Amy looked at her belly, then looked away. "So it's true," she blurted. The bell rang. "Cat, we need to talk; what's your first class?"

"English."

"Meet me on the football field at lunch, okay?"

"Can't, I'm only here mornings."

Amy Lee stopped her hurried walk. "Okay, Nutrition then, the field, okay?"

"We'll see," said Cat, turning into the hall. There were kids lined up in front of a row of lockers; all eyes turned as she walked past. "Who's the ho'?" taunted a boy she didn't know. She answered over her shoulder, "Not me," and ducked into the classroom.

English had been her favorite class before she left. She liked the young teacher, who was so excited about literature. Cat stood in the back of the room waiting for Ms. Lucky, as students trickled in and found their seats. A few turned in their desks and stared at her. Ms. Lucky entered the classroom.. She was about thirty years old, dressed in a pantsuit. her pretty face blank. She saw Cat standing in the back, and was obviously expecting her.

"Alright, Caterina, this chair is free." The girl moved down the aisle, feeling all eyes on her. She opened her backpack slowly and methodically, then folded her hands on her desk.

"Alright, everyone take out the questions to *Grapes of Wrath*..."

Only kindergarteners rode the noon bus. The little kids bounced in their seats, playing with each other and talking in loud, high-pitched voices. Cat thought about the morning. She had met Amy Lee during Nutrition. The football field was frozen, and they had stood under the bleachers talking.

"Cat, I want you to know I had nothing to do with the rape. You probably think I was part of the set up, but I knew nothing about the boys' plan."

"No, I never thought that you did," said Cat, looking at Amy Lee's relieved face.

"I was ripped off too. I can't believe my cousin let them drug me. I've found out a lot about what happened. I told Chuckie I would kick his fat ass if he didn't tell me the truth. He said he was drunk, but he remembers stuff. Believe it or not, he feels bad about his part in it...And Cat, I am so sorry that this happened to you, and like I said, I've wanted to call you so many times, but my mom forbid it. No one knows anything about you, who you are...I mean."

"You mean that...it wasn't my fault?" Cat said quietly.

"No, it wasn't your fault!" Amy Lee said firmly. "It was

RJ's idea; he got the drugs and everything. Chuckie said that RJ threatened them with something terrible if they didn't follow through. And Chuckie also said that Julien—you know, the Indian boy—didn't even know about the plan. He said that Julien was real drunk and RJ forced him to have...to be part of it," she paused, breathless. "Cat, what are you going to do?"

"Stay here until it's born. The woman I'm staying with is a nurse, and she's going to find a home for it. I'll go back to Arizona and finish my senior year."

"Emma is a really nice person; she's helped a lot of people here."

"Yeah, I know," said Cat.

The bell rang. "Give me your number at Emma's."

"Okay," said Cat, writing the number down on a little piece of paper.

"Cat?"

"What?"

"I'm so sorry. Do you believe me?"

"Sure," said Cat, looking away, "thanks."

Emma was writing a prescription for her last patient. "This should help with the pain, Abby. Take it only at night though, it might make you drowsy at work. It looks like it is healing well. I'll see you in two weeks to remove the stitches." Abby Walters thanked her and handed her a check. "I left a jar of sweet pickles by the back door," she called.

"Great!" said Emma. "My cukes were terrible this year. Take care."

She cleaned up the exam room, pulled a clean sheet of paper across the table. As she turned off the light, she heard the back door open. Cat stomped the snow off her boots and was hanging up her coat when Emma came in with a questioning look on her face.

"So? How did it go?"

"Oh, it was fine, no problem; hardly anyone noticed that I was there," she lied.

"Oh, good," Emma said. "I've got soup on—are you hungry?"

"Starving," said the girl.

Liam drove the river road in the late afternoon. He rarely went to Midnight's cabin, probably because she and Julien were in the valley so much. Every turn of the thirty or so miles brought back memories of his past. He and his sister had experienced very different childhoods, being born sixteen years apart. They shared the same beloved mother, Winnie Fisher Wood, a spirited and spiritual woman, who had not married either of their fathers. She chose to stay independent of that institution, yet loyally connected to her tribe and family. She was a strong, loving woman, like his Grandmother Swan.

Winnie had worshipped her boy, born William Night Bear Wood. His childhood had been a boom time in the valley, the end of the raping of rivers for gold and the beginning of the raping of forests for lumber. There was abundance for their small tribe during those years, with plenty of work for the men and full larders for their families. His father, Rue, didn't live with them, but doted on Liam and came each Sunday to spend time with him. He died in a logging accident when Liam was in the fifth grade. A hardworking, gruff man from the St. Cloud tribe, which was not so different from the Green River, he'd taught him to hunt and fish, to be *his* kind of man. But Liam had loved drawing ever since he could remember. Rue told him if he caught him with pencils and paper—girl tools—he'd beat him.

Liam had helped his mother and ailing grandmother around the homestead and worked after school. Wary of the white world, they had disapproved of his relationship with Emma throughout his high school years. After she'd gone to San Francisco to start college, and just before he was to leave for art school in Portland, he'd gotten Gretta Longacre pregnant. His mother and grandmother made it known that this girl, with tribal ties and bloodlines, was a better choice. They moved her into their cabin and helped her with her baby daughter while Liam went to school.

Maybe there were other reasons, he thought, that he didn't visit Midnight's cabin too often. Those had been torturous years, when he was trying to find himself and forget his obsession with Emma. He'd wanted nothing to do with logging, having seen too many clear-cuts along the river and in the mountains above it. After college he'd worked hard in the mill in Butte City and was able to buy his small ranch. "A hay growin' Indian?" his Grandma Swan had sarcastically said when he'd told her. But it was really his art that had supported his little family. He'd felt good carving something out of the huge, discarded tree trunks. His sculptures, mostly birds of prey or animals, were big sellers in some of the best galleries in Portland and Seattle.

Hypnotized by the winding road, lost in the past, he snapped out of it, becoming aware of the gushing river below. He loved his little sister and his nephew and did what he could to help them. Midnight had inherited her father's fiery spirit, and sometimes he thought she was too hard on the boy. This rape accusation though, this was serious business. Liam couldn't fathom the boy's involvement in a gang rape. At first the other boys had accused his nephew of being the sole culprit, but when the DNA tests came back, they were all implicated. And now the girl—how ironic—was staying with Emma.

The turnoff appeared; he slowed and drove across the big

sturdy bridge, pausing to look down at the fast melt-water. After a mile or so of climbing up the mountain, he saw the smoke from Midnight's fire spiraling up through the big cedars ahead. She was in front of the cabin as he pulled in, splitting kindling by the woodpile.

"Hey, Bro, come in. I've got water on for tea."

The cabin was warm and smelled of mountain mahogany root. He saw the prayer altar by the woodstove. Antlers, shells, a beaded strap, and a picture of Julien were strewn across the little table. Midnight was far more traditional than he was. She cherished the Green River ways and taught language and dance classes to the young. He was a member of the men's elder council, but he had to admit that his sister knew much more about rituals, customs, and their tribal spirituality. Mom and Grandma had seen to that.

"How is Julien, Sis?" he asked, fingering the beaded strap that he'd given the boy at his birth.

"I don't know. He's kind of withdrawn, quieter, if that's possible. Doesn't look me in the eyes. Sometimes he's defiant, but Liam, I still, in my gut, don't believe he did this. There's rumors that he was so drunk that the others boys were able to force him into it."

"That seems unlikely, not that they wouldn't make him, but that he could deposit...," he searched for the right word and gave up, "you know...sperm."

"Yeah, I know," she sighed, as she moved to the kitchen area and brought a small teapot and mugs to the table where Liam sat. "And now it gets even more complicated...the girl is pregnant."

"Oh, shit."

"I know, as if what happened to her wasn't enough. Her grandma died, the rape, and now this."

"Does Julien know?"

"He must, it's all over the valley. I want you and the elders to talk to him. He's so nonchalant about it, Li; he acts like he doesn't care."

"So you want us to come up with consequences, the old tribal way—face up and pay back?"

"Yes! I'll agree with whatever you decide, but I really believe he needs to face the girl. I can't believe she went back to school, can you? She must be tough."

Liam took a drink of tea. "So the girl is still at Emma's; she's staying?"

"Far as I know."

"Alright, I'll talk to the others. We'll think of something, and then shouldn't Emma be told?...Maybe you should be the one to let her know what we decide. If Julien has to face the girl, and the girl will allow it, shouldn't Emma know?"

"You call her, Bro, I know you're dying to. It's written all over your face, not to mention your quivering heart. God! Why don't you ask her to dinner or something?"

He sat quietly a moment, looking into Midnight's face, "Because it...she means so much to me...Because honestly, if she said no, I couldn't stand it."

"You'd rather suffer, huh? Remember the old tribal definition of fear: false evidence appearing real?"

He squirmed in the chair, "Yes...I do...and thanks for reminding me." He gulped the rest of the tea, "and with that said, I need to get back to the valley; it's almost time to feed."

"You are just a great big coward!" She reached out and patted his broad shoulder, "I'll walk you out."

"I'm perfectly capable," he smiled. "I'll let you know about the meeting with Julien." He glanced at the almost empty woodpile. "Tell him to come by after school tomorrow, and we'll load his pickup with wood."

"Liam? The girl plans to give the child up for adoption. You remember her mother, Dovie, don't you?"

"Yeah, I think so. Wasn't she pretty wild, left after school?"

"Uh huh. I know this sounds crazy, but she was full-blood."

It took him a minute to get it. "Oh, I see, what's the girl's lineage?"

"She's half Hispanic. Regardless of the father, the child would have a lot of Green River..."

He smoothed his hair back and tugged on his braid. "Sis, you think way too much. Let's take this a step at a time, okay?"

"Okay." She reached up and hugged him, "Thanks for coming." She watched him get in his truck and drive away. *He's right,* she thought, *I think way too much.*

Midnight drove up the muddy dirt road to her brother's small ranch. Julien sat staring out the window. He'd fought and argued after school about coming to the meeting tonight. The truck bounced in and out of deep potholes, and heavy rain slanted into the headlights. Midnight rounded the last curve and drove up the hill. She parked near the other cars. Julien protested again as she took a still-warm dish out from under the seat.

"Do I have to, Mom? This is stupid! What do these old men know about anything?"

Midnight turned towards him. "Let's get it straight about whom and what is stupid. Get out! And come with me now!" she ordered.

Inside, Liam took the dish from her.

"I had some canned blackberries, made you guys a pie. Hey, Denver, Adam, Bill, good to see you; hey, Frenchie."

The men sat around the square table. Liam motioned to Julien to take the empty seat at the end. "Thanks, Midnight." He gave her a hug. "We shouldn't be more than an hour."

"Okay, I'll go and do some laundry in town." She let herself out the door.

The big kitchen held a wood cookstove, range, refrigerator, and a stonework open fireplace. At one end was Liam's workbench. He worked inside in the winter instead of heating his studio. His carving tools were lined up neatly on a shelf.

Liam struck a match and lit the end of a dried brown root. The mountain mahogany caught and turned red; its pungent smell billowed with the smoke, which drifted up in a steady plume. Liam stood and moved towards Julien who was sullen, his eyes downcast, his large hands on the table. Liam positioned himself behind and above the boy. He waved the root in a figure eight over the boy's head.

Denver Budd began to speak, his deeply creased face half-lit by the fire. "Take it all, take all of the dark and impure; clean us until we are like the rabbit, cougar, deer and bear."

Adam Sizemore picked up his drum, a small bowl of polished wood with a skin stretched over it. He set a beat as Bill Plainsford, round in his flannel shirt, threw back his head and sang a two-syllable chant, "ay-ya, ay-ya," over and over. Frenchie Homes and Liam joined in. "Take it all, take all the dark and impure until we are clean like the rabbit, deer, cougar and bear." Liam moved behind each man, waving the smoking root over and around them.

Julien sat rigid, his copper hair in his face. He hated these stupid old-time rituals and these crazy old men who called themselves the tribal elders. *What tribe? Why crap, there were hardly any Green River left, and they didn't even have a reservation!*

The chanting stopped, and Liam sat down at the other end of the table, facing the boy. "Okay, Julien, when we met with you in November there were certain things you were to complete. Did you join the Alcoteen group?"

"Yes."

"And have you gone to every meeting?"

"Almost; not over Christmas vacation, they didn't have them."

"And have you stopped drinking?"

Julien froze. He had known this was coming. He had really cut back, but he knew that if he lied, somehow, someway, these men who had known him his entire life would know. "Almost," he answered. A collective air of disappointment was passed around the table.

"State your reason for continuing to drink," said Liam. "Explain why you think that after what has happened, it's okay for you to endanger yourself and embarrass us further?"

"I don't know," said the boy nervously, "all the kids do…"

Frenchie let out a big sigh and pulled his stocking cap down over his ears. Adam Sizemore shook his head slowly back and forth.

Denver asked, "How did your father die, Julien?"

Shit! Here it was again, the legacy of Rhett Smith. "He was drunk, crashed his bike into the river and drowned."

"And who was involved in an alleged rape a few months ago?" asked Bill. The boy didn't say anything.

"Julien?"

"The judge already let us off. Uncle Liam, come on!"

"Whoa, wait just a minute." Liam gestured towards his nephew, "If I remember correctly, your DNA was found along with the other boys'. You may not remember, but it got there somehow. I suspect somebody who does remember pulled some strings in the DA's office, and now there are other…," he paused, "complications. So, we have come to some decisions that concern you. One, you will be tested weekly at the clinic for drugs and alcohol. And two…as we have just found out that the girl in question is pregnant…"

Julien looked at his uncle.

"She will be staying at Emma's through the summer. You will not only go to her and apologize for your part in what we

161

now have reason to believe *was* rape, you'll pay back, as the tribe calls it. We are still deciding how you will do this. Paying back and facing up might bring you some redemption for your addictive, thoughtless, and irresponsible behavior. Do you understand?" The boy's head bowed, and he nodded. "You will meet with us every month now, agreed?"

"Yes, sir," mumbled Julien.

"Oh, and Julien, you are also to start attending your mother's Green River language and dance classes. You need to learn about your heritage and our world, before the other one kills you."

Shadows bounced off the kitchen's stone walls. Liam's latest sculpture was in the corner on a bench, a huge osprey with a wing span of five feet. Roughly carved, it looked as if it were emerging from the shaggy cedar trunk.

Liam served the pie and coffee, and the men talked for quite a while about the declining salmon runs and the water restrictions being implemented by the government. They spoke about the next tribal meeting.

Julien was mute, his food untouched. When he heard the horn on his mother's truck in the driveway, he grabbed his coat and bolted out the door.

Frenchie laughed, "That boy sure has a lot of Rhett Smith in him, don't he?"

"I see his mother's spirit too," commented Denver.

"I wouldn't be that young again for nothin'," said Bill.

"Well," said Liam, rising and picking a log out of the pile, "this is going to be a rough one for the boy." He looked thoughtful, "It's not just going to go away." He tossed the dry wood into the fire; after a few seconds it exploded into flames.

"Yeah," said Frenchie, "but it might be what saves him, too."

Spring

Chapter Seventeen

Spring began flirty and fickle, slowly seducing the land with a gamut of extreme weather from sun to snow. Emma rejoiced, glad the long winter was over, but also overwhelmed by the change-of-season chores required to run the farm. The orchard had to be pruned—she had shown Julien how to trim the tall suckers, so that each tree would leaf out and flower in an open umbrella shape. The garden needed to be tilled—she had already drawn up a map of what and where she planned to plant. This year, more carrots. She'd figured out how to dry them and loved how they held up in winter soups and stews. More potatoes, fewer beets. Trees had fallen in the little copse of woods, broken and battered by the huge windstorm in January. The oak, especially, would make good firewood. All the animals needed to be wormed. Mav's hooves were overdue to be trimmed; his barnyard should be mucked out. He required a yearly series of vaccinations. The hellion kitten would have to go to the vet to be neutered. Old Bear should get his yearly check-up. And those were just the outside chores.

Smoke from the woodstove had smudged the windows. The carpets needed to be cleaned, and the drapes taken down and dusted. The old wooden floors could use waxing, and the exam room would be much lighter with a fresh coat of paint. The front porch, batiked by muddy raccoon, possum, skunk, and cat paw prints, could use a power wash. The house had cobwebs in every nook and cranny, surrounding every window frame and doorway. She swore that if this chore wasn't done every season, the whole house would be encased in a giant interlaced and knotted web.

Just thinking about it all made her tired, and she decided to drive out to Heron Lane and walk while it was still light out. Bear watched her lace her shoes with resignation. "I know," she told him, "you want to go, poor guy." But his arthritic hips had ended their beloved walks. She drove the short distance across the valley and parked the truck on the side of the road.

Heron Lane ran across the width of the valley for about five miles. Huge old cottonwoods arched over it, their new chartreuse leaves tight-fisted. Emma loved the old trees. In summer their cool, deep shade formed a tunnel of relief from the dry heat; their feathered seed pods cushioned the road in thick piles. There were always many birds here. The Rawlin's ranch sprawled on one side, a wide irrigation ditch on the other. This land had been in Lilly and Clare's family for over a century. Today, the freshly plowed fields looked like shaved chocolate, but in another month they would be eye-hurting green with alfalfa.

A dim silver light fell alongside the white poplars as she walked, lost in thought, lost in no thought. Something in the road caught her eye. Two robin's eggs lay side by side on the ground. She paused, wondering about the how and why of it. She looked around into the budded branches of smaller trees but couldn't see any nests. Finally, the mystery unsolved, she reached down and scooped them lightly into her palm. They were cold. She stared intently at their serpentine color and fine brown speckles. She took this discovery as a sign, and put one in each of her pockets so they wouldn't bump into each other. She walked again, leaving the cottonwoods, moving towards White's bridge, its steel ribs arched above the water. As she stepped up onto the bridge, she noticed nail heads as big as quarters poking up through the worn, wide boards. The Green River frothed and tumbled beneath. Her eyes glanced at a lump on the bank, which turned out to be a great blue heron, his head bowed, his wings wrapped around him like a cape.

After awhile she turned back, noticing the sun sinking behind the mountains. A dozen or so turkey vultures, homing in for the night, flapped into the canopy of old trees. She heard a truck but couldn't see it because of a turn in the road. As it approached, she saw that it was Liam's pickup, and her heart, a wild animal, leapt into her throat. The moment he recognized her, he slowed down, his face breaking into a wide smile. Frozen, breathing fast, she tried to control the school-girl reaction of her body.

He stopped, rolled down the window, and looked at her for a moment. "Now I know why I came this way. How are you, Emma?" He stepped out of the truck and faced her.

"I'm fine, fine." She asked, not looking into his face, "And how are you? How was your winter?"

"Quiet," he answered, "but I've been going strong with the art." His graveled voice made her shiver.

"Oh, that's good; what have you been working on?"

"Uh, mostly animals. Right now I'm working on an osprey, life size, for the gallery in Canyonville." Their eyes met; she could feel the energy between them.

"Great, great," she said, toeing the ground.

He reached out and gently lifted her chin. "And what about you, Emma, are you still helping 'em come in and helping 'em go out?" His touch was so powerful she stepped back.

"Oh, it's been pretty quiet. I've got my hands full. Well, you know about the situation with Jenny Brown's granddaughter; she's staying with me."

"Yeah, Midnight told me. Julien is supposed to meet with her soon."

"Hmm, how is Midnight? I haven't seen her for a while."

"She's okay, had me over for dinner last week."

A truck passed them, but neither noticed or waved.

"It's really great seeing you, Emma. I've wanted to…call ever since Christmas, but I didn't know how you, um, felt…"

How could he not know how she felt? And damn it! Why couldn't she tell him? The old fear surfaced, and in spite of the chilly air she started to perspire. More turkey vultures flew into the tree tops above. She glanced up and saw one looking back at her, his beady eyes and red wattle condemning her for her silence.

"They are ugly old birds, aren't they?" He walked to the truck. "Well I better go, I've gotta feed," he climbed up into the seat. "Good to see you."

Her face was flushed, "You too, take care."

He looked down at her from the truck window with those intense hazel eyes. She didn't want him to go, and then she remembered.

"Liam, here, hold out your hand." His hand left the steering wheel; she dug in her pockets and gently placed the eggs in his palm. He stared at them for a moment.

"Happy spring! I found them on the ground."

"Well, I know just where to put these in my studio. Thank you!" He placed them on a handkerchief on the dashboard and started the truck. "See ya," he said, pulling away.

She watched him and saw his face watching hers in the side mirror. She turned, her legs like jelly, her heart racing. She looked into the ditch, the water flowed by as if nothing had just happened. The sun had disappeared. Pulling her jacket closer, she walked. Something, some movement in the blackberry bushes, alerted her. Stopping, she focused on the deep shadows. Another movement and then she saw it: a great horned owl, stone still, stared back at her. *Ah*, she thought, *now there is wisdom*—Liam's face flashed into her mind—*and here, here am I…*

Signs of change burgeoned with leaf burst and thaw. Emma noticed a clump of purple crocus blooming in the warm ground near the chimney, and daffodils were poking through the icy earth. There was always a false spring in the valley, and talk at the post office was jubilant but laced with caution. Yes, the sun was glorious, but there was still more winter to come. She felt and saw the shift everywhere, in the subtle changes in the horse corral from frozen patches to puddles steeped brown with mud. She noticed the change of energy within herself after the long winter, as if mirroring the sap that must be rising in the trees. On a cold and sunny Sunday she felt wild and restless as she worked in the garden, cleaning out beds, thinking about what and where she would plant this season. As she nibbled a kale leaf that had wintered over, sure enough, a gang of thick grey clouds sauntered across the sky, and the temperature dropped rapidly. She shivered as the first flakes began to fall.

Upstairs in her room snowlight spilled over the old wallpaper—cabbage roses in shades of pink, yellow and blue. She loved this room, unchanged since before she was born. It had been her aunt and uncle's bedroom. When she first bought Rock Creek Farm, she had brought Gran's gigantic, ornate Victorian dresser and bed with her. The west-facing windows looked out to the garden. She could see the creek racing along, as slow patient flakes fell above it.

She took a pair of jeans and a sweatshirt out of the dresser as she stripped off her lightweight clothes. She paused a moment in front of the mirror. Her body, strong and curvy, still had light tan lines from last summer's work in the garden. Her large breasts, although lower than when she was a girl, still had heft to them. For a second she thought about Briar, but then pushed the thought away. She ran her hands down either side of her waist and let them slide over her hips. She turned to the side view; her woman's belly had given her grief even as a girl. *What would Liam think of her body now?* She circled, looking over her shoulder at her butt, which flared into two white fleshy mounds. Turning, she jiggled them, frowning. She promised herself to start walking more. Moving closer to the mirror, she looked curiously into her fifty-eight-year-old face, lightly freckled, heart-shaped, the wide mouth with little lines above it. The years had made her eyes look smaller, but they still retained their gold and brown flecks. She usually wore her auburn hair brushed back, in a clip or in a bun. She let it down now, noticing more silver streaks than the last time she'd looked.

"Well, you're still Emma," she said out loud, "and he is still Liam." At the thought of his name, something shot through her. *Alright, enough!* she scolded herself, pulling on her clothes on her way downstairs.

Liam paced the kitchen. He had put off calling Emma to set up a time for Julien to talk with the girl. It was a harsh consequence for Julien to have to face her, and not just once. He put down his carving tool and looked at the stallion he was carving. Johnny Cash oozed thick blues into the big kitchen. Liam studied the rearing horse, every muscle a complex knot of tension, the animal's virility reflected in its arched back and wild eyes. "Whoa, boy," he said out loud, thinking that the horse's young, untamed spirit did seem to permeate its body. *I remember that,* he thought to himself, *but it was a long, long time ago.*

It had been three years since his wife, Gretta, had died. Although their thirty-seven year marriage had produced a wonderful daughter, Mandy, the relationship had been one of duty, responsibility, and the hard work of running the ranch. He had grown to love Gretta, her solidness, good mothering, and her devotion to him, but for the most part it had been a passionless marriage. She was sick for five years with cancer before she died, so it had been, he counted, *sweet Jesus, eight years of celibacy.*

The run-in with Emma on Christmas Eve had haunted him ever since. His feelings for her woke him from a dead sleep and made him forget what he was doing during the long winter days. Outside, he saw the snow coming down fast above the ranch fields. She'd seemed so aloof and quiet that night in the church, but the heat that she had passed back as they kissed played over in his mind again and again.

He walked over to the big carved mirror in the dining room and stood in front of it. Surely no young stallion, his dark face was lined from too much sun. His eyes seemed sad and tired. His long hair fell down over his shoulders; he liked it free when he carved. His big body was still muscled and solid. He rolled up his sleeve, revealing fine reddish hairs on a smooth forearm. He flexed his bicep, which bulged as he made a fist. *What would she think of him if... if they were ever together again?* God, he'd always wanted her, ever since they were kids. Actually, the desire he had felt when they kissed gave him hope, but what he didn't know was if she could or would ever forgive him for not marrying her so long ago.

Clare picked the cigarette butt out of the egg yolk on the crusty plate. An empty bottle of Jim Beam lay on its side next to the strawberry jam. Don's chew spittle stained a paper napkin. Another all-nighter. Dread swelled as she took her coffee out of the microwave. The small kitchen was spotless otherwise, but boxy and dark with only one window. The room had probably been added to the ancient farmhouse as an afterthought. She crossed to the old fridge, which either froze everything or left puddles and rotten food. "Falling Down Ranch" was what she called the place. Don, who would rather drink and watch television than fix fences or handle the necessary upkeep, said he didn't give a shit. And furthermore, it was a house and land, and she should count her blessings.

Their framed wedding picture sat on top of the piano in the small dining area. She had been so happy that day, giddy with joy, really. Don was handsome in his western tuxedo and white cowboy hat. They looked out, their arms intertwined, their faces full of innocent hope. Lilly had tried to warn her even then, recounting his past history with other women in the valley, the drinking and cheating, his tendency towards violence. But she was blind and young and in lust for the first time in her life.

At first she could rationalize his roughness in bed and his temper, and she truly thought that, with time and love, he would change. After their first baby was born, he started coming home late and drunk, saturated with the heavy perfume of the women who frequented the two dingy valley bars that always seemed to be filled to capacity with the lost and lonely. The first time he hit her she was nursing Josh, and he'd barely missed the infant's soft head. It was downhill from then on, and she was too proud to tell her sister, who always, ever since they were little, had both protected and belittled her. She didn't want her parents to know what a bad choice she'd made, even though the whole valley knew about her husband's escapades. He didn't pull his weight on the ranch. Her dad and Bud never said anything, But Lilly did; she just couldn't let it go. By the time Clare's second child was conceived accidently, she felt trapped and saw no way out.

A picture is worth a thousand words, but it can also lie like hell, she thought, glancing at the photo. She looked around the room again. Over the years she'd tried to make up for the dinginess of the house by painting the rooms fresh, bright colors and sewing slipcovers for the frayed furniture. Still, it never felt clean, with its frequent fly hatches and layers of damp, rotted wood that smelled of mildew and wood smoke.

She poured milk into her coffee and stared out the window. She could see the tall old oak, a victim of winter's big windstorm, tilted on its side. This had been one of her favorite trees on the ranch. Her view of it through the changing seasons had made the kitchen feel better. The night it fell she never heard a sound. She wondered if the ionized air had streaked through the leafless branches, causing them to sway, while the skeletal cups of last year's nests flew apart, becoming simple sticks riding the air. Did the branches creak and split and wave their terrified arms in alarm as the trunk moved like a house, shimmying, until the mossy bark shifted and broke like puzzle pieces? She wondered if it was just one event, or if every storm had somehow shaken the great, rooted foundation, causing tiny quakes, little rumbles that slyly eked out pockets of dirt, slowly, subtly, until one wind-filled winter night, the tree gave up its solid form and broke.

She heard Don yelling outside; a loud banging sound followed. She moved into her son Ian's room, which had a view of the barnyard. Don was wielding a thick, rusty chain in one hand, and trying to control Bandit with the other. Clare felt sick as she watched him swing the chain in a circle, lashing out as the terrified horse tried to dodge it. Don's face was purple, his eyes bulging with anger, as he tried to get the haltered horse to turn in a circle. The horse kept rearing and moving away from him, pulling with all his might to break free. Don raised the chain over his head and hit the horse hard on its back. The horse screamed, then froze in pain. Clare ran down the hall, across the kitchen, out the back door, and around the back of the house, yelling, "Don! Don! What are you doing?"

"Get the fuck out of here. I'm teaching him a lesson." He threw the chain into the horse's dancing legs, where it bit and whipped around the slender bones.

"Don! Stop it! You're hurting him!" Clare screamed.

"You're damn right!" he hollered back, breathing hard. He pulled the lead rope in tighter, shortened the length of the chain, and began beating the horse's face.

Clare rushed in, trying to put her small body between the man and horse. "No, Don! Stop!"

"Get out of here!" In a rage, he dropped the chain, grabbed her arm and jerked her into the air. She flew; pain burned into her shoulder as she hit the ground. Don picked up the chain and started beating the horse again.

Somehow she got up and ran back into the kitchen, where she dialed Lilly's cell. Sobbing, she yelled, "Lilly, Lilly! Where are you?"

Lilly answered, "At the feed store...what's wrong?"

"Come quick!" Hanging up, she ran back outside where the sweat-drenched horse stood in submission, panting.

Don came at her. "How dare you interfere! That horse needs to learn," He grabbed her collar and yanked her close to his face. "And so do you," he spat, his breath reeking of whiskey. He pushed her chest with all his might, and she fell backwards onto the ground. She was so dizzy that she just lay there, the tops of the big cottonwoods spinning above her, a warm wetness seeping into her hair.

Lilly's truck and trailer came barreling up the road. She slammed on the brakes and jumped out. "Clare, Clare!" She ran over to her sister, who was trying to sit up.

"Oh, Christ!" growled Don, under his breath.

"Clare! Are you okay?"

"I think so...something's wrong with my shoulder."

Lilly helped her stand. "What happened?" She turned to Don, then she saw Bandit, his head down, eyes closed, the bleeding welts swelling. She noticed the rusty chain on the ground, and looked from Don to Clare to the horse.

She bent and picked up the chain. "You bastard," she bellowed, rushing at him. She leapt onto his short body and squeezed her legs around his waist. She brought the chain down onto his back. "See how it feels, you asshole!"

"Get off of me, Lilly!" he shouted.

"Lilly, Lilly, don't," cried Clare.

Lilly had the chain around his neck. She slid down, her feet on the ground, her face close to his. "You ever touch her or that horse again and I swear to God I'll...," she caught her breath. "You're just goddamn lucky I couldn't find Bud!" Don wrenched back, and the chain bit into his neck. He pulled harder; Lilly let go and he fell backwards into the mud. She heard her sister crying. "I'm going to take care of Clare now, and I'm taking the horse. You ever do anything like this again, and I swear your life will be over!"

Don got up slowly. "Don't threaten me," he spat, "it's none of your business."

"Yeah? Well it's going to be the sheriff's business now." She turned towards her crying sister, "Come on, Clare, let's go take a look at you."

In the kitchen Lilly tried to call Emma. Her machine picked up, but Lilly knew she was probably with a patient. She left a message saying that she was bringing Clare over. Then she called Briar and asked her if she could meet them at Emma's. She called the school and left a message for her nephews to come to her house after baseball practice. She loaded the trembling horse into the stock trailer. As she helped Clare into her seat, she asked, "Is it broken, do you think?"

"I don't know, but it really hurts."

Lilly felt a swelter of heat rise from her feet to her cheeks. Beads of sweat prickled up between her breasts and thighs. Anger flared; she tried to stop the words, but they wouldn't wait. She even bit her tongue, knowing it wasn't the right time, but frustration overtook her and she heard herself screaming at her sister. "Clare! What is it going to take, goddamnit? What's wrong with you! Why don't you leave the son of a bitch?...I don't get it! What about the boys? Is this what you want them to grow up to be? Why are you so goddamned scared? One of these days he's gonna kill you! Don't you see that?"

Clare whimpered and leaned forward in the cluttered truck seat. "I know, Lilly, please don't, not now, please!"

They arrived just as Emma's last patient was leaving. They left the horse in the trailer until Briar could see to him. After hearing Clare's story and examining her, Emma surmised that the first time Don had grabbed her arm, he had probably dislocated her shoulder, and when he threw her to the ground it had popped back in. She assured her that although it would be sore for a few weeks, it would heal if she wore a sling and rested it.

While Emma stitched up the cut on the back of Clare's head, Lilly stormed around the small exam room, fanning herself, cursing the "goddamn hot flashes," and begging Clare to call the sheriff. Her anger at Don was beyond any excuses her sister mouthed. They were the usual rationalizations Emma had heard so often from battered women.

"He's okay when he's not drinking. I shouldn't have gotten between him and the horse. I can't do it to the boys, not now... Josh graduates in a few months, and then Ian in two years. I'll leave him then..."

"Blah, blah, blah," interrupted Lilly, turning to Emma.

"Don't you, by law, have to report it?"

"Technically," she answered, "and Clare, I'm very cerned for the safety of you and your boys…"

"Please don't, Emma," Clare pleaded. Lilly looked disgusted and said she was going out to check on Bandit.

"I do have to report it to Dr. Drew, Clare, and ultimately it's his decision. Now let me show you how this sling works."

Outside, Briar and Harry were checking over the horse. Lilly, still fuming, stood quietly aside. The exhausted horse stood still. At first he had been afraid of Harry, but calmed as Briar took over. The places where the chain had made contact were swollen.

"Nothing broken; what do you think, Harry?"

"I think you're right, bruised muscles, some tissue damage, but he'll heal."

Emma and Clare came out to the driveway. Emma watched as Harry lifted a leg to check for tendon damage. The horse laid his ears flat and backed away, then Harry moved in. "It's okay, boy, you'll be better in no time."

"At least physically," said Briar, under her breath. Exhausted, she knew she didn't have the energy to take in the horse, and offered an excuse saying, "Em, I don't have room right now. Could he stay in your round pen for awhile?"

"Sure," said Emma, without thinking, "that's fine." Inside, in a rare moment of feeling overwhelmed, she thought to herself, *Why not? Isn't this the Emma Cassady home for runaway, homeless, pregnant, ill, and abused animals and people?"*

Chapter Eighteen

Amy Lee and Cat drove across the valley. The cold blue sky, pimpled with clouds, looked unpredictable. Amy Lee yawned.

"Were you up late?" Cat asked, pulling her short denim skirt over her knees.

"Sort of—there was a party at the rodeo grounds until the dumbass cops showed up and made us go home." She looked over at Cat. "Hey! your hair looks good up like that."

"Thanks. Was it fun?"

"Not really, just the same old kids, drinking, trying to break the boredom of another Saturday night in the valley. What did you do?"

"Stayed in my room, read, did a little homework, watched T.V. Hey, Emma asked me to pick up a few things at the store—would you mind? After church is fine…"

"I can't; I've got to go to my aunt's house right after I drop you off." She looked at her watch. "We've got time now, and it's on the way. Will that do?"

"Sure, that's great."

Amy Lee pulled her mother's car into the parking lot of Willard's Market. "I'll just wait here. Would you get me a

Pepsi? I've got cotton mouth." She reached for her purse.

"That's okay, I've got money," said Cat, closing the car door. She pulled her coat together. Her stomach felt weird. *Should have eaten breakfast,* she thought.

She took a little basket and started down the aisle. She was looking for refried beans when a woman coming towards her slowed and gave her a dirty look. Cat looked away and took two cans from the shelf. The woman kept staring and made a disgusting sound in her throat before she turned and walked away.

Hello to you, too, thought Cat. She found the vegetables and put three avocados in a bag. At the checkout stand she took a Pepsi out of the cold case and set it down on the counter. The woman who'd stared at her whispered something to the cashier before she pushed her basket out the doors. The cashier rang up her items, and Cat handed her a ten dollar bill. The cashier made a point of not looking at her as she counted out the change. Cat watched as she bagged the items. First she threw the avocados into the bag. *Whoa,* thought Cat. Then the cashier took the cans of beans and the Pepsi and threw them in on top.

"You the girl staying at Emma's?"

Caught off guard by the question, Cat looked down and nodded. The woman twisted the bag and slammed it down on the counter. "There you go," she said, shoving the bag towards her. Shaken, Cat walked out to the car and got in.

"What's wrong?" asked Amy Lee.

Cat took out the Pepsi, which was covered in smashed avocado.

"Shit," said Amy Lee, reaching for the paper towels in the back. "Did you drop it?"

"Not exactly," said Cat.

"Oh...who was the checker?"

"I don't know," said Cat quietly, setting the bag on a paper towel, then onto the floor. "She had black hair and big earrings."

"Oh, that's Nita Jo; she's a bitch. Don't worry about it, okay?"

"Alright," said Cat.

Amy Lee and Cat walked across the parking lot of the church. They laughed together, leaning towards each other, as families pulled in and parked. Mothers herded scrubbed children towards the Sunday School room. Usually Amy Lee came with her family, but this weekend her mom and dad were out of town with her brother's baseball team. Amy Lee thought that her mother would be okay with her bringing Cat to church, and anyway, Cat had been so serious when she asked if she could come along that Amy Lee couldn't deny her request for a ride.

"So," Cat asked, "what do you do here? I've never been to church."

"You're kidding," said Amy Lee, "never?" Cat shook her head as they walked towards the big glass doors. "Well, we sing and listen to really boring sermons. Sometimes the minister, Reverend Rickabaugh, says some good things. And then there's refreshments, which is my favorite part, because I usually sleep in on Sundays and miss breakfast. Amy Lee laughed and tucked her blond hair behind her ears. She stopped on the walkway and her big blue eyes looked into Cat's face, "Don't worry, just do what I do."

The large church was considered modern when it was built in the sixties. Huge triangular panes of glass fronted it, and even the cross on top had a stainless steel look to it. The sign read:

Green Valley Evangelical Church
Reverend Garland Rickabaugh
This Sunday's Sermon – "The Lessons of Temptation"

Amy Lee read it out loud and giggled as people streamed by them. "Wow," she said. Cat heard someone call her name and turned to see Jason and Kerry, with little Jac in Jason's arms.

"Hi, Cat," said Kerry, coming up and touching her shoulder. "Hi, Amy."

"Cat, we never got to thank you for all you did the night Jac was born."

"Oh, it's alright," said Cat, looking into the pink-cheeked baby's smiling face. "He's so cute," she told Jason.

"Yeah, he's growing into a big boy, alright."

"Well, we better go on in, but good to see you and don't be a stranger," said Kerry, hefting the infant seat to her other arm. "I'll never forget that night. Say hello to Emma."

"Hey, Amy Lee? Heard from your dad yet? Did the boys win last night?" Cat recognized the man who worked in the hardware store owned by Amy Lee's father.

"Not yet, Tim."

They were close to the entrance now. Cat felt a twinge of nervousness under her coat, and pulled at the waistband of her skirt. Her belly had really popped out in her fifth month, yet her childlike frame was still stick thin.

Inside, Amy Lee shed her coat and hung it up. She looked at Cat who whispered back, "I'm keeping mine."

"Oh yeah, right," said Amy Lee, getting it. People stared as Cat followed Amy Lee down the aisle and slid in next to her in the center row. There was an altar with flowers and candles, and behind Reverend Rickabaugh was a mosaic cross made up of tiny, colorful tiles and pieces of glass. Cat turned her head slightly and saw Emma's friend, Lilly, with two men, seating themselves in a pew at the far left front. She was sure the woman, busy helping the elderly man, hadn't seen her. *Who else is here*, she wondered. A small silver-haired woman played the organ.

Cat turned to Amy Lee, "Does your cousin Chuck's family come to church?"

"Sure," she said, "see that lady third pew over in the front, the one in the flowered dress? That's my Aunt Carmine. Chuck is gone with the baseball team to Three Rivers. Uncle Jack probably went too."

Cat's stomach felt weird again, not nauseous or like she had to go to the bathroom, just really funny, like an itch deep down.

The minister took his place centered between two big vases of flowers that were giving off a sickly sweet perfume. Reverend Rickabaugh smoothed his smock over his paunch and raised his hands. People stopped talking and shuffling. The organ player abruptly stopped.

"Let us pray," he bellowed. Cat copied Amy Lee, who bent her head, eyes closed. "Dear God in heaven, we are thankful for this day to worship you in your glory. Let us all be thankful for the blessings in our lives and for our families and friends. Amen. Now my beloved wife, Elinor, will start with some church news and events."

The organist got up, took a piece of paper from the organ, and approached the microphone. "Hello, all, and welcome. Just a few notes before the Reverend gives us our inspiration for the day. There will be a rummage sale next Saturday starting at 9:00 a.m.; leave your bags and goodies in the basement please. We're having a potluck on Wednesday to raise funds for the youth group's trip to Sacramento. And finally, whatever tithing is collected today will be donated to our sister church in Guadalajara, which, as you know, operates an orphanage. That's all, enjoy the service."

The Reverend began, "Today's sermon is taken from two places in the Holy Book. Our title today is 'The Lessons of Temptation,' and God knows how we are inundated with temptation in our society. Ten minutes of television tells you how our youth is being influenced, what with sex, drugs, greed, and violence on every channel. Where are our role models of today? This is from Isaiah 3, verses 16-24, showing us how ancient times mirror our own."

The Lord said: Because the daughters of Zion are haughty and walk with outstretched necks, glancing wantonly with their eyes, mincing along as they go, tinkling with their feet; the Lord will smite with a scab the heads of the daughters of Zion, and the Lord will lay bare their secret parts; In that day the Lord will take away the finery of the anklets, the headbands, and the crescents; the pendants, the bracelets, and the scarves; the headdresses, the armlets, the sashes, the perfume boxes, and the amulets; the signet rings and nose ring; the festal robes, the mantles, the cloaks, and the handbags; the garments of gauze, the linen garments, the turbans, and the veils. Instead of perfume there will be rottenness; and instead of a girdle, a rope; and instead of well-set hair, baldness; and instead of a rich robe, a girding of sackcloth; instead of beauty, shame.

Cat pulled at the big hoop earrings she wore, reached under her shirt and twisted the jewel that pierced her navel.

"We must resist those ways of being. We must lead our youth down a strong and steady path, in their looks, thoughts, and actions. Let us not be hypocrites, telling our children one thing while statistics show fifty percent of couples are divorced. Usually twenty-five percent have affairs; alcoholism is rampant. We adults need to clean up our side of the street."

Amy Lee wrote Cat a note on the offering envelope: "Look how red his face is. He could explode at any minute." Cat put it into her coat pocket. It seemed that more people were looking at her, then glancing away. She thought she saw Emma's friend pointing at her, while Amy Lee's Aunt Carmine looked around the church.

"And, while we judge others for their iniquities, listen to Isaiah 5, verses 18 to 23."

Again, Cat felt that strange tickle in her stomach, like the feathery swipe of a fish tail against her insides. *What*, she wondered to herself, *is that?* And when it dawned on her that what she felt was "IT"—"The Thing," the child moving inside her—she thought she would puke all over the pew.

The Reverend bawled dramatically, every word echoing in her head.

Woe to those who draw iniquity with cords of falsehood, who draw sin as with cart ropes, who say: "Let him make haste, let him speed his work that we may see it; let the purpose of the Holy One of Israel draw near, and let it come, that we may know it!" Woe to those who call evil good and good evil, who put darkness for light and light for darkness, who put bitter for sweet, and sweet for bitter! Woe to those who are wise in their own eyes, and shrewd in their own sight! Woe to those who are heroes at drinking wine, and valiant men in mixing strong drink, who acquit the guilty for a bribe, and deprive the pure of his right.

Cat was breathing fast. She had wondered if she'd have the nerve when the time came. *No way*, she had thought to herself, as she entered the crowded church. But now, there it was again—the proven reality of "The Thing!" That woman in the store and the minister's words enraged her. She was shaking with all of the adrenaline pumping through her.

"You alright?" whispered Amy Lee. The congregation stood, palming the hymnals and looking for the page the minister called out. They sang, "Amazing Grace, how sweet the sound, that saved a wretch like me."

Pretending to look at Amy Lee's songbook, Cat slipped off her coat. When the singing was over and everyone sat down, Cat remained standing. She picked up her coat and edged herself along the pew.

"Oh, shit!" Amy Lee muttered under her breath.

Cat stood in the aisle for a moment. People poked each other. The Reverend had started to speak again but stopped in mid-sentence, while the congregation stared as if they were a flock of birds slanting in unison. All were looking at Cat's tight, white T-shirt cut off just below her breasts. Her naked and protruding belly with its diamond jewel rode high above the waistband of her denim skirt. A buzz rose from the congregation as they read what she had written on the shirt in red felt-tip pen: on the front, a big capital "I," on the back, the word "Innocent." The minister stood with his mouth open as Cat started to walk up the aisle towards the altar. She heard whispers and pieces of comments.

"That's her."

"What's she doing here?"

"She's the one who accused our boys of..."

When she reached the front, she turned in a circle and then stopped, looking out at face after shocked face. She crossed to the other aisle and made her way slowly to the back of the church. All heads were turned towards her exit, and then she disappeared from their view. The entire congregation heard the cushioned hiss of the big glass doors as they closed behind her.

Emma came home around six Monday morning. Letty Gilbraith had delivered a baby girl at the hospital in Butte

City at three in the morning. The young mother had struggled for three days in light labor, and finally, after a grueling time in the hospital, she had given birth without the C-section that had been considered in the late hours of the night. Emma was tired and edgy and made a cup of tea before she decided to check her messages. There were three: one from Dr. Drew, saying that he would be out of town and to call Dr. Sampson if she needed backup with a birth; one from a telemarketer; and the last from Lilly on Sunday evening. Emma listened to her friend's distraught voice during the long message.

"Emma, Emma, you there? It's Lilly; it's Sunday around five. I need to talk with you…Hello?…Are you screening calls? Listen, Emma, that girl pulled a stunt at church today that will have the whole valley talking by morning. Emma, you've got to control her! She stood up during the sermon, exposing her pregnant belly. She even had a jewel pierced in her navel. Anyway, she wore this shirt with a big red 'I' on the front of it, and on the back it said 'Innocent.' She made a spectacle of herself, turning and facing off the congregation, giving all of us this terrible look. Then she marched down the aisle and left the church. Emma, she made everyone feel as if *we* had done something wrong, instead of the way it really is. She's trouble, and I'm worried about you having her live there with you. Okay, this message is probably gonna run out soon, just wanted to let you know, ***it was not okay, Emma!*** Call me."

She sighed, remembering Cat's words a few months before, "*They are so not ready for the revenge of Caterina Ramos.*"

Chapter Nineteen

Emma told Cat about her conversation with Liam. She explained about the consequences the tribe had chosen for Julien's involvement in the rape, even though he claimed that he had been drunk and coerced into it. The tribe's order that Julien must "face up and pay back" was dependent on Cat's permission for him to formally apologize, help around the farm, and even "do her bidding" if she wished. Emma assured her that if she wasn't comfortable with his presence, all she had to do was say so.

Cat remembered what Amy Lee's cousin, Chuck, had said about Julien being forced into being part of the rape. Because Cat had no memory of the incident whatsoever, she often observed the boys at school, trying to imagine what they had done to her body. They seemed so normal, just kids laughing and goofing off. But not RJ; he scared her, giving her dark, ugly looks, sometimes following her around school. She knew Julien to be quiet and shy, and had seen him walk away when some of the boys harassed or teased someone.

Her voice was aloof as she told Emma, "Oh, I don't care; whatever, it won't bother me. I have to be around them all at school anyway, and...," she added, thinking of all Emma did

187

to keep up with the farm, "I'm sure you could use the help."

Emma used her professional voice when she called Liam back. She told him they would be out with the mare the next day after school, and she thought that might be a good place for the meeting between Cat and Julien. Liam agreed, and said he would be at the corral with the boy at four o'clock.

A weak sun blinked in and out of clouds as Emma, Briar, and Cat walked towards the corral. The horses were out in the adjacent field, grazing. The day's early fog had burned away, and the intermittent sun lit the new green grass.

"Want me to get a halter?" asked Briar.

"No, I'll just call Mav and he'll come." said Emma. "Mav, Mav!" The horse looked up and whinnied, as if he hadn't seen Emma in a very long time, and started running towards her. The mare, her belly round as a barrel, trotted slowly behind him. The blood-red bay cantered gracefully in front of them, his tail arched.

"God, he looks good, Emma! You would never know that he was twenty."

"Yeah, we're the same age in horse years. I hope I can age as well." The horse skidded to a stop in front of the split-rail fence and reached towards Emma's waiting hands. "Hi, you big lug," she said, rubbing his soft black nose. The mare stood behind him, huffing with exertion.

"God, she has gotten huge!" said Cat.

"Way bigger than when she first came here. She's supposedly due in a month or so," noted Briar. "I want to check her bag for milk. That will give us a better idea of her time."

"Poor thing," crooned Cat. She had never been around horses before she came to Emma's, but seemed comfortable in their presence—especially with a fence in between. "What's her name again?"

"Candy," said Emma and Briar in unison, laughing.

"I hope I don't get as big as you, girl," said Cat. Suddenly the mare lifted her head, her ears twitched forward and backward, and her eyes seemed to focus and clear. She looked right at Cat, who was hanging on the fence, neighed loudly, and walked up to her. The mare moved close and snorted and sniffed at Cat's little pot belly exposed between the rails. "Whoa!" Cat was surprised. "What's she doing?"

The horse nuzzled her stomach, then put her big sad face right in front of Cat's. A series of sounds came from the dark brown horse's throat, deep and low; the timbre rose and fell as if she were talking: "Huh, huh, huh." This went on for a full minute or more.

"I'll be damned!" said Briar, "I think she knows you're with child too. In the wild, the pregnant and nursing mares stay together, even babysit for each other." Briar ducked under the fence. "Hey, girl, let's see your teats." The horse tensed, then relaxed as Briar gave her a hand to smell and patted her neck. She walked towards her rear and bent to look underneath. "Yeah, she's leaking milk, won't be but a month or so."

The mare moved her hind legs and swung around away from Briar. Again she approached the fence where Cat was still leaning. "Huh, huh, huh, huh, huh, huh."

"Oh yeah?" Cat teased back.

"Looks like you've got a girlfriend," giggled Briar, ducking back under the fence. Her stocking cap caught on a splinter and came off, revealing her bald head. "Whoa, whoa there; I lost my egg warmer," she laughed, retrieving the hat.

Liam made the right-hand turn onto Emma's road. The cottonwoods along the creek were slick with new leaves. Julien had been silent since his uncle picked him up at school.

"What am I going to say to her, Uncle?" Julien's voice croaked with nervousness. "This is stupid; I don't even remember anything. Why do I have to talk to her?"

Liam, whose nature was to wait and think, mulled over the boy's words. "Well, son, maybe it's like this. Maybe you need to tell her you're sorry for being so drunk that other people could use you in a bad way. You'll know when the time comes. My advice? Ask your ancestors."

"Yeah, right." mumbled Julien under his breath. They pulled into the turnaround. Emma, Briar and the girl were standing by the corral.

"Hey," called Liam, striding slowly towards them, his long arms and big hands loose at his sides. The boy hung back behind him. "Hey, Emma, Briar."

Emma gathered herself. She looked up into his face and saw the cautious look in his eyes. "Liam, this is Cat."

The girl stepped away from the fence. "Hello," she said quietly.

He nodded, then looked at the horses. "That's not Maverick is it?"

"Sure is."

"Hey boy, you're lookin' pretty good. How old is he, Emma?" Julien stood back behind the women.

"He was twenty last month."

"Wow, I guess spoiling really pays off. You still her baby, huh?" he called to the alert horse.

"Em, I've gotta go. Harry and I are moving cows this afternoon," said Briar. "So you'll pick me up at...let's see, I've got chemo at 9:00 and then the oncologist afterwards. How about 7:45?"

"Okay, honey," Emma replied, "that works. I'll see you in the morning."

"Hey, how is Harry?" asked Liam, "I haven't seen him in a long time."

"He's wonderful," called Briar, getting into her truck. "I couldn't do it without him. Bye." She pulled out and they waved, then stood awkwardly for a moment.

"She okay?" asked Liam.

"I hope so," Emma replied.

The horses had wandered back to the pasture. Cat stood silently next to Emma. Behind them, in the shadow of a locust tree, Julien waited.

Liam cleared his throat, "Okay then, Emma, I was wondering if you might show me that place that gave way on the creek. Jack Dunbar said he might need my backhoe to fix it."

"Sure, a pretty big chunk of bank broke off. It's this way." She cast a protective glance in Cat's direction, then turned away to walk with Liam towards the water.

Julien's hands were jammed into his jacket pockets. He toed loose rocks with his boots. He felt nervous, even sick, with the girl so close. He had watched her at school, how she tossed her long black hair around in the lunch room, the proud way she held her small shoulders when she walked. He had heard some of the boys say awful things about her, heard how pissed off they were that she came back to school. RJ really had it out for her. Just now, when Julien glanced up and saw her pregnant stomach, it was all real, even if he didn't remember a thing about that night. The boys had said that she wanted sex, but Chuck had told him they had doped her. Julien's mouth twitched. He could never be a part of anything like that, and yet now...

"Okay! Tongue-tied?" Cat said rudely. "Let's get it straight and get this over with; I've got lots of homework to do!" Her dark eyes burned into his. "You're supposed to tell me something, right?"

191

The ground buckled beneath him; his palms were sweaty, and his mouth felt like it was full of glass. Minutes passed. "I...I was really drunk," he looked at her, his face in pain. "I didn't know anything about RJ's plans." She tossed her head. "I'd never do anything like that, I swear to you. I don't remember anything..."

"And I suppose that means that in your mind you're innocent?" she spat out.

"No," he said, "It doesn't... I just don't..."

She got in his face. "Well, I don't remember the rape either, but I'll tell you what I do remember. I remember waking up in the hospital after they dumped me on my Grandma's porch, unconscious, all bloody, with my pants slit to my waist. I remember Emma telling me that my Grandma died of a heart attack right then and there, after seeing me like that. I remember waking up as some doctor was putting twelve stitches in my... down there. I remember the rape kit tests, and some asshole cop standing over me, trying to get me to admit I willingly had sex with all of you jerks. And I remember not knowing a soul here and being all alone at Emma's, and how I felt when my period was late...No, I wasn't on birth control. And contrary to common belief, I wasn't a slut, I was a virgin. And I remember the disgust I felt when I found out I was pregnant. I remember the looks people gave me at the market and gas station—as if I were dirt, filth, some whore who'd come and seduced you poor innocent boys."

Tears filled her eyes, and she turned her back to him briefly and caught her breath. She spun back around, her voice low and precise with anger. "And I remember when the judge let you all off as if...as if," she hiccuped, "it never happened! And I remember throwing up for three months straight and not sleeping and not having the guts to have an abortion to get rid of *IT*. And having to live with *IT* every day, reminding me of that night, not letting me forget for even one minute what you all did to me. So don't fucking tell me you don't remember!...And that's the end of that!" She skewered him with her eyes.

Julien squirmed, helpless and paralyzed where he stood. Mav and the mare ran into the corral. The mare trotted over to the fence and started neighing to Cat. She took her eyes off Julien. "It's okay, girl, it's okay." She felt in that moment emptied out, relieved, as if some of the heavy pressure she was carrying had been released.

Julien stared at his feet, still shaken from her tirade. *How, he asked himself, how could he find the courage to speak, to say the words?* And then he saw his grandmother and himself as a little boy, standing over a broken ceremonial bowl. He heard her say to him, "Julien, ask—ask the ancestors for the words."

"God! I'm so sorry," he stuttered, "I'm so sorry for what you've been through." His eyes were wet, and Cat felt the panic in him. "And I'm so sorry for my part in it." Then he bolted, stumbled and caught himself, and ran for his uncle's truck.

Emma took a handful of carrot seeds and picked out five or six. She knelt in the newly-turned earth and sprinkled them in the thumb holes she'd made.

The evening clouds flared purple and orange in the western sky. She gathered her thoughts in the quiet, hearing only the creek rushing by. She wondered about the meeting that afternoon between Cat and Julien. A question of doubt had surfaced after the girl's brief explanation.

"Oh, it was fine," she'd said, walking back to the house. "He'll be waiting to hear about the work you want him to do."

"Why was he sitting in the truck when Liam and I came back to the corral?"

"Oh, I don't know," said Cat casually, "he's kinda creepy and quiet."

Emma stood and looked around the garden. Lettuce, beets, kale, and broccoli had all been planted. Her thoughts turned to Liam and their walk to the creek. After discussing how Julien would get out to the farm three days a week, he had bent and scooped up some rocks in his large hands. He began to throw them into the water one by one. The silence became uncomfortable, and Emma didn't know what to say. She felt the energy buzzing back and forth between them, like a living thing. Finally, after about a dozen rocks, he turned to her.

"Hey," he said, his eyes serious and intense, "would you have dinner with me sometime?"

She smiled, "Sure, when?"

"Tomorrow?" he questioned, intent on his mission now.

"Oh, I can't; I'm taking Briar to Bradford tomorrow."

"Is she going to be okay?"

"I don't know. We'll find out more tomorrow, but I don't have a good feeling."

"I'm sorry," he said under his breath. "What about the weekend, Saturday?"

"Alright, what time?"

"How about five? I'll pick you up. We'll have dinner in Mt. Cloud; there's a nice little Thai place. Does that sound good?"

"Yes," said Emma.

He was quiet again, contemplative. "Do you think it's been long enough?" he asked finally, looking at her.

She hesitated, wondering what he meant. "Do you mean the kids or us?"

"Both," he said, laughing and turning back towards the corral.

She couldn't stop thinking about the luxury of spending time together at the creek, how his eyes searched her face, and the sweet way he'd asked her to dinner. *Come back to earth*, she told herself, closing the garden gate. The cats were meowing at her heels; she needed to feed them and Bear, and think about the evening meal.

After dinner she went out to watch the sunset. She settled into an old wicker chair in the middle of the orchard. All around her the season unveiled itself. She noticed deer, signaled by evening, step cautiously and delicately into the field, the buck's antlers covered in umber velvet. A robin, busy with the season, flew by with newly-shed horsehair clasped in her beak. Each apple tree had a distinct posture and personality. Those closer to the creek bore coral-nipped aureoles still tight in bud; some in the warmer core of the orchard were frilly with pink flowers. Mixed in among the apple trees were a few plum and pear trees, their creamy blossoms a pale foam seemingly flung up into the tree tops.

She drew in deep breaths, inhaling the intoxicating air. A thin wind lifted the saffron petticoats of daffodils. Irises, still penile, showed purple veins along their firm green shafts. The bridal veil arched over in shy virginity. She wondered about this swift season of fertility. How dormancy reigned most of the year, followed by this abrupt quickening—all pistils and stamens—and then the momentous rush of rotund, yellow bees circling the heavy fruit. She felt a desultory longing at the full throb of fecundity; a random, aimless desire rose in her body. In the twilight, frogsong sang from the creek: *"Spring! Spring! Spring!"*

Chapter Twenty

Briar turned on her side as a wave of dread washed over her. God! She was tired of it all. The nausea was supposed to have subsided after three months. She got up, swinging her legs over the edge of the bed. She made the bed, tightening the corners of the sheets and spreading the blankets so that each side rose exactly one and a half inches from the floor. She found jeans and a sweater folded neatly in the pants and sweater section of her dresser. Turning back to look at the small sparse room, she noticed her horse pillow, a needlepoint gift from Emma, lying face down on the chair.

"There," she said, as she lifted it and sat it upright, wishing that her doctor's appointment today would be as simple.

Downstairs, she put the kettle on, took a bottle from the fridge, and shook it—one of Emma's concoctions: wheat grass, herbs, and peppermint for her stomach. She downed the green, greasy mixture in one gulp. The teapot spat more than sang, and she picked it up with an old orange and green potholder that her mother, Jean, had crocheted. Briar sat down. She missed her mother badly just then and swallowed hard to push the emotions down.

As she sipped the tea, the rerun part of her mind overtook her. Before being adopted at the age of eleven, she had bounced from foster home to foster home. One in particular haunted her. The foster mother's name had been Doreen. Briar saw herself at three or so, sitting at a big table with other children. It was a party, with balloons floating along the ceiling. She wore a frilly pink dress and white patent Mary Janes. *Oh God,* she thought, *I don't want to remember this...not now.* But her mind just hurried on.

Her pudgy little arm reached for a chocolate cupcake with rainbow sprinkles, and the glass of milk tipped over and spread its white river across the table. Doreen picked her up and whacked her hard on her bottom, carrying her down a narrow hallway.

"You retarded or something? No more party for you! Look what you done just to get the attention on you and off of Bobby's big day! That dress is ruined now!" She bustled her into a dark room and threw her on a bed. "No wonder nobody wants you! You just stay there till morning and think about what you done!"

Later, in the dark room, Briar called out to them, over and over, that she had to go to the bathroom. But no one heard or came. She remembered the humiliation she'd felt when she finally had no choice but to soil the big-girl panties with ruffles on the butt. She lay there knowing she would be beaten in the morning.

Briar moved the mug of tea across the table, remembering other mothers whose own children always came first. The years of ragged hand-me-down clothes. The names they called her—Freak, and Stork, and Skinny. Then there were the foster fathers, either gruff and detached or showing up in her room at night. "Shh, shh, just do what I say or else!"

By eleven years old she was completely withdrawn, trusting no one, a beaten down, sexually abused child with no hope that life was ever going to be any different. And then the miracle had happened: an older couple, really grandparents, adopted her and brought her to this ranch in Green Valley. It had taken awhile for her to trust them, especially the man, but they were kind and patient. She saw herself at twelve, riding her mother's mare across the fields, her pigtails flying, a blissful smile on her face. They were both gone now, dying within a year of each other. And now she felt like a little kid and just wanted them there in the kitchen, laughing and teasing, putting their arms around her. *God! What a pity party!* she thought, glancing at the clock.

Emma honked three times. While waiting, she looked around at the little ranch in the early light. The small two-story log house, the neatly fenced pastures, cows on one side drowsily chewing new grass, a small herd of horses browsing the field. She saw Harry driving his red pickup and stopping to pitch hay to the animals. He smiled and waved, his weather-worn face grinning at her. Briar came out dressed in black jeans, stylish boots, and a teal sweater. She moved slowly, closing the heavy door behind her. Emma saw the weakness in her, her pale skin, the deliberate way she walked.

"Morning," she said, heaving herself up into the truck.

A warm spring rain had fallen outside of Butte City. As they drove along the Interstate, Emma commented on the purple and green tinge of new growth on the rolling hills. They chatted over the hour-long drive, although Briar sank into moments of quiet before Emma brought up the next subject of conversation. They discussed the impending birth of the rescue mare and came up with a sort of game plan in case she had her foal at night. When the time seemed close, they planned to have Julien camp in the barn, armed with a cell phone so he could alert them. Emma talked excitedly of experiencing the birth, as she had never seen a horse being born. She asked Briar about Bandit and how Harry's work with him was going.

"He's done wonders with him; he's the original horse whisperer." She told Emma how he had spent patient hours taking the horse with him as he did his chores, renewing his trust in people, after the horrible beating by Don. "I wish he didn't have to go back."

"Yeah," said Emma, "I wish Clare didn't either."

"Harry has asked her to come and start riding Bandit in the arena. He thinks they would make a good team."

"Oh, that's great," said Emma, "Clare will learn a lot from the experience."

"Yeah, she really loves that horse."

They crossed the border into Oregon, and on the outskirts of Ash Creek they commented on all the fancy new houses being built on the hillsides and in the old orchards of the little progressive community. They hit some traffic outside of Bradford. The appointment was for 9:00 a.m. for chemotherapy, and then Briar was to meet with Dr. Carter, the oncologist, at 10:30.

"I'm glad you're with me, Em," Briar said, as they pulled into the hospital complex parking lot. "It will be nice to have an interpreter to translate the medical-ese. What will you do while I'm having my cocktail?"

"Oh, just wait for you. I brought my book."

The big glass doors slid open silently. Briar had never gotten used to the smell of hospitals. She breathed a mixture of coffee, a fetid waft from the gerontology waiting room, and the stinging pine scent of disinfectant. They got on the elevator which exited into a long plush hallway. A sign on the right said **Chemotherapy**. There were a few people in the waiting room. Briar walked to the desk to check in, and Emma settled herself in a comfortable chair by the window. She was taking her book out of her bag, trying to find her glasses, when she heard Briar say to the nurse, "No, there must be some mistake; I'm supposed to see Dr. Carter afterwards." She leaned in as the nurse said something that Emma couldn't hear, and then turned around and faced Emma with a look of confusion on her face.

"What's up," questioned Emma, as Briar approached.

"Dr. Carter requested I come to his office first. Do you think that means something?"

Emma put the book in her bag and stood up. "Yes, he probably has a golf game to catch."

They left and turned down the hallway again. Briar stopped in front of a door with **Dr. Daniel Carter** stenciled on it in gold letters. She went up to the receptionist's window.

"He's waiting for you," the receptionist told them, gesturing to a closed door. They went in. He sat behind his desk and nodded.

"This is my friend, Emma Cassady," Briar said breathlessly. "She's a nurse. I asked her to come with me; I hope you don't mind."

"No, not at all, come in, sit down." His voice was flat and his face expressionless. "I'm glad she came along with you. I'll get right to it, Miss Terry. The reason I had you skip your last treatment this morning is…," he cleared his throat. He was young, maybe forty; he still hadn't made eye contact. "I've got the test results from your CAT scan a few weeks ago. You remember we were going to see how well the treatments had worked, and well," he paused, "I'm afraid I don't have good news for you." He looked at Emma, who reached over and took her friend's hand. The room was so quiet. The clock on his desk ticked unmercifully. Still he didn't look at Briar, but shuffled papers in the manila folder before him.

Finally, Briar stood up and blurted, "Please…just tell me."

"I'm so sorry, but the cancer has metastasized." Briar looked at Emma. "Spread," said the doctor, "to your lungs, liver and brain." Emma gulped, her morning tea back-washing into her throat.

Briar sat back down slowly. "I'm dying." she said. It wasn't a question.

He looked at her. "We could do more chemotherapy, radical and aggressive radiation. You do have that option. There's a small chance of remission, but with it moving to all of these other organs, the odds aren't good."

"How long?" she whispered.

"Well, usually after a diagnosis like this, um...anywhere from two to six months. We don't like to put a time table on it; every person is different. But it's usually somewhere in that time frame."

"I see," said Briar. She stood up slowly, "Let's go, Emma."

"Wait, do you have any questions, honey?" Emma asked.

"No," she answered, moving towards the door. She turned and faced the doctor, "Thank you, I know that was hard for you."

He shook his head, "I'm so sorry."

"Come on, Em." Emma followed her through the small waiting room and out into the long, empty hallway. "God, those are awful paintings." said Briar, as they passed some gold-framed florals.

When they got to the elevator, Emma came undone. She couldn't stop crying, as old buried grief took her back to another time when death had claimed the most beloved people in her world.

Briar waited for Emma's tears to subside. She heard the elevator, its insular rise towards them. She put her hand on Emma's shoulder. "It's okay. I've felt it for about a month now. People know, Emma, like the horse that leaves the herd; people know."

After Emma dropped her off, Briar changed her clothes and hurried to the barn. She saddled Elvira and rode her out through the gates and up into the hills behind the ranch. They rambled over logging roads, climbing steadily through a thin mist of rain. She noticed a jack rabbit crouching in the manzanita, and the bright unfurled leaves on the oaks. The air was damp and spiced with the scent of new growth. A quail called, another answered. She nudged the mare with her heels and the horse broke into a trot. She loosened her hold on the reins and the mare shot up the two remaining switchbacks, reaching the ridge. Once on flat ground, Elvira jogged, snorting and moving out. Briar leaned forward, her arms holding onto the muscular neck. The mare's long mane whipped her face; she closed her eyes and gave the horse her head. Breathless, startled the first few moments by the sheer speed, Briar let go then and joined with the animal's body beneath her. The horse's hooves pummeled the rain-softened earth as they flew mile after mile.

It was well after dark when Harry came to the barn to settle the horses and feed. He was worried. After Briar had ridden off, he had called Emma who told him the sad news. All afternoon he yelled in anger and kicked at things as he did chores. On his way over to Briar's, he noticed that the house was still dark. In the dim light of the barn he cut a bale open as the horses nickered to him. He made his way down the center throwing flakes of hay and was relieved to see Elvira. Thinking that Briar might have come in, he called quietly, "Squirt? Squirt, you in here?"

Something caught his eye in the empty stall that had belonged to Swift. Briar was there, curled up, sound asleep on a pile of grain sacks. As quietly as he could, he searched and found a saddle blanket and went to her and covered her up. He looked at her face for a long time. He couldn't hold it anymore and slipped out of the barn. The moon was a cold, white stone above him as he stumbled towards his trailer and his bottle of whiskey.

Emma looked into the mirror, attempting to cover the dark circles under her eyes with make-up. She hadn't really slept since she'd taken Briar to Bradford on Thursday. The fact that Briar had accepted the prognosis with such dignity had churned up all of Emma's guilty demons.

She felt spent from all the crying she'd done over the past few days. She didn't really want to go to Mt. Cloud with Liam, if she was truthful with herself. She'd chosen a long brown skirt and a cream-colored sweater. She heard his knock as she pushed big silver hoops through her ears, put on a wide turquoise bracelet, and took a deep breath.

He was handsome in Levis and a blue cotton shirt. His after-shave was the same Old Spice that she remembered from high school. As he opened the truck door for her, he told her that she looked pretty. Their small talk lasted over the pass to Butte City. Mostly they discussed his daughter, his latest sculpture, and his plans for expanding his fields of alfalfa over the summer.

Emma kept the questions coming, not wanting to focus on herself, but as they turned onto the Interstate he asked her what was wrong with such quiet sincerity that she spilled it all out. He listened patiently, nodding his head as she spoke of the inevitable end of a beautiful human being at such a young age. She was determined not to cry, but when he put his long arm around her shoulders, tears fell. She brushed them away, and by taking big gulps of air she was able to dam up the emotions. She could tell he was thinking by the concentrated look on his face.

"I'm usually pretty strong when it comes to death," she told him. "I know it's part of life, but I've made the mistake of asking 'why'." She realized then that he had been through this with his wife just a few years ago. She felt selfish and indulgent for sharing her pain without consideration for his feelings.

"I'm sorry for you and your friend," he said in his deep, slow voice. "There just are no answers. And you're right, asking 'why' doesn't help. I learned that with Gretta." Emma winced.

The long fields and rolling hills were mauve in the waning light. Mt. Cloud still snow-clad, loomed ahead. "But, Emma," he said, "I do believe that everything happens for a reason, and I've got a feeling that death is mostly hard for the people who love us and are left behind."

Emma closed her eyes. She felt anger and resentment. She hated his cool, philosophical analysis, and she hated him for leaving her so long ago and for all the precious time wasted in their lifetimes. *God, what's wrong with me?* she thought.

Mt. Cloud's main street was charming, with its big trees strung with lights. The Thai restaurant had red lanterns hanging from the ceiling. A fly buzzed lazily in the window. A woman with bright eyes escorted them to a booth. Every seat was filled, and the Saturday night crowd was loud. People were drinking, and the smell of garlic, onions, curry and peanuts floated from the direction of the kitchen. Liam had obviously made a reservation. Their booth was in the back against a wall, more private than the tables in the middle of the room. They faced each other in silence while looking over the menus.

"Want a drink?" he asked.

"No thanks, water will be fine."

"Okay," he said, "I think I'll have one."

They discussed the menu, things he had eaten before. They decided on two entrées that they could share. She tried to be chatty and relaxed, but she knew he felt the strain. *He probably wonders why he invited me,* she thought. She was so disappointed in herself. Here she was finally, after literally a lifetime, sitting across from Liam. But she was scared. *I can't do this,* she thought anxiously. Her fingers traced nervous images on her water glass.

The food came, generous and steaming. They made little balls of the sticky rice and dipped them into a spicy red sauce. They commented on the unique flavors. He moved sideways in his chair; his long braid lay over his shoulder. He sipped his beer and asked her questions about her work, and how the girl, Cat, was getting along. Emma was telling him about the couple in Bradford who wanted to adopt the baby when his leg accidentally brushed hers beneath the table. He smiled then, but she looked away.

As he paid the check, she paused at the register and turned the little wheel to get a toothpick. A cool wind was blowing down from the mountain as they crossed the street towards the truck. He stopped, "Would you like to go somewhere else? Or drive up the mountain?" His face, his beautiful craggy face, held so much expectation and hope that she had a change of heart.

"Alright, yes, that would be nice."

He was obviously relieved. Turning towards her, his eyes serious, he said, "Emma, I know this is a hard time for you. I just hope you'll give me the chance to be here for you."

The Goldrush Cafe was packed, due to the annual Old Timer's Rodeo. Trucks and horse trailers filled the parking lot, and every booth was full by 7:30. Luckily the first of the regulars had saved the big table by the window.

"More people from outa the area, huh?" said Ralph, putting sugar in his coffee.

Bud put his cup down, "I think people are more willing to travel since there aren't many rodeos anymore, and the barrel racing competition brings 'em out too."

Bill said, "Hey, speaking of barrel racing, anyone heard anything about Briar? Now those were the days...I've yet to see a faster pair than her and Swift. Too bad about that accident last year; at least he went down doin' what he loved."

"Yeah," said Carey Jackson, "but the irony of it—their being awarded and all, and the accident happening the way it did in the arena in front of everyone; the way he just crumpled under that broken leg..."

"I'll never forget how she threw herself on him after Harry put him down. I felt like bawling like a baby right along with everyone else," sighed Ralph.

Bud said, "Yup, me too. One of the worst things I've ever seen." He looked up from his omelet, "Lilly says she's terminal, cancer everywhere." He wiped his mouth.

"Oh, God! That's awful. She's so young, what? Thirty or so?" asked Carey.

"Thirty-five; she graduated the same year as my Richard."

"My wife said she heard Harry's been tending the ranch, trying to keep up with her boarders and training."

"What a shame," said Bill, putting on his coat. "Be sure to ask Harry if he needs help. Shit, he's getting up there too."

"Yup, aren't we all. Poor Briar. Life's a bitch, ain't it?" grumbled Ralph.

Carey took his bill, "Yeah, and a bastard too."

Chapter Twenty-one

Midnight banked down the fire and put on her jacket. Her small cabin was laid out in two sections. The original one-room portion held the kitchen and living-sleeping area; she'd added another room for herself as Julien got older, and a small bath area with a composting toilet. They hauled water from the creek for their needs. A solar shower worked well in summer. In winter they stopped at Liam's in the morning before school and work. She zipped her jacket and scribbled a note to Julien. *Dancing all night; be good. Love, Mom.*

Outside she noticed sunlight playing over new, tight fern fronds, and a toothy grass sprouting between rocks. Full-on spring would come later here, but it was a relief to see the signs. It had been one of the hardest winters she remembered. The accusation that Julien had been part of a gang rape had knocked her off her center. Even though the judge had thrown the case out, it left her questioning the very core of what she thought she knew about her child.

Sometimes, even sixteen years later, she couldn't believe that she had a child. It was never her intention to marry or parent anyone. She had left right after high school, attending the University of Washington on a full scholarship that she'd worked hard to earn. She'd sworn she would never return to the valley; her goal was to go as far in school as she could. She loved Seattle, the elegant skyscrapers near the water, and the ferries coming and going. On rare days when she had free time, she would ride the ferry all day, mesmerized by the immense, mercurial ocean. She saw herself as a college professor, living on one of the San Juan islands.

By the time she was twenty-six, she had received her master's degree in history. The whole world lay before her. She'd come home that summer to care for her ailing mother. Why she had let Rhett Smith into her life was still a mystery to her, and then one night, after too much wine, she'd conceived Julien. It just hadn't made sense to drag an infant to Seattle to be raised in daycare while she worked.

Midnight climbed higher, the creek's melt-water rushing past as fast as her thoughts. Suddenly a group of low-flying Canada geese passed overhead. They were so close she could see the black beads of their eyes. They landed on the bank of the creek. She remembered what her grandmother had told her—that a flock of geese flying in V-formation more than doubles the flying distance of a bird flying by itself. She'd said that when a goose falls out of formation, it suddenly feels the resistance of flying alone and will quickly rejoin the flock. When the lead goose needs rest, it moves to the back of the formation and another flies point. The geese honk from behind to cheer on those in front, and if a goose gets shot or is sick, two others will fall out of formation and follow it down and stay with it until it's able to fly or it dies.

She had hiked this way many times as a young girl with her grandma, who had a ceremonial cave below the cliffs. The last time she'd come here, Julien was five. It was the day before he started kindergarten. Short of money as usual, she was grateful that Liam and Gretta had taken him to Butte City to buy him new school clothes. She'd been so anxious about his starting school, entering the white world of the valley, no longer protected by family and tribe. Oh, he would be teased; she'd known that. One, because he was Green River; two, because she never married his father; and three, because he had red hair. *A red-haired bastard Indian!* She knew the resilience of children, but she had wondered at the time if *she* would live through what he would experience.

She was a little out of breath as she climbed the last stretch to the cave. The cave was tucked back in the cliffs. She found the entrance, but she couldn't find the old circle of stones. She sat on a fallen log and watched the fog lift and float above the incense cedars below. Again, the fears she'd had all winter about Julien surfaced. She had questioned him a thousand times, sometimes not very nicely, about the details of that Halloween night. He'd stuck to his original story. He'd been drunk and didn't remember anything, swearing on his grandmother's grave, but the DNA tests said otherwise. She thought about other mothers who, in the end, gave their children the benefit of the doubt. Had Jeffrey Dahmer's mother somehow rationalized her son's overt sickness? Would Hitler's mother, if she'd been alive, have rung her hands, sighed, and forced herself to believe in her son's vision for a purer humanity? Maybe Clare was right when she'd said, "It could have been any of our sons, what with alcohol and testosterone."

The eerie vibrating call of a wild grouse brought her out of her thoughts. *Was it still there?* she wondered, getting up and turning towards the entrance to the cave. She saw bear scat and whistled, just in case. She had to duck low to go inside. It took a moment for her eyes to adjust to the semi-dark. She felt along the cool walls and there it was, a small recess in the rough interior. Her long fingers searched and found the leather pouch inside. She came out to sit on the log again. The leather was hardened and the drawstrings stiff as she opened the bag she had put there eleven years ago. She reached in with thumb and forefinger and pulled out the photograph of Julien at age five. He'd been such a quiet, happy little boy. In the picture he stood in the creek, his small feet straddling rocks; his little red braid fell over his back, and his brown face was open and smiling and trusting. For many minutes she sat looking at the picture. Overcome with emotion, asking for the presence of the ancestors, she held it to her chest and cried and prayed and called forth the innate goodness of her son.

That afternoon Midnight drove through the river canyon, which was said to be haunted by the Green River people who had been massacred there during the gold rush. The noonday sun cleared Scott Peak. She turned down a dirt road where deep shade speckled the forested grove. She parked the truck, shouldered her pack, and walked to the river that was in a frenzy of froth and tumult, muffling the voices of the dozen women that stood around a fire at its grassy edge.

Old Ella Larsen greeted her. "Another dance, another question, eh, Midnight?" She chuckled. "How long we been doin' this?" Her creased face dimpled in a toothless grin. "This one's a big question though, don't ya think?"

"Yes, it is," she nodded. "How are you, Ella?"

"Oh, better than dead," she said laughing.

Objects marked the four directions—an eagle feather in the east representing air; a chunk of obsidian for the earth in the north; to the west of the fire was an abalone shell for water; and in the south a bundle of dried yarrow root lay ready to be lit in honor of the element of fire.

The women had been dancing their rituals for, it was said, "a thousand years." They danced for births, deaths, to mark each season, and to seek guidance for tribal decisions. Today they met at Midnight's request to discuss the possibility of a Green River family adopting Cat's unborn child. All afternoon they sat together, talking and listening to one another. They spoke of the spirit of the unborn, the violent circumstances of its making, and what this might mean for the baby's life path. On the other hand, they considered the possibility of a new member with Green River blood, and which family might be best suited to raise it.

After a light meal, they each set out to find a private place to rest before the long night of dancing. Midnight walked to the river. She spread her mat in the shelter of a tall madrone and closed her eyes. Sleep came easily with the soothing rush of water nearby. She woke sometime later to loud sounds; she felt stiff and disoriented, the glare of red sun behind her eyes. The noise persisted, and she lifted her head in the direction of the annoyance. A raven was poised on a rock a few feet away. His eyes were on her, and he squawked and cawed to her with urgency.

"Wing, what the hell?" She raised herself up. "Where were you all winter?" He hopped over to her, ducking and dancing, flapping his ragged wings. He came to her hand and rubbed his sleek head under it, as he had done as a baby. "How are you, old crow?" she stroked his head and down his back. He began to screech angrily, flying up, ruffling the warm air between them. "Okay, okay, hello, you wonderful raven!" He made a gruff rustling sound in the back of his throat, and she told him, "I know, I should never call you a crow."

He flew away then, across the river and into the woods. In a few moments he came back, but not alone. A fledgling flew unsteadily behind him. They landed near Midnight, and he began preening the young one, who was still brown and pin-feathered. Wing flew up, cawing, and landed, strutting proudly. "Congratulations! He's very handsome." She heard a call from the forest, a plaintive questioning. The raven's iridescent head cocked towards it and he rose up, summoning the young one. Off they flew towards the mother bird. Midnight lay back down, remembering how the raven had brought her the tiny pink plastic baby last fall, and now this. *Was it a sign?*

211

Chapter Twenty-two

Ralph walked through the fields to his farm house. He had eaten too much at Lilly's and had to fight her off about going to church. *No way am I going to set in a pew that might be shared with a goddamned environmentalist.* He farted as he entered the front door. *A goddamned ghost house*, he thought, a museum, a tribute to seventy years of life lived, hard work, the satisfaction of ranching, and raising a family on his own land. He paused at the fireplace mantle, where portraits of Lilly and Clare at various stages of life were framed. The house was just as Dora had left it eight months ago, her memory gone south, her silent staring. He had hidden in the barn the day they drove her away to live at the goddamned Alzheimer's place — *what was it called? Meadowbrook? Blue Bird? No, something with birds though.* "WORK!" he ordered his feeble mind. *Wrenwood? That was it; such a pretty name for a house full of wackos.* He went into the bathroom and tried to shit but couldn't. Nothing worked anymore, not his mind, his ass, or his legs.

He lay in bed all night, the cramps worsening, until he just threw the thought of sleep out the goddamned window. He made coffee in the big cold kitchen, then went to check the cows over near Clare's house. Her goddamned useless husband did nothing to earn his keep on the ranch. If he did show up while they were vaccinating or branding or moving cows, his breath reeked like a goddamned whiskey factory, and he soon left Bud and himself to do most of whatever it was that needed to be done.

It was getting light when he came back to the house. He saw that Dora's peonies were blooming. She had loved her flowers and always won first prize at the county fair for her giant roses and zinnias. "Dora! Goddamnit!" He whacked at the tears in his eyes, but they wouldn't stop. "What the hell!" He sat down on the wooden garden bench he'd made for their tenth anniversary and cried into his work gloves. He could feel the sun behind and above him, could trace its slow rise by the shadows on the new grass. Goddamn it, he missed her, her perky ways, singing in the morning over frying bacon. The way she clucked at him because he had carried "half the dirt from the fields in on his boots." But most of all, he missed her slipping into their bed at night, her body warm and scented.

How long had it been since he'd visited her? Clare and Lilly always asked him once a week to go with them, but he usually said no. He couldn't take it, the fake smiles on the attendants' faces, the smell of dead air and dead food. But hardest of all was seeing her there in front of him, her blue eyes, tiny waist, her silver hair up in a bun on her head. He couldn't take it when she looked into space, expressionless, as he pleaded, "Dora, Dora honey, it's me, Ralph, don't you remember...?"

How long had it been since he visited? Christ! almost five weeks ago...*I'll go today. The girls will be at church; good—they won't be able to fuss about my driving."* He went in to run a bath.

After the Sunday attendant, Miriam, fed Dora her oatmeal with raisins and encouraged her to take her vitamins and medications, she helped her get out of her eyelet nightgown and get dressed. Dora, calm and passive as always, allowed the woman to rub lotion over her small muscular limbs, and cooperated throughout the clean underwear and slacks, even raised her arms so a knit top could be pulled down over her torso.

"Want something to keep you warm, sweetie?" Miriam asked. After no reply as usual, she just went ahead and pulled the soft pale blue sweater she knew Dora's daughters had given her last week over the woman's slender shoulders.

"Now, up we go," she said, helping her rise up off the end of the bed.

"It's Sunday, Dora; are you having any visitors?" Dora stood there, a look of confused contentment on her face.

"Let's fix up your hair next." Miriam guided her to the dressing table, seated her, and began to brush the long silver hair.

"You've got such a nice natural wave here in the front." She picked up some bobby pins from a little pink ceramic dish and put a few in her mouth. She brushed the long, fine, wavy hair, then took it up in her hand and twisted it, winding it into a bun at the nape of Dora's neck. Removing the pins from her mouth with her free hand, she inserted them around the circle of hair and put her hand over it to make sure it was secure.

"There, you're all set. Now, let's get you to your chair." She helped Dora rise and walk to the yellow rocking chair by the window.

"Want T.V. or the radio?...No?...Alright then, I'll check on you later, okay?"

After the door closed Dora leaned forward. The big white oak outside the window had tightly-rolled, shiny leaves that reminded her of the ears of baby mice. She slid the window along its track. It would only open a crack. The strip of screen allowed a sliver of cool fresh air to enter the room. The scent of turned earth caught in her nose. Something had changed, something had happened outside through the branches of the oak. She could see big cream-colored clouds; they reminded her of something, *but what?* She couldn't remember. Maybe it was the clear blue around them that made her think of… *what? What was it?* She put her face close to the window; the branches of the tree almost touched the glass. She smelled last night's rain. The morning sun's warmth was penetrating the ground below. She felt the inner force stirring. She saw that new leaves had unfolded. *What was it called? Photo realism?…no. Photographic sensitivity?…no that wasn't it.* She knew this answer. It was something she'd always taught her students, especially when it was that time of year…*called?…that time when everything is born…It started with an S…SSS.* She couldn't remember what happened to the plants and trees. *Photographic sustenance?…no…* or, what the season was called. She pushed a short clean fingernail into her palm and pressed hard. "Never mind, never mind," she told herself.

The white oak reached up to the second-story room. The building must have been constructed right next to it, because she knew the tree was old, really old to be this tall. On closer inspection she noticed a nest tucked between branches high up, almost out of her view. She looked at the arrangement of sticks and grass. There was something orange hanging from it, *ribbon…tasselies…yarn?* She wondered. She stood up and looked out the top corner of the window to get a better view. The trailing stuff moved with a slight wind ruffling the leaves. Caught by the sun it seemed almost metallic. *I know! I know!* she thought, *it's tape, cassette tape woven in the nest! Were there eggs or… bald flying things? So much happened in a tree.* She looked at the crusted trunk and knew that much of its vast bulk was actually dead. Only truly alive were the leaves, buds, flowers and roots. Hidden within the tree, the living cells, which made up only a tiny percentage of the whole tree, were always at work: the roots drinking moisture, the vessels under the outer bark carrying the nutrients needed to grow the tree. She looked closer at the tips of the branches. The new leaves were...*what was it called?...phyto nutrisis? The sun so important had something to do with it...the leaves breathed.*

She saw herself in her classroom, chalk in hand, standing before a blackboard with a sketch of a plant and a list of the elements:

Earth = Nutrients
Fire = Sunlight = Energy Converted to Food
Air = Gasses, Breathing Moisture Through Leaves
Water = The Basis of Protoplasm Contained in Cells

Underneath she read: **"Photosynthesis means putting together with light."** Below that, at the bottom, was written the chemical equation:

$$6CO2 \quad + \quad 6HO2 \quad \rightarrow \quad C6H12O6 \quad + \quad 6O2$$

Carbon Dioxide · · · · Water · · · Light · · · Glucose · · · Oxygen

She sat back in the chair and smiled. "Spring," she said to no one. She pulled her cardigan closer and whispered, "Photosynthesis, photosynthesis, photosynthesis."

Ralph turned into the parking lot. The driver behind him laid on his horn, making him jump.

"Use your turn signal, old man," the guy yelled as he passed.

The parking lot was almost empty. *I hope I'm not too early,* he thought. "Well then, I'll sneak up to her room, goddamnit!" he said, getting out of the truck. He took the flowers from the seat. He'd wrapped them in brown paper that he had found in a cupboard at home. He patted his breast jacket pocket to make sure it was still there, then lifted a little black case off the seat. He couldn't hold the flowers, the strap of the case, and lock the truck, so he just left the truck open.

"Take whatever you goddamn want," he said to invisible thieves. He wore his Sunday slacks and black tie shoes, which felt slick on the asphalt. He walked towards the entrance, noticing two men smoking at the end of the building. The lobby was empty, even the desk was deserted, so he rang the little service bell.

A young woman came out from the office. "Can I help you?"

He cleared his throat, "I'm here to see my wife, Mrs. Dora Rawlins; she's in room 303."

"Mr. Rawlins, I'm sorry but visiting hours don't start for another hour. Could you come back then?"

He shifted the bouquet of peonies to his other arm. "Well, not really, you see I've got seed to plant today, and..."

Something about the old man's clean-shaven face and Sunday clothes softened the girl. "Okay, let me check to see if your wife has had her breakfast." She picked up the phone. "Has Mrs. Rawlins been attended to yet?... She has? Alright, is she dressed? Okay, thanks." She turned to him, "Well, Mr. Rawlins, this is against the rules, but I'm going to make an exception—just between you and me, okay?"

"Sure," he said, "goddamned right."

"Those are gorgeous peonies; gosh, they're so huge! You know how to get there, right?"

"Yup," he said, turning towards the elevator.

He knocked gently. After two or three tries he went in.

217

"Dora?... Dora, honey?" There was no answer. He found her in her chair by the window. "Dora?" She turned then, more to see what the scent was than to respond to the voice. Ralph moved towards her and held out the flowers, a mixed bouquet of different colored peonies: creamy white, burgundy, and light pink. He looked around, put the flowers on the table, laid down the case, brought a vase from a shelf across the room, and filled it with water. Her eyes followed him. After he unwrapped the flowers, he dropped them into the vase. "Look, sweetie, they're from your garden. Ain't they purdy?"

She stared at them for a long time, then got up slowly. She cupped her small hands around a pink one, leaned her face into the bouquet, and inhaled deeply. "Oh, oh," she said, her eyes closed.

Ralph seized the moment, unzipped the little black case, and removed a cassette player. He took the cassette tape out of his pocket and put it in the player. She was totally absorbed in the flowers when the music started, smooth violins and cellos weaving around one another. Dora looked up.

"Remember?" asked Ralph, as the sweet music swelled into the mellow voice of Gene Autry. The lyrics filled the small room:

> *Have I told you lately that I love you?*
> *Could I tell you once again somehow?*
> *Have I told you with all my heart and soul how I adore you?*
> *Well darling, I'm telling you now.*

"Remember, Dora?" She was looking intently at him. "Our wedding day, remember? We danced to this song."

> *Have I told you lately when I'm sleeping*
> *Every dream I dream is you somehow?*
> *Have I told you why the nights are long when you're not with me?*

He moved towards her. "Remember me, Dora? Ralph… your husband." He put his arms around her shoulders and drew her towards him. They had always danced, every chance they got. She offered no resistance, but let him gently draw her closer. He started moving his feet.

She looked at him, "Ray? Ray?"

He held her a little tighter. "It's me, Ralph…Oh, Dora, I miss you so much," he said, his mouth against her hair. He turned towards the tape player, hit the eject button so he could start the song over.

Dora, quick as a thought, grabbed the cassette and started yelling, "Orange, orange, orange, Roy! Look!" With her thumb and forefinger she pulled out the thin tape, winding it out and out until it fell on the table in a tangled mess. Scooping it all up, she ran to the window. "Look, Roy, look!" She banged the black plastic case on the glass up high near the corner of the window and pointed. "Bed for bald flying things! Bed for bald flying things!…Look! In the tree, spring! Spring! Photosynthesis! Photosynthesis!"

He was struck dumbfounded. "Goddamnit, Dora! What the…?" His voice was low with anger. "What did you say? You ruined it! Shit!…Look what you done! You ruined it."

She let the case fall out of her hands to the floor. "Bed for bald flying things," she said under her breath. She turned away from him, walked slowly over to the yellow velour rocker. She settled her small body into the chair and pushed up the sleeves of her blue sweater. "Bed for bald flying things," she whispered one last time, then looked out the window, her face passive and blank once again.

Chapter Twenty-three

After gorging on leftover macaroni and cheese, salad, and garlic bread, Cat washed the dishes. It was Saturday, and she looked forward to a quiet day of rest and study. The teachers always piled on so much work the last month of school.

Emma and Briar had taken the two-hour drive south to Red Creek for an appointment with an herbalist. As Emma said, "Even in the dying process the mind and body can remain comfortable." Cat couldn't believe that Briar was dying. *God, life sucks,* she thought, drying the dishes and putting them away.

The baby lurched downward as if in agreement. "Stop it, you Little Thing!" she said out loud to her belly. She still called it that because, really, she couldn't and didn't want to imagine what it looked like. Emma told her last week that she'd found a nice couple in Bradford who wanted to adopt. Cat had looked at their resumé and pictures. A lawyer and a teacher, their photo revealed a nice looking couple in their thirties. The woman wore lots of make-up and had blonde-streaked hair. The man seemed somehow "withheld," Cat decided, behind his smile. There were pictures of their huge English Tudor home and grounds, in a fancy subdivision in Bradford. Christian, happily married, all they wanted was a baby to "complete" their life. They were willing to pay a lot of money for her expenses and her return to Phoenix, Emma had said. After looking through the photos and papers, Cat didn't know how she felt about them. Jokingly she had held their picture up to her belly, asking, "Well, what do you think, are these your parents?"

She dozed off after reading only a few pages in her history book. She woke up feeling dull and heavy, and suddenly remembered that Emma had asked her to check on the horses. On her way downstairs, she wondered if Julien was still on the property. He had come over early, as Emma was leaving, wondering what work she needed done. Ever since his uncle had brought him to the farm, he had driven his little blue truck to Emma's three days a week to work. At school, when she saw him in the hall or lunch room, he made brief eye contact accompanied by a fast nod of his head.

On Thursday, RJ had been lurking around her locker. She'd found a note inside that said, "Watch out, Bitch!" She had no idea how he'd gotten her new combination. When she closed the locker and turned to go to class, RJ was behind her, laughing in that demonic way of his. Julien was coming down the hall and had stopped and waited until RJ had moved on. She'd hurried off in the other direction to her math class.

Cat walked through the orchard. She had never really experienced the seasons in Phoenix, just hot and dry and maybe a little cooler in winter. The strong perfume from the trees almost made her dizzy. She unlatched the first gate and closed it, wondering where Julien was, or if he had already left. As she crossed the pasture she heard a chainsaw start up; the sound came from somewhere behind the house, maybe in the garden.

In the middle of the field she paused by the huge incense cedar tree, whose back side held a wide cleft where honeybees had built a hive. She listened to the deep vibration inside. She closed the second gate and heard the strong creek water coming from the mountains. Mav was grazing under the big oaks, but she didn't see the other horse. As she walked toward the corral, Mav caught up with her. She stopped to scratch his ears. He was such a friendly, calm horse; she wasn't afraid of him. *Where was Candy?* She looked in the pasture near the road, which was deep in shade, but didn't see her. She wasn't in the corral either. *Okay,* thought Cat, *she's in the barn.*

"Candy?" she called, "where are you, girl?" Behind the big open barn door was a dark, cavernous space. Squinting, trying to get her eyes to adjust, she went inside. Although she couldn't see the horse, she heard the mare's familiar call, "Huh, huh, huh, huh, huh, huh," coming from the back. Cat stepped forward cautiously. "Hey, girl, where are you?" Again the horse nickered. Cat approached and saw the mare lying on the ground on her side. Sunlight streamed through a broken window as the horse lifted her head, the whites of her eyes showing. She let out a series of grunts. *Oh, no,* thought Cat, *she's having her baby.* She moved around the horse to look at her backside, and saw two tiny hooves sticking out. "Holy shit! Are you alright?" The mare rolled onto her other side as if in agony.

Cat turned and ran. She saw Mav coming over to the barn and called out, "I'll be right back," as if he could understand. By the time she had crossed the ten acres, her sides were aching, and she could hardly catch her breath. She followed the sound of the chainsaw to the garden, where she found Julien cutting through a log. He couldn't hear her panicked voice, so she placed herself in from of him, jumping up and down and waving her arms. He finally looked up and turned off the saw. "Help, I need help! The mare is having her baby."

He took off his safety glasses and threw them down. "Where is she?"

"Follow me," said Cat, "she's in the barn."

Mav was standing just inside the door when they reached

the barn. "This is weird; they almost always foal at night," said Julien. They stood over the mare who was motionless, eyes closed.

"Is she dead?" blurted Cat. "Oh, God! see the hooves coming out?"

Julien knelt and touched the horse's neck. "Whoa, girl, it's okay." The horse opened her eyes and looked at him. After a moment he moved to Cat and said, "Something is wrong; call Emma."

"My cell is at the house."

"Okay, here's mine," said Julien.

Cat punched in the number, but there was no answer. "Emma, it's Cat, call me, it's about the mare. What's your number?" she asked Julien, then repeated it into the phone. "Who else can we call?"

"My uncle," said Julien, taking the phone. "Oh, I forgot, crap! He's gone for the weekend." The horse moaned weakly.

"What about the vet?" Cat suggested.

"Okay, I'll get the number." The horse's body spasmed. Julien dialed the vet with nervous fingers, then listened. "The vet's gone. Dr. Raintree is on call, but he's in Butte City. Let's see, my mom, but she's down river today."

"Look!" cried Cat. Blood was seeping from the mare.

"Shit!" said Julien, rubbing his head.

"I know! What about Harry, Briar's friend?"

"Good idea," said Julien, "he'll know what to do. What's Briar's number?"

"Uh, I think it's 460-3789."

"Damn it! No answer. Harry! This is Julien Smith. I'm at Emma's. The mare is in trouble; if you get this, come right away."

The horse was making a terrible sound. "What should we do, we can't just let her die!" Cat said trembling.

Julien thought for a minute. "Okay," his voice was determined, "I've only seen a couple of foals born, but I'll try." Under his breath he muttered, "Where are my ancestors when I need them?"

"Cat, get that halter hanging over there and put it on her." Cat fumbled with it and finally buckled it. "Now, just hold the rope lightly, she might try to stand, and be careful if she does, just move away." The boy knelt at the mare's rump, "Okay, girl, this might hurt. Cat, talk to her."

Julien started to reach inside the mare, stretching the opening as wide as he could around the little hooves, until he got his hands inside up to his wrists. "Here we go," he told Cat. He wiggled his fingers and grabbed the bony little legs. Slowly he pulled, inch by inch, downward. More of the foal's legs became visible, but then they disappeared inside again.

"Cat, god, I hate to ask you this, but could you sit on her belly and push down while I pull?" The horse was limp now, her flanks barely moving with breath.

"I'll try," Cat said, positioning herself.

"Okay, when I tell you, push down as hard as you can." Julien pulled again, and a stream of reddish water trickled out. "Okay, now push." Cat pushed and Julien pulled and the other two hooves appeared. "Let's do it again, when I say." Julien moved his body back and forth, thinking of how a car had to be rocked before it was pulled out of the snow. "Okay, push!" This time Cat laid her whole body across the mare's side and pushed down with her hands. "It's coming!" cried Julien, "once more!" He pulled gently again. An explosion of water shot out of the mare, and a slimy bag with four hooves sticking out gushed onto the floor. The mare groaned.

"Oh, it's deformed!" cried Cat, jumping up.

"Hold on," said Julien, taking his knife out of his pocket. He slit the grey membrane and pulled it apart carefully, revealing a tiny head. The foal's eyes were shut as Julien slid the sack off its body. The mare raised her head and delivered the placenta. Turning back, she nosed toward her motionless baby with a weak nicker.

"Is it alright?' asked Cat.

"I don't know." Julien's hands shook as he stood. The mare began to lick the foal and its eyes twitched, then opened. "Huh, huh, huh," she said to her baby, and the little black nose touched hers. The spindly legs stretched and the foal tried to stand, but fell back. Its eyes were alert now and wide open, its forelock and short mane spiked up.

"C'mon," said Julien, "you can do it," and the little black horse raised himself up unsteadily and stood. He let forth the highest-pitched whinny to his mother.

"Move back." Julien put out his arm to protect Cat, "She's getting up." The mare rolled and heaved herself upright and began licking the foal all over. "It's a colt, good sized; maybe that's why she had trouble."

Cat pointed. "Look at his butt," she said, admiring the big white circles.

"Appaloosa," said Julien.

Cat felt queasy. The fact that the mare and colt seemed alright sent a delayed wave of emotion over her. Tears filled her eyes, and she turned away so he couldn't see.

"Why are you crying?" he asked softly, "they're fine, I think."

Cat paused, "I'm just…happy. I was scared that they were going to die."

"Yeah," he said, kicking at the dirt. "I'm going to get her some water."

Julien was coming in with a bucket when they heard a truck pulling into the turnaround. Harry ran as fast as his seventy-year-old legs could carry him.

"Julien, Julien!" he called.

"In the back," Julien answered.

Harry talked on, "I never check Briar's phone, but she told

me to today…I hope I'm not too late. Well, I'll be damned!" he exclaimed, looking at the mare and foal, "everything turned out fine I see…"

"It was touch and go," said Julien. "She went down; the foal was stuck; there was blood; and she gave up, hardly breath'n…"

"And Julien put his hands inside her and pulled him out," blurted Cat excitedly.

"And she sat on her, pushed while I pulled," said Julien.

"Well," said Harry, putting a wad of chew in his mouth, "you kids did a great job." He walked over to the mare, "Hey, mama, you got a flashy young one there. Look at that color! Has he nursed yet?"

"Nope," said Julien, "he was only born maybe twenty minutes ago."

"Well, let's see now." Harry put his chew can back in his jeans pocket, where a perfect faded denim circle molded itself over it. He checked the mare, "She's a little torn, but she'll heal. Can I touch your son, mama? Get him goin'?" He approached the foal slowly. "If he's handled right away, he'll be trusting and easy to break. Come here, little fella." He squirted some milk from the mare onto the colt's face, and with his arm scooted him under his mother. "Tastes good, huh? Here," he guided the colt's head to the teats, "there ya go, alright." His voice was the kindest that Cat had ever heard.

The colt latched on and the mare jumped, and everyone laughed then at the loud sucking sounds. "You'll get to keep this one for a while," Harry said to the mare, moving the bucket of water closer. "Well, kids, nature'll do the rest. Emma and Briar are gonna fall in love. Couldn't get a hold of them, huh? Probably coming up the canyon from Red Creek when you called. He's a real beauty, big and strong. Bet they'll let you two name him."

Cat wiped her sweaty hands on her pants. She turned to

Julien, "What do you think his name should be?"

The boy paused, then let out a long sigh, "How 'bout, Lucky?"

Summer

Chapter Twenty-four

Emma sat on the front porch swing, relishing one of the first true summer evenings. The orchard lay before her, and beyond, in the fields and pastures, the gift of the long, wet winter and spring was realized in the waist-high grasses, whose heavy seed heads arched over and bobbed in a warm wind. The gnarled trees in the orchard had escaped the March frost and were studded with small hard green apples. The moist earth provided the foundation for an abundant garden, needing only the long summer days of heat and sunlight. Leaves had unfurled in their greening way, and the farm once again rested beneath a protected canopy. The quiet of winter and spring had given way to the noisy cadence of birdsong, crickets, frogs, and the rushing water that filled creeks, ditches, and streamlets to their brims.

The lawn around the house had greened and thickened and would require mowing soon. Days started at dawn. Now that the horses were in the pastures, the chore of feeding them hay was replaced with the morning ritual of watering. Help from Julien was greatly appreciated, since the pastures, lawn, and garden required moving sprinklers twice a day. The garden would take up much time—weeding, planting, harvesting, and, as fall approached, the drying, canning, and freezing of all the produce. The house in summer was easier in some ways, because a fire didn't need to be tended twenty-four hours a day. Still, in order to stay cool, windows had to be shut each morning, fans turned on, and drapes drawn to keep out the oncoming oppressive heat.

Crows swooped overhead, maybe twenty-five of them, cawing their way up the mountain to roost. As she sipped a glass of iced tea, she watched them fly over, inked against the fading sky. Her cell phone buzzed in her apron pocket. She fantasized not answering it, but when she saw that the number was one of her pregnant moms, she said, "Hello, this is Emma." Sara Harding's strong voice greeted her. "Emma, hi, it's Sara. Thought I'd call and give you a heads-up before dark, just in case, to let you know my pains are getting steady and closer together. Hold on a minute...Tyler, get off of that table now!...Sorry about that. Chris is out haying, and I'm trying to do forty things at once *and* corral this wild boy of mine. Anyway, if it's going to be like the other three, I'll bet this baby comes before morning."

Emma looked at her watch. "How exciting, Sara. It's about, let's see, 8:30 now. Do you want me to come over and check you?"

"If you don't mind; that way I can get my Mom to take the kids and make up the room and maybe I can take a shower. I'm pretty sure this is it. I'll bet I'm...oh, hold on a second..." Emma waited, listening to the woman's deep breathing. "Okay, it's over... I'll bet I'm five or six."

She knew that Sara knew her body, and her three other births had been fast, intense labors. "Sure, okay, I'll be there in a half hour or so; does that work?"

"Tyler! Get that rubber band off of the dog's nose!... Sorry, Emma, that'll be great. God, I never thought I'd think of labor as a vacation, but time away from this two-year-old will be a good thing. Bye."

Emma scribbled a note to Cat, who was already in bed, and left it on the kitchen table. When she arrived, Sara was huffing and puffing around her house. She progressed quickly, a centimeter or more per hour, and at 12:07 a.m., after three boys, she delivered a baby girl, whom they named Naomi. When Emma left, the proud and surprised parents were sitting on their couch, gazing at the child in awe. Sara's husband, Chris, looked up, "Thanks, Emma, we sure appreciate you! Do you think we'll know what to do with a girl?"

"Yes! I think you'll love it!" She bent down and stroked the little head, "Bye, Naomi, see you in a week."

On the ride home she thought about what there was to eat at the house. Always famished after a birth, she mentally scanned the interior of the refrigerator. By the time she finished her sandwich, it was after 2:00 a.m. She sank into bed, exhausted, only to wake less than an hour later. She'd dreamt of Briar, but couldn't remember anything else. She got up and went downstairs, made a cup of chamomile tea, and took a tepid bath.

Back in bed she rolled over and over for another hour, her mind wheeling from one thing to another. Something about Sara's birthing reminded her of her own labor so many years ago. Perhaps it was the fierce intensity and speed of it, or how Chris and Sara were so engrossed in their daughter's face. She and Ronnie hadn't been able to stop staring at baby Theo for months it seemed. The sheets were twisted around her legs, and when she got out of bed to straighten them, she decided to just stay up.

Slipping on a cotton robe, she crept quietly down the stairs and out the back door. The night was lush with stars. The sound of water surrounded her. Bear came out of his dog house and yawned up at her. A three-quarter moon lit the garden, casting dim shadows near the plum and pear trees. Dew from the grass wet her bare feet. She lowered herself into a rickety chair that had, for some reason, escaped the burn pile time after time. The neat rows of new plants were partly visible in the half light. Bats whirled in circles above the pear tree, and Bear lifted his head towards her hand.

Beneath her weariness were layers of worries and concerns. Her usual ability to cope with multiple people and situations had left her. Briar's inevitable death, Cat's birth, and the maddening approach-retreat, approach-retreat pattern with Liam weighed on her.

God, how to deal with her own grief, losing a friend so like a daughter. She just wanted to help her live as joyfully and as long as possible. She knew death could be an amazing and powerful transition when fear and resistance were minimal, but Briar was so young. Would she be able to surrender, or would she fight it in her quiet and spirited way? What about the others? All of them were having a really hard time dealing with the finality of their friend's life. Each had come to her asking questions, or as Lilly had done when they'd met for lunch last week, expressing anger and resentment.

"Goddamn it!" she'd said, brushing her bangs out of her eyes, "why her…why now?" Deep in the throes of what they referred to as "The Pause," she'd ranted to Emma. "I feel awful. Everything is changing—my body is in chaos; my mom is out of her mind; my dad's depressed and grieving; even our lifestyle is threatened. The boys told Bud and me that they weren't coming home this summer; they all wanted to stay on the coast and work. Jimmy told Bud that they were probably not going to be ranchers. I hate change, and now this with Briar…it's too much!"

Then Clare had brought her oldest son, Josh, in to get stitches. He had supposedly bumped his head getting into the car, but from the way the boy kept telling her, detail by detail, how it had happened, Emma suspected that Don had something to do with it. As they were leaving, Clare had turned her shy brown eyes to Emma and asked quietly how long Briar had to live.

"No one knows," she'd answered, "probably a few months." She had felt compelled then to ask Clare if everything was alright at home.

"Yeah," she had said half-heartedly, "pretty much the same; but we're okay."

"Are you going to Hidden Horse with us?" Emma had asked.

"Yes, I'm bringing Bandit, and I'm excited that Briar feels up to it; be good for us to all be together."

"Yes, she's really looking forward to it."

Emma looked up and saw the low bright canopy of the Milky Way as her thoughts circled around to Cat. She was due in about six weeks and still hadn't committed to the adoption with the wealthy couple in Bradford. The girl was working hard in these last few weeks to finish her schoolwork for the semester. She seemed tired and emotional, which of course was to be expected, considering everything. Soon they needed to talk about the birth and classes. She had decided to have the baby at Emma's house, but there were still many details to discuss.

It was starting to get light, and the lopsided moon hung lazily over the mountains in a purple sky. The cats had found her and were curled at her feet, which had become chilled during her reverie. What else, she asked herself, did she need to mull over before she went to sleep for a few hours? Liam? Yes; their dinner in Mt. Cloud had brought up many issues for her. The old hurt from the past had almost stopped her from having any hope for the future. But his persistence that night, his suggestion after their uncomfortable dinner that they drive up to the mountain, had provided an opportunity for them to really talk about the past. When he asked her to forgive him, she told him that she respected him for marrying Gretta when she got pregnant. They had stopped and kissed, long and deeply, as they walked through the forest, the old heat flashing through them. They had a date for a picnic the weekend after next. At the thought, she felt an excited, fluttery feeling in her stomach, but also a sense of...what was it? uncertainty? fear? vulnerability?

A rose glow bled over the horizon. She yawned, exhausted from the deluge of thoughts and worries. A lone trucker's jake brakes sighed, down on the highway. She stood up, wondering how life could be so beautiful and terrible in the same breath.

Chapter Twenty-five

Amy Lee and Cat had stayed in horse camp, unpacking the kitchen and babysitting Bear, while the women rode. It was Cat's first time at Hidden Horse, and she was taken with everything, from the hour-long trip spiraling up into the remote wilderness, to the mountains that rose around the meadows to a height of 6,000 feet. She loved the way the little campground was laid out, and how the women's trucks and trailers formed a circle like a wagon train. She'd never been camping before, and hadn't hesitated when Emma had invited her and Amy Lee to come along. Emma had explained that they usually never went in June, because it was cool and snow still covered the trails to the lakes. But this year they wanted to fulfill Briar's wish to go. "Every day counts," was how Emma had put it, not saying that it might be her last time.

After a quick lunch—Clare had made sandwiches—the women had prepared for their ride. Cat and Amy Lee had walked around meeting each woman's horse. Cat knew Briar's blue-eyed Elvira, and of course Emma had brought Mav. Lilly brought her gelding, Joe, and Clare, although nervous, was riding Bandit. Midnight, whom Cat found to be both friendly and mysteriously aloof, was riding a wild-looking mare named

Molly. Cat had caught a look of sadness from Amy Lee as they watched the women saddle Briar's horse and help her up. But Briar had joked, "This is the life—having my horse saddled and being waited on!" Cat had sensed their excitement as they left camp with Lilly yelling, "Yee haw! Yee haw! See ya later, girls!"

Cat and Amy Lee sat at the picnic table, Cat sitting sideways because her belly wouldn't fit under the table.

"Have you camped much?" Cat asked.

"Oh, yeah, you can't grow up in the valley and not spend a lot of time in the mountains in summer. I haven't been up here much though; my folks aren't horse people. We have a cabin up at Coyote Lake that has been in our family forever."

"Ouch!" said Cat suddenly out loud. "Knock it off, you Little Thing. God, this kid thinks I'm its punching bag."

"Can I feel it?" asked Amy Lee excitedly. "Is it still kicking?"

"Oh yeah, it never stops. Go ahead—I think there's a foot right there." She took Amy Lee's hand and put it on her stomach.

"Oh, my god, that's so strong! Does it hurt?"

"Sometimes my ribs get real sore."

"Have you found parents for it yet?"

"Kind of. Emma found a couple in Bradford who seem okay, but I'm really not sure about them…"

"It must be hard giving it up. I really respect you, Cat, for not getting rid of it when you could have. How much longer?"

"I'm due July 30th, so about…," she counted on her fingers, "about six weeks."

"Are you scared?"

"I would be lying if I said no. I just want it over with so I'm not reminded of the…you know…that night."

"Yeah, I'll bet," said Amy Lee, looking away. "That night was crazy. I never thought those boys…especially my cousin…could do anything like that. RJ, yes, but not the others."

"He still bothers me," said Cat, picking at her fingernail.

"Like what, just seeing him you mean, reminds you?"

"No, he stalks me, leaves notes in my locker."

"How did he get the combination?"

"I have no idea."

"What do the notes say?"

"Things like 'Watch out, Bitch,' or 'I know your every move.' And last week he wrote 'Why didn't you kill that kid? Want me to?'"

"Cat, have you told anyone about this?"

"No, like who?"

"He's dangerous! Tell Emma."

"No, I can't. She's got enough to worry about. He does scare me, but I'm not going to let him know it. I just ignore him and look the other way. Besides, school will be out next week, and I'll never have to see him again." They watched a chipmunk come into camp and investigate around the bottom of the garbage can.

"What's it like having Julien working at Emma's? Did you guys really birth a colt together? I saw it when my mom dropped me off. That's the cutest foal I've ever seen."

"Yeah, it was pretty random," said Cat. "We had no choice. The mare was dying. Julien...he's really quiet I think, different from the other boys."

"Yeah, he grew up fast when his dad was killed. He was drunk and crashed his motorcycle into the river and drowned. Julien drank a lot after that. He's quit partying though; I heard the tribe made him."

"Do you know his mom?" Cat asked, "Midnight?"

"Sure, she's lived down river forever. She's full Green River. She left to go to college but came back to help the tribe. My mom says she's a culture keeper."

"Is she nice?"

"Oh yeah, once you know her. She can be sarcastic though;

that's where Julien gets it."

"I'm hungry," said Cat, getting up and going to look in the cooler. "Do you want something?"

"No. Do we need to do anything to get dinner ready?"

"Not yet," said Cat, eating a piece of cheese. "I guess Midnight brought chicken to barbeque. What time is it? Do you have your watch?"

"It's 2:30," said Amy Lee.

"I've got to give Bear his medicine at four, don't let me forget, okay? I think I'll go lie down for awhile; my back hurts."

"Okay. I guess I'll read my book for English. How do you like *Silas Marner*?"

"In one word," Cat said, "boring."

The women rode out of the campground. Their mood on the outside was one of excitement and gaiety, but underneath the joking and good humor gave way to a silent collective thought—that someday soon Briar wouldn't be with them. They trotted downhill over well-traveled deer trails. Afternoon sun lay on the path and flickered through the trees, lighting up the new soft pine needles on the ends of the branches. At the bottom of the hill they rode across a snow-packed service road which, in another month, would have thawed enough to take them to trailheads that led to a number of high mountain lakes. In order to give Briar her probably last adventure, the most accessible option was the Big Meadow Wilderness Area trail, which plunged down through lush meadows crossed by snow-melt creeks and then rose up again over a series of rollercoaster hills. Sun-caught treetops were a glittery scrim above, as they rode in single file through the varying terrain. Enormous granite boulders sprouting dwarfed wind-bent trees flanked the path. The only sounds percussing the thin, clear air were the hammering of woodpeckers and the jubilant calls of outlaw jays.

They came to a section of brush strewn with downed logs that blocked the path. Clumps of grainy snow hung in shaded crevices between the long, criss-crossed slash. Without a word, they pulled up, grouped together, and waited as one after another cautiously led her horse through the dangerous litter. They crossed a flat meadow spiked with skunkweed, the tinkling din of streamlets slopping beneath the horses' hooves. Below a grassy edge the path dropped down radically, and they held their horses back as each one picked its way across the swirling water. In single file again, they loped up a fern-filled incline to a flattened plateau and a crossroads.

"Which way?" called Lilly, who was in the lead.

"The long way, uphill, to the right," hollered Midnight.

"How's Bandit?" Briar called to Clare, who was in front of her.

"He's fine, fine, following right along."

Briar watched perfect meringue clouds float above them and felt the sun warm on her back. She reached out and stroked Elvira's sleek neck. She let the moment fill her, something she'd been able to do often since the diagnosis a month ago. Sometimes, in the middle of the night when she woke with fear of the unknown, she wished she believed in something or had the comfort of religion. She'd never really thought about death until her parents died, but they were older and had lived good long lives. When her beloved horse, Swift, died she had questioned the circumstances, and shook her fist and cursed at an unjust God. It wasn't that she didn't believe in God; she didn't know what she thought about it all. She was going to die, no doubt about that, but when? No one really knew.

"Alright," she called out, "you slow old women, let's go!" Elvira shot forward, Briar whooping and screeching as she led

241

them. They galloped upward, gaining momentum. The horses were puffing and blowing as they crested the hills. Briar was still ahead. By now the horses knew it was a race, and at the wide points in the road they spread out five abreast, wild-eyed and snorting for position. Then Elvira would somehow jet out ahead again, and they would all fall back into line.

As they neared the top of the last hill, Lilly yelled out something that sounded like "Hell, hell, and good luck!" She was hunched forward and low as Joe ran, hooves pounding, now in second place. Suddenly she was catapulted into mid-air. They heard her scream as she flew over the horse's head, veered, and landed on the side of the road. Briar turned and caught Joe's reins. The horse, who evidently didn't know he'd lost his rider, was still heading for the finish. The other women reined in their horses, backtracked, and rode to where Lilly lay, dazed and gasping, on the ground.

Emma leapt off Mav and went to her. "Lilly, Lilly! Don't move, okay?"

Lilly's blue eyes opened; she saw their concerned faces above her. The wind had been knocked out of her, and she wheezed.

"Do you hurt anywhere?"

"No," she answered.

"Can you move this arm?...good, now this one?...your legs okay?...How about your back, any pain?"

She had landed in a big pile of dried pine needles. "No," she sat up, "I'm okay." She caught her breath.

"What happened?" asked Midnight. "I heard you yelling something."

Lilly stood up and looked at them, "You're not going to believe this. I tried to tell you. I yelled, 'Help! Help! I'm stuck!' My bra got hooked on the saddle horn, and I couldn't get it off. Joe was running uphill and I leaned back, and the next thing I knew it snapped me forward and I went flying."

There was a moment of silence, then suppressed giggles, until all of them except Lilly burst out laughing.

"A human sling shot!" shouted Midnight.

"I can see the headlines now," said Briar, "**Woman sent into orbit by brassiere.**"

"Shut up, you bitches!" Lilly rubbed her butt. "I'm gonna be so sore…"

"It was like slow motion," said Clare. "One moment we were all in the saddle, the horses hell-bent for victory, and then you just floated upward and over Joe's head like you had wings. I thought you were being cocky about winning and yelled something like 'Hell! Hell and good luck!'"

"Very funny!" said Lilly, now brushing off pine needles and dirt.

"Well, we're just glad you're okay," said Emma. "We declare you winner by default, only next time just know that flying is cheating. You should write to Victoria's Secret and tell 'em their new ads should say: *Try the new 'Western Wonder' bra, helping women leap over mountains in a single bound.*"

"I guess it was pretty funny," Lilly laughed, as she got back on her horse. "Now let's go finish this race, cause Joe wants to win!"

They were all still cracking up about Lilly's "flight" when they returned to camp. The horses were unsaddled, brushed, and put into their corrals. Cat and Amy Lee offered to feed them while the women changed their clothes and relaxed before dinner.

Midnight had started a fire, and the coals were burning down as Lilly handed Clare a glass of wine. "Hey," she whispered to her sister, "I didn't know Emma was bringing the girl, did you?"

"No, but what's the harm?"

"The harm is that I don't trust her. She's trouble, and Em still doesn't get it. I wonder if Amy Lee's mother knows who her daughter hangs out with?"

"Lilly, stop, the girl seems nice enough. She's really helped Emma, and Josh says she's quiet at school."

"That's not the point. The fact is she's an outsider who came to the valley and drug our kids through the mud! Do you think she's innocent? I don't, not after that stunt she pulled in church."

Briar sat down, pulling her sweatshirt closer. "What are you two whispering about? I hope it's not about me." She knew she looked terrible, thin and sick.

"Of course not! Do you want some wine or beer? Midnight brought soda too," offered Clare.

"I think I'll have a beer; you only live once you know." Briar saw their faces and laughed. "Hey! it's only an expression."

"Here ya go," said Lilly, handing her a beer.

"God, look at that sky!" said Briar, "isn't that gorgeous?" The sun was a fireball perched above the mountains; orange and red streaks sliced the blue behind it.

Midnight came in carrying a container under one arm and a paper bag under the other.

"What'd you bring, Midnight?" asked Briar.

"Marinated chicken breasts," she answered, setting everything down and poking at the fire with a long stick, "and fry bread."

"I'm starving," Lilly sighed, "where's Emma?"

"She's getting their beds made up in the tent. The girls are watering the horses."

"So what do you think?" Lilly asked, "did you know the girl was coming?"

"What does it matter?" Midnight said. "Did I miss something? Did she need a permission slip to join us?"

"I guess not," Lilly pouted, dumping potatoes and onions into a skillet. "How long for your chicken, Midnight? These will take about twenty minutes."

"The same for the meat. I hope Emma brought a salad; I'm hungry for greens." Midnight smacked her lips while she put the chicken on the grill. The marinade dripped, and the fire pit started smoking.

"Jeez Louise!" said Briar, moving her chair.

Emma and the girls came in then, each carrying a container. "Here's the salad. I picked these greens this morning; that first crop of lettuce is always so tender. And Cat's got the dressing," Emma said, pointing.

"And I've got the dessert," said Amy Lee. "I hear Briar is famous for these."

"Did you make brownies?" Clare asked Briar, grinning.

"What do you think?" She didn't want them to know she'd been so weak yesterday that Harry had to load up all her gear and bake the brownies.

Emma handed her a little bottle of something, "Here's your herbs, sweetie."

"Thanks," said Briar, opening the lid and downing the green liquid, "yum." She choked a little, making a funny face, "Yuck!" Bear came over to her as if in sympathy and put his head in her lap. "Oh, thanks, old guy," she crooned, petting his ears.

As the women chatted and the food cooked, dusk fell and gathered around them. A small herd of deer grazed at one end of the campground. The horses close by could be heard chewing contentedly, and wood smoke spiraled up through the branches of the big cedars.

God, I love this, thought Briar, *and all of them.* Midnight made a joke about how they "roughed it," saying car camping didn't count, and Clare's laughter rang out. Briar looked around at them then, Midnight's strong body, her black hair loose down her back, her beautiful proud face, her eyes flashing with amusement. She watched Lilly sip her wine, noticing the elegant way she held her glass and the way the fire played in her hair. And Emma, the most dear to her of all. This incredible woman who had been mother and sister and friend since she was a young girl. She watched Emma's face as she ate, the auburn hair curling around her oval face, her eyes taking in everything. And even Cat, this brave girl-child, whose rebellious nature so reminded her of her own. Someone passed her a brownie, and she let the moist chocolate linger in her mouth a moment, sucking at the bitter and sweet taste.

Stars appeared like big chunks of glittering cut glass. Everyone pitched in on the dishes, and then Lilly and Clare brought out their guitar and banjo. The sisters played, the strains of music floating over the camp. Clare's banjo sounded like a mandolin. They sang along to *Oh, Susanna*, slow and plaintive, *My Old Kentucky Home*, and Woody Guthrie's *This Land is Your Land*:

> *This land is your land, this land is my land*
> *From California to New York Island,*
> *From the Redwood Forest, to the Gulf Stream waters,*
> *This land was made for you and me.*

Then Lilly asked if there were any requests. Briar called out, "That Russian folk song, what's it called?...You know... *Hold Me, Hold Me?*"

A tense silence followed; finally Lilly said, "You sure, Briar? That's a sad one."

"I'm sure," she said, "I've never wanted to hear it more than now."

Midnight started it, her deep voice soft and low:

246

Hold me, hold me, never let me go.
Hold me like the leaves on the ends of the branches...

Tentatively the others joined in...

And when I die, let me fly, let me fly
Through the air like the leaves when they're falling...

Then Clare's high soprano...

Hold me, hold me, never let me go,
Hold me like the stars in the sky high above me.
And when I die, let me fly, let me fly
Through the sky, like the stars when they're falling

The song ended and all were silent. "Hey, you guys!" said Briar, "I feel like a big fat elephant around this fire. Everybody's so considerate and tiptoeing around the fact, the truth, I'm—we are all—going to die. I'm just going first. It's okay! Okay?...If it's okay with me, then please let it be okay with all of you. I'm going to miss you so much, and yeah, I'm scared and...curious. I never went to church, and I haven't really thought a lot about what death is or what dying means, and I have a favor to ask while I've got you all here. I'm asking you, each of you...please tell me what, what it is you believe?"

Lilly and Clare shifted in their chairs; Emma pulled her jacket closer. The girls gazed into the fire, not wanting to meet Briar's eyes.

"We believe in the longevity of the spirit," said Midnight, turning to face Briar. "We believe that the spirit or soul of a person is separate from the body. That the spirit is the fire that fuels the physical body, and that the spirit is the essence of the person. And that when you die the spirit is released, like a great 'letting go,' and then it returns to the source, the creator, the great mystery. The Green River sing and dance the spirits of their ancestors into and out of this life. Of course many of us were raised going to church too, but that's what the old ways say." Midnight turned to Lilly, who was on her left.

"Well," she said hesitantly at first, "um, well, as you know we've always gone to Green River Evangelical church. 'Evangelical' meaning we believe in the authority of the gospels. We know that the Bible is the word of God, and therefore follow it strictly. Our beliefs say that if you have been saved by the Lord Jesus Christ, and you live a good life, you will die and go to heaven. If not, then...," she paused, not wanting to condemn her friend, "well, we believe you will spend eternity in hell. But it's never too late, Briar, to repent and be saved by the Lord." Briar smiled at her in the firelight and nodded. Lilly turned to Clare, who laid her banjo across her lap.

"Gosh, Briar, I don't know what to tell you. I go to church sometimes. But I've always been real scared, since I was a little girl, of the fire and brimstone stuff. But I remember something my mom said once when I asked her what happens when someone...dies. She said that the church believes one way, and science looks at it differently. She told me that she thinks we must go on somehow, because energy doesn't die, it merely transforms, and we are all made of energy. I never forgot that. And I guess I'm telling you that I'm not sure; I mean, the older I get, the more I realize...I don't know." She looked into the flames.

Cat looked down and said, "I'll pass," and turned to Amy Lee, who shook her head in uncertainty. A log in the fire shifted, sending up a shower of sparks as Emma spoke.

"Well, as you all know, my grandmother, Genevieve, my mother's mother, lived with us while I was growing up. She was Catholic, and of course she and my parents never missed a mass, and so neither did I. But there was another side to Gran, whose mother and mother's mother had been midwives in a small village in England. Gran told me that, before Christianity, almost all of Europe believed in a Great Mother, a Goddess, who was the spirit of the earth. My great, great grandmother grew herbs and made medicine. She delivered babies and tended the sick and prepared the dead for burial. In this old religion they believed in the Summerland, and they believed that we live over and over, with the same soul but inside different bodies and at different times. Reincarnation was based on the way the cycles of plants and animals progressed from life to death and then to birth again. Like a leaf that sprouts and grows, then dies, and nourishes a new seed to be born again. So this is what I heard, from the time I could remember, about life and death and rebirth. Once I asked Gran which religion was right, and she said, 'Emma, as many souls, as many ways to God.'" She paused for a moment. "I agree with you, Clare; the older I become, the less I know, but personally I'm grateful for the mystery of birth and death. If we were supposed to know, or were ready to know, we would."

No one spoke as a cool wind lifted the splayed branches of the nearby trees. And after a moment, Briar looked into each of their faces and said, "Thank you, my friends."

Cat yawned, then pulled her sweatshirt tighter. She had lain awake most of the night. She wasn't used to sleeping on the ground, uncomfortable even with a pad, and scared of the night sounds in camp—the horses calling to each other, restless in their pens; wind rippling and rattling the rain fly on the tent; and near dawn, after she had just dozed off, the loud squawking of blue jays. All of the women except Midnight had risen early and gone for a short ride. Cat sipped tea by the fire while Midnight broke down the camp kitchen. She'd offered to help, but Midnight had told her, "No, just stay warm and relax." Amy Lee was still asleep as Midnight quietly packed up dishes and food and loaded them into her truck. Cat shifted in her chair, the baby moving low in her pelvis.

Midnight came back from the corrals and stood Molly's saddle on the ground. She poked at the fire, then sat on the picnic table bench. "Cat?" she said finally, looking right at the girl, "I wanted to speak with you. This might be a good time?"

"Okay," said Cat, the woman's serious eyes putting her on guard, "sure."

Midnight came and sat directly across from the girl. "I understand from Emma that you have decided to give the child up for adoption; is that right?"

"Yes," answered Cat.

"And have you found parents yet?"

"No, well not exactly. Emma found a couple in Bradford that are interested."

"Well, I'd like to give you another option." She took a folded envelope out of her back pocket and handed it to Cat. "I...I mean we, the tribe, were going to send this to you, but when I heard you were joining us this weekend, I decided to give it to you in person."

Cat took the envelope, unfolded it, and read the letter, which stated briefly that the Green River tribe was interested in adopting her baby, which would be raised by a native family, for the sake of preserving the Green River culture and adding a new member with tribal heritage. Cat glanced up at Midnight with a questioning look. "But...why? Why would you people want...it."

"Well, because," Midnight responded, "you, Cat, have the blood. Your mother is Green River and was raised in our community."

"Did you know her, my mother?"

"Of course! We grew up together. Even though my family was down river and hers was in the valley, we were in school

250

together until…she left in her senior year. I never saw her after that. But your Grandma Jenny was my mother's friend, and I've always kept an eye on her…well, until last fall. I think it's great that you're going to college; it will change your life. We would listen to any ideas of how to do this; for example, if you wanted an open adoption where you could have contact with the child, this could be arranged. I know you have a lot on your mind right now. Take your time and think about it." Midnight stood up, lifted the saddle, and walked towards her truck.

When she came back, Cat said, "Midnight?"

"Yes, Cat?"

"Could I ask you something off the subject?"

"Sure, go ahead."

"How did you get your name?"

"Oh, that," she said, tossing her head back and laughing. "Well, we have Sunsets, Sunrises, and Evenings in the tribe. The time of day or night you were born. I had an Aunt Noon and an Uncle Morning. That's all, nothing too mysterious."

"Oh," said Cat, "I was just curious."

"What about you? Is Cat your given name?"

"Caterina, after my father's mother, supposedly."

"Did you know him?"

"Not for one second; he left before I was born."

"I see," said Midnight. "I'm gonna get Molly now. Let us know, okay? You could even meet the family if you'd like. We just really want our own to stay with us, learn the ways, you know. Take care."

Cat watched her load her horse. Midnight waved as she drove out of camp. Cat's mind was overcome with thoughts and questions about this new possibility. She wondered if Emma knew about the tribe's offer. And then she thought of Julien—did he know? What would be best for…the Thing?

Chapter Twenty-six

Emma was packing the picnic basket when she heard Liam's truck. She only had a moment to brush her hair back with her fingers and put on lip gloss without the benefit of a mirror before he was at the back door.

"Hi," she said, letting him in, noticing that her hands were shaking.

"Hey, you look nice; are you ready?"

"Yes, I just need to let Cat know I'm leaving. I'll be right back," She gave him the basket. "Want to put this in the truck? I'll meet you out there," she said, over her shoulder. "Cat," she called at the bottom of the stairs, "I'm going now." The girl answered back, "Have fun."

They drove into a glorious day, warm and sunny. "Finally feels like summer, huh?" Liam said, rolling down the window.

"Yeah, it's always so cool in June; most of the trails to the lakes still had snow at horse camp last weekend."

"Did you have a good time?"

"Oh yeah, always, although bittersweet. I don't know if Briar will be able to go again—she's weaker every day. She's coming to stay at the house with us on Monday."

"You'll have your hands full, with the girl and all."

"Cat's no trouble; she's a big help actually. I'm really going to miss her."

He passed the little post office and turned left towards Serpentine Creek.

"Did you know about the tribe wanting the child?"

"Oh yeah, both the men's and women's councils have debated it for a few months now."

"What do you think?" asked Emma, looking over at him, noticing the way the sun lit the tiny hairs on the back of his beautiful gnarled hands.

He paused, "Hmm, I don't know what I think. I know why they want another tribal member to raise, but I wonder what it will mean for Julien? Is it a possibility even? Is Cat considering it?"

"She is. We met the couple in Bradford yesterday. They were nice enough, but Cat didn't especially care for them."

"Any chance she'll keep the baby herself?"

"I doubt it. She really wants college after she graduates next year, and with the circumstances being what they are, I don't think she's even considering it. She calls it the 'Little Thing.'"

They were both quiet as they started up a dirt road that climbed up through the canyon.

"Remember all the time we spent at the creek when I was up for summers?"

"How could I forget? You were the most incredible girl I'd ever met..."

"Isn't it weird that we're here today, forty years later?"

He took her hand, "Yup, pretty weird, pretty wonderful."

The Serpentine Mountains rose before them, the jagged peaks painted a mica-flecked gray-green. From terraced meadows water plunged down through the canyon, the creek strewn with giant boulders, the alluvial fan spreading wider into the lower gorge. They parked in a copse of trees and climbed down to a sheltered beach. The water rushed past, loud and fast, turning and foaming off the rocks, swirling and jetting into whirlpools. They both stopped for a moment, hypnotized by the raw power.

Warm sun lay on the sandy shore, and Liam smoothed out a blanket and took the basket from Emma. He sat down, his long legs stretched out in front of him, and smiled and gestured for Emma to join him. As she settled next to him, their shoulders touching, she reached inside the hamper and took out a cold bottle of wine. She uncorked it and poured some into the little glass tumblers she'd wrapped in cloth napkins.

"Comfortable?" he asked. She could barely hear his low, deep voice over the sound of the creek.

She nodded then and said, close to his ear, "God, the water!" They drank the Riesling, and a contented drowsiness came over them as the sun cleared the canyon walls. Emma brought out cheese and crackers and poured more wine. When they both reached for a cracker at the same time, heat flashed up between them.

They saw a small grey bird fly low over the water and land on a rock in the creek bed in front of them. He bobbed up and down, spreading out his wings. The dipper threw back his head and warbled, "*Bjeet, bjeet, bjeet,*" the clear notes rising above the water's roar. Liam took Emma's hand as the bird dove into the water, completely submerging. He popped up a little further downstream, only to bob up and down in his ecstatic dance again, as water rushed all around and over the rock where he was perched.

"Look," she whispered, "how he loves the water."

Liam's mouth was close to her ear; his warm breath sent shivers down her arms. "You are my water, Emma."

She reached up and loosened the leather tie on his braid; the dark mass fell down his back, silver streaks glinting among the black. She combed her fingers through it, her eyes

254

closed, savoring the moment, the nearness of him, his clean smell of soap and cedar. He stroked her nose and cheekbones. "Always loved these freckles," he whispered. He kissed her then, his mouth wide and soft. She felt his manhood rising between them as his tongue, playful and darting, found hers. He pulled her down onto the blanket. His hands lifted her sweater and he unhooked her bra. As the straps gave way, his hands cupped her full breasts and he called her name over and over. With a woodcarver's sensitivity, his fingers circled slowly; she could feel the gentle friction of the calluses on his finger tips.

She sat halfway up and slipped the sweater and bra over her head. The noon sun made her breasts glow with a translucent whiteness, and she saw the pleasure in his eyes as he took them in. He pushed her back gently on the blanket and buried his face in them. She felt his hardness rubbing against her hipbone as he pinned her arms above her head, holding them lightly. Slowly he kissed the inside of her wrists, moving his lips along the crook of her arm, then found her ear, ringing it with his tongue in fast circles. She was helpless beneath him, wild with desire, her heart echoing the fast water.

She put her hand down below the waistband of his jeans, and as her hand found him, he moaned. He sat up then and took off his shoes. Then he stood and pulled her up to face him. With her arms around his neck, she used her heels to slip out of her shoes. Embracing, each of them became a conduit, fire running up and down their bodies.

He stepped back and unbuttoned her pants, letting them fall to the ground. His shirt came up over his head, and hurriedly she slid his pants down. They were now naked and barefoot in the cool spray of water. He took her hand and reached for the blanket on the shore. He walked her to the center of the knee-deep creek. She felt the pebbled sand between her toes. He laid the blanket over the top of an enormous boulder, and guided her towards the sun-warmed stone. Her body curved as her back came into contact with it.

As he bent over her, face to face, she felt the warmth of his chest and belly on hers. His hands lightly brushed her sides and hips. Drunk on their nakedness, her head thrown back, he kissed her eyelids, then her throat, up one side and down the other. He worked his way down slowly, kissing her breasts, her belly, until, as he knelt in the water, she cried out again and again. He moved his mouth back up her body, belly to breasts, and kissed her. They were arched over the stone, his hair spilling over her, the water tumbling and thundering all around them. Her breath came in excited gasps as she opened her thighs and took him in.

Later, as they lay in each other's arms on the beach, the sun soaking into their skin, Liam took her face in his hands. His voice was tender and deep as he spoke, "Emma, sweet Emma, no more living without you…no more…"

Chapter Twenty-seven

Cat felt a deep twinge in her side. *Good!* she thought, *maybe this will make the Thing come out.* She pushed the wheelchair over the last rocky bit of ground, brushing sweat from her forehead. "You okay, Briar? It's a little bumpy, huh?"

"I'm doing fine; what about you? I think it'll go smoother on the grass. We're almost there. These mountain bike tires Harry put on really work well. I'll bet the horses will take notice."

Once through the rocks, Cat pushed Briar across the little footbridge and into the pasture. The huge oaks—like umbrellas above them—created pools of shade on the summer grass. They came to a stop, and just as Briar predicted, Mav, Candy, and her colt Lucky came trotting towards them. Mav skidded to a stop, snorting and circling them.

"It's okay, boy, it's just a chair with wheels." Briar pushed herself up and reached out to him. "Are you the protector, huh? Acting like the papa?" She reached into her pocket and gave him a piece of apple. Tentatively, the mare moved in for her treat. She nuzzled Cat's shoulder before delicately lipping the apple. "She just loves you, girl; what can we say?" Briar laughed.

"But why? I don't get it." The colt came in close, completely unafraid, searching out the sweet smell.

"Well, maybe she knew someone who looked or smelled like you, or maybe you remind her of someone who was kind to her once. Maybe she thinks you saved her. They have incredible memories."

"Have you always been around horses?" Cat asked her.

"No, well almost. I mean it wasn't until I was adopted when I was eleven that I even laid eyes on a horse."

"I didn't know you were adopted. Where were you...," Cat looked away, shyly, "you know, before...?"

"In about eight different foster homes." Briar reached out and let the colt nibble at her hands.

"I thought all babies were adopted right away."

"Oh...it's a long story. They found me in a parking lot, and without my mother to give permission, well, it took a long time for my adoption, and then I was too old. Most people want newborns. But when it finally happened, I got the best parents anyone could ever have. They were older, grandparents really, but they raised me here, and horses were just a way of life."

"I've never really been around any animals. Are they different from, say, cats and dogs?"

The little black colt kicked up his heels and ran into Mav's chest. Mav raised his head as if to say, "Watch it, buddy!" The colt did it again and then ran off, whinnying, across the field. Mav's tail went high and he chased after the foal. When he caught up with him, he bit his shoulder gently. A game of tag ensued, and both Briar and Cat laughed at their antics.

Arcs of water refracted in the sunlight as the old-fashioned free-standing sprinklers ticked around their orbits. The mare stood quietly by Cat with a look of contentment on her big face. She sniffed at Cat's belly.

"Well, dogs are great and very devoted, and cats are so independent," Briar paused, "but horses are different. I think

258

it's because of their size, partly, and their wildness. I always wondered why they let humans control them. They could have just run away. Although we humans never would have evolved the way we did if it hadn't been for the horse. They're smart and, of course, probably the most beautiful creatures in all the world. But they're also…let's see…they have this quality of… well, the best way I can say it is, horses are true. They're true to their ancestral memory, their environment, their instincts, and their herd."

She started coughing, and it took a few minutes before she could catch her breath. "In the wild they are prey animals and must adhere to a kind of pattern of togetherness to survive. In captivity, the horse stays aloof and wary. It will cooperate, but with reservation, and maybe only because it's afraid. They have been so abused. But if someone shows a horse respect and kindness, most of the time the horse will give of itself wholly and willingly. When this trust is established, you will never find a creature more loyal and honest."

Cat, her hand on the mare's neck, said, "Maybe someday I'll have a horse."

"Well, you're sure a natural with them. You have the right kind of energy, and if you were staying here, I would give Candy and Lucky to you."

The girl smiled, her eyes hidden beneath her long lashes, "Really? Thank you. Sometimes I wish I could stay."

After a moment Briar said, "Yes, I know how you feel; it's a pretty wonderful place. Whew! I'm ready for a nap. Would you take me back now?" She sat down in the wheelchair, slumping with the relief of not standing. The mare followed, walking alongside Cat as far as the fences would allow.

Over the next few days, Briar's weakness increased. And as it turned out, the day Cat had taken her to the pasture was her last time outside.

Emma had made the yellow room as comfortable as possible, layering feather beds, quilts, and big pillows to cushion her friend's emaciated and pain-filled body.

"There, honey, how does that feel? Are you comfortable?"

Briar closed her eyes and sighed, "Oh, it's nice Em, a real nest."

"Remember, you can push that button anytime you need to for more medicine."

Briar's wizened face scrunched up, "I don't like the morphine. It makes me feel all loopy and weird...But I guess it does help the pain...a little."

"I'm going to let you rest now. Ring the bell if you need anything. I'll be in the kitchen."

"Thank you, Emma...for everything. You've been so good to me."

Emma bent to kiss her cheek, "Don't be silly; you would do it for me, right? Now rest."

She drifted. Every once in a while she opened her eyes and looked at the trees outside the window. Small hard green apples studded the leafy branches. *When those apples are ripe,* she thought, *I'll be gone, even before.* The pain flared, a deep bone ache inside her whole body. She was so weak she could barely lift her head. Reluctantly she pushed the button on the morphine drip and waited. *What has my life meant? I haven't accomplished much,* she thought, *not even marriage or family.* She felt grateful for that now. It was hard enough to see the misery in her friends' eyes. She couldn't imagine a husband and little children gathered around her deathbed.

What is it going to be like, this dying? This big letting go? And would she do it with her body or with her mind? She'd asked Emma, who, after a thoughtful silence, told her the surrender seemed to happen not just physically but mentally and spiritually too. She'd told her it was different for every person. Sometimes it was peaceful, and sometimes people fought it until the very end. *I hope I'm not like that,* she thought. She hoped it would be soon. Her body needed it to be over, and her mind had almost accepted it. She drifted again, a ranting mantra repeating in her failing brain, "free of pain, free of pain, free of pain…"

For the next few days the women took turns staying by her side. Lilly, Clare, and Midnight sat around Emma's kitchen table. They heard Briar scream and cry, calling "Mama, Jean, Mama;" then Emma's soft voice comforting her.

Lilly's eyes were red and swollen. "I can't take much more. My god! How long does she have to suffer?"

Midnight flipped her braid. "Why don't you take a break, go home, Lilly, for awhile." She got up and took her cup to the sink. "I need to get some work done myself. Emma will call us."

Emma came into the kitchen just as the back door closed. She stood at the sink washing her hands, telling herself, "I cannot cry! I will not cry!" The weight in her chest was a solid thing.

The next day, Emma saw a change in Briar, a deeper sleep state and an inability to respond. Dr. Drew came and told her that she'd had a stroke; all systems were shutting down, and it would only be a matter of time. The women came and went. Harry sat vigil at night when Emma had to give in to sleep. A hushed cocoon of waiting enveloped the house. Sometimes Briar moaned or spoke unintelligible words. Harry and Liam sat in the kitchen drinking coffee in silence, not knowing what to do, but not able to leave.

On the last day, they were all there. Briar felt them all around her. She needed to be free of her body. Off and on she floated somewhere far away from the room. Once she saw the universe as one huge light, all of the stars like cells in a larger organism. She was closer now, and after all of the pain, she just wanted to go. When the moment came, rasping breaths wracked her in long intermittent wheezes. She leaned into Emma, who had climbed onto the bed to hold her. She could feel everyone in the room anticipating her deliverance and release. She felt the separation between spirit and body; a dizzying freedom filled her, and she floated momentarily above herself.

She was surprised that her body still felt physical and did not continue to rise, but instead bore her downward through the mattress as feathers tickled her nose. She was carried through the old oak floor, smelled the sweet rotten dank of the basement. She felt a sense of peace as she sank into the earth, moving through rich, dark soil, seeing animals—foxes and rabbits—burrowed and sleeping, taking no notice of her. She passed in and out of the intricate weavings of tree roots, and the enormous damp bases of boulders. She heard gurgles of artesian water rising up through the strata. Finally she found herself in a tunnel. She reached out, touching the smooth, cool walls, and stood still for a moment, her senses alive. She looked at her hand, still a hand, yet the flesh was becoming more and more translucent. A subtle wind billowed the white nightgown around her ankles, and at the edge of perception she heard a distant sound. Then it faded. Again she heard it as she stood poised, waiting. Whatever it was, it was coming closer. The sound was a hollow, rhythmic ringing, like metal striking metal. And then she knew; it was hooves, galloping hooves. She could see him, and as he slowed and came to her, she called out, "Swift!" Her arms flew up around his neck, and his sweet grass breath was hot on her cheek.

Afterward, the women gathered in the kitchen around the table, waiting for Norris Whelp to come from the mortuary to pick up Briar's body. The moment he and his assistant came out of the yellow room with the stretcher was difficult, especially for Lilly, who broke down and cried out, "That's it? That's what she gets? This beautiful person! An amazing life!... A plastic bag? A big black plastic bag?"

After they calmed her down, Cat poured everyone iced tea, and Emma opened a sealed letter from Briar.

My Dear Sisters,

And so it's over, and I want to tell you that all of your love and support over the years has meant so much to me. As you know, it's my wish to be cremated, and please—no public funeral or memorial. Emma knows where I want my ashes laid and will tell you of the right timing of it. As for the ranch, it will not be sold. I want Harry to stay in the house and have a comfortable place to live out his days. He and I have discussed the possibility of taking in as many promarin mares and their foals as he can feed, the goal being to find good homes for them once they are healthy. My last wish is that you all check on Elvira and give her a carrot now and then. She loves Harry but will need a woman's touch once in a while. Don't be sad, okay? It's been a lovely, wild ride.

Yee Haw, Briar

Afterward, Cat washed the iced tea glasses, dried them, and put them away on the open shelf above the sink. She crept quietly out and paused in the dining room, her eyes falling on the photo of all of the women laughing, sitting on their horses in the high summer meadow. She climbed the stairs. As her heavy body and swollen feet plodded upward, she wondered, *How could this be? However could this be, that Briar was dead.* Late afternoon sun filtered through the white sheer curtains in the library. She sat down in the purple chair by the window, her small hands resting on her belly, and as the Thing rolled within, she felt the undeniable sad, cold fact of mortality. She heard the dying wheezes and saw the emaciated face of her new kind friend, now…gone.

Emma's yellow cat, Sam, came out from under the bed. He'd moved there permanently it seemed, except to eat and go out once in awhile. She watched him stretch, his raised back arched. His striped front paws slid out on the wood floor in front of him as he yawned and flicked his ears. He looked up at her, a curious expression on his face, and, as if coming to some decision, he walked closer, then in one movement jumped onto the arm of the chair. He had to maneuver his body delicately, but managed to lie down in the valley between her chest and stomach. She stroked his fur, and when he began to purr, she told him, "I hate life, Sam. I hate it."

Afterward, when everyone had left and Cat had gone upstairs, Emma sat at the table, Bear asleep on the floor next to her.

Liam came in the back door. "Hey, I'm going home now. Just came to say good-bye. Are you alright?"

She stood and turned to him. When he saw her face he

said, "Oh, god, Emma, come here." He reached out for her, but she shook her head back and forth, buried her face in her hands, trying so hard not to break in front of him.

"Come here; you've held it in for so long." He put his arms around her. She pushed him away. "No, no, she's gone, Liam, she's gone. It should have been me, not her, not that most beautiful being...She had her whole life to live...It's not right," she cried. "Why wasn't it me? Why wasn't it me?" She moved into him and began to beat her fists on his chest.

He knew this was not just about Briar, but had everything to do with the loss of her husband and son so many years ago.

"Emma, listen," he took her face in his hands.

Her eyes were wild with grief. "Why, Liam? Why wasn't it me?"

"Because it wasn't, Emma; because you're meant to be here, for you, for all the people who need you...for me, Emma, for us...for us."

Afterward, Lilly and Clare drove silently across the valley, each in her own world. The pickup's windows were rolled down, letting in the heat-dusted July air carrying the scent of freshly-cut alfalfa. Without even a good-bye, Clare jumped down from the truck when they reached her house and closed the door. Lilly watched her in the rear view mirror as she pulled away. Her sister stood still, the truck's dust circling her in front of the ramshackle house.

After weeks and months of sadness, Lilly, her muscles tense, jaw clenched, felt waves of anger rise with the heat in her body. "Stop!" she screamed, as she dodged potholes in the dirt road. "Just goddamn *STOP IT!*" she ordered her body. A big black horse fly flew in the window and buzzed loudly around the cab. "Shut up!" she told it, reaching for an old *Ranch Gazette* on the floor. Steering with her knees, she rolled the yellow-edged paper into a tube and began swatting at the insect. "You think *you* get to live?" she yelled. It landed on the dash, where she smacked at it with all her might. "Missed! Goddamnit! Just wait, you horse-biter!" she screamed. The enormous fly lifted and flew crazily in circles around the cab. She waited, watching its descent as it landed next to her. "There!" The force of her printed weapon squashed it flat, leaving pieces of wings, eyes, legs, and green fluid smeared across the seat. "God, Lilly!" she said to herself, as she pulled into the turnaround, "god! I'm just so pissed!" Shaking, she knew she would go into the house and pick a fight with sweet, agreeable Bud, and that he would somehow know it wasn't about the underwear on the bathroom floor or the dog's empty water bowl.

Afterward, Clare stood frozen in front of the house, and stared at the ripped screen on the front door. She kept seeing Briar's body being carried out. She was brought back by Don's slurred voice behind her, "What the fuck are you doing? Don't you know it's past dinner time!" He pushed her forward. Numbly, she walked into the kitchen, past her sons sitting in front of the television. Their wary eyes looked up to her, full of fear, as their drunken father stumbled in after her, calling them "lazy fucks." She walked to the bathroom, locked the door, and stood before the cracked, silver mirror. She thought about how she'd failed her two brave boys and herself. She stared into her dark, tired, want-to-quit-the-battle eyes and knew that their stolen childhood was just as much her weak and fearful fault. She noticed a razor on the edge of the sink.

She stared at the long, black, stubbled hairs on its sharp edge. Picking it up, thinking of Briar, she brought it to her wrist and wished she could leave, just go and float away too, right now. Again she looked into her eyes for a few seconds and thought, *No, no, there's no easy way out for cowards.*

Afterward, Harry drove back to Briar's. He parked the truck, opened the glove box, and took out a full bottle of Jim Beam. With shaking hands, he unscrewed the cap and guzzled it halfway down. He wiped his dripping chin with the back of his hand and gagged. He felt his body sink into the torn upholstery of the seat. He didn't move, just let his weathered old claws rest in his lap. He stared through the cracked windshield at the house.

How I'll ever be able to go in there with her gone, I'll never know. The house, a cabin really, sat on a little swatch of green lawn. One of his chores since the Terrys had passed on was to water it in summer. He'd met Will in the Navy, and they'd become fast friends. They'd seen plenty of action in Guam and Japan, then returned to the states when the war was over. Both had dreamt of ranch life, and at only twenty years of age, their plans and goals seemed achievable. Will married Jean a few years later, and they'd built up this homestead in the valley. When his gypsy life had brought him near enough to visit, he felt they were the happiest, most compatible couple he'd ever known. They'd wanted kids so badly, but Jean lost a lot of babies over the years.

Then, when they were in their forties, they'd adopted Briar. He remembered the first time he saw her, riding Jean's old mare, the tallest, skinniest little girl he'd ever seen. She'd looked at him with her big, old-soul eyes and smiled, and that was that, he was done for. He'd had a brief disastrous marriage, then traveled from job to job, ranch to ranch, from then on. The only person he'd ever really given his heart to was that little girl. Watching her grow and become a supreme horsewoman—well, he couldn't have been any prouder if she'd been his own. They were his family, and when Jean and Will died a few years apart, he'd moved his little trailer behind the barn and stayed mostly full time to help Briar with the ranch and horses that she boarded and trained.

He stepped slowly out of the truck, his stiff body aching like a son of a bitch. Palming the chew can out of his back pocket, he opened it and scooped a wad into his cheek. The trainers and his Elvira slept in the shade of a big oak, their bodies still except for their tails, twitching back and forth at the relentless flies. After Swift died, Briar had really latched onto his big blue-eyed mare. It was mutual, and a relief that the horse was getting ridden, since his back couldn't take too much time in the saddle these days.

He looked back at the cabin. She wanted him to live there now. Humble as it was, it seemed like a mansion for a hard-drinking rambling man who threw his bedroll down wherever he landed. He thought staying put might be good for him though. She had written out detailed instructions on how to run the place. He needed to finish up the boarders and send them on. He was to get in touch with the lady in Canada and take in as many of those hormone mares as he could feed and house. Let them keep their foals, sell them to good homes, then use the money to get more. She'd even left money for him to live on. *Ah, Squirt! I'm gonna miss you so much.* Grief blinded him, along with the realization that nobody should outlive the people they love. Choking up, he leaned into the pickup and grabbed the bottle of whiskey. Taking the lid off, he brought it up to his mouth, then stopped. *No!* he told himself. *By God! If Briar left me this place, then I'm surely gonna do right by it!* He

268

tipped the bottle down and watched it glug out onto the dirt, then walked towards the lawn to turn on the sprinklers.

Afterward, Midnight drove down river in the plush summer evening, through the winding cleft of the canyon, the slow, silver riffles of the river beside her. A doe and fawn stood at one turn, and she braked to a stop and let them pass, the mother looking back as the young one crossed. Farther on, swallows swooped in circles, feeding and calling in midair, their peach underbellies flashing in the last light. *It was peaceful there at the end,* she thought. Briar's face had calmed as Midnight felt her surrender.

The last spark of sun sank behind the high, ribbed cliffs. She turned onto the bridge that marked the long, narrow drive to her house. Stopping her truck on the bridge, she got out and leaned over the railing and watched the river below, feeling a lightness in her body after the tension of the day. The clear, low water pooled over and around the stones and boulders randomly scattered along its bed. She thought about how the water's fluidity adapted to whatever environment or form it found itself in, without losing its essence. Because she believed that a newly-freed spirit might do the same, she raised her arms skyward, turned in a slow circle, and began to sing.

Chapter Twenty-eight

After working in the garden with Emma all morning, Cat went inside with a big basket full of huge red strawberries—a "bumper crop" Emma called it. She set it down on the kitchen counter. It was over a hundred degrees outside, and she was sweating and out of breath. She was used to hot weather in Phoenix; it sometimes reached one hundred and twenty in the streets in summer. But she wasn't this fat and had never been this tired. She slipped off her flip flops; the cool wood floor soothed her swollen feet.

She'd told Emma that she would trim the berries and put them in the refrigerator. *Crap! There were probably seventy-five of them.* She carried them to the sink, found a big silver bowl in the cupboard, and poured them in. She took a paring knife from the holder and got started. Her body screamed its exhaustion in her aching neck, back, and legs. Over at Lilly's in spring she'd watched the women making sausage. That's what she felt like—a sausage stuffed too tightly into its skin. She threw the green stems into the other side of the sink. *I hope I don't explode,* she thought.

The Thing kicked hard near her pelvis. *Ouch!* It seemed like it never stopped punching and kicking. She hated being pregnant, and wondered why some women did it over and over. She was never having a kid by choice. The due date was in a few weeks. She'd sort of decided to give it to the couple in Bradford, even though something about them bothered her. As far as the tribe, she didn't want it raised where the rape happened. She counted the berries...*thirty-five, thirty-six.* She ate one, letting the cool juice wash down her throat.

A series of yawns overtook her. *God! I'll be so glad when this is over.* Her belly made her look like a total freak. She wanted to have it and get it over with, but she was also scared to death of the birth. Having it at the house with Emma made her feel a little better, but still she knew it was going to really hurt. Anger flashed over her. *Screw those boys that did this to me! Forty-nine, fifty, fifty-one.* Her hands were stained red. The books said there could be a lot of blood. She hated blood, never even wanted to look when she had her period. She worked faster, finishing the last dozen. *Wow!* She felt like she was going to pass out. She put plastic wrap over the bowl and put it in the fridge. With heavy eyes she dumped the stems into the compost bucket on the floor. When she stood up she felt dizzy.

After washing her hands, she lumbered into the front room, lowering herself down into the big brown overstuffed sofa, noticing how her belly—a high round ball—stretched her tank top to its limit. The big white ceiling fan whirled above her. This was the coolest room in the whole house; it reminded her of an aquarium. Large trees shaded the old bubbled-glass windows. Green filtered light played on the walls. She sighed, settling into the cushions, in that moment feeling insulated and protected. She wondered if this was how the Thing felt inside her. She yawned, her eyes heavy. Through the screen door she heard the drone of a low-flying plane overhead, the hypnotic tick, tick, tick of the rainbird sprinklers, and the slow trickle of the creek passing by.

She dreamt that she was swimming in deep water. Weightless, her arms and legs fanned out, propelling her forward. She was searching for something in the cool, deep water. She passed through a forest of strange plants; the swaying leaves were shaped like hands, with long fingers pointing the way. *Where,* she thought, *where is it?* She kicked and glided, floating with the movement of the water. She swam deeper and deeper, feeling her small feet raise clouds of sand as she landed on the bottom.

As the water cleared, she saw a row of giant clam shells. Their great, white, ribbed humps all looked exactly alike. She waited, not knowing what to expect. She felt both afraid and curious. Then she noticed bubbles coming out of one of the shells. Its serrated jaws began to open. At first only a crack of black was visible, then slowly the shell opened more and more. There was something round inside. It moved toward the opening and floated out and upward. The pink thing suspended in the water was curled in on itself. Still floating, it stretched itself open.

"Here, I'm here!" she called, rising to meet it. As it came into her arms, she drew it closer. It tucked its soft head beneath her chin, and she whispered, "My baby, my baby."

Emma heaped freshly whipped cream over the strawberry short cake and put a spoon on each plate. "In my opinion, one should never eat something like this with a fork." She smiled and handed Cat a plate. "Let's go out on the porch; I think it's cooled down by now."

Cat waddled after her, and they settled on the big porch swing. In the orchard bats flitted in and out and over the apple trees, weaving through the welcomed dusk. They both relished the rich dessert in a contented silence. After putting her spoon on the plate and licking cream off her fingers, Emma said, "Well, that's quite a dream you had today. I appreciate you sharing it with me." Taking another bite, she asked, "What do you think it means?"

Cat felt nervous as she shifted her body and faced Emma. One of the horses out in the pasture called to another. Frogs began to bleat by the creek. "I don't know exactly. The strangest thing is, I've never been to the ocean. I don't even know how to swim, but it was so real, and I was really comfortable under the water." She bit off a piece of strawberry and swallowed it, waiting for the courage to tell Emma. She wiped her mouth with the napkin and laid it on the rise of her belly. "When I woke up I stayed on the couch for a long time, thinking about it and remembering it. For the first time since I knew I was pregnant, I thought of 'It' as a baby."

"I see," said Emma thoughtfully. Gray and white killdeer flew over the grass calling, *"Dee dee dee...Dee dee dee."*

The girl's voice was soft, her big dark eyes serious, "For the first time I actually considered not giving it up for adoption... you know? Maybe keeping it...I don't know how though. How could I take care of a baby, finish my senior year, and work?"

Emma moved the swing back and forth with her foot, "What about the circumstances, Cat? Does that bother you?"

"No, not anymore. Since the dream I've been feeling that the baby belongs to itself, no matter how...it came to be." A doe and fawn slipped through the fence, the fawn mimicking his mother's delicate steps.

"Do you see yourself here, or in Arizona?"

"Here...that is...if...?"

"Uh huh, but what about college?"

"Oh, I'm committed! I may have to do it slower, over time, maybe a junior college before university." She held her small hands out in front of her, "It is possible, right? Single mothers do get degrees, right?"

Emma nodded, but uncertain thoughts ran through her mind, mostly about her role in this venture. Would she be able to offer the girl and her baby the time, place, and energy? And help the girl complete her goals? She could hear Lilly telling her what a fool she was to trust the girl and to commit herself to this stranger. Even though she knew Cat would qualify for social services, she wondered if the girl would be too proud to accept them. If not, could she afford to support two more people? The cats found them and came up on the porch, purring around their ankles.

"I've been meaning to ask you, have you seen Sam lately?"

"Oh yeah, he's always up in my room. He sleeps under the bed when I'm not there."

Hmm? thought Emma. *Sam, who didn't like anyone, now lived in the library. Interesting.* Her mind went back to finding an answer for the girl, who really did seem sure about her decision to keep the child. What about Liam and her new involvement with him? Could their relationship handle the stresses of Emma letting the girl and baby stay with her? She suspected that Liam would support whatever decision she made.

In the end, it came down to the questions she *didn't* need to ask herself: Would Cat be a dedicated mother? Was she determined and strong enough to complete her educational goals? Could she, Emma, handle the stress and pressure of this kind of commitment? Since she felt that the answer to all these questions was "yes," she turned to Cat. "I've always wondered if the library was meant to be a nursery when the house was first built. You know...that small alcove by the window seat, a crib and rocking chair might fit nicely in there."

"Really? Really, you would let me stay? You believe I could do it? Be a good mother and work and go to school? Because if you believe in me, Emma...like you have so far...I think I could too!"

"Well, we have a lot to think and talk about. First things

first. It's going to happen fairly soon. Do you still want to have the birth here?"

"Yes, I do, no hospitals for me."

"Okay, but it's time to get ready. Have you read the books I gave you?"

"I've read them all," she said proudly, "Lamaze, LeBoyer; but my favorite was the *Calm and Peaceful* one. Even though the only two births I've ever seen were Jason and Kerry's baby and Candy's colt, they were the total opposite of peace and calm, more like intense and frantic. That's the book I liked best though, especially the part about the mind."

Emma laughed, "Intense and frantic, huh? Sometimes births are like that, but that's my favorite method too. The mind is an amazing tool. So what do you think? Shall we start practicing tomorrow so you'll be ready to have…," she paused, realizing that even she had become used to calling the child "It," "so you'll be ready to give birth to your baby?"

A few days before the due date the women gave Cat a shower. It took their minds off Briar, and gave them something else to think about and, of course, it was also an excuse to eat. Since it was unbearably hot by noon every day, they planned an evening party—a potluck dinner in the orchard. Cat, who was at first embarrassed, having never been the guest of honor at any event, relaxed into the moment. She helped Emma string white lights through the apple trees. They laid white cloths on the tables, and Cat had fun arranging bouquets of flowers she'd picked in the garden.

They prepared food all day: a curried egg salad with snips of chives and dill, a smoked salmon spread with red onions and cream cheese. Two gallons of lavender lemonade cooled in the old refrigerator outside. Emma sliced big thick tomatoes and layered them with fresh mozzarella and basil, then drizzled them with her garlic oil and vinegar.

All of the women had received the news of Cat's decision to keep the baby with a positive response except Lilly, who was still suspicious of the girl. At Emma's urging, she had grudgingly agreed to come. She and Clare arrived together, Lilly with fresh steaks to barbeque, and Clare with a carrot cake iced with lemon frosting. Emma noticed that Clare didn't take off her sunglasses. Midnight arrived with potato salad and cole slaw. Amy Lee and her mother, Eva, came into Emma's kitchen shyly. Amy Lee carried a present, and her mom two loaves of sourdough bread. Kerry, her arms full, handed six-month-old baby Jac to Emma, while everyone circled around admiring his blond curls and blue eyes.

They settled in the orchard, the women pretty and garden-tanned in their summer dresses. As they ate, they guessed if the baby was a boy or girl by the way Cat carried. They asked her what names she had chosen, giving their advice and thoughts about the role of motherhood. Cat looked radiant in a yellow blouse, her hair swept up. Emma had pinned some daisies around her thick bun.

After cake and ice cream, Cat opened presents: a soft quilt with fish on it from Clare; a gift certificate to Babies-R-Us in Bradford, from Lilly. Midnight had beaded a tiny cap used in Green River welcoming ceremonies. Amy Lee and her mother gave her a baby book. And Kerry, the most practical, a dozen little onesie outfits in pastel colors. Emma's gift was a car seat and stroller.

The sun had gone down, and Cat thanked them all. They batted at mosquitoes, sipping lemonade, their voices carrying across the fields and over the creek. To everyone's surprise, two male figures appeared in the shadows near the house. The women stopped talking and waited, curious.

"Hey," Liam called out, "dare we cross into the female ranks?"

"If you're brave enough," bantered his sister.

They heard Liam say, "You go first, Harry."

Harry came towards them, awkward and grinning, carrying something behind his back. He stepped up to Cat and bowed, then held out a small light blue halter in his hands. "This is for Lucky, and along with it comes help from me in training him. Briar spotted a horsewoman in you, ya know." Cat was overwhelmed and gave him a big smile.

Liam, who had disappeared around the corner of the house, came forward carrying a large heavy object covered with a blanket. Emma noticed how his biceps bulged as he set it down in front of the girl. It was about three feet long and two feet wide. Without saying anything, he uncovered it. The cradle had been carved from a single cedar log; the bed was scooped out and sanded smooth. The headboard curved up and was detailed with birds and butterflies. Along the sides he had carved rabbits and bears, frogs and flowers. On the footboard was a full moon with a gentle, smiling face. Everyone was speechless.

Finally Emma spoke, "Oh, Liam."

Cat got out of her chair and ran her hands over the soft wood. She rocked the cradle back and forth, then knelt down, tracing the birds and butterflies with her fingertips. "I don't know what to say...it's so beautiful." Liam beamed.

"There's cake and ice cream left," offered Midnight.

"Can't refuse that," Liam said, winking at Harry.

"Uh oh!" said Cat, a look of alarm on her face.

"What's wrong?" asked Lilly

"I can't seem to get up," said Cat, "could someone help me?" They all laughed as Liam lifted her to her feet.

Down at the Goldrush Cafe, a group of non-regulars gossiped about the impending birth.

"Heard she decided to keep it."

"Who would do that?"

"Someone who found a good thing. She'll stay with Emma, take advantage of her generosity, bleed her dry."

"I heard from Bill Plainsford's secretary's cousin that Jenny Brown might have left the girl her place."

"Well, Jenny only had them two, her drug addict whore daughter and the girl."

"Whose kid do you think it is? You know, they all did her, no matter what was said in court or who their fathers were."

"Let's start a pot—ten bucks to get in, and the winner takes all. I vote for Chuckie Gallegar. If the kid is fat and pasty white in spite of the mother's skin, we'll know its Chuck's."

"I think it'll be Calvin Drucker's. If the kid comes out blowing a blood alcohol level of eighty, it'll be Drucker's. In that family, they're born drunk and die drunk."

"Or, it could be the Butte City boy, ya know, the commissioner's kid? Heard he was expelled and had to go to school here."

"Doubt if it's the Ross kid; he wouldn't do something like that, I'm sure. They go to our church every Sunday."

"What the hell does that have to do with anything?"

"Word was that Indian kid was too drunk to get it up."

"I'll bet it's not any of 'em's kid. She came here pregnant, ready to scam. Come on, put in your money. Let's bet whose it is."

The baby knows. It sucks its thumb and presses its fat fingers into its palms and waits. The baby knows everything. Where it is coming from, why it is coming here to these people, why it is in this body, at this moment. The baby knows how the story of its conception will play out far into the future. The baby opens its eyes in the warm quiet dark and knows…that as soon as it is born, it will forget, forget it all.

Chapter Twenty-nine

Cat moaned, "How late am I...eight days?"

"A due date is just an estimation; the baby knows when to come."

"Well, it better be soon, or I'm going to die of a combination of gas and loss of sleep."

Emma shook out the sheet. "No mother sleeps at the end of her pregnancy. It's nature's way of getting you ready to be up all hours of the night. Here, help me put this sheet on. It's important to have a nice bed for birthing."

"I thought it was messy. These sheets are going to get wrecked, aren't they?"

"We'll put a plastic cover over them." Emma plumped the pillows and set them upright against the headboard. "It's pretty, don't you think? The lavender color with the quilts? I'm glad we have two sets. This room has changed from a library into a bedroom-nursery with a lot of books." Emma smiled.

"Emma," said the girl, "you know so much about birth and everything. Why didn't you have children?"

Emma walked over to the cradle, now lined with a soft mattress and blankets. "Well, Cat," she said pausing, looking out the window, "I did have a child...once."

"Oh, god! I'm so sorry, I shouldn't have asked."

"No, it's alright, I don't mind talking about it."

"Was it with Liam? I've heard the women say you two were together in high school."

"No, no, it was after that. I was living in San Francisco, where I was raised, finishing up midwifery school. I didn't expect it, but I met a nice man, Ronnie. We got married and had a child, a beautiful little guy; his name was Theo. He was two-and-a-half years old when the accident happened. Both he and Ronnie were killed instantly...I was driving the car."

Cat's voice was small, lost in the heavy silence, "Oh, Emma, I'm so sorry."

"Well, don't be, sweetheart. It happened a long time ago, and hopefully I've transformed the pain of it into something useful. Speaking of which, have you listened to your relaxation CDs today?"

"No, not yet."

Emma sat on the bed, "Anything you need to talk about? Share with me? Any questions? Comments? Fears?"

"Well, there are two things I thought of. More than anything, during the birth, I don't want anyone to see me...you know...naked."

"Well, I'll keep you covered as much as I can. You know it will be mostly you and me in the room, but at the end I'll need other hands to help. Dr. Drew will most likely be on vacation, but the women will be here."

"Emma, if I have complications, I'll go to the hospital in Butte City, right?"

"Yes."

"I hate hospitals...after...you know."

"Well, we want what's safest for you and the baby. Hopefully the birth will be here. We can plan and imagine how we want it, but birth is like a dance, and we don't always know the choreography...until we're in it. Anything else?"

"I'm scared that it won't come out, you know, that I won't open enough or something."

"Your body and baby know what to do, and I can assure you that no baby has ever stayed in there."

Cat smiled, "Okay, and then the last thing is, Emma, what if, what if…I don't…I don't love it? You know, right away, or ever?"

"Oh, honey, once in awhile bonding might take some time. But this is *your* baby, Cat, and becoming a mother is such a powerful, natural force. I predict you will not be able to let it out of your arms or take your eyes off its little face."

"Okay," said the girl, sighing, "you always make me feel better. Thank you. I'll lie down now and listen to my CD. What's the name of it again?" Out of all of Emma's music, she'd chosen a classical piece.

"Mozart."

"I'm calm; I'm relaxed; I'm confident," said Cat, laughing.

"Good girl! I'm going down to see a few patients; rest now, okay?"

Liam and Emma sat in the shade of the cherry tree. A fine spray from the sprinklers floated above the garden.

"So, I just came by to say, 'Hey.' I'm on my way to Butte City to pick up some parts. Wow! The garden sure looks great," he took her hand, "and so do you."

"It's wild isn't it? Always gets away from me by August. Don't you think it's like an impressionist painting—the way the herbs and flowers and vegetables all mingle? Can I interest you in some zucchini? or tomatoes? I'm in canning hell right now."

"No zucchini, Midnight dropped some off yesterday, and I don't even like the taste of it." He leaned in and kissed her,

"But I like the taste of you." They stood up then and held each other. "Tonight, you still coming over to my place?" he whispered into her ear.

Cat appeared at the gate, still in her nightgown. "Oh, sorry," she said, embarrassed.

"It's okay, honey, what's up?"

"Can I talk to you for a minute?" she asked, with a look of confusion on her face.

"Hi, Cat, I was just leaving. Okay, Em, see you tonight," Liam called over his shoulder. Emma faced the girl.

"I have cramps, and I just went to the bathroom and all this water came out."

"Was it clear?"

"Yes, there was a lot of it."

"Well, your water broke. That's great! It means you'll have the baby in the next twenty-four hours or so. Let's go get ready." She took the girl's hand, "You'll probably want a shower."

She froze, "Emma, I'm scared."

"I know, honey. While you're in the shower, talk to the baby, tell it how ready you are to hold it, ask it to come nice and easy. Go on up; I'm going to pick a birthday bouquet for your room."

As Emma's hands French-braided Cat's untameable hair, she thought about how, in a few hours, the girl's childhood would be over. Not that she'd had much of one. Perhaps raising the baby would help her experience some of the innocence she'd lost.

All afternoon her labor progressed, coming on irregularly at first. It was hot outside, so Cat paced around the cool house, as Emma suggested she keep walking and moving as long as possible. Emma called the women, who would arrive later. They weren't sure about Lilly, who was taking cows up to the mountains. By six-thirty, Cat had to stand still and breathe with her contractions, as she and Emma had practiced.

"Out, out, out, let your belly be a balloon."

Midnight arrived with a casserole and fry bread. She gave Cat a hug and told her that the native way was to squat as much as possible, and that she was in the best of hands with Emma. Clare came later carrying her camera. Cat had asked her to take pictures after the birth. Emma noticed that her make-up didn't quite cover the greenish-yellow bruise under her eye.

Clare was excited, "Look at those flowers! I'm going to take a picture; maybe I can paint from it."

"My grandmother believed that each flower had its own quality," Emma told them. "The roses are for love and unity, rosemary for remembrance, sage for strength, daisies for innocence, lavender for calming, and of course baby's breath for new life."

Cat grimaced, "Are there any flowers for 'hurts like hell?'"

Emma smiled. "Alright, how about some juice? It's important to keep hydrated. Clare, Midnight, let me show you the ropes. I've laid the things out that we'll need, and I'll be letting you know what to bring upstairs when the time comes. Here's Dr. Drew's phone number in case I need to call him."

Cat bent over and grabbed the back of a chair and began breathing. Emma moved closer, "Relax your hands now, just be loose all over, That's it." When Cat took a breath, Emma said, "Getting stronger, huh?" The girl nodded. "Why don't we think about going upstairs soon. Do you ladies want to see the birthday room?" Emma picked up the vase of flowers. They had started up the creaking stairs when Cat had to stop midway and breathe. "They're getting closer; that's a good sign. It's time to get you settled."

Clare and Midnight admired the room's transformation. The bed was piled high with pillows, and the turned-down quilt showed the new lavender sheets. Sheer white curtains hung in the windows, and the cradle and rocking chair waited in the alcove. Emma set the flowers on the dresser.

"Emma, something's coming out of me."

"That's normal; it's probably just fluid. Shall we light the candles and put on your music?" Cat nodded as she sat down on the bed. "I'm going to check you too." After Clare and Midnight left, Emma examined the girl, who was stoic and kept her eyes squeezed shut. "Cat, honey, you're a good five centimeters, halfway there." The girl groaned, then started breathing with concentration.

She labored throughout the night. Around midnight a full moon sailed over the house, and although she was tired, the girl remained strong and focused. Emma crawled into the big bed and Cat leaned against her, resting her head on Emma's chest in between each contraction. After a few hours the contractions were back to back, and Cat became agitated.

"I can't...breathe through them anymore..."

"This is good. The intensity means you'll have the baby soon," Emma said, getting down from the bed. "Look at me. Now, when one comes, you'll let everything go, all your muscles loose and relaxed, holding no tension anywhere. Blow out your breath nice and easy. I'll be here with you to remind you. I'm going to listen to the heartbeat now." Emma placed the fetal monitor on her belly. "It's perfect, strong and steady."

"Okay, here comes one," said Cat, closing her eyes.

Emma wiped her forehead with a cool cloth and held her hand. "That's it, easy, easy, up and up, focus on your breath. Good, good." The girl opened her eyes. "Honey, you're doing such a good job! At this rate we'll have a baby by morning."

By 4:30 in the morning, Cat was in hard labor, too antsy to stay in bed. She wandered the room between contractions, then stood and swayed with the pain. Emma held her. "Good, good, swaying is good; you're bringing the baby's head down with gravity."

Cat's concentration broke and she yelled out, "Come out, you Little Thing! Oh, Emma, I'm so tired, I can't do it anymore. OUCH! SHIT! SHIT! I can't! I can't!"

"Okay, come on and lay down, let's check you."

"Emma, I can't! I don't want to! I hate them! Help me! Help me!" The girl squirmed on the bed.

Emma rang the little bell to summon Midnight and Clare, who hurried up the stairs. "Okay, Cat, you're complete, the baby's head is right there. Now breathe, breathe."

She turned to the women, "I'll need the warm olive oil, the water, and Clare, could you lay out the bulb syringe and the scissors? Leave them in the sterile pack. Midnight, check the oxygen. Turn it on, do you hear a hiss?...good. I'll need you both here from now on."

"I'll be right back," said Midnight.

"Emma, I'm so hot! I'm burning!"

"Clare, open the windows, okay? And turn on the overhead fan." Midnight returned. "Give her some ice chips in between contractions. Alright, Cat, the baby's head is starting to crown. Do you want to see?" The girl nodded. "Clare, bring the mirror."

"Oh, my god! It really is a...head."

"Now, I'm going to massage warm oil around the opening to help it stretch, so lay back. Here, Clare, you support this leg; Midnight, hold the other. Okay, honey, just slow and easy. Sit up a little bit, put your chin on your chest. Feel one coming? Okay, breathe your baby down and out...that's good, good...Now rest and take a nice big breath until you feel the pressure again. You might feel some stinging; it'll be fine, just breathe through it. We're almost there."

Suddenly the girl thrashed, pulling her legs down. "What?

What is it, Cat?" Emma asked.

"I've got to get up. I'm so hot!" She raised herself up and swung her legs over the side of the bed. She stood up and ripped the nightgown up over her head, then stood there stark naked. *So much for modesty*, thought Emma.

"Clare, spread out that blanket on the floor, please. Okay, Cat, come here. Go ahead and squat, Midnight will hold you from behind." While she was in the throes of a contraction, Emma went down on her knees to the floor. "Okay, push when you feel like it." She had her hands cupped over the baby's head when it popped out. "Okay, Cat, the head's out, got to get you back on the bed now. Midnight, Clare, support her arms, that's it. Lie back on the bed."

Emma's hand circled the little neck, "No cord, good, okay, one more push, and the baby will be here." Cat groaned and the baby slid out onto the bed.

"Clare, the syringe. Well, hi there, little one." She suctioned the infant's mouth; the baby didn't cry, but was obviously breathing, its little chest moving up and down. Cat collapsed back against the pillow, her eyes far away.

"Cat, look, let's see what it is." Emma turned the dark slippery body over. "Clare, the blanket and hat, please. It's a girl!" She turned the baby back over and rubbed her gently with the blanket, then wrapped her in it. "Look at all that hair, Cat; she's so cute. Here, go see your mommy." Emma put the baby into Cat's arms, as a look of shocked wonder crossed her face.

"Let's get the placenta; I'm going to press on your belly now." The girl winced. "I know, it's almost over, okay, here it is," and the placenta slid out. "Clare, give me that basin. Cat, you were incredible! What an amazing job you did!"

"Really!" said Clare, "a great job!"

Midnight's eyes were glued to the baby. "Oh, my god!" she exclaimed. "*Ain na wa ha cawa!*"

"What?" questioned Emma.

Cat was ruffling the baby's thick damp hair with her hand.

"Look at her hair!" said Midnight. The child's hair was a bright red copper. Midnight was laughing. "Look at her face; oh, my god!" She danced around the room. "*Ain na wa ha cawa!* Gratitude! Gratitude! Old Ones."

"Let me see you," said Cat, holding the baby up to face her. "Your hair sticks up all over. It's so red you look like a little woodpecker!"

"You can do your DNA swab test or whatever!" cried Midnight, "but that child is the spitting image of Julien! Oh, my god! Old Wing was right!"

"This is how Julien looked?" asked Cat.

"Exactly!" said Midnight, "wait until you see his baby pictures."

Cat smiled then, and just like in her dream, she tucked the baby's soft head up under her chin and closed her eyes.

They tidied up the room as light grew at the windows. Someone came up the stairs. Lilly put her head in the doorway.

"Hey, come in!" said Emma, "look who's here."

Lilly moved towards the bed where Cat was nursing the baby. "How did it go? I couldn't get here sooner. Runaway cows, a whole other story. Oh, it's so little! Hi, Cat...Wow!"

Cat said, "Want to see her?" She moved the infant away from her breast so Lilly could see her face. She was asleep, her long lashes lay on her fat brown cheeks, her rosebud mouth was still sucking, and her hair, a wild red thatch, stuck out all over.

"Oh, she's beautiful! She looks like, um...doesn't she look like...?" She searched their faces; the women could barely contain themselves.

"Yeah!" said Clare, "go on! Who do you think she looks like?"

"She looks like..." Lilly guessed, "I don't know, but so familiar. Not like Cat though, hmm, all that red hair…?" Suppressed laughter traveled up through Midnight's body and exploded.

"We think," said Emma, her eyes on the infant's face, "that not only did Cat become a mother today, but that maybe Midnight has become a grandmother."

Autumn

Chapter Thirty

Emma brushed dirt from the overripe, cracked carrots. *A treat for the horses*, she thought, tucking the carrots into the bottom of her basket. After the intense summer heat, September had arrived as if a dimmer switch had been turned down. Warm weather continued, but cooler nights and chilly mornings insinuated autumn. The garden had overflowed all at once, yielding tomatoes, corn, cabbages, potatoes, kale, and the biggest crop of green beans ever. Red, pink and orange zinnias blazed, and sunflowers big as pie plates were seed-picked by numerous flocks of gypsy birds.

Broad-leafed trees glowed golden at their edges. The orchard hung heavy with fruit; another month and picking would be underway. The sixty or so mature trees put out hundreds of pounds of apples. She loved this abundance, but picking and boxing them required so much time that she usually just welcomed neighbors and friends who wanted to pick them. Harry would deliver many boxes of apples to the senior centers in the valley and Butte City. Perhaps Julien could help out this fall. He had already cut up the winter-storm-downed trees in the pasture, where the air was filled with the sour reek of fresh-cut oak.

Next week hunting season would begin, and Emma's usual

mixed feelings surfaced. Men dressed in camouflage, their big trucks pulling RVs fancier than houses, came to the valley in droves. They hunted the large docile herbivores from jeeps and pickups set up with armchairs in the beds of the vehicles — surely no contest. The men were often alcohol brazen, and it wasn't uncommon for them to miss the killing shot, wounding a too-small buck, and leaving the poor animal to limp into the forest and die a slow death. The locals, on the other hand, were conscientious and adept. Their families truly needed the meat, and they were skilled at cutting, freezing, and making jerky without wasting any part of the deer. Well, she'd have to make sure the **No Trespassing** signs were up and in good shape.

Emma's practice had been busy with an epidemic of stomach flu and sports physicals. There had been an unusual number of births, which she attributed to the big snowstorm in January. Cat had returned to school half day and seemed to be handling her studies and her role of motherhood well. She was in love with the infant, as was Midnight, who came to the house four mornings a week to care for baby Ruby. It was a relief that the child was here and thriving. Even Liam was captivated by the little girl and asked to hold her each time he visited. Harry, too, was sweet on her. But Julien, although he still worked on the farm, had shown no interest. Liam, who at times had a gift for clear logic, told Emma that a relationship with the child might not be a choice Julien would make. On the other hand, her relationship with Liam had blossomed, and they took pleasure in making up for all the lost years.

Life had finally settled and she felt content. Yet in the few quiet moments she had to herself she often fell into a bottomless grief, missing Briar. The emptiness felt like a hole in her solar plexus. Briar's name often came up when the Yee Haws gathered, and there would be that moment as if they were waiting for her to come through the door in all her tall, gorgeous elegance, saying, "Jeez Louise, ladies, sorry I'm late."

What is this death reality, she wondered, *this great inevitable absence. Just...gone. One moment we are here and the next somewhere else, with no clue of how, or why, let alone a glimpse of what we might become...or not.* She guessed that the puzzle of it, the fact that humans hadn't figured it out, affirmed that this knowledge was perfectly and intentionally withheld. Everything reminded her of Briar—early morning sun coming up over the Eastside Mountains, anything chocolate, even Mav. She recalled how Briar had helped train him. Passionate, fearless, patient, always seeing everything from the animal's point of view. *Mary Mother of God,* she thought, *I hope there is some reason, some divine logic for the world to be without her.*

She picked up the basket of vegetables and closed the garden gate. On her way to the back door, she noticed a trail of crushed grapes. Raccoons. She'd heard them rummaging through the vines the night before. The Concords were still sour, but the masked bandits probably didn't care. She'd have to get out the juicer/steamer next month. She hoped they'd leave her enough for juice. Bear had followed her, and as he waited by the door she noticed how stiffly he moved. His arthritic hips had gotten worse; she wondered if this might be *his* last winter. She pushed open the heavy dutch door and saw Cat sitting at the table, a look of concentration on her face. The baby slept in the little woven basket that Midnight had made and decorated with shells and flicker feathers. Emma set the vegetables on the counter. "Homework?" she asked.

"No, look." The girl laid a pink birth announcement on the table. "I wondered if I should do this...you know, under the circumstances. But then, I decided, why not? She deserves to be welcomed like any baby. And this picture is so cute." She smoothed the edge of the card.

Emma leaned over the table. In the picture the baby's wild red hair was caught up in a bow; below the card read:

Caterina Ramos is proud to announce
the birth of her daughter
Ruby Dawn Ramos
Arrived August 9, 1999, 5:04 a.m.
6 pounds, 3 ounces, 18 inches long

"These are pretty, Cat! She's changed so much already. I love the flower border around the picture."

"Thanks, I found it on the computer. I'm sending one to Kerry and Jason, one to Amy Lee's family, one to the Monsoons, one to the library ladies in Phoenix, of course the Yee Haws, and Liam and Harry, one to my mom, and one to the high school."

Emma raised her eyebrows at the thought of the school secretary opening the announcement. "Hmm, how did the phone call with your mother go last night?"

Cat put the cards in a neat pile and squared their edges. "Alright I guess. She was surprised to hear from me. She sounded really far away. I think she was in some kind of glass booth at the prison. She was quiet when I told her about Ruby. I didn't tell her how I got pregnant. She seemed happy for us, said she was glad I was safe, and to say 'Hi' to Midnight and to thank you...She said she's been clean for 10 months. Well, we'll see." She glanced up at the clock and grabbed her backpack. "I've gotta go." She bent and kissed the baby. "Tell Midnight there's breast milk in the fridge."

RJ looked both ways down the hallway—no one around. It was a few minutes until lunch. He needed to get to his locker and snort another hit of crank. He had to have it more and more or else he got those weird flashes of light behind his eyes or his hands started shaking. He didn't eat or sleep much, but he got off on the high, the way power seemed to flow through his veins making his body feel like a superhero. Even the football coach had commented on his improvement. *Ha! If he only knew why.*

Mostly he craved the way it made his mind feel, like speeding bullets, the thoughts faster than shit and right on target. And horny? Oh, man! He opened his locker, found the old aspirin bottle in the back, and slipped it into his pocket. In the bathroom he snorted it in a stall, came out, washed his hands, checked his nose for powder. He looked at his watch—exactly 12:01. The bell would ring in two minutes.

He was going to find Cat today. He knew she'd come back to school. He'd seen glimpses of her between classes, but only in the mornings. After school he couldn't find hide nor hair of her. He dreamt about her and fantasized about her, the way he'd felt standing over her, his knife poised to slit those tight, tight black leather pants. He felt a rush and stiffened, pulling his long sweat shirt down low. *She deserved it again.* He walked the hall and all of a sudden he got it. She was only there half day! That's why he never saw her after school. He'd heard she'd kept the kid. The noon bus came from the elementary school, parked in front of the office. *Oh yeah, busted!* He walked past the office, giving the school secretary a big ol' RJ smile. *Stupid fat bitch.*

Cat shifted in her seat. Mr. Robbins droned on and on about the industrial revolution while her eyes grew heavier and heavier. "The industrial revolution changed our society and the way we humans saw the world." She caught herself nodding off and threw her head back. That was close. Yesterday she did fall asleep in PE, leaning back against the gym wall. She wasn't allowed to play volleyball for another two weeks. Ruby still woke up to be nursed at least two or three times a night. Sometimes Cat couldn't go back to sleep after she laid her down, so she worked on the homework she didn't have time for after school. She was so exhausted. But looking at her baby's face made up for it all. Emma had offered to give Ruby a bottle for one of the feedings, but she was determined to handle it herself.

She yawned while jotting down the dates for quizzes and tests that Mr. Robbins had written on the board. Her stomach growled. Breakfast had been only a bite of toast. Emma told her she needed to eat more because nursing burned up an extra six hundred calories a day. Her mouth watered, wondering what Emma had made for lunch. She caught the snotty look Carrie Ross gave her across the room. Her brother Hubert was there at the rape, and she had taken it upon herself to send hate towards Cat ever since school started. Pretty much the whole school was shocked she'd come back. Amy Lee had remained her loyal friend, but even she had lost friends over her relationship with Cat. Cat guessed that just her being at school, still in the valley, reminded them all of that night. *Well, too bad!*

The period ended; she gathered up her books, notebook, and backpack and headed towards the office. The hallway was full of kids at their lockers and people going to the cafeteria or heading out to the waterfall to smoke or whatever. She passed the office window, shifted the heavy backpack to her other shoulder, and pushed the big door open. She sat down to the side of the top step. There were still almost ten minutes before the noon bus came, so she took out her calculus homework and started doing problems. If she could finish her homework today, she could spend more time with Ruby and maybe even help Emma with chores. She wondered how her baby was and couldn't wait to hold her. After finishing the rest of the problems—math was easy!—she put the pencil and notebook in her backpack and yawned. She stared out at the street and watched groups of kids walking to the store or diner. She didn't hear him but felt someone come up close behind her. She turned around, her stomach tumbling.

RJ glared at her with a sick smile. "Caught ya!…Well, looky here, if it ain't Mama Cat. Weren't you in that old timey singing group? The Mamas and the Papas? And just where is the Papa today? Off to some powwow or other?" He reached down and grabbed her arm. "How's your little rape baby?"

She looked to her right and left but no one was around. The bus wouldn't be there for another few minutes. Scared as she was of him, she stood up, hefted the backpack, and faced him. She tried to pull away. "None of your business!" she spat out. "Let go of me!"

He gripped her tighter. "That's not what you told me on Halloween, little girl. You never said 'let go of me.' You told me, 'more, more, do it more and…harder…RJ…harder.' Don't you remember how horny you were after you took that drug you'd brought along?" She yanked away with all her might, but he was too strong.

He paused, lowered his voice, his eyes scary and intense. "Is your itsy, teeny rape baby just so cute? I'd like to see her, you know, hold her, see if she looks like me. Maybe throw her up in the air and not catch her, ya know, drop her and watch her little baby brains splat all over the ground. Come on, Mama Cat, share your rape baby with me, pleeese!" The bus belched out exhaust as it turned the corner. "If you ever want me to rape you again let me know. Or I could come to that farm where you live and kidnap your little one when nobody's looking." He let go of her arm as the bus pulled into the parking lot. "See ya later, slut."

He sauntered off, turning once to look back at her, grinning. She rubbed her arm and climbed into the bus. The kin-

299

dergarteners were wild and loud, bouncing on their seats. She rushed to the back and sat down, her whole body trembling. She slipped her calculus book out of the pack and held it up to her face so the bus driver couldn't see her in the rearview mirror. She couldn't catch her breath, and big stifled sobs were stuck in her chest. *Breathe*, she told herself, *like during the birth, breathe.*

Outside, alfalfa fields were littered with fresh cut hay. She heard the trill of redwing blackbirds through the open window. The kids had settled down, but her mind was going crazy. What if he did do something to Ruby? His horrible threats repeated themselves. *"I'd like to hold her, throw her up in the air and not catch her, drop her, watch her little baby brains splat..."* Fear overtook her and she felt like screaming. Her feet twitched inside her shoes, her knees knocked together, her stomach cramped, and she felt like she had to go to the bathroom right then and there. *Breathe*, she told herself again. She closed her eyes and saw his scary face before her. *He's insane*, she thought, and the truth of it made her teeth chatter. *Totally, sickly insane.*

What should she do? How could she protect her baby? Should she tell Emma? Should she tell the school? If she did, would anyone believe her? Probably not, since they didn't even believe her about the rape. The bus stopped to let kids off every few minutes. Now there were only a few left, and she stared at a cute little girl with blonde hair. She was laughing at the boy across from her, and Cat suddenly pictured Ruby in five years. *God help me*, she thought, *please, I don't know what to do.* Tears slid down the page of her book. *I hate him, I hate him, I hate him.*

Chapter Thirty-one

Mr. Justice opened the door of his room and peered out, craning his long neck to look down the hallway in one direction, then the other. He retied the blue-striped seersucker belt of his robe and gave the knot a good tug. They tried to get him to put on clothes every day, every day for four and a half years now, but every day he refused. When his son had him locked up in Wrenwood, Mr. Justice told him that was it! He would waste away there. Die inside. So what was the use of putting on clothes when he'd spend all day in bed!

For forty years he'd gotten up at 5:30 a.m., showered, shaved, and put on a clean white shirt, slacks with the seam pressed exactly down the center of each leg, a suit coat and tie, and his polished and buffed wingtip shoes. Sales was his game, and he never regretted a day of it. Out in the fresh morning air, the city still asleep—well, it was like you owned the world. He'd start up his car, always a Chevy sedan, hit the freeway, and begin his rounds. His briefcase and order books lay on the passenger seat next to him like a passport to success. Wholesale liquor was his trade, and being a sociable man, he enjoyed stopping and chatting with his clients, whether they were in upscale neighborhoods in downtown Sacramento or tucked away in the back alleys of poorer neighborhoods. Forty years; and he was an award winner, always receiving the prize for most new accounts at his company's annual Christmas dinner.

He stood still and listened, but there wasn't anybody around. He stepped out, closed the door quietly, and turned stealthily down the hall. Today he was on a mission, one that had taken a few weeks of planning, and he was looking forward to seeing the look on Dora's face when he accomplished it. His room was on the first floor; his son Bob had insisted on that, since in the last few years of working, when he began losing time, or his way back home, he had often been found on the top story of some parking garage without his car or briefcase, teetering at the edge of a concrete ledge, peering down at the choked traffic below. After he'd been reported as homeless or demented, they'd find his wallet in the left breast pocket of his blue suit coat and call Bob to come and get him.

"Dad, what were you doing up there all day? Where is your car?" his boy would ask, his eyes scared and sad.

"I don't know," he'd answer. "It's just that I can think better the higher up I am."

He smelled bacon cooking and heard the breakfast crew clanging pots in the big stainless steel kitchen. Right after he passed by, one of the windowed double doors swung open. He ducked around the corner just in time, so the girl setting tables in the dining room didn't see him. He ran down the empty hallway, his navy blue slippers slapping his heels like a friendly follower. As he passed Mrs. Ravelli's door, he heard her screaming and swearing like she did all day long, "Shit. Stop! Damn you, bastard! Get away from me!" Then he heard the soft voice of the female attendant trying to calm her down.

Only a few more steps and his favorite escape route to the outside world would be visible. The big orange metal door with a sign above it that said EXIT ONLY came into view. This was the way he always got outside; no one ever noticed that the door could be propped open just a smidgen by the slim bar of soap he kept in his pocket. He looked both ways again, gently pushed the metal bar ever so quietly, and opened the door. It used to squeak loudly, but he'd snuck into the janitor's supply room and sprayed it with WD-40 last year.

The little carton of milk in his other pocket bulged and almost fell out when he bent to put the bar of soap between the edge of the door and the jamb. *Whoops.* He caught it and tucked it back in. *Can't lose that,* he thought, slipping out into the warm autumn air.

Dora, fed, groomed, and dressed, sat in the yellow velour rocker. The attendant, Miriam, had left with a cheerful goodbye and a promise to look in on her later. Morning sun streamed through the window. Her oak tree's leaves were a faint crimson . Deep quiet filled the room, and she sank into it like warm water. She let her left foot slowly rock the chair, back and forth, back and forth, the rhythm lulling and hypnotic. The attendants always wanted her to watch the toaster, or listen to the refrigerator, but there was nothing good on anyway. She couldn't read any more; the words—an army of enemies—marched all over the page and hid their meaning from her. And mangozines—the colored pictures hurt her eyes, and they were all perfumey, the pages sticky and sharp. No, she loved the quiet, the nothing. Dumbtimes she fished for companions, but mostly no. Mr. Rightness from downstairs came to talk, but he never wore clothes and that made her uneven.

Mr. Justice circled the giant garbage bins calling softly, "Here kitty, kitty, come on, come and get some milk." He waited, knowing the kittens were wary and would not make a sound or show themselves until the mother cat saw his blue seersucker robe and told them it was alright. He retrieved the plastic bowl he hid in the bushes nearby, took the milk carton out of his pocket, and poured it all out.

"Come on, kitties, it's okay." The black mother came out from under the bin. She looked good for a wild cat, and he felt satisfied that the milk and meat he sneaked to them from his meals were helping. Not quite tame, the mother cat slipped beneath his outstretched hand and drank the milk. Her three kittens let him hold them once they ate. One by one, a striped, a calico, and the runt, a silver-gray, gathered around the bowl. He felt so happy inside, watching them lap the milk hungrily. *Useful,* he thought, *I've done something useful today.* A delivery truck pulled in behind the kitchen, so he crouched in the bushes. He could still see the cats, the mother now cleaning herself, licking her paw and rubbing it over her ears and head.

Dora heard a soft knock on the door. The attendants never knocked, just came right in. Usually they were already telling her why they were there before they were even in her room. She waited, another knock, then another. She watched the door open slowly and saw a man in night clothes shut it behind him.

"Ralph?...Ralph, is that you?" she asked.

"No, Dora, it's me, Mr. Justice. How are you today, my dear lady? Did you sleep in the well last evening?"

Dora looked at him. *Why was Ralph in his PJs?*

"Dora, I brought you something. Remember how I told

you about my project, the one outside by the garbage bins?"

"The garbage man comes on Thursday, Ralph! The cans are full, so don't forget." She rocked faster in the chair, sighing with indignation and dropping her nervous hands into her lap.

He walked closer to her and knelt down on the thick carpet. She saw him reach into his pocket. A silver furry thing was in the palm of his hand.

"I told you, Ralph, to set the traps. The barn is full of mice, and Clare and Lilly keep forgetting to do it." She heard a tiny sound and leaned forward. The rat in Mr. Rightness's palm did it again, then raised its head. She saw the littlest face, sleek and silver, tiny ears set wide and downward on its head. It opened its pink mouth and yawned, its thread-thin whiskers twitching. She reached for it gently, taking it in her two hands. "Oh, Ralph, a cattin. It's so adored. Where did you find it? In the barn?"

Mr. Justice watched her face soften and open, heard her voice crooning to it. "You keep it for a while, Dora. Its belly is full of milk so it will sleep in your lap. I'll come get it later after lunch." He heard the voice of the Activities Director on the intercom announcing the day's activities. "I've gotta go." He stood up and walked to the door. Turning and looking back, he saw the kitten curled in her lap; he could hear its tranquil purr.

Dora's head was bowed. She said, "*Felus Catus*, any of the Felidae family. Carnivorous, usually solitary and nocturnal mammals, such as the domestic cat, lion, tiger, leopard, jaguar, cougar, wild cat, lynx or cheetah…"

He walked to the door, pulled his robe over his shoulders, retied the sash. He glanced at Dora once more. *Useful*, he thought. He opened the door slowly, peered down the hallway in both directions and, since the coast was clear, made a run for it.

Emma watched Liam pull the flatbed truck loaded with hay through the gate, then closed it behind him. Mav, Candy, and the Appaloosa colt Lucky came running, whinnying, and excited. "Oh yes, we've got the groceries," Liam told them from the truck window. He drove the short way to the barn and parked.

Mav walked next to Emma. She ran her fingers through his long black mane. "You need a brushing, boy." Thunderheads, eerily imprinted by sheet lighting, crackled overhead. The colt jumped and ran ahead of his mother. The horses gathered around the truck.

Liam got out and stood there laughing at the way they tried to tear hay from the tightly bound bales. "Not getting much, are you?" He gripped the ties on one of the bales with his gloved hands and pulled it off the truck, letting it fall to the ground. Reaching in his pocket for his knife, he sliced the three lengths of twine and the bale gave way, splitting into several flakes. "Here you go, beasts." He scattered it in front of the horses. "There, maybe you won't bother me while I unload the rest and stack it." The horses chewed contentedly as a few raindrops fell on their dusty coats.

Emma came closer to Liam. "Oh, you are such a nice guy; look at how happy they are!"

"Yeah, well, I aim to please, you know." He reached out and brushed her cheek with his gloved hand. It made her shiver under her jacket. He lifted her chin up towards his face and kissed her. His full lips were hot against hers. He put his arms around her waist and pulled her towards him. When their bodies touched she felt him hard against her. "Oh no, Ms. Cassady, you've managed to distract me again." He moved back. "Now take your wanton self and stand over there before I ravage you and forget what I came here to do." She laughed and obeyed, stepping back towards the barn door.

"There's four tons, Em. That ought to keep your charges fat and happy over the winter." He reached into the truck cab for hay hooks. Emma watched him unbutton his cuffs and roll up his sleeves. His hard, muscular arms contracted as he gripped the hooks, leaned forward, and in one swift motion stabbed the hooks into the ends of a bale. He lifted it, his biceps straining against his flannel shirt. "It's a really good crop of grass hay. Aren't you going to help me?" For a minute she didn't know if he was serious or not. His face broke into a wide grin as he saw her hesitation. "Of course I'm joking," he smiled down at her.

"Well, good, because I'd rather watch you."

"That right?" he said.

It took him awhile to lift the bales and stack them in the barn. She watched him and loved him, amazed that he was there in front of her. Thunder boomed and lightning splayed electric fingers across the darkening sky.

"Well, there you are, my lady—grown, delivered and stacked for the well being of your ravenous steeds."

She flirted back, "Thank you, sir, what do I owe you for services?" The air crackled with static; a nearby boom of thunder scattered the horses.

He eyed her up and down, stepped in and kissed her mouth. "I suppose you could pay me in trade. I've been known to be open to barter and such."

As their bodies met, the kisses progressed from mouths to necks to wrists to eyelids. When he found her breasts under her jacket, she sighed. He picked her up and carried her into the barn. Without setting her down, he kicked the loose new-mown hay across the floor into a pile. His strong arms still held her as he took a horse blanket from a rafter and laid it on the floor. When he set her down, she slipped off her shoes and let her pants fall. Her jacket and blouse came off slowly. Liam, never taking his eyes off her, undressed, tossing his pants and shirt over his boots.

The horse blanket spread across the hay made a love nest for them. They held each other, still thrilled by the silken contact of their skin. She stroked him, tracing circles around his mouth, and he bit her gently on the neck. He ran his fingers through her hair and smoothed it back from her forehead, then kissed her faint freckles and even the delicate lines around her eyes. His tongue found her ear and circled the spiral interior. He looked into her face and saw that she was lost, moaning, begging him to take her.

"Not yet, Sweetheart, not yet," he teased her, running his hands across her belly and down her thighs. They turned belly to belly. They kissed, their tongues darting fire. Breathing fast, sweat soaked, they slid over and under one another. Their wild urgency and excited cries peaked with the sound of thunder and hard rain pounding the tin roof.

Afterward, timeless and floating, spent in each other's arms, they lay there, peaceful. Emma turned to spoon him, then burst out giggling.

"What? What's so funny?"

"Look," she pointed. Mav's big face was framed in a paneless window. Rainwater dripped from his forelock and mane as his curious eyes stared down at them. Emma shook her finger at him, "Maverick! What are you doing there?"

They broke up laughing as the horse stuck his head further in the window and nodded up and down, his lips curled in a toothy grin. Liam quickly covered them up with the horse blanket, which made them laugh even harder. He rose up on one elbow and told the horse, "Oh, I see how it is! You equine lech, you old voyeur."

Chapter Thirty-two

Emma lifted the scalding jars out of the water bath and placed them on a towel. "Fifty-two, fifty-three, fifty-four," she counted. Feathered dill and garlic cloves floated around the green beans. "Well, this is the last of them." Midnight, decked out in one of Emma's flowered aprons, screwed the lid onto the vinegar bottle and swept the dill stems across the kitchen counter and into the compost bucket.

Cat sat at the table, Ruby asleep in her arms. "Midnight, would you hold her while I go to the bathroom?"

"Oh, I think I can handle that. Come here, Little Flicker, come to grandma." She tucked the baby into the crook of her arm and carefully sat down. "Sleep, Precious, that's the girl."

Emma looked over her shoulder to make sure Cat had left. "So, Midnight, what does Julien think since the DNA tests came back. Was he surprised?"

"Surprised? Shocked is more like it. Still says he doesn't remember anything. Maybe it is true what Amy Lee told Cat… that he was forced into it." She patted the infant's back. "He doesn't seem interested, hasn't seen her yet. I don't know. He did say he's looking for another job for the winter; he doesn't want Cat to have to go on welfare." The baby let out a tiny cry, and Midnight shifted her up over her shoulder. "There, there... Isn't it strange, Em, I have a granddaughter?"

Emma looked at the baby's peaceful face, "God, she is so sweet, so good natured."

"Of course, all our babies are happy, right, Ruby?"

Cat returned. "Oh, she's still sleeping! Would you mind watching her while I fold some laundry?"

"Would I mind? Would I mind? Go, girl, take your time."

"Thanks, it shouldn't take long. Call me if she wakes up; it's almost time for her to nurse."

"She's a busy girl," said Emma, "and proud. She won't let me help with the night feedings, laundry, or anything. She wants to do it all herself. I know she's exhausted—did you see those dark circles under her eyes? But that baby girl is clean and well fed and cared for. She gained back her birth weight right away. I'm a little surprised. I've seen grown women have a harder time. She's a good mother, Midnight."

"I know it, especially considering what her mother was probably like."

There was a quick knock at the back door, then Lilly rushed in. "God! It looks like a grocery store in here—strawberry jam, pickled beets, dilly beans...You two have been busy! I'm skipping canning this year. Bad planning on the Lord's part, picking the hottest time of the year to put everything up. I'm sweating like a pig, as usual." She fanned herself with a newspaper she held. "Oh, Midnight, you look so good with that baby. Let's see her." She moved around and peered at the baby's sleeping face. "She's just so pretty! Look at those eyelashes...Where's Cat?"

"Folding laundry. Want some iced tea?" asked Emma, taking glasses out of the cupboard.

"Sure. Have you two seen the paper?" Lilly was suddenly serious.

"No, why?" Emma clunked ice cubes out of the tray.

"Look at this!" She spread the paper out across the table. The headline read: **RJ Dobson Arrested for Alleged Rape.** "It says that he drugged a Butte City girl and raped her in his car. They were parked up behind the Y, caught in the act. It says that he used the same date rape drug he used on Cat."

Midnight read through the article. "His county commissioner daddy won't get him out of this one." She read on. "They found crank on him too. The girl was a minor; they don't say her name."

"Is she alright?" asked Emma. "Was she admitted to the hospital?"

Midnight hefted the baby higher on her shoulder. "How could she be alright after something like that?"

Lilly looked at them, her face flushed, tears in her eyes. "I feel like shit! I didn't believe Cat...I thought she was lying. I'm so sorry, Emma. I just couldn't picture those boys doing anything like that." She got up and paced the kitchen. "Especially the Ross kid or Amy Lee's cousin Chuck. Why, Bud and I coached them in Little League. This RJ kid must have had some power over them, or...I don't know," she sniffed, "or threatened them with something. And Cat was so...," she searched for the words. "I didn't listen to you either." Her face was red and blotchy. "Damn, here comes another one." She pulled at her collar and blew down her blouse. "I need to apologize to Cat. I can't believe I didn't know."

Emma handed her a glass of iced tea. "It's okay, Lilly."

"No, it's not!" she protested. "I was an ass. I don't know who I am anymore. Do you think she'll forgive me?"

"Go talk to her," said Emma, "she's in the laundry room."

"Okay, I guess now is as good a time as any."

After she left, Emma turned to Midnight. "I'm happy for Cat. Lilly wasn't the only one; the whole valley suspected her. You'd be surprised how people treated her...or maybe you wouldn't. You know how they are: if they like you, there's none more wonderful, but if they don't…Maybe the girl will find some justice now."

Midnight took a long slow swallow of tea and put her glass down. After a moment she said, "Yeah, well, the Green River have a saying, 'The innocent have no need for justice, only protection.' That boy—I don't like to use the word evil; I've heard a lot of definitions of it like 'LIVE' spelled backwards. Some say evil is derived from a lack of love, a sort of non-feeling vacuum. The dictionary says, 'morally wrong or bad, wicked, harmful.' I've looked all of these up, by the way, over the years, while I worked on myself, trying to exorcise my anger over what has happened to my people. My Grandma Swan's last words to me were, 'Don't hate them, Midnight, for they know not what they do.' Yeah, okay…but sometimes there are people who do know what they're doing and just don't care. This boy, RJ, I wonder what he's experienced to make him this way?"

Emma listened to Midnight while she packed the cooled jars of jam into a box for her to take home. She took a damp wash cloth and wiped the overspill from some of the lids. "A lack of love, I think; that pretty much says it all, doesn't it? I see so many kids who have been branded. Most of the time they're not—bad I mean. But once in a while I'll see something in their eyes, and I wonder if this child is destined for no good."

Lilly walked to the dining room and stopped. Her heart was beating fast, another symptom of "The Pause", but also because she was nervous about facing the girl. She'd been so leery of her ever since she'd come to Emma's. She'd never really trusted people from outside the valley, where it was said that you had to live for a hundred years before you were considered a local.

She'd been so sure that the rape hadn't really happened, especially since she'd known all the boys since they were little,

312

except for the Dobson kid. The girl was so hard and rude. And her mother was, after all, a prostitute. She'd completely misread Cat's actions at the church. At the time it had seemed like a desperate teenage attempt to redeem herself at the expense of all the nice people in church that Sunday. She saw now that it was one of the most courageous things she'd ever witnessed. God, she hated being wrong. But this had to be done because evidently she *was* wrong, really wrong. She took a breath and opened the door to the laundry room.

"Oh, you scared me!" cried Cat, holding a tiny shirt in midair. Her eyes questioned, "Does the baby need me?" She added the shirt to one of the piles of baby clothes that were neatly folded on the dryer.

"No, she's fine. She's asleep, snuggled into her grandma Midnight."

"Oh, good." She reached over, took a diaper, snapped it in the air, and folded it into fourths.

Lilly saw caution in her eyes. "Cat, I think you'll be interested in this." She spread the newspaper out over the clothes. The girl read the headline, her eyes growing wide. Lilly waited, watching Cat's expression as she took in the article's contents.

"Where did you get this? When?"

"At Willard's; just came out this afternoon."

Cat looked up at her. "Really? Is this really happening?" A smile spread across her face, "Oh, please, let it be true…My baby…" She finished folding two more onesies and stacked them, then burst out, "Lilly, this is the best news! Does Emma know?" Not waiting for an answer, she rushed on, "Because I've been so afraid of him!" She bit her lip. "All this time… he stalked me…still is…even last week. He threatened me after, you know…it happened…Told me he wanted to kill the baby…I'm so relieved…Thank god it's over, it's really over. Let's go tell Emma."

She grabbed the newspaper and ran past Lilly into the

kitchen. "Emma! Midnight! Look! They got him! They got him!"

"We know," said Emma, smiling. "It's great news."

She and Midnight both looked at Lilly, who sat down. Sweat beaded her face. She picked up the newspaper, folded it, and started fanning herself nervously. She looked over at Emma and Midnight for reassurance. Emma nodded at her, but Midnight flipped her braid and began to pat the baby's back rhythmically.

"Cat?...I owe you an apology. I didn't believe you about... you know, the rape and everything. I thought you lied." She wiped the back of her hand over her forehead. "I didn't trust Emma either, and I never gave you the benefit of the doubt. Now that I know what you've been through and how you've dealt with it all, I just feel like...I'm so sorry." Her voice was shaky. "Can you forgive me?"

Cat walked over to Midnight and looked down at the sleeping baby. After an uncomfortable moment she said, "Sure, Lilly, don't worry about it...I can understand why you didn't. Ruby is teaching me a lot about forgiveness and..."

"Oh, thank you, Cat." Lilly lunged awkwardly towards the girl and threw her arms around her.

The baby stirred and fussed, searching with her mouth. "Oh no, Ruby," Midnight told her, "I don't have what you need, Precious. Go to Mama." Midnight put the baby into Cat's arms.

"Yup, it's time again. I'm gonna go upstairs to nurse her; huh, Honey Bunny?" She started out of the room then turned. "Lilly, don't worry, okay?" She left, and they heard the baby fussing as she climbed the stairs.

"Whew, I'm glad that's over! She told me in the laundry room that RJ stalked her even after the rape and threatened her!"

"I didn't know that!" said Emma, alarmed.

"And he threatened to kill the baby!"

"Just let him try!" hissed Midnight.

Lilly looked at them. "Well, you don't have to worry about him anymore. I can't imagine what Cat's been through. That girl, she's something else, isn't she?"

Midnight didn't look at her but nodded, and Emma, proud as any mother, thought to herself, *Yes, yes, she sure is.*

Julien emptied grass clippings onto Emma's compost pile. *Man! she had a big yard to mow.* He'd be glad when summer was over. *It would have been a lot easier if she owned a riding lawn mower.* He took the grass catcher back to the mower and re-attached it. He'd only have to mow maybe three more times. He'd been working at Amy Lee's dad's hardware store too, and that would go on through winter.

He wanted to help Cat as much as he could. She still hardly looked at him at school, but she nodded if they passed each other in the hallway. He still couldn't wrap his head around the fact that she had a baby. Ruby supposedly was *his* baby! He'd see Cat sometimes at Emma's, out in the yard or on the porch. She wore the kid in a pack in the front, like a kangaroo. Cat told his mom he could see the baby anytime. *No, thanks! Giving her money was one thing.* But the test said she was his. His mom said she looked just like him? *Shit! What were the odds of that?* He tipped the water bottle up and guzzled some. *How the hell did this happen? Oh, yeah, he knew... the evils of alcohol.* He still had to go to the Alcoteen meetings. *But a baby? It was just too unreal.*

He pulled the throttle and mowed in circular runs around the apple trees, getting as close to the trunks as he could. His mom was obsessed; all she talked about was "Ruby this," and

"Ruby that." He made a pass in front of the house. Well he'd give the girl money but he'd keep his distance. God, his friends pimped him unmercifully at school. "Here comes Papa Julien." "How's diaper duty, dude?"...*Assholes.*

He stopped the mower. How annoying—the catcher was full again. On his way to the compost pile he heard the kid crying, which he often did as he worked around the place. *Damn, she's loud*, he thought. "Wha, wha, wha," she screamed. He saw it then, the stroller parked next to the front porch. Her cries reached a high-pitched squeal. *Where is everybody?* he wondered. *Shit.* He approached the stroller and looked inside. He didn't see Emma, Midnight, and Cat hiding behind the lace curtain in the living room and watching him. *God, she was so little and ugly crying like that, her face all red and scrunched up, her little legs kicking and punching in the air.* "Where's my mom, damnit? Or anyone?"

"Shh, shh, shush," he said to her, "what's wrong?" But she was gone, lost in some kind of baby freak out. He looked around for someone, anyone... "Wha wha wha." Now she was hicupping. He wiped his sweaty palms on his jeans and reached in and picked her up. Her head was all wobbly. "Whoa!" he said, putting his hand on her head, "steady there." He lifted her up over his shoulder, but still she wailed. "Hey, hey, it's okay." He put his big awkward hand on the baby's damp back. She quieted. He'd seen people pat a baby's back, so he tried it, thump, thump, thump. She hiccupped again but was quiet. He looked around once more—where was everyone? He was afraid to walk with her; what if he dropped her?

Curious, he lowered her into the crook of his arm. She was scary tiny, didn't seem to have any bones. She had a round brown face with really fat cheeks. Her soft red hair spiked up from her head. Her dark eyes were open, and she looked up at him with a serious stare. *Crap*, he thought, *she does look like me... poor baby.* She smiled, her little pink mouth upturned.

Was that real? he wondered. *Do they smile this soon?* With his free hand he touched her cheek. "Did you smile?" She grabbed his finger and held on tight. He was surprised by her grip. "You're strong, aren't you?" he whispered. She flashed him the biggest grin; then sounds came out of her. She cooed and gurgled, still staring right at him. "Is that right?" he asked her.

From behind the curtain Midnight said, "Well, there it is, love at first sight."

"Uh huh, look at his face," said Emma. "Baby magic; I've seen it over and over with the biggest and gruffest of men."

Cat moved towards the door, "I'd better go out there."

Julien was still face to face with the baby when the screen door banged softly. "She was crying; I couldn't find anyone...I think she's okay now. She's making sounds..."

Cat walked towards him. Seeing them together, right next to each other, she thought, *spitting image.* "Yeah, she does that now. Sounds like she really knows what she's saying, huh?" He handed her to Cat. "Hi, Ruby." She held the baby girl out in front of her, "Did you meet Julien?...Well?" she said, looking at him shyly, "what do you think of her? Do you like her name?"

He toed the grass and plunged his hands into his pockets. "Yeah, it's okay. She's so little...I guess she does kind of look like me...I guess she's cute...Haven't been around too many kids. Babies make me sweat. She's got a lot of hair, doesn't she?"

Cat laid her back down in the stroller. "Yeah, tons of hair... Well, thanks for picking her up...I need to go feed her now." She wheeled the stroller towards the side of the house. "If you ever...um...ever want to hold her again just let me know."

Julien walked back to the mower and fiddled with the grass catcher. Just before she disappeared around the corner he called out, "Cat? Wait a second." She looked over her shoulder. "I might take you up on that...sometime."

Something inside her dissolved, a hardness dislodged. She

Chapter Thirty-three

Clare stood in the kitchen listening to the loud voices of Don and the boys arguing in the next room. She could almost see their ruddy faces, the wild whites of their eyes. She knew better than to interrupt; if she intervened, someone would accuse her of taking sides, and the war would only escalate. Or even worse, the anger would turn on her. She scribbled a note, *Hiking up the hill,* and put it on the table.

She moved to the coat rack near the back door and grabbed her red thermal sweatshirt. *Best to be visible,* she thought, since it was a few weeks into hunting season. She sat down on a wooden chair, hurrying, putting on woolen socks and hiking boots. The voices became louder. Quickly she strapped on her fanny pack and thunked a full water bottle into its sling. Then, as if she were a thief leaving a crime scene, she quietly turned the old porcelain doorknob and slipped out the door.

Arrow, the McNab, was instantly at her side, dancing with excitement over their daily walk in the woods. The autumn air was a brisk shock to her face and hands as she dug for gloves in her pockets. They moved out over the cattle guard and down the dirt road. The sky was a clear robin's egg blue, one of her favorite colors. She took a mental picture of the soft gold sunlight to use in her next painting.

She turned into the new subdivision; Arrow, in a frenzy of run-and-sniff, was far ahead of her. The encroachment of the tract houses hurt both her eyes and her heart. She walked up the road that led to a little stretch of woods at the base of the mountain. Walking along the old irrigation ditch that fed a small pond, she paused for a moment, watching graceful chartreuse duckweed swirl in the clear water. The trees—mostly oaks with a few scattered pines—were tinged with autumn, the bright red and gold a tribute to the occasional beauty of death. The crunch of her footsteps released the earthy scent of acorns and pine needles.

She always felt free here, not judged or needed. There were often animals. Once a bobcat sat just above her, only yards away. Unafraid, she studied his inquisitive eyes, the pen and ink ears. She had spoken to him, his ears erect and listening. She had told him not to be afraid, that she really did not want the freshly-killed rabbit between his paws. Once in winter a peripheral darkness had caught her eye; a black bear and her cinnamon cub were climbing up the hill. The young one's coat resembled a fuzzy pumpkin against the snow. The day she came across a heavy-teated young mother coyote, sadness had filled her. These creatures would soon be driven out to make room for the ongoing intrusion of humanity.

She moved along the path, breathing in the pure air. Arrow was still far ahead, darting in and out of sight. After scanning the sky, she decided there was enough light left to stay a little longer. She turned up the mountain, weaving between giant manzanitas, stopping to stroke the smooth burgundy skin of a twisted trunk. Her small, muscular body climbed the steep incline without much effort. She knew that the dog would find her. As she moved up into a treed cleft, she felt her strong calf muscles flexing inside her blue jeans. She reached the plateau and paused. This was a favorite place. Light slanted through the grove of trees in pale silver bars. She could hear Arrow crashing through the brush. A gray squirrel sprinted, levitating to the top of a pine, while the dog flew in quivering pursuit. They sang to each other; Arrow's yelping and the squirrel's raucous scolding reached a pitch so frantic that she laughed out loud. After a few minutes, the dog lost interest and began nosing the ground.

The circle of oaks was perfectly placed, as if by a landscape architect. She sat down, her back against a tree. The deep quiet and fading light lulled her. Arrow lay nearby in his nest of leaves, taking her in with quiet dog calm. The air was still and cool. Finally, knowing her time here was up, she stood and zipped her sweatshirt, then bent over to tie the undone lace of her boot.

It hit her from behind. The powerful force of its streamlined body knocked the wind out of her, ramming her face hard into the ground. Her knee shattered in pain; she scrambled on all fours like a crab. Arrow was barking and whimpering. Turning her head in panic, she caught a flash of tawny fur. She screamed as the cat lunged again, its claws slicing, cleaving into the skin of her lower back, while its teeth simultaneously hooked the fanny pack strap and one belt loop of her jeans.

The lion bounded through the oak circle in a graceful lope, then paused and raised his head. Clare dangled in mid-air, limp and unconscious. Engulfed in the lavender glow of twilight, he moved slowly up the mountain.

The lion patiently made his way up through the steep cliffs. Night had fallen; above him arced a filigree of stars and an almost-full moon. Sometimes in his exhaustion he dragged her over brush and boulders. The top of the mountain was in sight, but the closer he was to the ledge, the weaker he became. It was midnight by the time he dropped her into his lair. He struggled, loosening the fanny pack strap and belt from his teeth. He didn't bother to inspect the motionless prey. His legs crumpled under him, and he surrendered to sleep.

Clare's son Josh called Lilly at eight o'clock that night and told her that his mother hadn't returned from her walk and that his dad was drunk. Lilly and Bud went to the house, where Josh and his brother showed them Clare's note and told them that the dog had returned alone. Don was passed out on the couch. When Bud tried to rouse him, he sat up bleary eyed, yelling that he didn't give a shit if Clare ever came back.

They took the boys with them, questioning them about the places that Clare liked to hike. They drove through the subdivision even though it was dark, stopping near the path that led up the mountain. They called her name, even honked the horn, but to no avail. Once back at the house, Bud called the sheriff, who said he'd organize a search party first thing in the morning.

Clare woke at first light, wondering if she had died. The landscape was eerily unfamiliar. She lay on a rock ledge that jutted out over a small canyon. Above her was an overhanging stone that seemed like the opening of a cave but only provided a small shallow shelter. The lion was nowhere in sight. She could not move. She had never known such extreme pain. Even in childbirth there were moments of reprieve. This was a tight, hot cocoon of constant pain. Besides the crushed knee and clawed back, she was covered with wounds, scratches, bruises and welts. Her clothes were torn, her hair tangled. She wore only one hiking boot. Infection bloomed pinkly in her body, and the oncoming fever made her eyes sting.

She heard a distant rustling across the canyon, then saw the lion weaving his way back to the ledge. She felt her bladder let go, and a stream of tears slid down her face, landing in soft puffs of dirt. Her heart pounded inside her small chest. She could not slow down her breathing. She managed to move herself, curling inward to protect the soft inner part of her body, even though she knew she was going to die. Instinct and adrenaline running deep in her brain bent her into a womblike position, waiting.

The lion moved towards the ledge, lingering at a stream. He paused, enjoying the sun on his back. More and more, his old bones needed warmth. He drank the clear, cold water and stretched.

The search party met at the base of the hill. Midnight and Liam had trailered over with their horses, Molly and Red. Lilly and Emma had saddled Mav and Joe. The sheriff brought mules, three men, and a team of hounds. They carried basic provisions in case they ended up camping for the night. The hounds were given one of Clare's coats to smell; they picked up the scent right away.

Clare could not stop shaking; spasms washed over her. The lion moved so quietly, so quickly, he seemed to be a mirage. She had to blink to be sure it was really there. Ignoring her, she saw him nose around a pile of leaves by the cave and uncover a carcass. The scream rose in her throat like a scream in a dream. Her mouth opened but no sound came out. The lion glided over to her. He sniffed her back. She could feel the stiff whiskers as he scanned her with his face. She heard a deep, low noise come from his throat. She did not move. He circled her, his long limbs each ending in terrible flowered claws. He sniffed and circled, and sniffed again. He changed directions. She could barely breathe. Her eyes were squinched tightly shut. Then she felt a subtle shift in the lion's presence and slowly opened them. He stood frozen, staring, his haloed coat backlit, the topaz eyes drilling into her. Turning, he walked a few feet away and lay down. He yawned, showing the efficient weapons of his teeth. Lowering his head onto his paws, he closed his eyes and seemed to sleep.

Fear took her away. Once she woke up to see the lion twitch. The thick fur rippled and shimmered as the shiver ran its course. The sweet safety of darkness beckoned, and she drifted. She saw flashbacks of her life randomly placed in time. She knew the shape of time—that it was a spiral—not linear, but layered, past, present, future, coexisting simultaneously, all time being one time at the same time. She was a girl, a mother, then an old woman with long, white braids.

About ten miles in they found Clare's hiking boot. Although it was confirmation that she'd been there, speculation about how and why further increased their fears. Lilly broke down, cradling the little boot in her lap. They remounted and set out looking for deer trails that led upward through the thick brush. When a narrow deer trail ended, they had to break through terrain choked with slash and boulders. Often there were no flat areas to rest the horses, so they pulled up on the steep incline, facing uphill, until the sweat-soaked horses could climb again.

The fever dream broke in late afternoon. Her thirst was an obsession. The lion was not on the ledge. She glowed with a low, slow combustion. She felt swollen all over, the wounds still clean but ringed in scarlet. She was lit so hot, so bright. She gazed across the canyon where the oaks climbed up the mountain like fire: ochre, amber, and rust. She felt the colors burn into her as she flamed into them. All around a mist rose; it grew and frothed at the base of trees, arranging itself, spreading like smoke, floating up the tree line.

The shot rang out, startling her. The sound bounced between the canyon walls, ricocheting in a zigzag pattern. She heard a voice somewhere near the mountaintop, a male voice calling, and then another answering from a different direction. The two men yelled loud, unintelligible messages back and forth. A few moments of silence—they were closer now.

"Shit! I know I got it, bastard buck!"

"Have some whiskey, asshole. It'll make you a better shot."

They laughed drunkenly.

"There it is!"

"Where?"

"Over there!"

Muffled by the canyon, the explosive pop of the second shot snapped the air like a wet towel. Its echo was overlaid by panicked screams, "Holy shit, man! Run, run!"

For hours in her dehydrated stupor she waited for the lion. Surely the anticipation was worse than any death she envisioned. It was almost dark now, the moon and the Pleiades overhead. A sound pulled her eyes away from the sky, a slow, soft, scraping sound.

In the late afternoon the search party heard distant gunshots up high, near the back side of the mountain. More than likely hunters, they guessed. But the fact that there were people in the vicinity made them nervous. The hounds ran ahead criss-crossing the terrain but finding no signs. They stopped just before nightfall, setting up camp in a small flat meadow. Liam and Midnight strung a tie line between trees for the horses and fed them hay and grain that the mules had carried in their saddlebags. Sheriff Thomas and his men set up the tents while Lilly and Emma threw a makeshift meal together. Then, discouraged and exhausted, they all turned in early.

The lion approached, dragging its left front leg, limp from the shoulder down. Clare watched him, fascinated by this transformation. The hunter's bullet had pierced the bone and ruptured his lung. He collapsed, panting heavily, his tongue lolling outside of his mouth, his breath coming fast and shallow. His eyes were dull and half-lidded. Blood trickled steadily from the fleshy hole. Soon exhaustion swept over them. Deep night found lion and woman asleep on the ledge, each bathed in the featherweight pearl of the moon's light.

Clare dreamt of water, winter's rain of stinging, slanted shafts, and spring's soft globes pooling on new green leaves.

She remembered the cup of her womb snapping as an amniotic gush released the body of her secret, stillborn daughter. Never would she forget the silky, paraffin skin, the tightly-shut eyes, fringed with dark lashes. *Would this being be there waiting for her when she died?*

She knew the river's ecstasy, the cascading snowmelt of bubbles and foam. She saw a fluorescent dragonfly vibrate across the molten rim, heard trees sucking deep in the earth. She looked into the still bowl, circles within circles, as hungry fish dimpled the thick soup of the pond. She sank into it, at home; she kicked and floated like a water bug across the limpid expanse.

The vertical plunge of glassy sheets, the waterfall thundering in deep, bass tones, damp moss in rocky clefts. Her body demanded it, wanted it, needed it, begged for it: water, the coolest weight that slides, the sweetest taste to thirst.

She awoke in the nether time, moments before dark became dawn. Stars seared coldly overhead. Birdsong claimed the day; a ribbon of coral stained the horizon line. She could hear it gurgling somewhere in the canyon. Her raw throat ached for it; she was dying for it. Turning slowly, she tried to shift her body. Perhaps she could sit or stand. Stabbing pain met the effort, and she rolled back, fetally curled. Something met her hip in hardness—a rock or a piece of wood. She reached behind to grab the obstruction. Her ragged hands gripped something round and cold, too smooth to be a stone. The water bottle was still attached to her fanny pack!

With effort, she twisted the fanny pack belt around and over her back. Breathing hard, each movement a marathon of energy, she managed to lift the bottle. The sound of Velcro scratched the air, startling the lion. She popped up the spout and dribbled water into the corner of her mouth, then gulped the icy liquid. Tears flowed. *How like life,* she thought, *for it to have been there all along.*

The lion watched her, the slurping sounds triggering his own need. His tongue felt thick and wrong. The wound in his shoulder jabbed and throbbed. Blood bubbled from his mouth, staining the white muzzle pink.

Without thinking, acting purely on impulse and instinct, with all of her will she pushed herself towards the lion. She moved in tiny increments, scooting, resting, scooting, resting, until she held the bottle up and squirted a small stream into his mouth. He swallowed only a little. Again she tipped the bottle, and this time he swallowed wholly, his agate eyes never leaving hers.

Later in the morning a thick fog rolled up and over the mountain. The water had heightened her clarity, but the lack of numbness brought back intense fear. She was so cold, her body stiff and sore from lying on the ground for so long. The bare foot felt bruised and swollen, and she couldn't move her toes. As fog thickened around the ledge, visibility was limited to a radius that included only herself and the lion. He seemed to be sleeping, his breath creating clouds of warmth in the damp, cold air. Even with his devastating injuries, he was still capable of mortally wounding her in an instant.

Why hadn't anyone come looking for her? Yesterday she thought she'd heard the high-pitched whine of hounds, but the sounds had faded after only a few minutes. She curled tighter into the ball of herself, wondering what story had been told about her disappearance. She thought about how half-truths and assumptions fed gossip like a game of telephone in the valley. No one would ever guess her true circumstances.

The lion raised his head and yawned; again the lethal weapons of his teeth made her heart beat fast. He rose, struggling, breathing hard, and slowly limped to the side of the ledge, disappearing behind a clump of buckbrush. She could hear the strong stream of urine. He fairly dragged himself back and collapsed into his place, facing her.

She played a game with herself, an old game she had learned in art school, memorizing physical details, colors, textures, and patterns so that she could paint from her mind's eye. Even though she would never paint again, she drank in his beauty. She noted the powerful head and black-tipped ears; how the upturned eyes were ringed in kohl like an exotic dancer's, the pupils small dark dots floating in green-gold. His nose was wide, capped with an hourglass pad of pink. The vee-shaped mouth and white muzzle were studded with long, thick whiskers. *Regal,* she thought, *exquisite.*

The morning's exertion had taken its toll; her lower back ached and stung. She slept all afternoon. When she woke it was dusk, and she was disoriented. Flailing up out of sleep, her mood was dark and hopeless. Her cries came from deep inside her; they shook her body and she let them. She wailed for her every loss, her pain, her sons, the unlove of her husband, her short life.

She never saw the lion move, didn't realize he was standing over her, until she felt the weight of his body as he dropped behind her. She felt the thick fur of his belly press against her back and she screamed, praying it would be over soon.

Wrapping his body around her spoon-fashion, the lion's huge paws pummeled her back, slowly, gently, the claws retracted. He pushed and kneaded and kneaded and pushed, the purr vibrating in his throat. The cat's huge tongue began to lick her. Every time it touched her bare skin through torn cloth she felt its roughness chafe against her. And then he licked her wounds in contented slowness. Everywhere the damp tongue snaked, her skin rose in gooseflesh.

Throughout the night she woke and the lion was still there. By dawn she could feel his body cooling and his blood seeping all around them. When his breathing changed to a strangled gurgle, she began to cry. Finally his body slumped against her in heavy stillness.

The search party had ridden for two days, traveling over twenty-five miles into the mountains. At dawn they discussed the fact that soon the horses would not be able to handle the steep incline. But in late morning the yelping hounds rediscovered the scent from the day before.

As they came up above the ledge, the dogs became agitated. The sheriff leashed them and handed them over to one of the men. Midnight, Emma, Lilly, and Liam dismounted and stood stunned and silent. Below, the bodies of Clare and the lion lay curled together, motionless, in a pool of blood.

They traversed down to the ledge. Liam approached cautiously, kicking at the cat just to make sure. "Biggest one I've ever seen." With no expectation, he bent over to feel for Clare's pulse, then shouted, "She's breathing! Bring the stretcher down!"

"Look what he done to her," one of the deputies said.

Clare curled tighter into herself. Her eyelids twitched. Then slowly she rose up on one elbow, her eyes wild, her other arm reaching behind to hold onto the lion.

"Jesus God in heaven," Lilly said to no one in particular. She knelt down. "Clare, Clare," she sobbed, "oh, Clare, are you alright?" She took in the ravaged body of her sister. Bloody cuts and scrapes covered her face and arms where the red sweatshirt was shredded and tattered. The cat lay curled behind her. "Please, somebody, move her away!"

"We can't move her yet, Lilly," said Emma, "we've got to examine her first."

"It's my knee," Clare moaned.

"Make sure she stays in this position when you move her, Liam." The bare foot was hot and swollen. "Can you move your toes?" asked Emma.

"No."

"Okay, what about this hand?"

As Liam and the sheriff lifted her away from the lion, more blood seeped onto the ground.

"It's from the cat," Emma reported.

They were able to move Clare to a portable stretcher. She took a few sips of water and swallowed the pain medication they gave her. While they were stabilizing her injured knee she heard one of the men ask if he could take the lion for a trophy.

"No!" she cried out.

Liam was putting a blanket over her. "What is it, Clare? Did I hurt you?" He could see that she was trying to say something, but her voice was barely audible. He leaned his face in even closer. "What, what? Tell me again."

"Don't let them take him, please." She took his hand, hers small and torn, the knuckles scabbed. Her eyes, wild again, looked into his. "Leave him here; he must stay...here!" Her words trailed off.

As two of the men carried the stretcher up the bank, Lilly broke down. Emma put her arm around her.

"Is she going to die? Oh, God, please no, I couldn't bear it."

"She's going to be alright, Lilly," Emma told her. "She'll be air-lifted to Bradford. It's a miracle that she's alive. Don't worry. Come on, let's help pony the horses so she can be carried to a place where the helicopter can land." They started up the hill.

Midnight remained, standing over the huge cat. It looked to be an old one. She wondered what had happened between Clare and the cougar. Whatever it was, she knew it would change Clare's life forever. Having never been this close to one, she studied the body, the strong square head and artful markings, the bullet hole in its chest. The lion looked almost content, curled on the ground, the enormous paws studded with long, black, crescent-shaped claws. She sang to it, calling its ancestors. Then she bent down and knelt next to it. After several minutes she stood and hiked up the hill to join the others.

The two men carrying the stretcher walked out on foot while the others followed on horseback. The downhill ride was slow going, as they picked their way through brush and litter-strewn slopes. After five miles or so they found a flat area on a ridge top where a helicopter could land. It was late afternoon, the light waning, when they radioed and sent up flares so the pilot could find them. After more than an hour the helicopter hovered above them, spooking the horses and mules, before setting down in the clearing.

Lilly begged to go with her sister, but there was only room for two paramedics and the pilot. Clare, semi-conscious, was loaded in, the doors shut, then the craft lifted off above the thick overstory of trees. The search party once again turned the horses downhill, kicking and spurring them along, focused on making it down before night fell. No one spoke as they rode the deer trails through the forest and meadows, but every once in awhile one of them sighed loudly or shook their head in dis-belief at what they had seen.

Chapter Thirty-four

Bud met Lilly in the yard when she returned and took Joe's reins as she dismounted. "He's whipped, Bud," she told him. "I didn't think he was gonna make it down. Had I known what we'd go through with that terrain I wouldn't have taken him. Give him oats and rub him down, okay? He's really lathered up."

After Bud came in he told her that Clare's boys Josh and Donnie were at her dad's watching movies. She broke down, falling into his arms, telling him in dramatic detail how it looked when they found Clare lying with the huge mountain lion in a pool of blood, and how scared she'd been that her sister was dead. "She wouldn't let go of it, Bud! She had her arms around it like it was a teddy bear. Her body was a bloody mess, and she looked out of her mind. She was up there for three nights, Bud! God knows what she went through."

He held her tight while she cried again and told her, "She'll tell you someday, honey, or maybe she won't remember, since she was dehydrated. Is her knee broken?"

Lilly nestled against him. "I don't know. I just called the hospital and she was in surgery."

He fed her some spaghetti he'd made for Ralph and their

nephews and drew her a hot bath. She dropped into bed right after but tossed and turned the rest of the night.

When the alarm went off the next morning Bud brought Lilly coffee in bed, sat down on the edge, and took her hand. "Didn't sleep much, huh?" He stroked her hand while she sipped the French roast with just the right amount of sugar and cream. Bud asked her what time she was picking up the girls.

She threw back the covers and said over her shoulder, "Soon; I need a shower."

Bud sat there while she showered. Of all the people to have lived through what Clare must have experienced, his sister-in-law, so timid and shy and scared of everything, was the most unlikely.

Emma fed the cats and Mav, who was still tired from the long last few days of extreme riding. The sun floated up above the Eastsides, splashing their peaks with light. She came back to the house, remembering that she wanted to bring flowers to Clare at the hospital, and opened the gate to the garden. Lilly was picking her up soon. She took the clippers off the nail where they hung in the potting shed. There were still zinnias, red and orange, and small, late sunflowers. She added some Shasta daisies and arranged them quickly into a bouquet. These would surely brighten Clare's room.

She kept seeing the image of Clare and the lion curled together on the ground as the riders came up over the ledge after two days of futile and hopeless searching. It was a miracle, as she had told Lilly, but she wondered what exactly had happened, and worried about Clare's mental state. Clare was so fragile and already traumatized from living with Don. She hurried into the house, dumped dry dog food into Bear's bowl, and searched through the junk drawer for some ribbon. She rubber-banded the flowers and tied them with raffia.

Lilly had called her at ten last night reporting that Clare had just gone into surgery. She told Emma she was just too tired to drive to Bradford, and Emma assured her that her sister was in good hands and would be heavily sedated and in the recovery room probably all night. They planned to leave this morning, and Lilly had said she'd call Midnight. It was quiet upstairs—Cat and the baby were most likely still sleeping. She'd heard Cat up with Ruby a few times in the night. Emma hastily washed her hair, put on some mascara and lipstick, grabbed an apple, and was swilling the last of her coffee just before she heard Lilly's car pull into the driveway.

Midnight rode with Liam back to his place. He told her that he'd deal with the horses and she should go on home, since she still had a half-hour drive down river. A full moon lit up the low, slender, silver river, and as she made each turn and bend of the winding road she thought about Clare and the cougar. The image of them lying together was forever tattooed on her mind. When she'd taken the time to look at the lion after the others had lifted Clare onto the stretcher and carried her uphill, she knew that the lion was old, very very old. An elder.

Cougar medicine was a strong and powerful one in the Green River tradition. It represented courage and strength and the ability to lead, none of the qualities Clare seemed to have so far in her life. Midnight knew without a doubt that with the cougar, or catamount as her grandmother called them, as Clare's totem, her life would change. Unless, of course, the fear and trauma she had experienced up there blocked the medicine and made her even more afraid of the world. She'd seen this happen in the tribe when she was a little girl, when her Uncle Early had been mauled by a bear. Instead of embracing the medicine, he'd quit hunting and was never the same again.

But something had come over Midnight as she'd knelt beside the cat, and she'd taken her knife out of her pocket, asked permission, then pushed back the furred sheath on the lion's paw and cut a vee to remove one of the big, black, crescent-shaped claws. Telling no one, she'd swiftly wrapped it in her bandana and tucked it away in her jacket pocket.

Once home, she made a fire, ate a sandwich, and, grateful that Julien wasn't there, went right to bed. In the early morning hours, snug in the cabin's warmth, she dreamt of the cougar when he was young. She followed him through his hundred-mile range, into old-growth forests, across high-water creeks, along steep river canyons, into meadows where he lay with his mate rolling in the pristine morning dew, his sleek, tawny body shiny and muscular. As she woke to light softening the dark windows, she knew what she had to do.

Midnight parked and locked the truck in the parking lot of the gas station on River Road. Lilly's car pulled in; Emma was driving. Midnight opened the back door of the older Toyota sedan, ducked down, and scooted across the seat. Lilly turned around and asked her if she'd been waiting long.

"Nope," she answered, "just got here; no worry."

Lilly ran her fingers through her short curly blonde hair. "Are you as tired as we are? That's why I asked Em to drive."

"Yeah, it was a pretty big few days, wasn't it? How are you, Emma?" Midnight asked.

"Okay, beside the fact that I can only sit on one butt cheek at a time. I haven't ridden that long and hard since I was a teenager."

They started up the mountain towards Butte City. Lilly looked over the seat and told Midnight, "I called before we left; they said the surgery was a success. I guess Clare's knee was crushed, but the ICU nurse said she was comfortable and resting. I wonder how long she'll be in for, do you know, Emma?"

"Oh, maybe a week; then once she's home there will probably be months of physical therapy."

Lilly's cell phone rang. "Hello... Hi, honey... What? They are? You're kidding! What network? San Francisco? But how did they know? Wh...huh? Oh, God! Dad did that? Bud, please, honey, take Josh and Donnie and Dad and leave the ranch. Those boys have been through enough! Go out to breakfast or something, maybe in Butte City. That's so crazy, Bud!...And the *Chronicle* too? Okay, I'll call you after we see her. I will. Love you, bye."

Lilly turned to the girls, "Do you believe it? KSAN reporters with camera crew and everything showed up at the ranch. Told Bud they heard about the woman who killed a mountain lion with her bare hands! Ha! Bud told them to leave, but they wouldn't. He said Dad yelled at them and scared 'em off, running at them with his pitchfork. Good Lord! What is happening?" She laughed, and then Emma and Midnight heard the timbre of her voice change and she was crying hard.

Emma reached over and patted her leg. "It's okay, honey; it will pass. Take some breaths. It's just that it is such an incredible story, and the media is a relentless..."

From the backseat Midnight swore under her breath.

Emma finished with, "a relentless machine. The only thing that's important is that Clare is alright." Emma pulled onto the freeway. "Here's a Kleenex."

"Yeah, but *is* she alright, Emma? She's so fragile and..."

Midnight leaned forward, "Lilly, I have a feeling that

what happened up there will change your sister's life in a good way."

"Me too," said Emma. "And she will have us for support. If we helped Briar die, then surely we can help Clare live."

They were quiet as they climbed the summit towards Bradford. The rolling hills were covered with long brown grasses swirled like cowlicks. Their silence was overlaid with the grinding noise of diesel trucks hauling their longbeds up over the steep, winding pass. They crossed into Oregon, drove past Ash Creek, and entered Bradford. Low grey clouds threatened rain as Emma pulled into the hospital parking lot and found a space.

Midnight looked out the back window at the hospital entrance, "Uh-oh...Look! There's a whole swarm of reporters, camera equipment and all."

"Shit!" Lilly muttered to herself, "I just want to see my baby sister."

"It's okay, I know the back way in." Emma put the car in reverse and pulled around to the back. They walked towards the entrance which was surrounded by a courtyard planted with flowers and greenery. An ornate fountain splashed soothing sounds.

"Look!" said Emma. By the quadruple glass doors was another group of people, one holding a camera with WT3-TV lettered on its side. A short man rushed up to them, microphone in hand. "Are you Lilly McClaine? Any of you related to Clare York, the woman mauled by a mountain lion?"

Midnight stepped up, towering over him. She ripped the microphone out of his hand in one fell swoop and clicked the Off button. She grabbed him by the collar, bringing his terrified face close to hers. "No! We are not related to anyone in the hospital. We are all surgeons, here for a conference on how to dismember and lobotomize members of the media."

She released him. As he stumbled, she handed him the microphone, and the women rushed through the big doors. The TV crew members followed them, but they made it into the elevator just in time. They laughed as the elevator rose up but became serious as it approached Clare's floor. They bumped to a stop and the delicate ding sounded.

The ICU nurse at the desk told them that Clare's surgery had gone well. She said that she would be in a cast for about six weeks but would be able to walk with crutches soon. The nurse warned them not to stay too long.

Clare was asleep, her face and arms a mass of bruises and welts, her cast leg resting outside of the blankets.

"Hi…" Lilly approached the bed. Clare's eyes flew open in panic, then seeing her sister, Emma, and Midnight, she smiled and sank back against the pillows.

"Hey, honey, how are you?"

"I'm alright…just still in a lot of pain…" Her voice drifted off.

"Well, we won't stay long; we know you need your rest," Emma said as she set the vase of flowers on the nightstand.

Midnight laid an envelope on the foot of the bed. "From the tribe…a card."

"Nice," said Clare, seeming to become more present as she shifted her body.

"Here, let me adjust the bed for you." Emma pushed the button.

"That's better," said Clare in a small, weak voice. "Lilly, how are my boys?"

"They seem fine. They've been staying at our house. Don came over, but we threatened him with a restraining order. Dad and Bud are taking the boys to Red Creek tonight for the football game. They want to come see you Sunday."

With effort, Clare said, "Thank you, Lilly and Emma and Midnight, for not giving up…for finding me."

Lilly, tears in her eyes, said, "I'm just so happy that you're alright. Clare, *are* you alright?" Clare looked towards the wall. "Honey, what happened up there?"

Clare looked into each of their faces, her own unreadable. The quiet beeps of the machines filled the room.

"I can't...talk about it yet...I hope you understand...I need time to...," she paused. "Lilly, I want you to move mine and the boys' things over to dad's house. I know it's asking a lot..."

"No," said Lilly, "not at all! Consider it done."

"And Midnight, would you call Bill Plainsford and ask him to draw up divorce papers?"

"Sure will," said Midnight, tossing her braid.

Clare closed her eyes.

"C'mon, ladies." Emma moved towards the door. "Let's let her rest."

"Oh, and one more thing," Clare whispered. "What did they do with him?"

"Who?" asked Lilly, puzzled.

"The lion. I heard someone up there say that they wanted him...for a trophy."

Emma turned to her. "Liam made sure he was left there on the ledge like you asked."

Clare sighed, "Oh, good, that's good. Tell him thanks." She closed her eyes. "Sorry, I'm just so tired."

They tiptoed out.

Chapter Thirty-five

The women rode out from Hidden Horse in single file, taking the back way down through the forest. Late afternoon October light lay pale and golden on the beaten-down deer trails. Emma and Mav led the way, their communion easy yet solemn, Mav's tail raised high as he pranced. Next came Cat, who had left Ruby with Amy Lee. She sat comfortably on the broad back of Candy. Her colt Lucky ponied behind, his black-and-white spotted rump dancing from side to side to stay close to his mother. Lilly followed, her hand resting on Joe's dun-brown withers, grateful for his steady predictable ways. Then Clare, on a willing Bandit, her cast leg secured in a lengthened stirrup, her crutches tied on back. Around her neck she wore the small leather medicine bag Midnight had made with the lion's claw inside. Midnight, deep in thought, rode the half-wild mustang, Molly. Last of all came Elvira, the big taffy-colored, blue-eyed mustang mare, riderless and carrying Briar's ashes in her saddle bag.

They traversed a steep hill, riding around big fallen logs and slash. At the bottom they trotted out onto the Forest Service road. The Trilogy Mountains loomed all around, rising dramatically to over six thousand feet. Their dark rugged cliffs punctured a cerulean blue sky. Instead of the longer way through Big Meadow, the group stayed on the road, racing daylight for the next few hours.

After a short distance they turned up a stony path and onto the trailhead, where the terrain was terraced like stair steps, up through old-growth forests laced with creeks and streams. The horses settled into a rhythm on the path, walking through the silent wilderness into the gloaming woods. Overhead ancient trees, some five hundred years old, rose and swayed, allowing glimpses of the sky above. Then suddenly they came into an open area flooded with light. Here a jack rabbit abruptly crossed their path; the comic boing-boing of its hopping startled the horses momentarily. The rabbit's ears were a translucent pink as it leapt through the illumined glade.

Mile after mile the women rode, mostly silent, as they guided the horses through scant autumn creeks and around giant boulders. They climbed for a long while sheltered by the woods, listening to the tinkling trickle of seeping tributaries and inhaling the pine-scented air. In the waning light a clutch of grouse spiraled up out of nowhere, the sound a whirling, quivering WHOOSH, as their feathered legs descended into the protective brush again. The horses shied and snorted at the ruckus, their eyes bulging, feigning fear.

They climbed the rocky paths, switchback after switchback, up through wide, mica-flecked, marbled steps. Three-quarters of the way up, as they stopped to let the horses drink, an eagle circled above. Back on the narrow trail, the horses' hooves turned up the rich scent of fallen leaves and moist earth. As they emerged from a tunnel of trees in a cleft of high meadow they found deer grazing in tall yellow grass, and listened to the distant sound of cowbells from a herd that hadn't yet returned to the valley. The women watched a falling sun poised above their destination, where the mountain walls sheltered a hidden lake.

Urging the horses on and upward, they crossed the last creek, whose eroded banks were hung with dangling roots and frost-tangled grasses. As they climbed higher, the forest thinned out into a series of sparse ridges where small wind-bent evergreens, their branches clumped with knobby cones, grew in between lichen-covered boulders. Pausing so the horses could catch their breath they could see below the terraced tree tops and snaking trail of the path they had climbed; they could see across the valley to the other side, where the Pacific Crest Trail was stitched along the tops of the eastern mountains. Emma dismounted and tightened her saddlebags, which were tied to the back of her saddle. Lilly hopped down and checked Clare's cinch and stirrups. The others followed suit, quietly going over bridles, cinches, and bedrolls, then stretching their bodies for a moment before the last leg of the journey.

Onward they rode, up through brush and scree, the trees farther apart and the ground stubbled with random clusters of smaller granite rocks. As they turned up a steep roundabout, a large buck leapt onto the path and stood facing them. A set of six-point antlers branched up above its head. The deer's round, dark eyes seemed passive as it stared back at them. Then in an instant it rose up, all four legs off the ground, and bounded off the edge, downhill. They could hear its rhythmic leaps breaking through the brush.

The horses panted up the spiraled rise, their bodies slick and lathered with a foamy sweat. They gave off a sweet yet gamey scent. How precisely they stepped amongst stones and stumps, with a graceful sure-footedness in spite of their weariness. In their true dedication, they would have traveled far beyond their ability to endure, even suffered pain without yielding, for their riders. Now and then the women patted them, reassuring the beloved beasts that soon the path would end.

The sun sank down behind the farthest peaks, and night birds sang in the cool air as Venus floated into focus above.

They climbed the last incline to the uppermost point and sat silently for a moment as filtered glimpses of the lake became visible through the trees. One by one stars glittered the darkening sky, and finally the women dismounted. Lilly helped Clare down and untied her crutches. Midnight strung a line between two trees, knowing that the horses would stay calmer throughout the night if they stood together, herd-like, with their shaggy shoulders touching as they dozed. The women moved, legs stiff and rumps saddle sore, around the horses, untying saddle bags and bedrolls. They undid the cinches and chest straps and lifted the saddles off, propping them upright against boulders or tree trunks, as the horses blew through their lips and sighed with relief. One by one, except for Clare, they led the horses down to the lake to drink, then back again. They brushed the horses' manes and tails, dried their sweat-stained coats, and picked their hooves free of stones. Bridles were removed and hung over the saddle horns. Then they buckled on halters and lead ropes and fastened the horses to the tie line. The colt butted his head against his mother's flanks, anticipating the warmth of her milk. The women removed flakes of hay and grain from the saddle bags and spread them in front of the hungry animals, topping each pile with an apple and carrots.

With the horses settled for the night, the women shouldered their bedrolls and saddle bags and walked to the west side of the lake. They spread the horse blankets and pads dry side up and gathered kindling. The lake lay before them, its mercurial surface one moment a shimmer of copper, the next an emerald flash. Midnight collected rounded stones, and Emma set them in a circle. Lilly stacked pitchy pine cones in the center and laid criss-crossed sticks on top. Clare, comfortable on her blanket with her cast leg outstretched, passed sandwiches around, while Cat set a pot of water on a small grill for tea.

Afterwards, still mostly silent, the women sat as night fell around them, their hearts and minds conjuring precious images and memories of Briar. Then Midnight opened her bundle, delicately removing layers of big, crisp, dried oak leaves, each upturned like a hand. The center of each leaf held tallow wax and a cotton wick. She passed them to the women as Emma uncorked an old glass bottle that held Briar's ashes. Each woman poured a small amount of the ashes around the leaf boat candles, then lit the candles and carried them to the edge of the lake. In unison they let them go and watched for a long time as they floated out over the still water, their flames mirroring the light show above. And then they held each other's hands and sang:

Hold me, hold me, never let me go,
Hold me like the leaves on the ends of the branches.
And when I die, let me fly, let me fly
Through the air like the leaves when they're falling.

Hold me, hold me, never let me go,
Hold me like the stars in the sky high above me.
And when I die, let me fly, let me fly
Through the sky like the stars when they're falling.

Gratitude

Gratitude to all who have inspired and believed, my family, Jane Lewis-Nichols, Jackie McNamara and the Writing the Ox Home ladies, Jennifer Middleton, Donna Wildearth and Lani Phillips, "Imagefairy" thank you for a beautiful book design and cover and of course the real Hidden Horse Sisterhood and Mav the Wonderful.

About the Author

Melinda Field is a writer/poet/playwright who lives on a farm in the mountains of Northern California. A version of her short story *The Ledge*, excerpted from *True*, won an honorable mention from the Lorian Hemingway International Short Story Competition. She has authored three sets of wisdom cards with photographic artist Lani Phillips, that were created to inspire and empower women of all ages on a daily basis. They are *Wisdom of the Crone*, *Wonder of the Mother* and *The Journey*. The cards can be viewed at www.wisewomenink. com. Melinda is currently working on her second novel. Visit her blog at http://truemelindafield.blogspot.com